Wars, particularly civil wars, are truly h...
communities against one another and causin...
the effects of which can be felt for generatio...
all those people still suffering in civil co...

# Chapter 1

*He hath cast me into the mire, and I am become like dust and ashes.* Words from the book of Job whirled in my brain as I looked down at the corpse of my sister-in-law, lying below me in the ditch.

'Loveday, I've served six years for nought!' This girl had been my sweetheart once.

Not brought to dust and ashes yet, but I judged she had been lying two days or more beneath the June sun. In those conditions a corpse will quickly start to become one with the sedges, rosy campion, and the sickly scent of meadow sweet. The damp decay of last year's leaves lined the bottom of the ditch.

So, this was my welcome home. Rob Haddon, cavalryman with the New Model Army. Who tried to get himself killed for love at Naseby, was mentioned in dispatches at Drogheda, and wounded, not beyond repair, but beyond soldiering for the present, at Dunbar. Oliver Cromwell, our general and chief of men, who had been in poor health himself these last few months, was still skirmishing in Scotland. It would be August before he began his great march south, to trounce the remnants of the dead King's party for the last time at Worcester. Now, in mid-June, I had pleaded injury and family business, and received permission to take leave, and ride over the border, skirting the Westmorland hills, and making for my home in the Lune Valley. Tucked into the lining beneath the pommel of my horse's saddle was the letter I had received two weeks ago from my mother, urging me home. The New Model Army prides itself on excellent communications. In it, she had expressed misgivings about my brother's marriage to Loveday, who had chosen him to wed, not me, and worries about the farm, the hay crop, the livestock. But no hint of this. Never this.

'Dear God, Loveday, was there no one left to bury you?' I asked aloud. Turning off the drover's road to ride the last few miles for home, I had found myself wrapped in the peace of my valley. My home place. Cloud shadows sailed across the green and purple of the fellsides, warblers gurgled in the bright summer foliage, and the river Lune purred contentedly over its limestone pavement at the foot of the meadow. But Loveday Haddon, my brother's wife, lay at my feet, dead and decomposing in a ditch. With the shock of this discovery, the colours of the lovely June day were bleached to leaden grey.

I had seen many men die these last six years, cut down in the heat of battle, or lingering for weeks or months with festering wounds and fevers. But never abandoned, uncared for, sent to Heaven or Hell without anyone to say a prayer over them, and turn sufficient clods of earth to give them a rough burial. It must surely mean my family were all dead? My brother

Miles, my mother, and my young sister, Ann. The livestock slaughtered, the farm burned to the ground?

Yet even as I leaned against my horse's flank, cold with shock despite my heavy leather jerkin and the warmth of the day, I could see that this last was not the case. Lowflatts still stood, house and barns serene in the sunshine. Cattle grazed at the water's edge. Two of our brindled cows had waded out into the stream, where they stood, heads down, drowsing the afternoon away until milking time. Someone had milked them this morning; their udders were not yet distended. A mile away on the hillside, I could make out grey-white clumps of grazing sheep amongst the moving cloud shadows, and now that I shaded my eyes, a tiny speck of blue. This I recognised as the smock of Lanty Briggs, the shepherd, seated, his back against a rock, his hat forward on his brow. Nearer at hand, beyond the slope of the hill, I could hear the distant sound of wood being chopped, and someone whistling, tunelessly.

'Well, Caesar, what sort of homecoming is this?' My horse, swivelling his ears at the sound of his name, turned his great head, and gazed at me. With his broad roman nose and sceptical rolling eye, I fancy he would have made a fine Emperor. 'Where are they, boy? Where are Miles and Mother and Ann?'

I had ridden across the fields from the drovers' road, and was now within sight of the stone mullioned windows of the farmhouse, built by my grandfather in the latter days of good Queen Bess. Yet no door flew open, no one rushed to meet me. Something was terribly amiss, although the evidence of the browsing cattle, the sleeping shepherd, said otherwise. Dreading what I would find, I took Caesar's bridle, and began to walk him towards the farm.

Lowflatts was in good shape. The barn was swept, ready for the new hay, the cow byres clean and freshly whitewashed. Hens scratched in the yard, and in the home garth the late born lambs were playing king of the castle, jumping on and off an old tree stump. The geese nibbled at the greensward. The old gander was engaged in nipping the heads off Mother's gilly flowers. But where were my family? I hitched Caesar to a post and made my way to the kitchen door, by which we habitually came and went, calling their names. No one answered. Then I saw that the studded oak door hung slightly ajar, creaking gently to and fro on its hinges in the light summer breeze.

I went in, telling myself I must. Memories of the butchered bodies of men, women and children piled high in the market place at Drogheda swam before my eyes, and I began shivering, almost retching, at the thought of what I might be about to find here. Grasping my sword hilt, I gingerly pushed open doors. Mother's sewing lay neatly folded beside her work basket in the parlour. A dove grey gown lay flung across the bed in Ann's room. On the kitchen table a receipt book lay open at the page which told (in my Grandmother's crabbed writing) how to prepare a gooseberry fool, a favourite dish of my brother's.

I could picture Loveday standing there, strands of her fine fair hair falling from beneath her white linen cap, absentmindedly licking the juice of the stewed gooseberries off her fingers, as she puzzled over the instructions. She had never truly mastered the art of reading.

Then I heard it, a faint sound coming from the still room, which led off the kitchen down a short stone-flagged passage. Shuffling sounds, as though someone was dragging themselves across the flagstones, and the muted chink of metal. They must be in there, my family, bound in chains, left by their assailants to die. My wounded thigh was stiff from my long ride, but I limped down the passageway and pushed at the door. It resisted me. Cold fear griped in my guts. Was one of them dead or unconscious behind it, having crawled so far and then collapsed? I called their names. No one answered. I pushed again, and still the body behind the door resisted, soft, yet firm. The chain chinked again, ringing on the stone floor. I pushed harder. There seemed no alternative, though I might be causing further injury to whoever lay there. The stillroom had once had another entrance, but it had been closed off, years before. I yelled again, 'It's me, Rob!' and suddenly the resistance gave. The door flew open. I fell into the room, landing heavily on my hands and knees.

And found myself gazing into the evil yellow eyes of Tabitha, my mother's old nanny goat. Bored, perhaps, by the lack of opportunities for wickedness afforded by the garth (the gander had beaten her to the gilly flowers) she'd managed to upend the stake that held her chain. Then she'd wandered indoors to explore. What she had found was a basket of ripe gooseberries, no doubt those Loveday had been intending to use. Tabitha had already eaten most of them, as the sea of filth on the still room floor testified; all except those that had cunningly worked their way behind the loosely woven strips of willow that formed the base of the basket. She'd been overcoming that problem by eating the basket. I had interrupted her meal with my ridiculous shouting and shoving at the door, and she wasn't the slightest bit pleased to see me. I, in my turn, had been desperate with fear, so sure that I would find the mutilated bodies of my mother, brother and sister in this room, that my first giddy relief turned to anger. I unbuckled my sword and whacked Tabitha across the rump with the sheathed blade.

'Out! Out, she devil!' I bellowed. The animal jumped sideways and began to gallop madly around the room. I charged after her, skidding in the goat shit, my arms flailing as I tried to remain upright and belabour Tabitha at the same time. After the second circuit of the stillroom she exhibited more common sense than I had, and bolted through the open door, down the passage, and out through the kitchen door to the garth beyond.

Gasping for breath, drained, and ashamed of my stupid ill treatment of the goat, I followed slowly. My whole body was shaking with aftershock. My legs felt palsied, as though I were an old man in his dotage. My wound throbbed. I laid my sword on the scrubbed kitchen table, and stood a while, supporting myself on my hands, head down, until my heart's rhythm slowed, and my rasping breath came more easily.

The house was empty and undisturbed. Whatever had happened to Mother, Miles and Ann, must have happened elsewhere. Were they dead, like Loveday, in a ditch somewhere? Or fled to safety?

Then a mixture of fear and exasperation curdled within me once more, and I hurled my hat across the kitchen and flung myself against a doorpost, howling my anguish to the Redeemer.

'Lord God, where are they? *What has happened here?*'

I yelled loud enough to be heard in Sedbergh, let alone Heaven, but received no answer except the tick-tocking of Mother's beloved clock in the hallway. It was still working, which told me that they were less than three days gone.

*In the time of their trouble, when they cried out to thee, thou heardest them from heaven...*. I'd been six years with the 'New Model', first with General Tom Fairfax, and then under old Ironsides himself. Everyday had begun with a Bible reading. We had gone into battle primed on prayer. But am I a true believer? I know I never felt more inclined to defect to the Devil's party than I did that June afternoon in the deserted kitchen at Lowflatts.

So, if the Lord God wouldn't help me, who could? I considered the possibilities. A healthy young girl does not lie down in a ditch and die for no reason, and I had seen no sign of sudden contagion. Murder. Loveday had been murdered. Three adults don't disappear, plucked from earth by boggarts or brownies, whatever the old wives say. I needed to report these things to the Authorities. In this part of the Lune Valley the law was represented by Colonel Benson Moreland, Justice of the Peace, at Lings Hall. He lived a mile or so away across the river. I knew Benson Moreland and liked him. He'd been a Colonel under Black Tom Fairfax, had fought bravely for the Parliamentary Cause, but was no regicide. The execution of Charles Stuart had sickened him, as it had many of us. So nigh on six months ago he'd resigned his commission, and returned to his family and his lands in Lonsdale. I respected the man, agreed with him for that matter. I'd wanted to resign and come home myself. Especially after Drogheda. I still have nightmares about Drogheda.

I didn't, because Loveday had married my brother, and I couldn't bear to see them happy together. My Mother's recent letter had hinted that things were far from well between them, but I could have borne that even less, to see Loveday *un*happy, and be forced to stand by, unable to come between man and wife. Despite Mother's vaguely worded misgivings, if I hadn't received that pike thrust to my thigh at Dunbar, I wouldn't have chosen to come home.

But even as I was telling myself that I should ride straight for Colonel Moreland, an inner voice murmured, 'Hold hard, Rob Haddon. What if your brother killed her? Miles has a fierce temper when driven hard. You know that, none better.' As boys we had sparred like fighting cocks. 'Or has he accused some other man, publicly, of lusting after his wife, as your mother seemed to hint, and this killing is that man's revenge?'

Who would know what has been going on here? The Postlethwaites? If Miles and Mother and Ann were forced to flee for their lives, they *might* go to Highbiggens, it's closest by far. Someone was chopping wood and whistling over the brow of the hill not half an hour ago. Which means at least one of them may be sober enough to tell what he knows.

I tethered our wayward nanny goat, locked the door, hid the key behind the rain barrel where we'd always kept it. Then I unhitched Caesar, who was tossing up his superior roman nose at the hissed insults of the gander. The snort he gave as I swung into the saddle, and turned his head towards Highbiggens, seemed to indicate that he thought poorly of Lowflatts' hospitality so far.

'This wasn't the homecoming I hoped for, either,' I told him, patting his arched chestnut neck, stained with sweat and dust from a long day's travelling. I was sweat drenched and dusty too. My thigh was stiffening up, and hurt like the devil. 'Like you, old fellow, I was looking forward to a good meal and a comfortable bed, but now we must steel ourselves to try and get some sense out of the Postlethwaites. Let us pray that drunk or sober, they can throw some light on this business.'

# Chapter 2

I let Caesar pick his own way along the, to him, unfamiliar trackway to the Postlethwaites' farm. This lay just out of sight, its buildings hidden by the rising land and a stand of fresh-greened larch trees. My one thought was to find help. My spirits were too agitated to care what path I took. Had my family scrambled, harried and desperate, pursued by evil men, along this path, to seek shelter with the Possies? I was sorely troubled, hardly aware of my surroundings, yet my campaigner's eye noted little evidence that anyone had passed this way in a hurry. Caesar was having to place his hooves carefully, experienced trooper though he was, along a track beginning to be overgrown with fresh tendrils of bracken which no one had cut back so far this year. Did this tell me that I was wasting my time? The path had been trodden, true enough, but there were no signs that anyone had come running in fear and haste, catching their clothing on bushes and briars, to seek protection. Yet I could not bring myself to turn back, and take the lane to the next nearest human habitation, the hamlet of Beckside. That would mean passing the place where poor Loveday's corpse lay.

Though harsh winds can suddenly sweep down from the fells at any season, in summer our Lune valley is generally a lush and pleasant place. In the pastures the cows stand up to their udders in the rich grass, starred with purple mayflowers and golden kingcups. The hedgerows hang pink and fragrant with dog roses and honeysuckle. I saw none of this that day, only the image of a dead girl whose corpse lay rotting at the bottom of a ditch.

I urged my tired horse up and over the hill that forms the boundary of our land, and along the edge of the wood, to Highbiggens. Once on the steep upward slope beyond the trees, it becomes apparent why Highbiggens is one of the less prosperous farms in the valley. The thin soil barely covers thrusting outcrops of limestone, white as the bones of the monsters that lived before Noah. Not land to grow fat on, for man or beast. Yet the Postlethwaites are a numerous tribe. Josiah Postlethwaite once had a wife, though I have but the dimmest recollection of her, and he had three sons and two daughters living with him. On my last brief visit home, riding north, nearly a year ago, to join Cromwell's troops in Scotland, the news was that the two eldest daughters had left home. They'd hired themselves out as farm servants over in the next dale.

'No surprise there,' said my mother. 'Dorcas and Marjorie have neither looks nor siller to catch husbands, and at least they'll be decently fed and clothed on someone else's farm, which is a good deal more than they could hope for at home. Possie and his sons drink every penny Highbiggens makes.'

Getting hold of strong drink was all too easy for the Postlethwaites.

George and Malachi brewed it themselves. It was good ale too, and they could have made a profitable business of it, if they hadn't drunk most of it themselves. What state would I find them in today? Would they know what had happened, have news to give me of Miles and Mother and Ann? Or would they, lounging about in a drink sodden daze, have failed to notice if the Devil and all his Imps had swooped down from the flat top of Ingleborough, and carried my family off? Surely, if they knew of her death, they would have roused themselves and made some attempt to bury poor Loveday?

Approaching the farmyard, deep in my own anxious thoughts, I saw at first what I expected to see, meagre grazing; sheep, and a few thin cattle, but then I noticed the sheep were freshly sheared, and the fences in better repair than the last time I'd been here. Could the shock of Dorcas and Marjorie upping sticks, and going off to find a place where they might get some thanks for their labours, have had a salutatory effect on their menfolk?

Rounding the barn, I decided it must be so. I'd never seen the yard at Highbiggens so well ordered. Surely no Postlethwaite cockerel had ever crowed atop so small a midden heap? The yard had been cleared of its usual clutter of bits of broken wagons and old furniture, and a neat pile of split logs was stacked against the house wall. There was a sharp scent of new lime coming from the open door to the cow byre, and an attempt had even been made to patch a hole in the barn roof which had been there since I was in petticoats.

I got down from the saddle and looked around. Of the Postlethwaites themselves there was no immediate sign, although a bright edged axe lay beside the wood pile, and on a chair under one of the windows of the farmhouse a book lay open, its pages lifting gently in the breeze. I was surprised that the Postlethwaites should own a book. When I got close enough, I saw it was a King James' Bible.

Then old Josiah came shuffling around the end of the house with a pair of spectacles on the end of his nose. I had to blink twice to recognise the old reprobate. He was clean, neat, and sober, and someone must have taken the sheep shears to his beard.

'Robert Haddon, my dear friend and neighbour!' he cried, picking up the Bible and hugging it to his chest. 'The Lord be praised that He has brought thee back safe from the battlefield! How is thy dear mother? Is she back from Lancaster? Was she successful in getting thy poor brother out of gaol?'

Then George and Malachi and young Benjamin appeared, and one of the two daughters who were still left at home, all austerely clad in black, the girl with a freshly starched collar. They all praised the Lord for my deliverance, and quoted Scripture, and the girl — I decided she was

Hannah — struck up a psalm in a sweet piping voice.

I was so dumbfounded that I suspect I stood there, a complete gapeseed, with my mouth opening and closing like a river trout. Caesar, sensing my confusion, laid his ears back and showed his teeth, snickering in alarm. He couldn't have been more taken aback than I was. My sober sides brother, it seemed, was a gaolbird, and the Postlethwaites had got religion.

'Nay, lad, don't look so 'mazed,' cried Josiah, 'to see us walking in the Lord's way! We've been six months now, on the path of righteousness, ever since our Dorcas and our Marjie got work with Major and Mrs Thornley over at Newbyres, and we were brought to the Light.'

'M-my apologies!' I stammered, hastily removing my hat, 'I didn't know, I've just got here...'

'Nay bother, nay bother, and tha' needn't doff tha' hat, laddie, we're all on a level now. We give Hat Honour only to our Maker, isn't that so, lads?' He turned to his sons for confirmation, and the great lummoxes nodded solemnly. As drunks, George and Malachi had been what the Irish would call roaring boys. Sober, they were evidently tongue tied.

'Oh, never mind that, Father, can't tha see our neighbour is troubled?' piped up Hannah. Mother always said the Postlethwaite girls had more wit about them than the men.

'It's Loveday! She's dead... and the house is deserted!' I blurted. 'You say Miles is in Lancaster gaol? ...and Mother's gone there... but someone's killed Loveday and left her in a ditch!'

For a long moment there was silence in the farmyard, except for the ring of iron on stone, as Caesar shifted his hooves impatiently on the cobbles.

'Nay, nay, that can't be!' whispered old Josiah, clutching his Bible as though it were a floating spar, and he a drowning man. 'A lawyer wrote to tha mother. There was an inheritance from an uncle, brother to your mother, and Miles went to Lancaster to claim it. There was a dispute, some other fellow, some relative, thought he should inherit, and there was a fight, and they landed in gaol. Your mother took the pony— Miles had the cob — and went off three days ago to pay the fine. She walked over to tell us that the girls were going to manage on their own. Lanty Briggs was to help them with the milking, and fodder for the beasts....'

'And we sent our Rachel!' interrupted Hannah, her voice suddenly rising, 'Where's my sister, Rachel? She went to keep them company!'

'The Lord keep us and save us!' rumbled George Postlethwaite, speaking for the first time, 'We'd best come o'er and see what's t'do. Loveday dead, tha says? And no sight of t'girls? Happen we'd best send for t'Magistrate if there's bin murder done!'

Hannah, who had already gone as white as her own starched collar as the import of my news sank in, now bust into wailing and weeping. 'Oh! 'tis just as Loveday prophesied! *The winds shall take me, and I shall lie, three days beneath God's unclouded sky!'* Her voice rose to a shriek as she recited this piece of doggerel, and when her father and brothers said nothing, but merely shuffled their feet uncomfortably, she poked Malachi in the stomach. 'She did, after church, on the Lord's day, two weeks back, *thee* remembers, Malc?'

Malachi, looking even more discomforted, muttered, 'Happen. Happen she did. It sounds like her. She said a lot in that fashion when she had the prophesying fit on her... but Ah niver took it to mean she were expecting t'die.'

I must have looked as befuddled as I felt, because Josiah took it upon himself to explain. 'Oh, aye, she was quite the female prophetess, was tha brother's wife, just like they have 'em in Lunnon town. She were getting known for it, up and down the dale.'

'Was she? Mother never mentioned it — in any of her letters.'

He scratched the side of his nose thoughtfully before replying, 'Aye, happen she wouldn't. Tha mother doesn't— didn't — hold with it... but tha brother didn't mind. Thought it gave her an interest, like, since she didn't seem able to breed babbies.'

'We'd best do sommat,' stated George, dropping his large hand on Hannah's shoulder. 'Weeping won't mend owt, and t'day's wearing on. Our Benjy, thee set forth for Lings and fetch Colonel Moreland. Malc and I'll come down with a hurdle, and help coffin t'poor lass.' He paused as a thought struck him, the same one, as it happened, that had just struck me.

'What of Lanty Briggs, then? Don't 'e know what's t'do?'

# Chapter 3

The sun was dipping down behind the western hills into the Irish sea by the time George and Malachi closed the lid of the rough-hewn coffin, and hitched one of Colonel Moreland's farm horses to the haycart to take Loveday's body to church.

Young men of our district take pride in being lithe runners over rough terrain, and Benjamin Postlethwaite must have reached Lings almost as soon as his brothers, carrying the hurdle, and myself, leading Caesar, got down to Lowflatts. We left Josiah, reading aloud from the psalms, seeking to console the weeping Hannah.

We found the coffin boards stacked in the barn — every family living on a remote farm keeps a spare coffin about the place, for winters can be harsh, and sickness comes suddenly. I stalled Caesar and busied myself knocking it together, whilst George and Malachi went and lifted Loveday out of the ditch. I, who had supervised the burying of many a brave comrade, could not bear to watch. They carried her up to the house on the sheep hurdle, a piece of sacking covering her face. I was grateful for that, although for her loveliness she should have had a silken shroud. I had to turn away, tears starting in my eyes. Then Colonel Moreland rode into the yard on his big roan, together with his steward, Jem Robinson, mounted on a cob, with Ben Postlethwaite clinging on behind.

Leaving the rest of them in the yard, I signalled Benson Moreland to follow me indoors. I led him into the parlour. At the back end of the year, Mother dries lavender and rose petals and places them in a treasured blue delftware bowl, and the sweet musky scent still hung in the empty room.

'This is a day of lamentation, Major,' said Colonel Moreland, giving me my title in the New Model, though I'm loath to use it away from the battlefield, knowing that I earned it by stepping into the boots of brave men now dead. He placed his broad brimmed leather hat on the table, and, plumping himself down heavily on one of our oak dining chairs, demanded, 'Is this right, what young Ben Postlethwaite tells me? Mistress Loveday dead, and your family all missing? I knew nothing of it! No word of any trouble has reached us at Lings. Although my wife mentioned only this morning that she hadn't seen your mother in Church, and wondered if all was well with her.'

No, I thought. There would never be a time when Mother would be happy to have your noble wife poking her nose into our family's affairs. She wouldn't have wanted her to know that Miles is in gaol. Mother had no patience with Lady Brilliana Moreland and her superior airs. But I had to tell the Colonel the whole story now, so I did, briefly, wasting no words, the way I'd been taught to make a report to a commanding officer. No emotions, no feelings, no guessing what might have happened, just the facts. Benson Moreland had been a good officer, and he listened without interruption until I finished.

'So, Miles and your mother are probably safe enough, if not happy with their lot? The Lord God be praised for that. But Mistress Loveday dead… and those two young lasses missing,' he sucked in air through his teeth. 'This is a bad business, Major, I can hardly credit it. You and I have both seen terrible things, on the battle field and off, but here … Oh, there was trouble enough in Lancaster, back in '43, but this valley has been scarcely touched by the war. There was the castle sacked down at Tunstall, and a while ago we had reports of a few Scottish mercenaries, cut off from their comrades, marauding in the hills, but in recent days, nothing. You may be sure I encourage my farm tenants to pass on news of anyone sleeping rough, any cattle or sheep taken. There's been naught like that. I cannot understand it.' He shook his head in puzzlement and ran his palm down his face, flattening his great bulbous nose. 'I suppose I must go and take a look at the poor girl's body. Then organise a search party for the other two.'

'Colonel, you won't mind if I don't come… to look again at the body?' He studied me for a moment. 'Yes, it hits harder when it's one of your own,' he remarked, and strode out of the room, the tops of his great boots creaking as they chafed against his breeches.

I sat for a while staring into space, watching the dust motes settle on the Colonel's hat, which he'd left on the table. When I was a boy I wept easily over a dead puppy, or on receiving some hurt in a scrap with Miles, but now I am a man, and must put away childish things. I got to my feet and made my way stiffly through the door to the yard. I hoped Colonel Moreland would have finished his examination, and be ready to start the search for my sister and Rachel Postlethwaite. We must make some attempt to find them before the light failed.

However, Colonel Moreland and the Postlethwaite brothers were all still standing around the open coffin. Jem Robinson stood to one side, his eyes fixed on the barn's rafters.

'The skin discolours within a short time of death,' Benson Moreland, was saying, 'I've seen it, a hundred times on the battlefield. But, see here, in the hair line. Bruising, and, yes, quite a deep indentation. Her skull cracked like the shell of an egg.' I watched from the doorway as his gloved finger probed, felt my gorge rise, and closed my eyes. 'Easy to say what was the cause of death. A blow with some narrow edged weapon with a knob or a metal protrusion of some kind. A poker, some tool around the farm here. But as to what exactly it was, or who dealt it… she was face up in the ditch?'

George Postlethwaite answered. 'That she was, and her clothing undisturbed, thanks be to God, and may He have mercy on her soul.' His brother chimed, 'Amen.'

'So we can dismiss the idea that she was the victim of ravishment. Or that it was a simple accident, where she tripped and hit her head on a sharp stone. You didn't see anything that made you think she had been carried to that place — or dragged there?'

'No, she lay as if she'd fallen there,' George stated. There was no discourtesy in his tone, he was merely matter of fact, as one man speaking to another, but I noticed he didn't call Benson Moreland, 'Sir' or name his military title. The Colonel straightened up, taking off his gloves and slapping them against his thigh boots to dislodge any hairs and particles of skin from the corpse which might have sullied them.

'I'd better see the spot where she lay, and then we'll search the fields round about for any sign of the other two,' he nodded to his steward, 'See to it, Jem.'

'Yes, Sir. Where do you suggest we start?' I could not read the steward's expression, nor fathom his tone of voice. In contrast to George Postlethwaite, though he called his master Sir, he sounded world weary, almost insolent, as though he thought the task a waste of time, and wanted the Colonel to know it. Yet I had, many a Sunday in church in days gone by, seen his eyes rest on Loveday's beauty. Rumour had it he would have offered for her, had she not been promised to Miles. So why did he not care what had happened to her? Or to Ann, who had been growing into a pretty maid the last time I was home, and he still without a wife?

'Fields roundabout. Ditches.' Benson Moreland glanced at me, 'Have you looked in your beck?' He meant the small tributary stream that drains from our land into the Lune. I replied that I had not, feeling a fool to have searched so little before I rode to the Postlethwaites for help. But then I had believed everyone had fled, including Miles and my mother, from some attack. It was all too possible, I now conceded, that we should find the girls' bodies lying hidden below the undercut banks of the stream. Jem swung himself up onto the magistrate's tall horse, and set off across the meadow, Benjy Postlethwaite running at his side. George and Malachi, receiving the nod to go ahead, harnessed the cob to the haycart, and set off for Beckside and the church. I watched, bereft, as Loveday left Lowflatts for the last time.

'I've been thinking, Major.' The Colonel waited until they were gone, and he was sure Jem Robinson and Benjy were out of earshot, 'Have you heard that Mistress Loveday had set herself up as a Prophetess these last months? Quite a way she had, my daughter and my servants tell me, with rhymes, and phrases that sounded as if she'd taken them from the Bible or the prayer book, although my daughter insists they were of her own devising. It caused a considerable stir up and down the dale, as you can probably imagine. Could she have angered someone? You know how the people are around here... anything that smacks of witchcraft, or supernatural matters?' He was watching me out of the corners of his eyes. 'I know these Prophetesses are all the thing in London, even Parliament listens to 'em... whether they take any notice is another matter! But people here are still living in old King James' time as far as these things... things that cannot easily be explained, are concerned. What my daughter repeated to me, what she remembered, of what your sister-in-law said, was harmless. Vague stuff that sounds as though it means something, but no one can quite say what. But she'd only have to, accidentally, hit on something that someone didn't want to hear, or didn't want others to know. If you take my meaning?'

I understood, only too well. 'It was news to me, this prophesying. The Postlethwaites told me. I get the impression it was a just a young girl trying to make herself interesting. According to Josiah Postlethwaite my brother thought it harmless...'

Hearing the tinkling of bells, we both turned. Sheep were streaming over the grass on the other side of the Lune. The bellwether was already skittering down the bank to lead them across the river at its shallowest point. Behind them came Lanty Briggs, waving his stick and emitting the high pitched cawing sound which is his only means of communication.

'Does Lanty know the girls are missing?' In the distance, Jem Robinson was riding slowly along the bank above the beck. Ben Postlethwaite, whose energy seemed boundless, veered from hedge, to bush, to a stand of trees. If the girls were dead, their bodies were not to be easily discovered.

'I know not,' I replied. 'Lanty was way up on the hill when I first found Loveday, or I'd have questioned him. Mother asked him to help the girls with the milking, or so says Josiah.' We watched Lanty's approach. Benson Moreland emitted a gusty sigh. 'And what can he tell us, a deaf and dumb idiot?'

'He hears a little, and understands signs. Mother taught him. Names for example. Loveday. Love Day.' I pressed my hands on my heart, and then raised them to form the arched rays of the rising sun, although today's sun was dropping fast now, its rosy light glinting on the tops of the fells.

'Enough to interrogate him?' He used the language of the army.

'I hope so.'

The rumbling and skittering of the sheep's' hooves as they descended the bank and crossed the beck towards us concealed all other sounds, so that both of us jumped, startled when a voice spoke behind us. Lady Brilliana Moreland and her daughter had ridden up the grassy lane without us hearing their approach.

'Husband, it's as well we are not an enemy troop,' stated Lady Brilliana, from atop her bay mare. There was a glint in her grey eyes, and a suggestion of sarcasm in her voice, as though it gave her pleasure to catch her husband unawares. 'Is this the place where the girl was found?' She noticed me for the first time, and said, 'Robert Haddon, the soldier son? I'm sorry to hear what has happened to your sister-in-law. We met with George Postlethwaite and his brother as we came through Beckside, and they told us the sad news.' She spoke the correct words, formally, but her voice held no note of warmth. A cold, proud woman, my mother had always said, but I had put that down to Mother's prejudices. Lady Brilliana was the ninth daughter of an impoverished Earl, and Mother had no time for those who thought birth alone afforded them special treatment, especially where there was no money to pay for it. Lady Brilliana must have been a very handsome woman in her youth, with fine black lash-fringed grey eyes, but now lines of disappointment, or a peevish disposition had settled around her mouth. She remained seated on her mare, gazing down into the empty ditch with its broken flower stems. Judith, her daughter, slid down from her horse and came to stand beside her father.

'This is dreadful. Poor Loveday. She was so beautiful, wasn't she?' she remarked, glancing at me sideways and then quickly away as though something about me made her nervous. I hadn't seen Judith Moreland for three years or more. Then she'd been clumsy, plump, puppyish, a child not yet grown to womanhood, though even then she had her mother's fine eyes and neat straight nose, and her father's broad brow. Now she was taller, and slender as a flag iris. A young woman — no, a young lady. I was surprised they hadn't found a husband for her. Perhaps they had, though news of a betrothal was just the sort of item I would have expected Mother to include in a letter. Then again, it might not be easy to settle on the right man, despite her good looks and her father's position. Her father had fought for Parliament, but her mother's family for the King. And even though her birth was good, money must be tight. Difficult times for young women wanting to wed.

'And the child,' she murmured, glancing sideways at me again, 'was there a child? Loveday was sure she was going to have a child at last, but your mother said it might be wishful thinking.'

I shrugged my shoulders. 'I don't know, Mistress... Moreland.' What to call her? As a little girl I'd called her Judith, but she wasn't a little girl anymore.

'Here's Lanty with the sheep, maybe he can tell us how it happened,' I began, as the flock swarmed passed us up the slope towards the farm garth, and the bent, wizened old shepherd limped towards us, his hobgoblin face split in a wide grin.

'Rah! Rah!' he greeted me, apparently delighted. Rah was his name for me, the nearest he could get to Rob. 'Ma ghh!' he added, pointing down river.

'Mother's gone to Lancaster?' I interpreted. He nodded.

'And the girls?'

'Yah, ghh!' he affirmed, but his expression became more doubtful.

'You think they went to Lancaster too?' He nodded, shrugged; spread his hands, indicating that he was unsure.

'How many days ago?' I asked. He held up two fingers, confident at first, but then seeing something in my expression, and that of Colonel Moreland, he hesitated, and a look of fear stole across his face.

'And Mistress Loveday?'

Now he knew there was something wrong. His eyes slid first to one of us and then another.

'She's dead, Lanty.' I signed cutting my throat, and putting my hands together in prayer. His jaw fell open, and he emitted a strange whimpering sound.

'Deh? Nah, nah!' Suddenly his eyes rolled back into his head. His body twisted sharply, wracked by a convulsion, and he fell backwards onto the ground, foaming at the mouth.

'Possessed. The devil has him fast!' remarked Lady Brilliana.

'I have to do it. You know I do, Major. Protective custody. For his own safety,' Magistrate Moreland stated quietly, not liking it, any better than I did. But Lady Brilliana had spoken, and we had all seen Lanty thrashing on the ground, limbs twisted, and foam and spittle issuing from his mouth. And of course we had all seen, the Colonel's wife and daughter; Jem Robinson, the steward, back from his fruitless search of the beck, Benjy Postlethwaite, shaking his mop of hair, a self-righteous, 'Lord, have mercy on a poor sinner,' on his lips. There was nothing for our man of the law to do, but arrest the shepherd.

# Chapter 4

I knew Lanty had the falling sickness, had had it from a child. Colonel Moreland knew it too. Knew that his falling into a fit on being told that Loveday, whom he adored, was dead, and the girls missing, was most likely the result of shock and fear rather than guilt. But he and I were soldiers. Hardened campaigners. We knew what terrible news— the death of a dear comrade — could do to the most robust of men. Lanty was far from that, a poor dumb half-wit at the best of times. The charge of being possessed by the Devil, knowingly or not, with the implication that under that possession he had murdered Loveday, my sister Ann, and Rachel Postlethwaite, could see him dead. Either legally, or strung up from a tree by the local toughs. Being locked up in the Magistrate's cellar at Lings Hall might kill him anyway. But as Colonel Moreland had indicated, many people hereabouts cling to the old ways, the old beliefs. The Devil is very real to them; they see him peering out at them from every shadowy corner. Every child born with a deformity, every ailing cow, every churn of good milk turned sour, confirms that *he* is at work in the world. Lady Brilliana had named the Devil. Those words could not be unsaid.

'I agree,' I told the Colonel, 'it's best you take him. For his own sake.' It was the last thing I wanted, but there was no choice. If my mother had been here... she would have tried to keep him with us. Insisted he was too ill to be moved. Put him to bed in the spare room and let him sleep off the effects of the seizure. Cooled his blood with a special concoction of herbs she brewed. And then, when he was fully recovered, taken him gently through his story, using the system of hand signals she had devised to communicate with the poor dumb fellow, until she was sure she knew everything he knew. He must surely know more than we did. But my mother wasn't here. I didn't have her skills. I had no idea which herbs she had found so beneficial in treating Lanty in the past. I could summon to my aid only a few of the many intricate signs they used to talk to one another. So I let them take him, still unconscious, slung across the saddle of the big roan. Jem's sour expression told me how little he relished having to lead the horse home. I feared Lanty would be thrown down the cellar steps when they reached Lings Hall. The magistrate took his daughter's horse while she hitched up her skirts without complaint, and rode pillion behind her mother.

I didn't stand about to watch them go. I had problems of my own. Woolly ones, skittering off up the lane without their shepherd to guide them. Getting into the uncut hay any minute, if I didn't head them off. And there were cows to milk. Hens and geese to feed. A nanny goat with goosegog flux, and a valuable cavalry horse, who was used to being treated like a Roman emperor, and who wasn't impressed with the welcome Lowflatts had provided so far.

'Ah'll stop an' give thee a hand,' offered Benjy Postlethwaite, as the rest of my flock disappeared down the lane into the dusk. ''Tis the Lord's work, an' our George said a' can stop, if tha' wants? Ah've bin helping tha' brother many a time of late, when he were needing a pair o' hands.'

I surveyed his eager face in the dying daylight. I was exhausted, mentally and physically, but this youth, who had run getting on for two miles to Lings and back, and then tracked about across fields and meadows looking for his sister and mine, seemed indefatigable. I suppose it had been an exciting day for him. Something out of the ordinary rut, and the Lord's work into the bargain! If he was worried about Rachel, it didn't show.

'Ever thought of enlisting, Benjy?' I enquired. 'Oliver Cromwell could use an energetic lad like you.'

'Ah've thought of't, agreed Benjy, his eyes glittering beneath his uncut fringe, 'Aye, Ah've thought on. What's t'pay like?'

I told him, and his eyes grew round. 'Ah might then. Go for a soldier!'

'The only slight disadvantage is, you might get killed,' I warned, a fact recruiting sergeants somehow never mention. The other thing they never mention is that the job involves killing other people. Folks you've never set eyes on before in your life, and with whom you have no personal quarrel. That's the bit I'd found difficult. But Benjy didn't want to hear any of that just now, and if we didn't get the sheep penned soon it would be dark. We'd never get them rounded up, and the wily grey hill foxes would tear the throats out of the half-grown lambs before the night was out.

We got them penned. We dragged clumps of grass out of the hedgerows as fodder for them. We fed the other animals, and I rubbed Caesar down and fed him. We went indoors and wasted what felt like an hour, hunting for the flint to light the tallow dips. Then we sat at the kitchen table eating cheese and drinking small beer. There didn't seem to be anything else.

'In the morning, Benjamin, the sheep will need to be taken up to the high ground...' I began.

'Aye, Ah've thought on,' agreed Benjy, who obviously had, guessing perhaps that I might suggest he take them there (and stay with them). 'Ah'll go t'Beckside at first light, and get twa o' Luke Procter's young 'uns. Them'll go, if tha'll fix 'em with some o' this cheese o' Mistress Loveday's, an' a pint o' small beer in a pot wi' a stopper. Ah'll bide here wi' thee, and milk t'cows. We might get word o' tha' sister an' our Rachel. Tha'll be wanting to put scythe t'grass, happen?'

'Yes, Lieutenant Postlethwaite!' I grinned weakly at him, 'but with my wounded thigh, I'd better sit on the three legged stool and milk, and *thee* had better scythe!'

'Major, S'ah!' He grinned back at me, sketching a salute.

I ordered us both to bed. He refused to go without a passage from the Bible. I fetched it from the parlour, and read it aloud. Psalm ninety one, verses two to five, if you should want to read it yourself.

'He shall cover thee wi' his feathers, and under His wings shalt thou... trust,' Ben repeated the words after me, and kept repeating them, committing them to memory, as he stumbled upstairs to the small bed space off the linen room, where Mother used to put Lanty after one of his turns. A prayer for the safety of his sister and mine. I understood that he cared more about Rachel than he'd allowed himself to show.

I slept in my old attic bedroom under the eaves, and dreamed, I'm sure. All the old nightmares of killing and ugly death, but exhaustion had me in its grip, and in the morning I didn't remember any of them.

I woke to the cockerel crowing on an orchard branch, and the chink of pots in the kitchen. Benjy was up before me. I found him paring rind off the cheese.

'Ain't much,' he told me. 'Ah' found some butter, but t'bread's gone mouldy in't crock. Dust tha know how to mek bread?'

I replied that I did not. He shook his head. 'Our Marjorie sez women is the equal of men, because though a man may reap and sow, 'tis women puts bread on t'table, and if there be no women, a man would be eating berries along with birds of t'air.'

Surveying our depleted larder, I thought Marjorie had a point, though I wasn't sure I wanted to admit it, so I took up the Bible and read Matthew six, verse twenty five, where it says, 'Take no thought... what ye shall eat... what ye shall drink', and sent Ben loping off to Beckside to rouse Luke Procter's young 'uns.

Then I turned Caesar out into the paddock, fed the hens and collected the eggs (Marjorie wouldn't know, but though a man may not be able to make bread, the army teaches him to fry eggs) milked five cows and the nanny goat, drew water from the well, and swilled out the befouled still room. Then I closed, but did not lock, the back door, and followed the cows across the meadow and down to the river.

There is a spot, under a clump of overhanging alder bushes, where grit stone boulders have worn away the limestone of the river bed and created a deep 'washpot'. Here I stripped off my travel stained leathers, shirt, and small clothes, and lowered myself, gasping, into the cold clean waters of the river Lune. First I submerged myself, holding my breath for as long as I could, and ducking down under the surface two or three times, so that any lice who had travelled down with me from Edinburgh should appreciate the kind of welcome we give to blood suckers in these parts. Then, grasping the smoothed limestone edges of the 'pot', I lay back against the river's current, and tried to think.

The reason, I'm sure, that the Parliamentary army has been successful against that of the late King, is that we've become disciplined. All that bible reading and discussion, while we sat around in camp, had a purpose. It taught us to think, to reason, to put our thoughts into words, to place our ideas in some sort of order. To draw up a list of what we needed to do, whether it was save our souls, besiege a castle, or buy in stores. I needed those skills now. A list of things to do, actions to take, ease a troubled mind and make a man feel he is in some sort of control of his destiny, no matter how chaotic and dreadful the events that surround him.

I tried, now, to think out a strategy, as I had when directing a troop of men. What were my priorities? What should I do first? What should I direct others to do? What others? There lay the nub of my problem. Given that the Postlethwaites had loaned me Benjy, I had one rather inexperienced, though willing, lieutenant. Even now, shaking river water out of my ears, I heard enthusiastic yells, and drumming hoof beats. Luke Procter's young 'uns, two grubby ragamuffins armed with ash plants, were driving a rather surprised flock of sheep up to the hills. As the baas and yelps faded into the distance, I heard the rasp of the whetstone on the scythe blade, as my one man prepared to mow our meadow.

I resorted to counting on my fingers. I must contact Mother and Miles, and break the news of Loveday's death. I needed to mount a proper search party for the missing girls. I must speak to the priest and make the arrangements for the funeral. But how could I do those things and keep the farm going? Farm animals can't be left to care for themselves. Cows have to be milked twice a day. Sheep need shepherding against predators while they graze on the open fells, and extra fodder in the fold at night. A horse needs hay, water, grooming, and exercise. Hens need corn, and their eggs must be gathered, or they'll cease laying. A goat will forage for herself, but you'll soon be sorry if you let her, and even she needs milking. Benjy, however energetic, couldn't do all this. Even if the Postlethwaites would lend me Hannah — and why should they, who would cook and do their dairying? — we'd barely manage. Perhaps there might be someone in the village? Even so, I could not be spared to ride to Lancaster to find my mother and brother... therefore...

Therefore, my priority must be to keep the farm going and *at the same time* make efforts to find Ann and Rachel, alive or dead. Mother might never forgive me, but I could see no alternative.

'Good morning, Major Robert!' I hadn't seen her or heard her approach, any more than I had the day before, and now she was squatting amidst the lower branches of an alder, just above me on the bank. Bright grey eyes, green velvet riding habit, and a tall hat with a feather in it.

'Mistress Judith!' How is it, that caught without clothes, the hands fly to cover the dowsetts, even though I knew she could not possibly see my private parts through the swirling current?

She giggled at my discomfort. 'I was just thinking, *Judith and Holofernes!* Because I can only see your head above the water,' she explained, perhaps intending to put me at my ease. My ease! What if anyone should see her conversing with a naked man? The story would run round the neighbourhood like wild fire. Her reputation would be ruined, and I would be blamed. I would probably have to marry the wretched girl, although I certainly wasn't the aristocratic catch Lady Brilliana would be looking for.

'Mistress Judith, I don't think you should... believe me, you must go. At once.'

'Oh, fiddle faddle!' she swung an insolent foot out over the water, the low-bent alder branch swaying beneath her. 'I've seen naked men before. My brothers and the farm lads always strip off and jump in the river if the weather turns hot. Anyway, I can't *see* you, as I said. Only your head, and it's your head I want. I want to talk to you.'

'No, Mistress Judith. Go away and I'll dress, and then we can talk if you wish it.'

'Oh, fie and fiddlesticks! I know how that would be. You wouldn't listen half so well as now, when I have you at my mercy! Your mind would be on the farm. With half an eye you would be watching Benjy Postlethwaite to see is he scything the hay properly, and half an eye would be scanning the hillside to notice if those Procter scamps are driving the sheep too close to the edge of the ghyll. One piece of your mind would be getting ready to call on the priest to arrange Loveday's burying, and another on how will you spare the time to ride to Lancaster to find your mother and Miles. You would not be listening, really listening, to me!' She paused, chewing her indignation.

'Nobody listens to me at home, not even Papa, so I am forced to take drastic action. I shall stay where I am, and you will have nothing to do but hear me.' Having said this, she was silent for several moments, kicking at the dusky pink wood avens on the river's brim with her glossy boots, and showing a good deal more of her trim calves than any well brought up young woman should do.

'Lanty's all right by the way,' she stated, after a while. 'He came to, none the worse, my father says. Frightened out of what wits he has of course, but one of our stillroom maids was kin to his late mother and she understands him to a certain extent, so she's not afraid to go down there and give him his meals.'

I nodded. This might not sound like good news, but Lanty was being treated as fairly as could be expected in the circumstances. Judith kicked at the avens once more, and changed the subject.

'You know we're ruined?' she asked, and for a moment I thought she meant we two, because of my nakedness. 'Papa's at his wits' end. This war

*24*

has cleaned out our coffers. Lings has gone to wrack while Papa was away fighting, and it's come out that my brothers have run up terrible debts in the Low Countries — where Papa sent them to keep them away from the war — and now I think he may have found out that Mama has been all the while selling her jewellery, to send money to her brothers who fought for the King.' She swallowed and turned her head aside, but not before I saw tears well up in her eyes. 'But never mind that. What I came to talk about is Loveday. My father told you she'd set up as a prophetess?'

'Yes, and so did the Postlethwaites. What exactly did she prophesy?'

'I don't know,' replied Judith frankly, producing a fine linen handkerchief from her sleeve, and dabbing her eyes, 'although I heard her do it often enough, mostly in the church yard after the service on Sundays. It all sounded... exciting, strange! She used to go into a kind of trance, and whirl around a few times, and then gaze towards the distant fells and speak verses! At the time it sounded... portentous? Is that the right word? As though it must mean something important, warnings that people should take notice or something terrible would happen. But then, afterwards, it was difficult to say what it did mean, or who the warnings were meant for. Even Loveday didn't know, once she'd come out of her trance! Or so she said.'

I was beginning to feel that there would be no need to hide my manhood much longer as my parts would soon drop off. My wounded thigh too, throbbed with the exquisite pain of being immersed in icy water. 'Mistress Judith, I do want to hear what you have to say, but ...'

'But you have been in the water long enough, and wish me to turn my back while you clamber ashore!'

In truth I wished her in Hades, but now I realised it was imperative I hear her out. She disentangled herself from the alder tree and walked over to where her mare was grazing, some distance off, so that I was able to pull myself out of the pool and struggle, floundering like a newly caught salmon, into my shirt and breeches. Then, positioning myself down stream of the washpot, on a boulder in the sun, praying my shirt would dry out, and my teeth would stop chattering, I called her back.

She came to the brim of the river opposite and sat down on the bare turf, curling her feet neatly under her.

'Mistress Judith, you spent time with my sister in law. Do you believe that her prophesies may have upset someone, perhaps made somebody angry enough to kill her?'

Now she was clear of the shadowing leaves of the alder tree, I could see dark circles under her eyes, tight muscles along her jaw. I've carried out enough interrogations, of those suspected of keeping information to themselves which the Parliamentary army wished to have, to spot the signs. Mistress Judith hadn't been sleeping too well, her conscience was troubling her. Now was the time to put pressure on her to tell what she knew.

The stream bed was narrowed by great jutting boulders at this point, but the water swept on, deep and strong between us in its restricted channels. I couldn't have used any of the methods of physical coercion the army had taught me, but often you don't need to. Wait quietly, and the story comes pouring forth. So it was with Judith Moreland. It appeared that whilst her father, and I, and half the men of the neighbourhood, had been away campaigning, everything had changed. Before the war, she freely admitted, Judith Moreland of Lings Hall would not have been allowed to ride about the countryside calling on whom she pleased. One might have supposed that a delicately nurtured girl would have been placed under even tighter restrictions in a time of conflict, but not so. Once she would have had a groom to escort her, who would report to her mother where she went, and whom she saw. But as it was, there were no able bodied men to spare, and the battlefields were a long way off. Judith was not the kind of girl to sit quietly in the parlour with her embroidery for the duration, and the risks must have been judged trifling. Lady Brilliana might heartily dislike her spending time with the poorer sort in their farmhouses and cottages, she undoubtedly did, but she had no means to prevent it. Also the Morelands' well-known divided loyalties must have posed additional difficulties. Not that they were the only household where such differences had occurred. In some families the father fought for the King and the sons for Parliament, in others it might be brothers who took opposing sides. By mutual consent, social gatherings amongst the 'best families' of the district were suspended. There could, in any case, be no parties or assemblies whilst no acceptable young men were available to lead the young women onto the dance floor. Lady Brilliana must be at a loss to come up with any suitable entertainment for her only daughter. Better she should spend her days in the kitchen at Lowflatts, with Loveday, Ann, and Rachel, learning to churn butter, make gooseberry fool, or turn sheets sides to middle. At least, Lady Brilliana must have calculated, my mother was there to keep an eye on them.

Unfortunately, or so I gathered now from her somewhat confused narrative, my mother was relying on Judith to distract Loveday, who had grown fretful at her failure to conceive a child, and who was, Judith artlessly reported, furious with Miles. Miles was too busy keeping the farm going to spend much time with her, too tired to make love to her when he did. Loveday fretted and complained, and even wondered aloud whether she had chosen the wrong brother.

'And Ann and Rachel?' I interrupted; not wanting to hear a detailed a description of Loveday and Miles' marital difficulties.

'Oh, Ann's so quiet and shy, and Rachel... sometimes it was Hannah. They were both interested in Loveday's prophesies. I think they thought they were genuine warnings from Heaven. Especially as they concerned their brother, Malachi!' Judith giggled, but then grew serious, describing once more Loveday's antics in the churchyard.

'And did anyone else take these utterances seriously? Was anyone visibly upset by these warnings?' My mind skittered away from my worst fear, that Loveday was involved in some kind of witchcraft, or had allowed others to believe she was. Not so many years had passed since a group of women, hardly more than a day's march from here, had perished as a result of accusations of black magic from their neighbours.

'Oh, many were made *uncomfortable*. Malachi Postlethwaite... I do believe Loveday had some part in the Postlethwaites' reformation! Jem Robinson, my father's steward. Sam Woodley at Bartonriggs, Deborah Snaith, the miller's widow... there may have been others,' agreed wide-eyed Judith, calmly. 'One rhyme I recall was, *"On her will fall the wrath of God, who meets her lover in the wood."* I remember that one, because we never worked out who it might be.'

And you encouraged her, you silly little...! I felt fury rising in me. It was fortunate for her that a deep rushing channel of water separated us, or I might have forgotten military discipline, and shaken Judith Moreland until her teeth rattled.

Had she not thought it might be dangerous? Had it not occurred to Loveday, or to any of them, that someone might be sufficiently upset by these warnings to want to silence her? No, apparently it hadn't.

'Your mother counselled that perhaps it wasn't wise, but Loveday didn't take much notice. Besides, your mother thought perhaps it was genuine, or at any rate she supposed Loveday thought it was. It gave Loveday an interest, stopped her complaints against Miles. Your mother was desperate to keep the peace between those two.'

Yes, her letter had indicated as much. And if Mother hadn't fully realised the danger, hadn't been able to make Loveday see the foolishness of her actions, then perhaps it was unfair to blame Judith. I placed my hands over my eyes, seeing inwardly Loveday's loveliness, now blotted out for ever. Nothing was audible above the river rushing and gurgling over the rocks, but when I looked up again I saw that Judith was weeping, shoulders shaking, tears flowing unchecked down her cheeks.

'I really loved her, Major Rob! And Ann and Rachel, and your dear mother! They've all been kind. They were so patient with me, teaching me how to make butter and cheese. They never resented my wanting to learn their skills, or said it wasn't fitting for a young lady like me, like our own maids at home do. We sang, and talked, and laughed, the time flew by, and none of the tasks seemed irksome at all! Loveday was so beautiful, so full of life. And the baby! She really thought she was expecting at last, and now she's dead, and the baby too. You think it was partly my fault, don't you?'

'I think quite a few people could have done more to prevent it,' I told her, through stiff lips, 'but perhaps not. Loveday was always wilful.' I myself had loved Loveday with all the passion of a young blade of twenty, but in truth I'd always known she was not as wise as she was beautiful — that she was silly and headstrong, and must always be a star in the firmament, no matter what trouble it brought.

'But what's done cannot be mended,' I stated. 'What we must hope is that no serious harm has befallen Ann and Rachel.'

'Lanty Briggs...' I began, and then stopped. Even if I could imagine Lanty harming Loveday, which I couldn't, he would never harm Ann. I remembered Mother letting him hold her in his arms for a few moments when she was a tiny baby. He loved her as much as if she had been his own.

'Lanty thought the girls had followed my mother to Lancaster, and he must have a reason for believing so, though he cannot tell us what it was. We must pray he's right. Though I don't see how they were to get there, unless they went on foot. And why would they set out on such a journey without letting Rachel's family know?' I was thinking aloud now, almost forgetting Judith, crouched on the river bank opposite.

'I know nothing of Ann and Rachel,' she said sadly. 'Mayhap they saw... *him*, the murderer. And ran away?'

I nodded, for this had occurred to me. 'But where?' I asked, 'I thought myself, when I arrived home and found Loveday dead, and the farm deserted, that some violent attack had overtaken them and everyone had fled, so I rode straight to Highbiggens, only to find the Postlethwaites knew nothing. They didn't come to you at Lings, nor have they been seen in Beckside so far as I can gather. Where would they go? Where could they go?'

'Perhaps *I* could ride to some of the farms and ask...' Judith began, but then her gaze slid away, spotting something beyond me in the distance. I turned and looked over my shoulder. A horseman, cantering along the grassy ride, his cloak billowing gently in the summer breeze, was making straight for Lowflatts.

# Chapter 5

He was mounted on a slender black thoroughbred, a good mover, an expensive piece of horseflesh. He wore a russet cloak, and a hat with a broad brim, shading his face. The horse's coat shone glossy in the sunlight, and a sword hung from his belt. This much I could tell from afar. I didn't recognise him, although I was sure I should. He sat easy in the saddle, confident, as though he knew the road to Lowflatts, and expected to find a welcome there. In the hayfield, I saw Benjy pause in his rhythmic scything, and stiffen into stillness, warily eyeing the man's approach. I snatched up my abandoned clothing, bundled it inside my jerkin, and left the lachrymose Judith without a word. I half ran, half hobbled, favouring my wounded thigh, across the water meadow, in a fruitless attempt to cut him off. I would have called out, demanded his business, but was too laboured of breath to do so. Might this be the man my mother had hinted at, who had been paying Loveday amorous attentions? Could this be the killer? I had no weapon on me, not even my clasp knife.

By the time I caught up with him, he'd ridden into the farmyard, dismounted, and found himself challenged by a grim faced farm boy. Benjy had left off hay cutting and, shouldering the scythe as though it was a pikestaff, galloped down through the orchard, ready to defend our property to the death.

I came on the tableau from the stranger's rear and realised what I should have realised all along — I did know who he was.

He was leaning against his horse's girth, apparently relaxed, yet wary, surprised, no doubt, by Benjy's aggressive welcome. I hadn't seen the black mare before, or the cloak. He was weighing up the situation, one hand on the mare's bridle, while the other rested gently on his sword hilt. I knew he would be smiling, quite unperturbed. Yet if Benjy had tried to take him on, the boy would have been dead, skewered on this man's sword blade, in less than a minute.

'Gentlemen! At ease!' I gasped, breathless from running, and the soldier turned, his face lighting up with pleasure.

'Rob, God be praised!'

'Gervase, you scoundrel! It's good to see you!' To Benjy's open-mouthed astonishment we threw our arms around one another. I think Benjy seriously doubted my political loyalties, and possibly even my manliness, at that moment. I was Parliament's man, wasn't I? So why, his bewildered expression begged, was I embracing a man whose hair curled over his lace trimmed collar, whose top lip boasted a magnificent blond moustache, whose fine woollen cloak, thoroughbred horse, and decorated sword scabbard, all screamed... Cavalier. Royalist.

'All's well, Benjy! Put that dangerous weapon down, and come and shake the hand of my friend and comrade, Gervase Fenton. Gervase, meet my new lieutenant — indeed my sole supporter, Benjamin Postlethwaite. Ben, don't be deceived by this rapscallion's appearance! Gervase is as loyal to the Parliamentary cause as a man can be. You see, Gervase is... one of Parliament's agents. It's sometimes necessary for him to appear to be what he is not!'

'One of ours, pretending to be one of theirs! A spy, in fact!' chuckled Gervase, showing his even white teeth, 'I don't always look like this, mind you. My hair grows at an alarming rate, which can be a curse as well as a blessing in my line of business. Five weeks gone, and I was clean shaven, with my hair cropped above my ears. Standard issue Roundhead. Very severe!' He made a mock frown. 'Questioning a noble family in... Staffordshire? I think it was Staffordshire, on the whereabouts of the Head of the household! Interesting answers. Didn't believe a word they told me!' His blue eyes twinkled, but then the laughter ebbed.

'I'm afraid I'm the bearer of bad news, Rob, old lad. I was in Lancaster — never mind why — and met your dear mother in the street. She didn't recognise me at first, understandably, me being in disguise, and she more than somewhat distracted, but when I made myself known she told me...?' My friend glanced from me to Ben and back, unsure whether to continue.

'Speak freely, Gervase. Benjy here knows all our shameful secrets. My brother Miles is in gaol.'

'Not anymore. Your mother paid the fine and got him out. But not, unfortunately, before he contracted a fever from that filthy place. She's nursing him in a room over a shop selling herbs and spices. Some relative has left the shop and the business to your family. Indeed, I believe it turns out that he has left it specifically to you, Robert.'

This was surprising news, but I nodded, hardly taking in its significance. 'Uncle William Sedgwick, Mother's half-brother. He was many years her senior. Ben's father, Josiah, told me there was some dispute about it with another relative, and Miles and he were taken up for affray. Though how that came about, I'm not sure. Miles is seriously ill?'

'I fear so. Your mother is determined to pull him through, but stout hearted as she is... it rests in the hands of the Almighty. She asked me if I could call here and speak to your sister-in-law, Mistress Loveday, and warn her...'

He saw it in our faces. 'Something is wrong here?'

'Loveday is dead. Murdered. I arrived home yesterday and found her.'

Gervase closed his eyes, screwing up his face as if in response to a blow. 'Dead? That lovely lass?' His arm fell across my shoulders in a vain attempt at comfort. I think Gervase always knew how I felt about Loveday, although I had never told him. 'How did it happen? Marauders? Is your sister safe?'

'I was praying you could tell me that. I *hoped* Ann was in Lancaster with my mother. Lanty Briggs, our shepherd, believes she was going there, together with Rachel, Benjy's sister. My mother didn't mention them?'

Gervase slowly shook his head. 'They're missing? Dear God!' was all he said. We stood, all three, in unhappy silence for several moments, and then I remembered my duties as a host.

'Come indoors, both of you. We'll eat, and I'll tell you the whole story. There's no bread. Fried eggs or cheese ?'

Gervase laughed and slapped my shoulder, 'Yes, we must eat, keep our spirits up. Eggs and cheese, if you can spare them? But I've eaten this man's camp cooking, Benjamin, and it's not to be tolerated! I shall cook. You shall expound, Rob, and then we'll plan our tactics.'

It was a comfort, having him there, talking of our tactics, as though he meant to be part of them, although I supposed he'd be unable to stay long. He was riding forth in these parts in this guise for some purpose, though he probably wouldn't tell me — at least not fully — what it was, and that purpose would call him away. Benjy, relieved of the various fears he had been harbouring, offered to unsaddle the mare and turn her out in the paddock. Caesar's head was already up, ears flicking, looking at her over the wall.

'Her name is Venus, not for the pagan goddess, but for the blaze on her forehead, which is said to represent the evening star,' Gervase told Benjy, and turning to me, 'your big fellow is gelded, isn't he? Only I don't like the way he's looking at her.'

'He is,' I grinned, 'but he sometimes likes to pretend it never happened.'

'Ah! We can all dream!' chortled my old comrade. Benjy looked faintly shocked. The lad would have to get used to soldiers' talk, if he was serious about enlisting. Not everyone in the New Model is a Friday faced saint, don't ever believe it. Both Gervase and I had had our adventures, he, I think, more than I. Though I spared a thought for a certain inn keeper's bonny widow, whom I had left behind in Edinburgh.

'Lord preserve me from pious adolescents,' I muttered as he walked away, leading the mare. Gervase and I raised our eyebrows at one another in mock commiseration. We'd both known our fill of milk-and-water youths who thought the answer to everything was in the Bible, and that God would send his angels to minister to their every need. 'The lad's a hard worker,' I added. 'I can't fault him in that respect.'

Or as a provider, as it turned out. Benjy came back from the paddock swinging a dead rabbit by its ears.

'Ah' set some snares early, before us broke us fast,' he announced, laying the corpse reverently on the kitchen table. 'Ah'll skin it, happen tha'll know how to cook it?' he asked Gervase, who roared with laughter again, pulling off his top boots and elaborately stitched jerkin, and rolling up his fine lawn sleeves to take on cook house duties.

As we ate at the kitchen table, I told the whole unhappy story — no, not quite the whole — for I left out the circumstances of my conversation with Judith Moreland, not wishing to shock young Benjamin again, though I related the main points of the conversation itself. Gervase listened and said little, moving between the hastily lit fire on the hearth and the kitchen table, skillet in hand. The time for a heart to heart conversation would be later, and I could see him wondering what task we could set Benjy, to get him out of the way.

'This afternoon, while the sun is at its height, we need to turn the hay Ben has already cut,' I announced. Otherwise it won't dry, and if there's a heavy dew it could rot.'

Benjy nodded agreement. 'Ah'll finish scything t'bottom end. If tha' starts turning half way down, Ah'll stook t'top end when Ah' finish.'

Gervase raised his eyebrows. I would hazard he has turned his hand to most things since he joined the New Model. His father has an estate in Huntingdonshire, but the finer points of farming practice might be a mystery to him. His sire can afford to employ a dozen people to turn the hay.

'Am I needed for this, or do I concentrate on rabbit stew?' he enquired.

'You're needed for this. Everyone's needed when we're haytiming. The crop's ready and we have a spell of fine weather. We must do as much as we can. Even my mother and the girls help... normally,' I swallowed, thinking of Loveday, who would never again complain of a sunburned nose. 'We three can manage this field on our own, but next week, when the rest is ready, I'll have to get extra hands from somewhere. This particular meadow slopes south and gets the best of the sun, and so is ready for cutting before the others.'

Benjy was wriggling on his stool, anxious to be up and doing. Three fried eggs topped with melted cheese, and that lad was ready for anything. We held him back long enough to skin the rabbit.

Out in the meadow, the two of us armed with hay rakes, and clad in old smocks and breeches belonging to Miles; were freer to talk, my old comrade and I. The regular swish of the scythe and the scraping of our rakes over the dry ground prevented Benjy from over hearing our discussion.

'I've called here several times through the winter and spring,' Gervase remarked, looking up from his raking to see my reaction.

'I realised that,' I replied, 'when I saw how familiar you were with where my mother keeps her skillet! I think I half realised when I saw you riding up to the farm. I didn't know it was you at that distance, but I sensed that this was someone who was expecting a welcome.'

I also thought, but did not say, no doubt you are the fellow who has been dallying with Loveday. Nothing serious intended on your side or— probably— on hers, but guaranteed to set Miles' teeth on edge.

'And have always received one. Your mother is a most excellent woman. Was she twenty years younger I'd throw her across my saddle and carry her off to wed!' Gervase chuckled, adding, 'It's a blind, of course, as you have no doubt guessed. I've had reasons to frequent this valley and the dales roundabout of late.' He pulled a face, meaning he was not at liberty to tell me what they were. 'And what is more natural than I should call at Lowflatts with news of my old comrade at arms, or to ask if they have news of you?'

'And you came in a variety of guises?'

'Indeed. Soldier — one of ours of course, packman, tract seller, horse dealer. I'm an excellent horse dealer. I believe I could get my living that way! Venus is my best purchase to date. I traded two chestnut yearlings for her as I came through Preston. I wish I could be sure the man who sold her to me had the right to do so! Your household always made me exceedingly welcome. The girls have tried to question me — girls always ask questions! — but your mother and brother kept their council. I think they guessed why I was here.'

'I can't!' I challenged him, just to see what he would say. Gervase leaned on his hay rake and squinted at me under the brim of my brother's old straw hat.

'No, but then you haven't been around in these parts for a year or more. Your mother and Miles have. They know, or guess I think, why Parliament is uneasy.'

'Which is?'

Miles shrugged, 'Sedition. Unbridled religion, mixed with politics. Folk banding together; prayer meetings in remote farm houses. Itinerant preachers whipping up ... what? True religious feeling or anarchy? People refusing to pay tithes to the Church. Not that that's new, but the protests are more organised. And letters have been received, some merely denouncing their neighbours from malice, but one at least…'

'Tithes? But surely, Oliver Cromwell himself...' I began, but we were interrupted. A figure in black was scurrying towards us, stumbling and tripping over the swathes of cut grass. He was bare headed, using his shallow crowned black hat as a fan against the heat of the afternoon.

'Major Haddon! Major Haddon!' this apparition cawed, in a voice as rusty as his black habit, and then began to sneeze, exploding at regular intervals as he covered the last few yards to where I stood. 'Major Haddon! I am come — *atishoo !*— to speak with you — *atishoo*! — about the — *atishoo*! — funeral arrangements!' he gasped between bouts of sneezing.

The Reverend Lemuel Drysdale, curate of Beckside Church. I half turned, intending to introduce him to Gervase, but saw that Gervase had undergone one of his personality changes. Suddenly he was a bent figure, one shoulder hunched higher than the other, with his hat pulled over his eyes. An anonymous farm labourer. Gervase knew I would take the hint. He didn't want to meet Lemuel Drysdale. I laid my rake aside, and took the exploding curate by the elbow.

'Come, Sir! Let me take you away from the hay, lest you succumb to a fever!'

I led him down to the farm house and seated him in the parlour, first removing the bowl of lavender and dried rose petals. He produced a kerchief from the recesses of his clerical garb, blew hard upon it, and wiped his streaming eyes. 'Alas, 'tis the grass pollen. It has affected me this way from a child!' he wheezed.

Lemuel Drysdale was one of those souls who seem to have been born old. I doubt he was more than five and thirty, but he always acted as though he was past fifty, and indeed always had, as long as I'd known him. He was a placeman, a poor curate who didn't look likely to advance in the church, but was keeping a pulpit warm for someone of higher rank. A wealthy female relative of the Morelands owned the living, and meant to keep it (and the tithes it brought in) in her own hands. In his beliefs I imagine he thought himself a Puritan, or perhaps an Arminian, but I doubt he had any real understanding of the arguments forever simmering between different branches of the church.

'The Postlethwaite brothers came to me last evening,' he croaked, once his eyes had ceased to water, 'bringing your brother's wife in her coffin to be housed in the church ready for burial. She was murdered? Terrible! I knew nothing of it! Terrible! But they gave me to understand that Magistrate Moreland has given his permission for the body to be interred?'

I assured him that this was the case. Much against my will, for I knew him to be worse than any old woman when it came to gossip (and I was no more anxious than my mother to have our affairs talked abroad) I told him how things stood. Miles lying sick in Lancaster (I didn't give the cause of his illness), my mother there nursing him, my sister and her companion missing, possibly travelling (I still hoped) towards Lancaster to join them.

'The Lord God has laid a heavy burden on your shoulders, Major Haddon,' the Reverend Drysdale sighed, but I saw by the glint in his reddened eyes that he was enjoying our misfortunes. So far as I knew, Miles had paid his tithes regularly, although he had no love for Lemuel Drysdale, whom he considered a clod pate, and my mother had been ever wont to point out to him his short comings, both in the matter of visiting and giving comfort to the sick, and the preaching of spiritual guidance to his congregation. So Lemuel Drysdale, though he had nothing, so far as I knew, against me, was enjoying my family's misfortunes.

'I wish I could say something of *comfort*, in the matter of your sister-in-law's death,' he remarked, peering at me over the hem of his nosewipe, 'but alas!' he sighed gustily, though his sorrow did not convince me, 'Mistress Loveday Haddon was a foolish young woman. We must pray that the Almighty will forgive youth and misguided enthusiasm.'

'I understand she had taken to uttering prophesies?'

'Imprudent! A very imprudent and foolish young person, I'm sorry to say,' the priest mumbled into his rag. 'However, we read that God is merciful unto sinners in the Day of Judgement, and we pray that it is so.'

I nodded, suppressing my anger. If he thought her so foolish and sinful, why hadn't he taken some action? What is a man of religion for, if not to guide his flock?

'Do you suppose, sir, that she may, unwittingly, have uttered some... prophesy, so called, which gave offence, angered someone to the extent that he — or she — was moved to kill her?'

Lemuel Drysdale looked startled, and discomforted. 'Her prophesies? That had not occurred to me. It was all a lot of meaningless rhyming. I doubt if anyone made sufficient sense of what she said. I certainly didn't!'

But I knew from the alarm that had leapt into his eyes, that he was lying. Something she had said must have cut him to the quick, perhaps even frightened him, and if so, might she not have left others equally disturbed? Could he himself have wielded some weapon, a staff, a cane? He was a cold fish. It was hard to imagine him hitting out in anger with sufficient force to kill someone, although I knew that he was handy with his cane across the legs of the village children if they were unable to recite the catechism, or even worse, if he caught them stealing plums from his orchard.

A strange expression now slid across his old-young features, a mixture of excitement and cunning. 'Your mother and your poor brother know nothing of Mistress Loveday's death?' he asked. I admitted that they didn't, and that I couldn't go, or spare anyone to go, to Lancaster at present.

'But they must be told! I feel it my duty, Major, as your parish priest. What I am about to suggest — I have already spoken with Luke Procter, and he has begun work, digging the grave — I suggest we hold the funeral service at first light tomorrow, and then I'll take my old nag, and ride to Lancaster. You would perhaps wish to write to your mother? I could carry the letter to her if you give me her direction? And when I return I hope it will be with news of your sister's safe arrival!'

I didn't like it. I didn't like Lemuel Drysdale, and I didn't relish the thought of his offering insincere pity to my mother and brother. He had been no friend to Loveday, and I suspected that his reaction to her death fell somewhere between indifference and relief. However, it was wrong that Mother and Miles should remain in ignorance, and whom else could I send?

# Chapter 6

With the dawn, a pale mist rose over the river and the low lying fields, giving promise of another hot June day. In that early light in Beckside churchyard, it wrapped itself about us as tenderly as a baby's shawl. I hadn't thought there would be many at Loveday's burying, since there could be no husband present, no mother or sister-in-law. Loveday had no family of her own. So I was grateful when Gervase and Benjy tumbled out of their beds and came with me. Halfway across the fields Benjy realised we'd come without the family Bible, and ran back for it.

The night before, while the rabbit stew bubbled in the pot, Gervase had commanded me to cut his hair in a ragged bob, and shave off the blond moustache. We moved to the parlour where the evening light was better, with razor, bowl, and soap suds. I took up my mother's dressmaking shears to complete the task. She wouldn't be pleased when she heard what they had been used for, but I'd nothing else to hand.

'I shall be an army groom,' Gervase told us, lounging on the settle at his ease in Miles' old patched and threadbare shirt and breeches, whilst smoking tobacco in a long stemmed clay pipe (a vile habit to my mind, but he had it) 'taking my master's horse back to his estate in the north — that will explain Venus, who is too fine a mount for the likes of the shabby fellow you are about to make me! What could be more natural than that I should call on you, my old Brigade Major, on my way, and then ride on to Colonel Moreland at Lings Hall with some trifling message from my master, the owner of the horse?'

He did not say who this master was supposed to be, or what he really intended with Colonel Moreland, Benjy being present and all ears — and eyes too — now that I had practised my barbering on him, and sliced a good inch off his fringe. I didn't try to press Gervase. The various hints he had dropped had made me uneasy. I'd been his friend nigh on five years, and I hoped our friendship held, yet I wasn't sure I could follow the road he seemed intent to travel.

I'd been Parliament's man, and still was, having sworn a variety of oaths when I joined the New Model Army, but doubts had assailed me, at Drogheda, at Wexford, and most of all when we heard that the King's head was cut off. Where was all this killing taking us? And now this talk of Fifth Monarchy men, Levellers, plotters and traitors, people who might be planning uprisings in lonely farm houses. Gervase appeared sincere in his belief in all this. I found it hard to credit. Why? Perhaps because these dwellers in remote dales were my friends and neighbours, related to my family by blood in some cases. Men made uneasy by the times, fearful about what had been done to our country, to our King. Who would lead our nation now, and what might the future bring? King Charles had been a weak and foolish man, but who could replace him as head of state? A self-appointed band of men up in 'Lunnon', of whom most people had never heard? The men of our district, yes, and women too, had much time for quiet contemplation as they carried out their daily tasks. Who could wonder if they did not like where their thoughts took them?

Though Gervase could not know it, and I was not ready to enlighten him just now, these were some of the same men and women who gathered around us in the churchyard, come to pray with me for the repose of Loveday's soul. They came silently, drifting across the fields out of the mist, gathering under the dark branches of the ancient yews in the burial ground. Quiet people, plainly dressed, who stood with heads bowed. Some had carried with them hay forks and shepherds' crooks which they left against the wall by the lychgate. We had chosen an early hour, in part so that the working day would not be wasted. Inside the church Lemuel spoke the words of the prayer book, and preached a short sermon, making no mention of Loveday's prophesies. I read verses from the Bible and managed a few strangled expressions of sorrow on behalf of my sick brother who could not be there to say them himself.

We laid her to rest beside my father and my grandparents, in a sunny corner of the churchyard plot, where she had a right to be, as a member of our family. The grave was lined with branches of green larch, so that we set her roughhewn coffin down in a leafy bower, slid the ropes from under it, and stood back, sighing with relief and sorrow mingled. Lemuel said what he must say, and I — well, I am not sure what I did say, but no one seemed surprised or alarmed by my words, so I must suppose it sufficed, and sprinkled a handful of earth over my brother's wife, my dead love.

Until that moment I hadn't noticed Judith Moreland. No other members of the Moreland family had come, although I had supposed the news of the time of the burial would have reached Lings, and had half expected that Benson Moreland and his wife might feel it their duty to be present. Jem Robinson, the Lings steward, who was a churchwarden, was well to the fore, but Judith, dressed in sober black; no feather in her hat today, must have hung back amongst the womenfolk during the service. Now she stepped forward with a nosegay of meadowsweet, clover and pink Campion, which she tossed lightly into the grave, and then raised her eyes to meet mine, challenging me to deny her right to do Loveday this last service. I said nothing, but nodded to Luke Procter, to begin the awful work of shovelling back the displaced earth, and turned away. I did not wish to speak with Mistress Judith, let alone get into an argument with her. I counted her responsible for encouraging Loveday's foolish pretensions to be a prophetess, which must surely have had some bearing on her death.

As we moved away from the graveside Lemuel Drysdale murmured eagerly in my ear that his horse was saddled in readiness for his to ride to Lancaster. Had I brought the letter for my mother? He seemed excited. No doubt his life as a country parson was a dull one. As a congregation, we do not even commit remarkable sins. I, who was battle weary, could think of nothing better than to sink down into the lush summer peace and solitude of Lonsdale, but I realised, that for Lemuel, a trip to Lancaster might be the highlight of his year.

'I forgot to bring it,' I hissed in reply. I'd scribbled a number of hasty lines before I slept the night before, but had left the letter behind on the kitchen table.

'No matter,' he responded, 'I will ride up to Lowflatts and collect it on my way. I'm anxious to be off before the day grows hot, but many of these good people,' he waved his arm to indicate the mourners, 'will bear you company for an hour or two on this sad day.' With this, he hitched up his black gown, and scurried away to fetch his horse.

The custom, in our small corner of the world, is to invite the mourners home after the funeral, to break their fast at a table groaning under the weight of home baking and small beer. It was this that had distracted me, and made me forget the letter. All through the service I had been conscious of discomfiture, wondering how to tell them that I could not entertain them to a funeral breakfast back at the farm. Mother would be mortified when she heard of it. I just hoped our neighbours would understand. But now I came to realise that we were not going to be allowed to slip away. One by one, as the menfolk fell into step behind me, I saw that the women had gone to gather up laden baskets from where they had left them in the shade of the churchyard yews. Custom would be followed, but the guests had been canny enough to bring the funeral baked meats with them.

Aside, I muttered to Gervase, 'These folk are coming back to the farm! They're our neighbours, blood kin to me in some cases, men and women our family has always known. I can't refuse them. Do you want to get away? Hurry ahead and saddle up if you do, otherwise you're due for a dreary few hours going over every word that was said at the graveside, and hearing how badly the crops are faring this year!'

Gervase hesitated, chewing at his newly shorn top lip. Should he stay and support me, as a friend and soldiering colleague, or should he take my advice and go whilst he could? But before he made his decision, a sudden startled shout broke the funeral calm. From the rectory yard a horse broke forth, dashing into the lane as though demons were after it. At the moment of its bolting, the rider was evidently only half in the saddle, and as the beast swerved into the road he was flung forward and over the animal's shoulder, landing on his head on the hard packed dirt. I heard the crack, as his neck broke, and the horrified gasp of the throng at my back. Gervase stepped quickly forward and knelt beside him, but we knew the answer before he spoke. Lemuel Drysdale would preach at no more funerals.

The horse, having shed its rider, came to an abrupt halt, and now stood, head down, trembling. It was, as Lemuel had described it, a poor old nag, sway backed and long in the tooth. Looking at it now, as Benjy Postlethwaite went to its head and snatched at the bridle, it seemed impossible that such a sad old creature could have found the energy to bolt. All around us people began to exclaim, asking one another what had happened. I looked around hurriedly for George and Malachi, and caught George's eye. He nodded, and touched his brother's arm. Together they went to find a hurdle from the rectory stable. A woman I felt I should be able to name came forward, loosening her drab cloak to cover the dead man. We were already subdued, coming straight from a fresh grave, and now stood about, irresolute, exchanging shocked whispers amongst ourselves. The woman with the cloak began to weep, quietly, another woman passed her a kerchief.

'Thank you, neighbour!' she mumbled, scrubbing at her face with the cloth, 'He called me a harlot and a sinner, but I never wished him harm!' When she spoke I recognised her. She was the Widow Snaith, Deborah Snaith, wife to the late miller, Jabez Snaith. Judith Moreland had mentioned her yesterday, as someone who might have been disturbed by Loveday's prophesies. George and Malachi appeared with an oak bench top, which they laid in the dirt beside the corpse.

'Happen we should hear a prayer afore we tek him up?' remarked George, straightening up and addressing himself to Jem Robinson.

Jem seemed startled, his swarthy face flushing darker. 'Why...?' he began, gazing around rather wildly, as though unable to understand why George had fixed on him, though he was churchwarden and sides man. 'I have not my prayer book.'

''Tis here, Lemuel's own copy', remarked one of the elderly shepherds, rooting it out with his crook from amongst a tangle of dusky cranesbill at the side of the lane, where it had flown from the priest's coat as he fell. 'Here, Jem, tha can read, happen tha can find t'page.'

'I... it should be someone in Holy Orders!'

'Happen,' agreed the old fellow, 'but there's nonesuch here, and thee lived in Lemuel's pocket, so thee'd best do it.'

'Shock, or guilty conscience?' murmured Gervase in my ear. The woman who had given Widow Snaith her handkerchief took the book and found the place for him, and Jem began to stumble his way through the prayer for the dead. 'He may be able to read, but you'd never guess,' Gervase said, adding, 'I can't slip away now, or they'll think the priest's death was my doing. Being present, and a sinister stranger?'

I looked at him with raised brows, 'Not an accident, you think?' I murmured back. I knew in my heart it couldn't be. Lemuel's horse had probably never bolted as a young and frisky colt, which I doubted it had ever been. I signalled to Benjy with a raised finger, and he led the horse a little way up the lane. Once the prayer stuttered to an end, and the assembled company had '*Amened*', and gathered round to watch George and Malachi lift the dead man onto the oak board, we followed.

'Undo the girth,' I told Ben, 'gently, don't put any pressure on the saddle or his flanks. Now lift the saddle. Lay it on end, here in the road.' Benjy did so. Gervase hissed through his teeth.

'Of all the foul contrivances!'

'Burrs. A simple country recipe for murder,' I agreed. 'Take a dozen fresh burrs from the nearest hedgerow. Attach them to the cloth lining of a saddle. Walk away calmly to attend to your affairs. Make your condolences at a funeral perhaps. Until the rider mounts, and presses his weight down on the saddle, the beast will feel nothing much amiss. When he does… there is every chance the horse, maddened by the sudden pricks, will throw the rider. As he did.'

'An evil deed. Who so hates —hated — your priest?' asked Gervase, sombrely.

'Naebody!' snapped Benjy, before I could get a word in, 'He were nowt. Harmless old…blatherskite. Naebody had cause to kill him!'

'But somebody did, Ben. Somebody has. Those burrs didn't get there by chance.'

Benjy's brothers had now lifted the corpse on to their improvised hurdle, and the congregation was giving them advice, arguing whether the body should be taken straight to the Church or to the priest's house, there to be prepared for burial. He had no wife or housekeeper, but there were several women present willing to assist in laying him out. Opinion seemed to be evenly divided. Voices were rising. One or two even glanced towards me, as though they expected — or hoped — that I would take charge of the situation, and give orders. Having the title of Major raises expectations, even amongst those who had known me since I was knee high to a rabbit, and formerly had no more opinion of me. Suddenly, the clear voice of Judith Moreland rose above the hubbub.

'Someone should inform my father!'

'Nay, lass… M'Lady…. 'twere an accident,' someone else replied.

'Never the less…' she began, doubtfully. She turned until she caught my eye again. I shook my head, and pressed my lips together, meaning, no, it was not an accident, and yes, your father should be informed.

'Ah'll go!' announced Benjy, thrusting our Bible and the horse's reins into my hands, and setting off at a fast lope. He didn't give me chance to point out that Judith had a horse, and could have gone herself.

'The divil! That lad goes off like a musket. Happen he's in training,' remarked the old shepherd who had rescued Lemuel's prayer book from the hedgerow. 'Ah'd put my money on him ginst ony from Haythorpe!' He named a larger village up the dale, famous for its athletic young men, and their fell running prowess.

It was time for me to take charge, loath as I was to do it. I was, after all, chief mourner at the funeral we had all just attended, and there was no one else to say what should happen next. The faction that thought Lemuel's body should be taken to his house seemed to be in the ascendant, so I gave them the nod, and urged the rest to continue with me to Lowflatts. All acknowledged the sense of this. There was food in those baskets which should not be wasted.

'I'll bring the saddle,' said Gervase, 'and turn the horse loose in the rectory paddock.' His tone told me he had now decided to stay around, at least for today. His expression was extremely thoughtful. Something about this second murder had worried him, or at any rate caught his attention. I thought it might be the fact that Lemuel was in holy orders in the established Church, and could have been in conflict with one of these groups of whom he had suspicions. He might well be right. I knew, because my mother had told me, that Lemuel had preached loud and long against those who protested against the paying of tithes, and in addition, I thought he was probably jealous of his office. He would have felt threatened by new ideas, especially by those who were now insisting that they had no need of a priest to intercede for them with God, and that they could meet, to pray and study the Bible without his assistance. I was uneasy, too, about Benjy's reaction. He'd seemed annoyed, even embarrassed, by the priest's death, as though he might well know, or guess, the culprit. Burrs suggested a boy's trick. Had someone really intended Lemuel to die, or was it a lad's prank gone horribly wrong? I didn't suspect Benjy himself, for he had been at my shoulder every minute since we left the farm, and such a knavery did not match his new cloak of righteousness, but I wanted to ask him a few questions. And I thought he knew that. Certainly he'd seized on the first excuse to dash away from the scene.

There was nothing I could do about Benjy until he returned, and nothing more anyone could do for Lemuel Drysdale, until Magistrate Moreland took charge of the situation, so I signalled to the shocked mourners that we should now fulfil our original intention, and make our way to Lowflatts.

And this we did, Gervase carrying the saddle, and the rest of the company falling into a ragged column behind us. The mist had lifted now, and the sun shone brightly on the verdant meadows, starred with golden kingcups, pink tipped daisies and early purple orchids. In contrast, we must have made a sombre spectacle, processing through the fields all dressed in funereal grey, brown and black garb. I wondered how visible we would be to my two urchin shepherd boys, high on the hillside behind us. I had a horrid fancy that from their viewpoint our procession must resemble some dark, loathly worm, crawling across the green meadows of paradise. I shuddered involuntarily.

Gervase, at my side, glanced sharply at me. 'Someone's there — at the farm — got there ahead of us,' he remarked. 'Were you expecting anyone?'

My eyesight is good, but his is better. He was right. There was a heavy dray, with two draft horses harnessed to it, standing in front of the house. A small, plump woman in a brown travelling cloak stood beside it. She was giving orders to a man, urging him to lift something down from the cart. It was he, up atop the dray, who pointed, drawing her attention to the approaching procession. Seeing us, she first countermanded her previous orders, signalling him to leave his burden where it was, and then hastened forward to meet us.

'Robert! Oh, my son, thanks be to God, you're here! I thought from the peddler's description it might be you, but he didn't know you, couldn't name you.' Breathless, my mother took in the crowd of neighbours at my back, 'You're just come from the churchyard? From burying Loveday? It's true the poor child is dead?' She took hold of my hands, and gazed up into my face, looking for denial.

'Yes, Mother, it's true.'

'And the girls are missing? The peddler said no one could find them.'

'Yes, Mother, I'm afraid we have no news of them yet.'

'Ann and Rachel may yet live, Mistress Haddon, we pray that they do,' Gervase intervened.

'Oh, 'tis you again, Master F...!' she exclaimed, taking in his changed appearance. She was about to say something further, but closed her lips. Evidently she had a good inkling what Gervase's various disguises might mean.

'A peddler came to you in Lancaster and told you how it was with us?' I asked her, my heart sinking. I was realising that poor Lemuel Drysdale's journey would have been in vain, and he need never have tried to mount his pony.

'Why yes, Totty Critchlow. You remember Totty? Perhaps you wouldn't, for he didn't know you. He's little lame fellow that whittles spoons and clothes pegs and sells them up and down the dale. He heard all about it in the ale house in Beckside the evening before last, after seeing George and Malachi Postlethwaite taking poor Loveday to church. He got a lift with a carter at first light yesterday, and came into Lancaster — where I suppose he intended going anyway — and found me last evening. And so,' said my redoubtable mother, 'I hired a cart to bring your brother home.' She glanced towards the dray, adding doubtfully, 'I hope he is no worse for the journey. We came on slowly, so that he shouldn't be shaken and jolted to death on the road. His fever is down, but he's as weak as a new born kitten... Oh, but I haven't introduced you!' she signalled to the man standing on the back of the dray, 'this is your cousin, Ezekiel,' she included the crowd of neighbours standing around in the introductions, 'Ezekiel Masterson, my late sister's son.'

He was a short fellow, some years my senior, whip thin, with a nose bent sideways, and the sun burnt into his skin from working in wind and sea spray in all weathers. His expression, as he jumped down from the cart and took my hand, was rueful.

'You're the one that fought my brother!' I exclaimed, suddenly understanding the reason for his ruefulness. How typical of my mother, that she had commandeered the cause of his misfortune to help bring Miles home!

'And landed us both in gaol,' he admitted with a wry grin. He had a strange twang in his voice that I couldn't place, and rotten teeth. 'I'm none the worse for it, but your brother caught the fever. I suppose mebbe I'm used to fevers, being a seafaring man— travelled in all parts as you might say, and lived in foul conditions below decks — I don't easy tek a fever — but your brother,' he looked towards the blanket wrapped form of Miles, lying prone on a pallet of straw in the back of the dray, pursed his lips and shook his head, 'is another matter. Your mother, Aunty Sarah to me, *would* bring him out of Lancaster, but I don't know, *I don't know*. He could die on us yet. We hafta face it.'

The kind hands of our friends and neighbours reached out to help Ezekiel lift Miles down, and carry him indoors. Gervase led them through to the back parlour where the womenfolk proposed making up a makeshift bed.

Mother and I stood alone, watching them, her hand on my arm. I saw, and felt a twist of dread in my gut at it, the grey pallor of Miles's face as they lifted him down, the black shadows around his sunken eye sockets.

'Oh, Robert, my son! Is this the burden that the Lord has laid on my shoulders? Are you all that's to be left to me, Ann lost, and Miles at death's door?'

I put my arms around my mother and held her to me, as she had held me many times when I was a child.

'I'll find Ann, Mother!' I vowed, 'You care for Miles. With God's help and your care he may pull through. I'll find Ann.'

# Chapter 7

It was good to have Mother home. I am a grown man and like to think myself a hardened warrior, but in this time of sorrow I felt comforted, as I had so many times in my boyhood, by her calm and practical presence. She was devastated by Miles' illness, stricken by the loss of Ann, her baby, but after that brief embrace she accepted from me, she threw back her shoulders, unclasped her cloak, and prepared to trot in doors to greet, and care for, her guests on this terrible day. I told her, in as few words as possible, what had, within this last hour, befallen Lemuel Drysdale. She closed her eyes, almost unable to take in this latest disaster. Mother had always been highly critical of the priest, but like all the rest of us (I felt certain), she had never wished him dead.

'What of this cousin, Ezekiel?' I called after her, as she turned to go.

She looked back at me, 'Zeke? Oh, Zeke. My sister Letty's boy. Well, hardly a boy, now. She and my brother William were many years my senior. Zeke must be nearing forty. He wants to give up the sea. He says your uncle promised him a safe berth. Meaning, I suppose, that he expected to inherit the shop, a foolish notion for one who probably knows little of spices, only that they carried them on occasion in the hold of ships he sailed with from the Indies,' she paused, her head on one side, considering, 'He was disappointed, when my brother's Will named you, and made many wild threats, so Miles said. I thought it best to keep him with us, don't you?'

I smiled and shrugged my shoulders. How like Mother. What a tactician. Oliver Cromwell could have used her! The man made threats, but he was family, so she sought to keep him close, under her eye, where if he meant further harm, she at least knew where to find him! The thought floated through my mind that I, too, knew little of spices, and I was baffled as to why the shop had been left to me, but there was no time to ponder on that. I followed Mother indoors, to the funeral feast.

How did we do it? Play host and hostess, Mother and I, that day at Loveday's funeral gathering? Clasp folks' hands and thank them for their condolences? I do not rightly know. Yet we did. We had help, of course, from our good neighbours. By the time we got indoors Hannah Postlethwaite, Widow Snaith, and others of the womenfolk had laid out the funeral feast in the front parlour, and Judith Moreland, for some reason best known to herself, was supervising the hanging up of cloaks and the stowing of empty baskets and farm tools in the hallway. Cousin Zeke, who seemed in no way put out to find himself part of a household in mourning, applied himself to what he described as 'galley duties,' passing plates of food around amongst the assembled company, though it appeared to me that he ate as much as he passed.

It all seemed to go by as in a dream. Friends and acquaintances approached us, shaking their heads in sorrow, offering us their prayers, and practical help too. George Postlethwaite took me aside to let me know that he and Malachi would come and help with the hay. Highbiggens, being situated at a higher altitude, has more moorland grazing than hay grass, and they could spare me time in the coming week. Benjy, he assured me, I could keep for as long as I cared to have him. I did not commit myself on that score! Even Jem Robinson, still sweating and uncomfortable after his enforced reading of the prayers for the dead, sidled up to mutter at me that Colonel Moreland had told him I might have use of one of Lings' horses and a wagon if I should need it. I overheard Deb Snaith, and Luke Procter's skinny wife, Martha, offering to come and help Mother with the dairy work, and Mother thanking them, with only the slightest tremor in her voice when she said, 'Of course we hope my daughter and Rachel Postlethwaite will soon be returned to us.'

At some point I realised that Gervase was missing, and I wondered if he had taken the opportunity to steal away on his secret mission after all, but when Mother asked who was sitting with Miles, and I went through to the back parlour, where a temporary couch had been made for him, I found Gervase there, sitting silent at the foot of the bed.

'I've seen worse,' he said, nodding towards my sleeping brother, whose skin shone with sweat, yellowish grey against the snowy linen pillowcase. 'He survived the journey, by God's mercy, and by His grace may yet recover.'

'Mother shouldn't have moved him so soon, brought him here like that,' I fretted, 'but what else could she do, once this peddler fellow told her how it was with us here? However, she is here now, to nurse him and attend to the household, and our neighbours are falling over themselves to offer me help with the farm work, so if you want — if you need to be gone?'

Gervase shrugged. 'No, by your leave, I'll stay around a day or two more. The killing of that priest... There is something going on here that I don't understand. I had thought — I was led to believe — but no, it could be that these killings come from some source of which I have no knowledge,' he grinned, without mirth, baring his fine molars, 'and I should know, that's what Parliament pays me for.'

'What do you fear, some political uprising?' I began, thinking that I had a right to know at least something of my old friend's mission if he was going to stay on in these parts, using my home as his headquarters, and no doubt indulging his hearty appetite at my mother's table. He did not reply, but turned his head to listen. The hubbub in the dining room had stilled, and now only one voice could be heard, that of Josiah Postlethwaite, beginning to read aloud from the Bible. I could not distinguish individual words, but from the rise and fall of his cadences I guessed he was embarking on one of the psalms, and presently people began to sing, the women's voices rising above those of the men. The door opened. Mother slipped into the room. Floating in over her head we could hear the words,

*'Though I walk in the midst of trouble thou wilt revive me: thou shalt stretch forth thine hand against the wrath of mine enemies, and thy right hand shalt save me'*

'Psalm one hundred and thirty eight,' said Mother, closing the door behind her, 'I hope it may do as much good as Josiah believes, for we are indeed in the midst of trouble. Hannah has a lovely voice, has she not? How does Miles go on?'

She did not wait for an answer but went over to the bed, and laid the back of her hand on his brow. 'His fever is up again,' she sighed.

'I'll fetch another wetted cloth, Ma'am, to cool him,' said Gervase, rising to his feet and slipping out of the room. Mother thanked him, sighing again, and went and plumped herself down on the stool he had vacated. 'A good fellow, your friend, don't you think?' she enquired. 'I think we may trust him?'

'I think so, Mother, I hope so,' I responded. We gazed at one another ruefully.

'A time of trouble!' she repeated, 'And Deb Snaith tells me Colonel Moreland has arrested Lanty on suspicion of doing away with poor Loveday, and perhaps Ann and Rachel too. Is that so?'

I admitted that it was. 'Colonel Moreland didn't wish to arrest Lanty, but once he fell into a fit, he felt he had to, for Lanty's own safety — since Lady Brilliana thought it a sign that he was possessed, and said so before us all.'

'Ah, so *she* was there!' said Mother. 'She has no love for our household, thinks we're beneath her ladyship's haughty nose. She'll have hard words for Judith when she finds that she has absented herself from home to come here today.' She sniffed. 'I hope the Colonel gave orders that Lanty was not to be abused?'

I assured her that the Colonel had done so, and that I had had word via Judith that he was as well as could be expected, with his kinswoman from the Lings' stillroom making sure he got enough to eat.

'Well, at least her Ladyship cannot say Lanty caused the death of poor Lemuel Drysdale. Not unless she believes he can send the power of the evil eye from out the cellars at Lings all the way to Beckside churchyard!' said Mother tartly. Mother is unusual for a country woman born in the time of King James, in that she has no patience with those who ascribe any unfortunate or unexplained event to witchcraft. Human beings, she believes, are more than capable of conjuring up their own wickedness without any supernatural aid. She insists that ailments like Lanty's falling sickness are burdens laid on their sufferers by God to test their faith, and that of those who care for them, rather than proof of possession by the devil.

I repeated my belief that Lanty had played no part in Loveday's death or in my sister's disappearance. 'He didn't know Loveday was dead, I'm sure of it. It was a dreadful shock to the poor fellow. And yet she had been dead two days or more when I found her. Of course he had been sleeping in the barn, and attending to the animals, as you asked him to do. He had no need to have gone down the lane and found her body. He knows something, that much the Colonel and I established. The girls told him they might be going somewhere, presumably all three together, Loveday, Ann and Rachel, but he didn't seem very sure where. I understood him to be saying he thought they had followed you to Lancaster. Unfortunately, at that point in our questioning he fell down in one of his fits, and I have not your skill, Mother, to bring him about.'

She sighed again, 'I wish I might see him. *I* could get from him what he knows.'

'Your old shepherd is surely innocent, Ma'am, and I think he will come to no permanent hurt,' said Gervase, coming quietly back into the room with a folded dampened cloth which he laid on Miles' forehead. 'Colonel Morehead is keeping him out of harm's way. Feelings are running high about your daughter-in-law's death, but now, with the murder of the priest, the village folk will be looking elsewhere for the culprit. The Colonel is here, by the way,' he nodded towards the door, beyond which the psalm singers had fallen silent again, 'ridden over to hear an account of the priest's death from those of us who were present. I told Benjy to show him the saddle.'

'Colonel Moreland! Mercy! Robert, go see what you can find in the cellar, we must offer him a glass of wine!' cried Mother, scrambling to her feet in alarm. For all her oft stated belief that we are all equal in God's eyes, she always feels at a disadvantage unless she can offer something other than home brewed small beer to the Colonel and his like. She smoothed down her skirts, and straightened her cap. 'I must go and welcome him. Rob, go quickly, and fetch a bottle of the Rhenish! Will you...?' she turned to Gervase.

'Of course, Ma'am, I'll stay and sit with Miles. I cannot tell the Colonel anything more about what happened this morning than Rob can.' He winked at me. Gervase's family are wealthier, and perhaps of more ancient lineage than the Morelands, for all Lady Brilliana's father was an Earl, but Mother does not know that, and Gervase prefers it that way.

I found Colonel Moreland in the stable doorway, examining the priest's saddle in the late morning sunlight.

'A filthy trick!' he grunted, savagely, pulling at one of the burrs, and finding it clung firmly to the cloth lining of the saddle. 'What devilish creatures are we harbouring here abouts that would do such a thing? To a man of God? My opinion of Lemuel Drysdale was that he was a poor thing, but he was honest. He did his best to uphold his office with what small talent he had.'

I said nothing, there didn't seem to be anything I could add. He changed the subject.

'How is your brother? I hear your Mother has brought him home — to die? Or will he mend, do you think?'

I told him it was touch and go, but that I hoped Miles might survive. 'He will if Mother's prayers and potions can save him.'

'A good woman. You are fortunate, the pair of you, to have such a woman to run your household.'

I did not comment on this. I noticed now, in the bright outdoor light, that Benson Moreland looked tired, drained. I remembered what his daughter had said, that they were 'ruined', that her father had come home to find Lings in poor shape. That she believed her mother had been selling her jewellery to support her husband's enemies. And that her young brothers had run up debts in some foreign land where they had been sent to keep them out of the war. Out of this family quarrel, so that they should not be forced to choose between their father's cause and their mother's family allegiances. Judith should not have babbled to me about such things, but having done so, I could not unknow them.

'Tomorrow,' he continued, 'I'm asking all the men down in Beckside, and all the farmers roundabout — all that can be spared from their work — to search the woods and fields for your sister and the Postlethwaite girl. They may yet live, may be being held somewhere,' he looked at me, assessing whether I still held out any hope that this was true, saw that I didn't, or not much, and continued. 'We mustn't forget them because of this new tragedy. We'll have the men quarter all the district between Lings and Highbiggens on this side of the river, and assign those who know each area best to search it.' A good soldier, he knew how to get results out of such troops as were available to him. 'Can you spare Ben Postlethwaite and that... soldier you have staying with you?'

'I can, both of them, and will ride out myself if we get the hay stooked in the south meadow by tonight,' I assured him, hiding a grin with regard to 'that soldier', since he was pretending not to know who Gervase was. 'It will be what we in these parts would once have called 'giving a day to the King,' is it not? Everyone giving up his own work to carry out some unexpected task in the community. What should we call it now? Giving a day to Oliver Cromwell?'

'I'm sure he would approve such an undertaking,' he replied, quite seriously, making me feel a heartless clod, that I should even attempt to joke while my brother lay between life and death, and my sister was lost, perhaps for ever. 'But I mustn't hold you up.'

So he went indoors, and sat in my father's great carved oak chair behind the dining table, drinking a glass of the Rhenish, and listening to various accounts of Lemuel Drysdale's death as told by those who had witnessed it. It was no surprise to him, I imagine, that these accounts differed. Like me he would have heard countless descriptions of skirmishes and routs, on and off the battlefield, witnessed by many, yet hardly any two identical in the telling. His conclusion remained the same as mine, no matter how the details might differ. Someone had deliberately set out to kill or maim Lemuel Drysdale, and had succeeded, and no one here claimed to know who that person might be.

Despondent, I left Mother, seconded by Hannah Postlethwaite, to see the Colonel and the rest of the funeral guests off the premises. I collected up Gervase, Benjy, and a selection of hay rakes and pitch forks, and went to stook the south meadow. A farmer can always claim he is too busy to attend to anything but the crops, and thus leave his social responsibilities to the womenfolk. Perchance the weather might turn, is always his excuse. The weather showed no sign of turning, overhead the dome of the midday sky shone blue and cloudless. It was obvious as we tossed the dry, sweet smelling grass that it would be ready for the barn by tonight.

'Tomorrow we ride out to search for the girls,' I told my companions.

'Excellent,' said Gervase, examining his sweat blistered palms, 'Venus is in sore need of some exercise. Your big fellow too.'

'Will tha have a beast fer me?' demanded Benjy, eagerly. I nearly joked, why would you need a horse, since you run so fast, but bit my tongue. His sister was missing as well as mine.

'Ah could have the cob?'

'No, Benjy, my mother may need the cob. Colonel Moreland has given her permission to visit Lanty, and try if she can find out from him where the girls told him they were going. And the pony cast a shoe on the journey back, Cousin Ezekiel tells me. Think you could manage one of those big dray horses Mother hired to bring Miles home? We'll be paying for each day of the hire, and we cannot at present return them to Lancaster, so we might as well put them to work. Cousin Zeke can take the other. It won't be a comfortable ride, mind, bareback!'

Benjy's face split into a grin as he thought about it, 'Happen ah could! Ah niver rode a four poster bed afore! God willing, we'll get news of the girls, *someplace* up the dale or down!'

'Amen to that!' said Gervase and I, in unison.

# Chapter 8

Morning brought its own troubles, though they were small in comparison to those of the previous day. Miles had been feverish and restless during the night, and Mother, of course, had been the one to hear his groans, and feel she had to sit up with him through the early hours. Now she was lying down, catching up on her rest. We men (and boy), tired out from our exertions in the hay field, had slept the sleep of the heedless, and piled down to the kitchen at first light, expecting breakfast to be put before us. We tried not to be put out when it was not, and we had to get our own, as we had, after all, being doing for two days now.

Cousin Zeke, who had not offered his services to haymaking the previous day, seemed particularly put out by this. ''Tis not like Auntie Sarah,' he grumbled, 'she's a rare cook, and I never knew her fail to put victuals on the table while we were at Uncle William's house in Lancaster. And your brother was much worse then aways!'

I gritted my teeth. I had suspected all along that Zeke was not going to be an asset to the family. While Gervase fried eggs I asked him, 'Can you milk? Feed livestock, Cousin?'

He stared at me, affronted. Perhaps he supposed that Mother had asked him here for a holiday, as a compensation for Uncle William's failure to provide for him in his Will. 'I can milk a goat,' he admitted, grudgingly, 'we kept 'em on ship board. I know goats. Mebbe cows is much the same?'

'Aye, them is,' confirmed Benjy, who was slicing cheese with a particularly foul looking pocket knife, 'but a cow'll kick yer harder, is all!'

Judging by the look Zeke shot him, he and Benjy were not going to be as David and Jonathan, any time soon.

'Major Rob's in charge,' remarked Gervase, who was still pretending to be a farm hand, and giving a fair imitation of our local way of speech. 'What he says goes, hereabouts!' He held a plate of fried eggs at Zeke's eye level, but just beyond his reach.

'That's how it is,' I confirmed, deciding to go along with this tarradiddle. 'So, you milk the goat, Cousin, since you know goats, and collect green stuff for her and the lambs. Oh, and when you go picking greens in the hedgerows, take a basket and collect any eggs you find there. The hens are laying away, and at the rate we're going through them we need every egg you can find. Benjy and I will milk the cows. Gervase, you catch and saddle the horses, ready to ride out as soon as word comes from Colonel Moreland what ground we're to cover.'

'Err... don't know as I can help you with this 'ere search,' said my cousin, mumbling a mouthful of fried egg. I'm a seafarer, remember? Sailed out of the port of Lancaster since I was nobbut a lad. Never bin on a horse.'

Gervase and I exchanged exasperated glances. These naval fellows!

'And I don't know the lay of the land, or where I should look,' he added, lamely.

'Then you'd best stay behind and sit with Miles,' I said, 'You can relieve my mother. If she's feeling up to it, Mother wants to go over to Lings Hall and talk with our deaf and dumb old shepherd, Lanty, to see what he can tell. Mind, I expect to find my brother still breathing when I return!'

''Twas a mistake,' Zeke muttered, 'I never meant him harm. I'd a drop too much taken, and I lost my rag. Anyhows, it would be you I'd need to do away with, not your brother!' Though he grinned as he said it, displaying his mouthful of black and crumbling teeth, I had the impression he would not be loath to dispose of me, if a good chance ever presented itself. I didn't intend to allow a chance to present itself.

'Well, try not to do away with anyone or anything this day, Cousin. We've had more than enough deaths. And you'd better show me the green stuff you forage before you give it to the livestock. Goats are hard to kill, but lambs have more delicate stomachs.'

Before my troop had the farmyard tasks completed, we heard the rattle of iron bound cart wheels approaching, and one of Colonel Moreland's farm hands drove in with Luke Procter's two young 'uns hanging off the back boards, having stolen a lift up from the village on their way to collect the sheep.

Everyone crowded round to receive their instructions for the search. Colonel Moreland, being an experienced campaigner, had wisely written them down, and even sketched maps, so that there should be no confusion, or forgetting of some vital piece of information. In the Army we'd heard plenty of cautionary tales of instructions passed on down the line by word of mouth. Sometimes what came out at the end had turned out to be quite the opposite of what was intended! While I was digesting the Colonel's marching orders, George Postlethwaite came riding down the track from Highbiggens on his ugly, rough coated piebald, with his brother Malachi up behind, to join the search. I gave Malc the second hired dray horse I had originally intended for Cousin Zeke. As Benjy had remarked, riding these great creatures looked rather like being bestride a four poster bed, but they were gentle giants (though it turned out they had mouths of iron), and they seemed perfectly willing to be put to this new task. Fortunately for their riders, they enjoyed the company of other horses, so that although it was difficult to guide them with the use of either bit or heels, they followed after the leading horse where ever it went.

My miniature shepherds, Saul and Timmy Procter, sensing that what we were about to do might be more exciting than driving the sheep onto the fell, begged to be allowed to come with us. I sympathised, but was firm.

The sheep must be taken to their grazing ground. However, I let them hear the search instructions, and told them that they could look around them whilst keeping an eye on the sheep.

'You'll be the only ones searching across the river,' I cajoled. 'Colonel Moreland judges that the girls wouldn't have crossed over, as there is no bridge and they had no horse. Three days ago, he says, the river was still high after last week's rain. If they had crossed the ford by the stepping stones at Beckside, any number of people would have seen them. But you never know lads, the Colonel could be wrong! I'm relying on you to spot anything unusual over there. If you find something, wave your shirts and holler!'

I didn't, of course, expect them to find anything, since I could think of no reason, any more than the Colonel had, why the girls might cross a swift flowing river here, when there was no village or habitation across on the other side within a mile or two of rough walking, and if they were bound for one of those, they would surely have followed the path on this bank downstream to the ford at Beckside. The boys were no more convinced than I was. But as it chanced, before they could work up an argument about it, Mother, heavy-eyed from lack of sleep, but resolute as always, emerged into the yard with a basket containing bread, cheese, a flagon of small beer, and a punnet of fresh raspberries for the young shepherds to take with them. At the sight of those plump juicy raspberries, we adults all fell guilty to the sin of envy, and young Saul and Timmy, grinning, made haste to seize the basket, let the sheep out of the garth, and start for the hills.

I climbed onto the cart, reviewed my men, and made my deployments. It felt quite like old times. Times I would rather not recall, mostly. Times when I had sent better men than these into perilous situations, and where lack of experience on my part had led to the deaths of more than a few. Today was not going to be like that, though in my heart I could envisage no happy ending. Today, at least, the outcome would be no fault of mine. Or so I thought.

My original plan was to split my teams of searchers into pairs thus: one who knew the ground well, and one who did not. For one who knows the terrain will know its hidden places, whilst one who does not brings a fresh eye to the search, and may spot little signs and indications simply because he sees it for the first time. So, I sent Malachi and Gervase to search the larch plantation that formed the boundary between the Postlethwaites' land and ours, and all the fields to the south and east, including the birch and alder groves that ran along the river bank. Also the coppice beyond the south field, already cleared of hay, and its hedgerows informally searched. We agreed (although the Colonel had included it) that there was little point in searching Highbiggins' land, since if the girls had got as far as the track beyond the larch grove, George and Malc would already have found them.

Once on that track they would have made straight for the farm. Off it was bare sheep grazing ground, with nowhere for a murderous attacker to hide one body, let alone two. I had then intended that George, who knew our land well enough, and Cousin Zeke, who knew precious little, except perhaps how to splice a main brace, should cover our home wood, the water meadows and the steep bracken and bramble covered slopes behind the farmhouse. This would leave Benjy and myself to cover the two northerly fields, and Hardcastle's farm, Withins, up to the great wood which divided their land from that of the Lings estate. Benson Moreland owned land on both sides of the river, and was using his own people to search the environs of Lings. However, having decided to proceed without Zeke's questionable help, I had either to leave George to search on his own, or give him Benjy. Our leaders in the New Model Army had always been willing to hear the men's suggestions (although not noticeably willing to follow them) so I asked George what he thought.

'Tek our Ben if you want, but send him wide, doan' tek him up t'farm,' he rumbled, 'Hardcastle doan' tek kindly to our lot, God save his soul.'

I nodded my appreciation of this point. Mason Hardcastle was a disagreeable old termagant, more often than not engaged in a ferocious quarrel with somebody in the dale. Quite why he should be feuding with the Postlethwaites, whose land did not border on any of his, I did not know, and did not intend to waste time enquiring . 'He's given his permission for a search of his land,' I told George, 'but Colonel Moreland makes it clear that he doesn't intend to offer any help. Is his son at home?'

'He ain't,' replied George, shortly.

'Dick's gone a preaching into Westmorland,' volunteered Malachi, 'amongst the Seekers.' I noticed Gervase prick up his ears at this. The Seekers, from what little I had heard about them, were a devout religious group (though who knew what their political beliefs might be?) given to meeting in each other's houses to meditate in silence, or listen to travelling preachers. Richard Hardcastle had evidently become involved with them. This did not altogether surprise me, since he was a youth with a melancholy cast of mind, and life with his hard bitten, hard drinking, hard cursing father couldn't be easy. It also explained why old Mason might be at odds with the Postlethwaites, since their recent enthusiasm for Bible reading and psalm singing might well be Richard's doing (it certainly wasn't Lemuel Drysdale's), and success with such unlikely converts would have encouraged him to take his message further afield.

That thought reminded me, and I sent Benjy to fetch the Bible from where I'd left it on the mounting block. I'm not a man for spontaneous prayer, but after three years in the New Model, I know my way around the Good Book, and while I fear my faith is a weak shallow thing at best, I was prepared to call on the Lord's assistance in our search, and knew my helpers would expect it. So I read them the parable of the lost sheep (I'd marked the place before I slept, determined not to be found wanting by young Benjamin). Then I told them to search until noon, and return to report how they had fared. George should take Benjy, at least to begin with, since he could best assist his large brother by crawling through rabbit runs into the midst of the brambles. If any of us should find some sign (pray God, not corpses), he should holler and whistle to attract the attention of those searching the next patch, and they the next, and so on. I would go alone and tackle the two northern meadows — and Mason Hardcastle.

I watched them mount and ride away, and the Colonel's man drive off back to Lings. Then I took the Bible back indoors, intending to leave it on the parlour table. There I found Mother, contemplating the old cradle in its familiar place by the empty hearth. I suppose Miles and I, in turn, once occupied it, and I remembered the tiny scrap who was my sister Ann, lying there, her mewling gradually ceasing, as Mother rocked it with her foot while she sat patching Father's breeches by the fire. Since Mother bore no live children after Ann, it has been used these many a long year for the storing of logs in winter, and in summer as a catch all for her knitting, Ann's lace bobbins, and Loveday's botched attempts at darning.

Mother looked round at the sound of my footfall, and gave me a wry smile.

'I wonder,' she said, as I stood beside her, 'was Loveday really with child? I didn't believe her. She'd thought she was, so many times, and her hopes proved false. She didn't show the signs. No vomiting in the mornings, or thickening at her waist. So I didn't believe her, but now... I pray God she was wrong! I can't bear to think of the child, dying inside her womb, as she lay dead. And now Ann, lost who knows where! My poor babbie!'

We are not a demonstrative family, we Haddons, but I could think of nothing to comfort her, except to lay my arm across her shoulders, and draw her close to my side. 'Try not to think of it, Mother. Cousin Zeke is willing to sit with Miles. He says we may trust him! If you feel up to it, why not put the side saddle on the cob and ride to Lings? Lanty must know more than he was able to tell me of Ann and Rachel. He was in such shock, when we faced him with the news that Loveday was dead, that the fit came upon him before we could question him properly. He seemed quite unworried about the girls when first we asked him, just pointing towards Beckside and perhaps beyond, towards Lancaster, saying, 'Gah, Gah!' as if they had told him where they were going. He'll be overjoyed to see you, and if anyone can make sense of what he has to say, 'tis you.'

I felt Mother's shoulders lift and her spine straighten beneath my embrace, 'Yes, poor soul. I hope the Colonel will soon judge it safe to let him go. I'll go to him, and take him one of your father's old coats. Even in this haytiming weather it must be cold at nights in those cellars at Lings. Would you heave the saddle onto the cob for me, Rob? 'Tis a struggle to lift it, I find, these days. As your old aunt Lizzie, your Grandmother's sister, used to say, 'With all this weight of trouble I'm feeling my age!'

'Did she have a lot of trouble?' I asked, smiling, as much to distract Mother from her own troubles as because I wanted to know about this long dead aunt.

'No, but she liked folks to think she did! Mind, she was grandmother to Loveday through her son Roland. I reckon Loveday inherited some of her play acting ways from Lizzie, and her love of being at the centre of the world, be it for good reasons or bad! How some ever,' she sighed, long and deep, 'let's go and do what we must do, son.'

She took down an old frieze coat of my father's which had hung behind the kitchen door for ten years or more, and her light summer shawl from the peg in the hallway, and followed me into the yard, where we found the cob already saddled (Gervase having evidently guessed Mother's likely errand), and tied to the fence next to Caesar, who was looking aslant at this rough haired country stumble shanks. 'Was this creature indeed a *horse?*' his rolling eye seemed to be enquiring. I ignored his snobbery, and led the cob to the mounting block, where Mother heaved herself aboard, laid the coat across the cob's neck, planted her stout boots on the step of the side saddle, and took up the reins.

'Loveday was as tiresome as a kitten tangling herself in a fresh wound skein of wool,' she remarked, with a smile and a sigh, looking down at me. 'She broke your heart, and she broke Miles's too, in the long run, and made a bad blood between the two of you. 'Twas a black day when I took her in, but how could I not, when she was kin, and the sweating sickness took her father and mother?'

'Never fear, Mother. My heart has mended itself,' I assured her, and found, in the saying of it, that it was true. 'It was a dreadful thing, finding her dead in that manner, but as to love, that was just a boyish fancy!'

'I'm glad of it! Don't quarrel with Zeke, but bid him take good care of Miles,' she said, smiling down at me, and reaching down to pat my shoulder before she rode away.

I was about to mount Caesar, but her words reminded me that I had not seen Zeke, nor had he come to show me what greenery he had foraged, but even as the thought struck me, he appeared round the corner of the barn, in possession of a pail part filled with goat's milk, two eggs, and a grievance.

'Will you look what that spawn of the devil of a goat of yours has done!' he grumbled, setting down the milk pail, and pulling forward the tail of his jerkin for my inspection, 'While I'm milking the beast she's turned her head, and eaten a hole in it. And it's good leather!'

I forbade a smile to creep across my face. 'You speak true there,' I said, solemnly, 'that goat is the spawn of the devil.'

'You might have given me some warning!'

'I thought you knew goats?'

He gave me a disgusted look. 'I only hope Aunty Sarah may have a little bit of leather put by she can use to mend it, that's all. This jerkin cost me good money! And you need not fear I have given those lambkins poisoned green stuff. That overbearing farm hand of yours, *Jervis*, or whatever he calls himself, took it and looked it over. Why do you employ such insolent fellows? That young Benjy is another. You and your brother will never be masters here if you tolerate men like that.'

At this I had to smile, 'You would give them the cat o' nine tails? Gervase is not in our employ. He is a comrade from the army. And Benjy has heard too many Bible passages read, and is overcome with a sense of his own righteousness. He's fifteen. He'll grow out of it.' Zeke snorted his disgust and turned away, 'I'll put this in the dairy. I only found two eggs,' he told me over his shoulder, 'I'll draw myself some beer and go and sit with your brother until such time as my aunt comes back.'

'Do that,' I told him, putting my foot in the stirrup and jumping up into my horse's saddle. Caesar threw his head up, urgent to be off. He was woefully short of exercise, and this was the first chance I'd had to give him some.

As we made for the gate to begin our search of the northern pastures I thought of this, and wondered if I might have to part with him if I was to be stuck here on the farm for weeks, perhaps months. Caesar was a horse bred for hard riding and the battlefield, not for ambling around the meadows each morning whilst I looked to the livestock, and then spending the rest of the day eating his head off on rich June grass. I thought, once we had cleared the gateway and I pressed my heels into his sides to urge him into a trot, that my wounded thigh was mending at last. I noted that the day was bidding to be another hot one, and that I should have brought a hat. I thought of Tabitha the goat chewing a hole in Cousin Zeke's jerkin, and allowed myself to chuckle. I tried not to think of the search I was embarked on. That I might at any moment find my little sister dead.

Caesar began to stretch his legs, eager to break into a canter. His neck arched, his ears pricked, swivelling to catch distant sounds that he alone could hear.

'Easy, you old fool!' I told him, laughing, 'We're not riding into a skirmish, you know!'

But my horse, of course, knew better.

# Chapter 9

I'd decided to start my search on Withins' land. I would ride to the furthest extremity, on the edge of Lings' woods, stopping on the way only to let Mason Hardcastle know I was conducting it myself, and assure him that I would do no damage and disturb his livestock as little as possible. Then I'd work my way back over his land to ours, and (assuming I found nothing) be home for bread and cheese and beer at noon as I'd arranged with the others. But as we rounded the small hazel spinney that marked the edge of Lowflatts' most northerly strip of meadow land, I began to hear the sounds Caesar's sharp ears had already picked up. Shouts and yells both male and female, the clash of metal on metal, the thud of wood against something equally solid. And soon I saw that, on the scrubby drying green in front of Withins' farmhouse door, a pitched battle was taking place. Only eight persons (and one small child) were actually involved as it turned out, but from a distance it looked more. Caesar automatically lengthened his stride to a gallop, eager for the fray. I, not having the faintest idea what was going on, and having come without sword, pike, or even a stout stave, was a good deal less enthusiastic.

'Whoa boy, whoa!' I muttered, attempting to rein him in. 'We should reconnoitre before we charge!' Extremely reluctantly, he slowed to a walk. I held him at a stand on the brow of a small hillock whilst I weighed up the situation.

It was certainly an unusual affray. Even from this safe distance I could see that. Chiefly because most of the antagonists seemed to be female, or at any rate were wearing female apparel. Only two wore breeches, and one of these was engaged in attacking the other with a hay rake, whilst his opponent (or his victim), fended him off with what at first I took to be a wooden shield with a metal rim and hand grip, against which the wooden tined hay rake with its metal collar alternately thudded and clanged. One of the women was on a horse, on which she kept advancing, whip at the ready to poke the aggressor's eye out, only for the horse to shy when they got close to the hay rake, and cavort away. The other women, on foot, also rushed forward at irregular intervals. I counted five of them, trying, I decided, to intervene on the side of he who held the shield. One of them was wielding a heavy metal saucepan. All were forced to back off rapidly when the tines of the rake were thrust in their faces. After watching in bafflement for some moments, I realised that the improvised shield was in fact the lid from a grain bin. The young female on the horse was Judith Moreland. I recognised her mare, and the feather in her hat, although she seemed in danger of the losing the hat, which had already slipped sideways over her left eye. The furious man with the hay rake was Mason Hardcastle himself. The old fool was puce of face, and bidding fair to cause himself heart seizure. The five women backing and advancing as though taking part in some crazed country dance, must be his wife and daughters. A small child in petticoats, sex unclear from this distance, dashed hither and thither in the melee, wailing at the top of its voice, and in grave danger of being trampled under somebody's feet. The identity of the man with the grain bin shield was unknown to me. I thought at first he must be Mason's evangelising son, Richard, but he was too stout of figure, too rosy of countenance, and surely too furiously active in combat, to be that spare, introspective youth. No swords, pikes or staves seemed to be involved.

'Very well, Caesar, let us advance, but warily!' I cautioned my horse, 'we don't yet know whose cause we wish to espouse.' We cantered gently down the slope to join the throng. If nothing else, I felt I ought to remind Judith Moreland that her father would disapprove of her intervening in this kind of affair. The daughter of a magistrate should refrain from gouging out his neighbour's eye, however much she disliked him. Mason was a wiry little fellow, and much fuelled by his furious temper, but he was over fifty years of age, and tiring. His swings with the hay rake were becoming wilder, and more apt to land blows on the heads and shoulders of his wife and daughters by accident (well, I took that charitable view) than on the fellow with the grain lid shield. As Caesar and I approached (no one seemed to notice us) Mason suddenly hurled the hay rake away in disgust, and turned and ran through the front door into the farmhouse, leaving his opponents open mouthed, and in the case of the daughter with the heavy saucepan, struggling to halt in mid charge. I rode up and asked what was going on. For a moment there was a shocked silence whilst they stared up at me on Caesar's back, apparently wondering if we had dropped from the sky. Then they got sufficient collective breath back, and told me. All at once. Almost immediately they realised the futility of this and stopped again. There was a short silence filled with a lot of noisy gasping, as they fought to refill their lungs with air. Then Mason's eldest daughter, Nan (she of the saucepan), took the lead in putting me wise.

'Our Dad's reet mad wi' Sam,' she informed me. 'Being as he's got our Prue in duff agen. 'Light began to dawn. Mason Hardcastle's four daughters were Nan, Joan, Leah and Prudence. The least prudent, it was well known locally, being Prudence, who had already made her parents grandparents (while I was away at the wars, but my mother had kept me informed) to the small child, Christopher, who had been running about weeping and wailing, and was now clinging to his mother's skirts. The considerable bulge beneath her apron confirmed that Sam, now grinning, only slightly shame faced, shield in hand, had indeed 'got her in duff' again. I now knew who Sam was. Sam Woodley from Bartonriggs. Mother has said in her letter that there was no secret about who had fathered Prue's child. Judith Moreland too, had mentioned him as someone who featured in Loveday's prophesies, though not what she had prophesied. Divine or human retribution perhaps, and Mason Hardcastle certainly meant to put the latter in hand. Unfortunately for me, who had not figured in anyone's prophesies, or despoiled anyone's daughter (alas, we officers are required to set such a priggish example in the New Model), it didn't work out the way he envisaged. Seeking further clarification, and intending to issue that stern warning (more priggishness) I turned in the saddle to speak with Judith Moreland. But, at that moment, the vanished Hardcastle flung open one of the upper casements of the farmhouse, and took wavering aim with an ugly looking weapon, a matchlock harquebus, dating back, I found later, to the conflict of Wittenmergen. The wick of this vile device he had already lit, and balancing it on the sill, he began angling the barrel towards Prue's seducer. Sam and the womenfolk, evidently guessing he meant business, flung themselves flat on the grass. Mason, stepping back, probably to avoid the recoil when the ghastly weapon fired, tripped over something, perhaps his own bootlaces, and the gun went off. Caesar screamed and staggered, his back legs buckled under him, and I was thrown to the ground. Landing on my shoulder and unprotected head, I lay benumbed, while Caesar, injured and terrified, struggled desperately to rise to his feet.

Everyone around me jumped up and began shrieking and screeching. Mason had disappeared, struck dead, I devoutly hoped, by his gun's recoil. I lay on the ground, my vision blurred by the fall. I no longer knew or cared who was attacking whom, or why. From the corner of my eye I could see blood running down Caesar's quivering flank. Poor old boy, I thought, through a haze of my own pain, you never took so much as a scratch on the battlefield, and now we're undone on my lunatic neighbour's doorstep.

The Hardcastle sisters and their mother crowded round me. Sam Woodley issued instructions, and remarkably sensible ones, 'Tek his left arm, *left*! Can't yer see he's put his shoulder out, woman?' I tried to protest, leave me be, look to poor Caesar, but Mother Hardcastle and Joan hauled me to my feet, and Sam seized my right arm at the elbow and shoved my shoulder joint back into its socket before I had time to realise that what he said was true, the fall had dislocated it. The hurt was horrendous, but all I cared about was Caesar.

'My horse!' I gasped, my voice grating with pain, 'that madman's shot him!'

'Aye, Ah alus knew t'old fool were crazed,' admitted Sam, calmly, 'Ah'd marry Prue if Ah had t'money, wouldn't Ah? No need to go shooting folk, any road.'

Judith Moreland must have dismounted from her mare when the gun went off, and she and Nan and Leah had somehow managed to get Caesar on to his feet, although I doubted whether this would help the poor beast.

If his hind leg was shattered or his spine damaged he would never walk again, and I would be forced to put a pistol shot in his brain. I had seen other men do it on the battlefield, when a horse broke a limb or was disembowelled by a cannon ball, and had dreaded that the day would come when I must despatch Caesar, though it would be a kindness. I'd been prepared to do it in the heat of battle, but never expected to lose my comrade on a sunny morning in the peaceful Lune Valley. I staggered over to look at the wound.

'It could be worse,' remarked Mistress Judith brightly, at my elbow, settling her rakish hat more firmly on her dark curls. Her mare must have trotted away when she dismounted, and was now grazing at the edge of the wood, wisely keeping well out of this catastrophe. Devil take this wench, why couldn't she do likewise, why must she be forever interfering!

'The ball's there look, in his quarter! It's not too deep in. You'll need to get it out quickly though, or it'll fester, but there's a good chance you'll save him.' I glared at her. Damnation, did she think she was a horse doctor? Had I asked her opinion? Had she ever tried to dig a lead ball out of a seventeen hands charger's flank? Through a haze of pain from my shoulder, and my muzzy head, I could at least see that Caesar had all four feet on the ground, although he was favouring his left hind, the one below the wound, as was natural enough in the circumstances. More tactful than Judith, Sam Woodley took a knife from the sheath in his belt, and silently proffered it.

'Or mebbe try to walk him home first?' he enquired, quietly. I gazed blearily at the knife in my palm. Caesar's hind quarters quivered, my hand shook. I was in no fit state to do this properly here and now without damaging the poor beast more and a glance at his accusing eye informed me that Caesar shared that view. This had never happened on a well regulated battlefield, and he blamed me. The knife wavered in my hand.

'Damn it, I'm not steady enough… even if you hold his head, I can't...' I think I mumbled. There was a mist before my eyes and the knife fell into the grass. The ground seemed to be shaking too. The ground was shaking, with the steady rhythm of approaching hoof beats. Caesar whinnied, plaintively, as another horse approached.

'Christ's bollocks! What in the devil's name goes forward here?' Gervase isn't easily astonished, but he was, as this most unparliamentary language betrayed.

I forced my head up to find my eyes level with the white star on the forehead of the mare, Venus. Gervase was staring down at me, thoroughly alarmed. In front of him on his saddle prow he clasped a grubby, half naked child, who grinned in gap toothed triumph, and dangled a pale pink ribbon before my wavering eyesight. The child was Timmy Procter.

'Ah've found 'un Mister!' he gloated, too excited even to notice that anything was amiss, 'Tis yourn sister Ann's, happen! Ah found it cross t'river, like tha said Ah shouldn't! Our Saul niver seed it!'

'Quite soon after they crossed over with the sheep,' Gervase confirmed, 'I'm surprised you didn't hear them hollering. The two young demons ripped off most of their clothing, which they claim you told them to do, and shrieked and danced about like hobgoblins until I rode across. But what in the name of Almighty God has happened here?' His sharp eyes took in Caesar's bleeding quarter and my befuddled state.

'Our Dad shot 'im,' said Nan Hardcastle flatly. "E niver meant to, mind. 'E meant it for Sam here.'

'I've somehow got to... hold him still, get the ball out ...' I began, forcing the words out, but it was no good. The ribbon dangling from the child's filthy fingers floated before my vision, and I blacked out.

I came to, lying on the bed of a cart. Mason Hardcastle's dung cart, and recently used for that purpose, from the smell of it. Judging by its slow progress and tendency to tilt to one side, it either had odd sized wheels or there was something wrong with the axle, and since the ground we were covering was a mass of cart ruts, I was constantly being jolted onto my damaged shoulder. My ungrateful waking thought was, why didn't these idiots, knowing the cart was lopsided, lay me the other way round? In fairness, some rough sacking had been placed beneath me to protect my shoulder, but to little effect. This too had an extremely unpleasant odour, which I identified as chicken shit. What with the pain and the smell, and the throbbing of my head, it was all I could do not to cast up the contents of my stomach. But what of poor Caesar? I struggled to raise myself on the elbow of my good arm, to find Gervase was walking beside the wagon, leading him.

'The ball's out,' he told me, grinning beneath the slouch hat he had donned as part of his farm labourer disguise. 'Just as well you passed out when you did. It would have been a damned nuisance if you'd tried to help doctor him, and then blacked out while we were doing it. As you very likely would! We ended up barricading him in a stall in old Hardcastle's apology for a stable, and I had to climb up and lie across the roof beams and come at him from above, or he'd have kicked my head in! Nearly demolished the stall as it was, and that was after this Sam Woodley fellow managed to force some horse physic of Hardcastle's down his throat to quiet the beast! I've packed the wound with moss. The scar will spoil the perfection of his glossy coat somewhat, but he'll live to go campaigning another day, won't you, Caesar?'

Caesar, hearing his name, turned his head to roll a lacklustre eye, and bared his teeth. I flopped back on the chicken shit sack, and wished I hadn't.

'Is Hardcastle dead?' I demanded, from the bottom of the cart.

'Dead? Not he! He'd merely stunned himself falling over, after tangling his feet in the draw string bag in which he keeps that revolting old contraption. A *matchlock harquebus*, for the love of Christ! Did you know the old fiend went as a mercenary back in the thirties, and fought — or so he claims — all over the Low Countries, and then for some Italian Condottier'e, leading a mercenary army somewhere on the Rhine? That's where he got the unspeakable weapon he shot at you with. I never saw such a loathsome thing, and devoutly hope I never do again!' He could not hope it more devoutly than I.

'He apologises, by the way, says he never meant to shoot anyone, just scare the breeches off Sam Woodley.'

'I'm well aware of that,' I replied, hollowly, from the bottom of the cart, 'You can't be sure of hitting a barn door with one of those things. You end up killing your own men and your own cattle.'

Flintlocks are marginally more reliable, but as we had found to our cost at Dunbar, the slightest bit of damp in the air and they jam solid. And if you're unlucky, blow up in your face.

'I hope you took it off him?'

'No, because I hadn't the authority — at least I didn't want him to know I had. I doubt he'll try it again,' said Gervase. Then he chortled, 'I pointed out to Hardcastle that Sam seems all too willing to take his breeches off. 'Twould be better if he kept them on! And I also reminded him that a cavalry horse of Caesar's stamp costs a pretty penny, and you'd be after him for compensation if the horse was permanently maimed. That gave the old wretch furiously to think!'

I lay in the bottom of the dung cart and gazed at the sky, which was a milky blue with just a suggestion of cloud above the distant fells. No change in the weather just yet, but this also meant the hay would be ripening fast. There were many things I didn't want to think about just yet, so I thought of that.

'I won't be fit to cut hay in the next day or two,' I remarked gloomily, 'I put my shoulder out when Caesar fell. Sam shoved it back again, but it'll pain me for a week or more.'

'No more you will,' Gervase agreed, equably, 'but I've no doubt your righteous and er, peculiar neighbours will continue to offer their help.' He looked down at me thoughtfully over the side of the cart, and winked his right eye. 'Tell me,' he glanced back over his shoulder and lowered his voice, and I understood that we were part of a procession, there were other hoof falls and subdued voices following the cart, 'are all the folks in these parts of a freakish cast of mind? To be honest,' he looked back again, and lowered his voice still further, 'Sam Woodley is about the sanest one I've met so far!'

I reflected that Gervase had spent the first part of the morning searching the alder grove with Malachi Postlethwaite, who had probably remained entirely silent, apart perhaps from reciting the odd verse from one of the gloomier books of the Old Testament. Now he'd encountered Mason Hardcastle. Little wonder he thought the whole district was made up of the moonstruck.

'Farming can be a lonely life,' I remarked, and closed my eyes. My head and shoulder were throbbing. I struggled against seeing any of the events of the morning once more in my mind's eye, but still the pink ribbon dangled there. 'What became of the Proctor lad, young Timmy?'

'Riding back there,' he jerked his head, 'clinging on behind Mistress Judith Moreland. Going to show her just where he found that piece of ribbon he declares to be your sister's. Whether it is or no, I know not. I never noticed her wearing such a thing these past times when I called at the farm.'

No more had I. Ann wasn't a girl to wear ribbons in her fine spun, hazelnut hair. A neat starched cap, setting off her clear complexion and pansy brown eyes, was more her style, but I now recalled that when I'd first got home and found the farmhouse deserted, I'd seen a dress, lying across the bed in her room. A dress in the process of being trimmed at the neck with pink ribbon. I had taken little note of it at the time, and couldn't swear it was the same ribbon, for the matching of silks was never a task in which my womenfolk had instructed me. But it might be. Ann could have set her sewing aside to attend to some more urgent household commission, coiling the spare ribbon in her apron pocket the while, and then...

I hadn't meant to think about this. After this morning's ludicrous events I wasn't stout enough, but I couldn't stop myself.

'Was there... any other sign? Where Timmy found the ribbon? Across the Lune?'

'Nothing wondrous,' said Gervase, slowly, but I knew from his tone of voice that there was something. Something he, as an experienced army scout, had thought notable.

'Last week there was rain here they tell me, and three days ago the ground was soft enough to hold a few faint marks. Just a suggestion, you understand, Rob? And largely destroyed by the hoof prints of your sheep passing by every morning and evening, but someone took a cart that way. No sign that it was ever on this side of the river, though.'

'That land across the river is Colonel Moreland's. But he has always granted us the right to take the sheep that way, up to the moor, when the river is low, to save driving them round through Beckside. His farm hands could have had a cart over there... for any number of reasons.'

'At this season of the year, Rob? I've been trying to think of one. It's open grazing land, and there are no crops or beasts on it at present.'

He was right. I couldn't think of a reason, either.

'The tracks, such as they were, seemed to be travelling upwards, towards the hills. Not the way your shepherds go, yet not towards one of the villages either,' said Gervase. 'Which is not to say they didn't change direction further on. I didn't stay to follow them, but rode back to fetch you.'

'And found me, an experienced cavalryman, brain-addled, and with my horse shot from under me, in a stupid domestic dispute!'

My head and shoulder still hurt as though the Devil was poking at them with a red hot toasting fork, but the whole ridiculous incident danced inside my eyelids, and I began to laugh.

# Chapter 10

I was no longer laughing when Mother came home and found me propped up on the settle in the parlour, my head and shoulder throbbing, frustratedly waiting for the return of the search party. They went (save Caesar and myself) plashing across the river, some on horseback and others on foot, led by young Timmy Proctor. Gervase, the three Postlethwaite brothers, Judith Moreland, even Cousin Zeke. Sam Woodley, who seemed to have added himself to the strength, stayed long enough to settle Caesar into his stall. Miles, Zeke assured me, before he dodged off to join the hunt (evidently he saw the point of it, now that there was something definite to hunt for) was sleeping, calm enough. They refused to let me go with them.

Gervase had roughly strapped my arm across my chest to take the weight off my injured shoulder, but I was as wretched as a wet house cat. Mother took one look at me and went straight to the spice cupboard in the corner for her willow bark concoction, and ordered me to drink it down. It tastes vile. When she caught sight of my expression, I thought she was going to scold, and so did she. The last time I remembered her forcing the stuff on me had been in my twelfth year, when I fell out of a tree and cracked a bone in my wrist.

Instead, her face softened, and she chuckled. "Twill ease the pain, and you know it! And then, most like, you'll sleep. So tell me first, what happened?'

I told her, making as little as possible of my calamitous excursion to Withins (though she got most of it out of me, as she always had of my youthful peccadilloes) and more of Timmy's find. 'Didn't you see them, searching across the river, as you rode home?'

But Mother had come through the lanes, and round by Beckside, and indeed had stopped there, to get news of Lemuel Drysdale's burying from the villagers.

'It's to be tomorrow at ten in the forenoon, they tell me,' she remarked, settling herself in an old fireside chair, and taking up her knitting. 'I must make shift to go, though I had little enough patience with the man while he lived. Two burials in Beckside churchyard inside a week!' She shook her head in dismay. 'That young parson, Mr Rogers, from Barbondale is to take it, they say. Colonel Moreland sent for him and gave him the order, although folks say he is not best pleased, having Royalist sympathies, and not being in charity with Lemuel over some matter concerning a tithe Lemuel had pocketed, which he believed was his by right. So, what signs does your friend Gervase believe the Procter child has found?'

It was interesting that she never doubted that Gervase was leading the hunt. No matter in what disguises he had presented himself in the neighbourhood over the last year, Mother must always have identified him as a figure of authority.

'A piece of pink ribbon. Timmy declares he had seen Ann sewing ribbon of that shade onto a dress one day when he was sent here by Martha to get milk.'

I told Mother now, as I had not before, about my search of the house when I came home and found them all missing. She nodded. 'She was trimming her new gown with pink. She bought the ribbon from a market stall in Sedbergh, at the hiring fair, and there was a little left, so she planned to sew it in the neck of her Sunday dress. I think Judith Moreland persuaded her the colour would suit her complexion. You know your sister. A shy thing, she holds herself back, hoping not to be noticed, but Judith is all set on bringing her out. She told me such a pretty wench should not be overshadowed.'

Mother pressed her lips together, and folded her knitting with a sigh. 'And now, God willing, she won't be. Ann's style of beauty isn't the showy kind. A hedge flower to a garden rose she was, next to Loveday. Pray God they find her and Rachel Postlethwaite too. Two young things that did no harm to anybody. I'll go and check on Miles now, Robert. You try to get some sleep to mend your hurts.'

'Wait!' I called after her, 'You haven't told me, what did Lanty have to say?'

She paused in the doorway. 'Little enough. You already had the gist of it. Apparently the girls were talking of getting a lift with a carrier's cart, and following me to Lancaster. Loveday was restive, because she'd had a fierce quarrel with Miles, before he set out to see the lawyer. That much I knew. It was the reason she didn't come with me to pay the fine. When I failed to return after two days, it seems she panicked, saying she knew from a dream she had, that Miles was dying, and she must go to him. She was afraid to go alone, and wanted Rachel to go with her, but that would mean leaving Ann here on her own. They knew Hannah couldn't be spared from Highbiggens. Lanty understood most of this. Ann had learned some of the signs I use with him, and must have told him. However, he thought nothing was decided. Then he came back one evening, he thinks four days ago, although it could be more, and found them all gone. He was surprised, because nothing had been said the night before. There was no note left, but of course he can't read, so they wouldn't think to leave one. He supposed that they'd had word from me, and taken the chance of a lift on a cart, all three together. Perhaps they did. Some carter or peddler may have offered to take them, and they thought it too good a chance to miss. They'd have believed themselves safe enough, three of them, even with a man they didn't know. That was all Lanty could tell me. He's been milking, and feeding the stock, waiting for them to return, and this was all the thanks the poor man got, to be accused of possession by Lady Brilliana! However, once Lemuel is buried, Colonel Moreland thinks to let Lanty come home. Folks know well enough he didn't kill Lemuel Drysdale, and that death had more of the Devil's hand in it than Loveday's, which could have been an accident that someone is afraid to own.'

I ran my hand across my aching forehead. 'But why and how did the girls cross the river? If they set out, as perhaps they did, either on foot, or riding in a cart, and Loveday met with an accident, or was killed, why cross over? Could not one of them make for Beckside to get help? It's hard to believe that even as vile a scoundrel as this attacker must have been, could kill one girl and abscond with the other two, without their screams being heard all over the dale.'

Mother closed her eyes and bent her head over her clasped hands. 'Dear Lord and Father, I ask that we may know all, in Your good time?' Then she went quietly away to check on Miles.

I prayed, that if my own worst fears proved true, we could spare her knowing all. Perhaps there had been two rogues, one to kill, and one to bind and gag? But why kill beauteous Loveday, who was surely the bigger prize to men of that stamp? It was useless to tease my brain with it until the search party returned with more information. So I did, until Mother's physic took its effect.

I woke to find the searchers returned, and standing over me. Timmy Proctor's shrill voice broke into my befuddlement.

'Major Rob! I found yer sister's ribbon, and *then* I found a piece o' lace trimmin' that might be Rachel's! An' we seen the tracks of a cart!' he squeaked, 'but we niver found no bodies,' he added, sounding disappointed. I looked at Gervase for confirmation.

'George here thinks the scrap of lace might have been torn from Rachel's collar,' he affirmed, 'but we'll know for sure when Hannah has seen it. Benjy's gone running up to Highbiggens to show her.'

I roused myself and sat up, rubbing my eyes with my unbound hand, forcing myself awake and ready for the fray, as had happened so many times on campaign. 'Do you think they may have thrown these things down on the ground, as a sign to lead us to where they were being taken?'

Gervase shrugged. 'Mayhap. The scrap of lace we found above the marks of a cartwheel that had passed that way recently. I sent Benjy to speak with Jem Robinson, Colonel Moreland's steward, and he came back with word that no one from the surrounding farms, which are all of them leased from Moreland, admits to sending a cart that way. Why should they, he says? There is nothing up there to be harvested, no reason go there except to check sheep, which is better done on foot.'

'Ah reckon someone's tekken 'em prisoner!' blurted young Timmy, his eyes gleaming through his dirty mop of hair. This poor scrap of a lad could never have had such a splendid day. Bread and cheese and Mother's raspberries, and all this excitement to boot, with himself the sharp-eyed hero of it all.

'We followed the tracks as far as we could,' continued Gervase. 'but after a mile or two the ground turned steep and slippery with loose shale. We couldn't see where the cart went. The light was fading, so we came back. What is there up there, anyway? George here says he doesn't know of any barns or dwellings.'

'The Lord niver made me to walk in those ways,' rumbled George, 'being labourers in our own vineyard, and bearing the yoke thereof.'

Sanctimonious lummox. In the past he would have climbed those hills fast enough, if he'd thought he would find a stream gushing forth strong ale up there. However, a notion was coming to me. Not a pleasant one, but it made sense.

'Colonel Moreland mentioned that there have been a few stragglers from the Scottish army of the Royalists hiding out in the hills. He thought they were all gone now. No reports of any sightings, or livestock taken, but there are sheep running wild up there. Not every farmer rounds up every stray and checks them, once the lambing season is over. Could there be a group of renegades camping out up there, and living on mountain mutton?'

Gervase and George, Malachi and Zeke (neither of whom had said a word) looked at one another. It was Timmy who blurted out, 'Me Dad sez there's caves up yonder, an' pot holes, where the Divil bides!'

Gervase placed a hand on Timmy's shoulder, 'Is that so? Could your father show them to us, or tell us how to find them?'

Timmy's eyes grew round at the enormity of this request. 'Nay, Mister! He'd happen tell yer, what me grandfether told him, but he'd be afeared to go there!'

# Chapter 11

As evening drew on I fretted over the farm tasks, the milking, foraging for the livestock, but I was assured that these would be done, and I should rest, in the hope that I'd be well enough to take part in the continued search on the morrow.

'Though, out of respect I suppose we mayn't set out until the priest is buried?' said Gervase. 'A pity, for I fear the day could be extremely hot.'

I told him there was no need for him to attend the funeral, having seen Lemuel only once.

'I shall go, none the less. Someone murdered him, and I'd give much to know why. Will the killer will be at the service? He would hardly dare to stay away, but if he does, his absence will be noted.'

Useless to tell Gervase that there are many reasons why a man of this district might excuse himself from attending a funeral — hay liable to rot and mildew if left any longer unturned; a sick cow, a wife newly delivered of a child — or simply dislike of the priest, who might have rubbed against a raw place in one of his homilies. The people of this dale, though they may touch their forelocks respectfully to Colonel Moreland, or indeed their parish priest, have a hardy streak of independence. Although it does not, in my view, necessarily lead to treason. Gervase was convinced, I realised, that our neighbourhood harboured someone of a traitorous mind. Someone with hidden Royalist sympathies. Or perhaps a man who in his secret heart cried, 'a plague on both your houses!' and plotted for revolution 'gainst the state itself. I knew also, from the enquiring sideways glances he sent in my direction, that he thought I could provide names, if only I would.

I sat at Miles' bedside, thinking. Mother was brooding over saucepans in the kitchen. Gervase and Benjy were milking and feeding the livestock, Benjy having returned with Hannah's opinion that the torn scrap of lace was 'very like' that to be found on her sister's collar. Those poor, terrified girls! Kidnapped, and being driven away, to what fate I dared not imagine, they must have tried with what little means they had, to indicate the way they were being taken, hoping that someone would follow and rescue them. If only I had thought to look for them across the river as soon as... How could I, how could anyone have known? I fretted, feeling my idleness, but accepting that no further searching could be done until after the funeral on the morrow.

Cousin Zeke, I hoped, after repeating his morning's exercise in finding green fodder, was forming a fast friendship with the goat, Tabitha, since I felt those two were meant for one another. George Postlethwaite and Sam Woodley were gone home to attend to their own beasts. Malachi had suddenly announced an intention to hoist the young Proctors (Saul having returned from the fell with the sheep) onto his saddle, and carry them home to Beckside. The children were bone weary, and the offer a kindly one, although George muttered something about 'falling into sin' which led me to suspect that Malachi's true destination was a visit to the Widow Snaith.

Why, I wondered to myself, does he not marry the woman; why all this secrecy? Her husband, the miller, must have been dead nigh on a year. She has no dependants, and a snug cottage where they can live, if she has no wish to move to Highbiggens.

Country matters, country mysteries, none of which seemed to have anything to do with revolution, or murder. Their love affair, if I could call it that, seemed to have been the subject of one of my sister-in-law's prophesies, but so had many other people. The very fact that Malachi still visited the lady, suggested that he and Deborah Snaith felt no personal guilt over Loveday's death.

Presently dusk fell and the hills that ringed the river valley turned a darker green, then gold, then violet in the twilight. The house and the barnyard grew quiet. Mother brought me a plate of stew and some fresh bread. When she had found time to bake it, I couldn't guess. She must have set the dough to rise during the watches of the night.

'His breathing is better,' she remarked, nodding her head towards my recumbent brother. Miles lay still, his chest rising and falling. 'I thought I'd done wrong, bringing him home. It set him back aways, but now I believe he's picking up again. Could you stay with him a while? Get him to swallow some water if you can.' She looked slightly uncomfortable, 'We're going to wait on the Lord here in the parlour later — a prayer meeting amongst our neighbours, since we're so afflicted. Deb Snaith is coming, and Martha Proctor, and Josiah and George, and Benjy, of course. Gervase said he'd be interested. He hasn't been to one of our meetings before.' She seemed apologetic. 'Of course, you haven't been either, son. I don't know... 'twas young Dick Hardcastle who introduced us to the idea. He's spent time with people over in Westmoreland who call themselves Seekers; seekers after true religion, like they say the first Christians were. They maintain that men and women can grow close to Our Lord without need of priests or set forms of words. We won't disturb Miles tonight, there'll be no preaching or singing of psalms. The idea is to seek the Will of the Lord God in silence, to see our way clear. Someone may read a passage from the Bible, or speak some words that come into their heart from the Lord.' She smiled, ruefully, and patted my good shoulder. 'I don't know what good it will do, but I feel so helpless. All we can do is ask for His mercy for Ann and Rachel, and for the souls of Loveday and Lemuel too.'

'Never fret, Mother. If you feel a prayer meeting with our neighbours may help, by all means do it. I'll sit and watch over Miles.'

I felt awkward, dishonest even, giving her this reassurance, knowing that Gervase was looking for signs of treachery amongst these pious, anguished souls. What did he imagine? That these people's occasional vocal offerings concealed secret information, being passed from one to another under the guise of prayer or exhortation? That if someone quoted a verse from the Bible, the chapter and verse number constituted (to those who understood it) a hidden code, revealing the whereabouts of weapons, or numbers of supporters? Surely he must realise that there were easier ways for men with such notions to meet and plot? Two men riding or walking in this countryside could simply arrange to meet in a stand of trees, or a lambing shelter in the hills, and speak freely, without having to spend an hour or more in silent contemplation amongst their womenfolk in order to share information?

Later, when the little band of worshippers had settled in the front parlour, I tiptoed stealthily round through the hallway and observed them through the open doorway. It amused me to see Gervase, tense and wary, seated uncomfortably on one of our upright oak dining chairs amongst this silent congregation of simple folk, their heads bowed in prayer, their calloused hands clasped before them, 'waiting on the Lord'. Presently, Josiah read from the Bible in a low voice, and then Hannah, red faced with anxiety, her fingers twisting in her apron, gasped out a prayer for God to deliver her sister and her friend. Her words were barely coherent, but when she fell silent my mother's hand reached out to squeeze hers, her smile thanking the girl, not so much for her jumbled words, but for the good heart that lay behind them.

'There may be plots against the Commonwealth,' I thought, 'but I doubt you'll find them in our parlour, Gervase.'

# Chapter 12

Next morning our hopes were raised, only to be dashed again. Martha Proctor came stumbling, breathless, into the farm kitchen soon after daybreak, bearing a message that two young women had been seen riding on a cart as it passed through Kirkby Lonsdale the previous day. A man travelling up the dale with a mule loaded with pots and pans, who had spent the night at the ale house in Beckside, had offered up this information over his breakfast crust. He was there still, Martha reported, but packing his traps. If we wanted to hear more we must hurry. I was in no case to hurry anywhere, having spent a rough and largely sleepless night with my damaged shoulder. Gervase and Benjy went. And returned. The carter described the girls he'd seen as 'the gypsy sort, all gold earrings and flashing eyes.' Gervase said he judged the man's eye sight was good, and his account reliable. Rachel was dark, but possessed no earrings, and nobody, even if their sight was failing, would describe shy, fair-skinned Ann as the 'the gypsy sort.'

'It wasn't our lasses,' he told Mother.

'I feared it wasn't,' she replied, apparently calm, but she turned her head away, blinking back tears. 'They've been gone how many days? Four? Perhaps five. Long enough to have reached Lancaster before we left. And if they stopped on the way for some reason, we came through Kirkby on our way home, surely we'd have met them on the road?'

'We'll get this funeral out of the way, and then we'll start combing the fellside again,' I promised, although the last thing I felt ready for was a stiff hill climb.

I wouldn't describe the turn out for Lemuel Drysdale's funeral as large. Our parish priest had not been the most well-loved of men, and a number of his parishioners had, as I'd suspected they would, found reasons to be absent. Mother, Gervase, Josiah Postlethwaite and I, represented our small corner of the dale. Cousin Zeke declined, reasonably enough, since he had never set eyes on the man. He offered to busy himself with farm tasks and checking on Miles without having to be asked, an improvement in his attitude that I was pleased to note. I was somewhat surprised when George rode into the yard, announcing that he, Malachi and Benjy would start scything the West meadow. True, the hay there was ready for cutting, and the day could not have been fairer for the purpose, but with their new found enthusiasm for religion, I'd expected them to attend the service.

Gervase, I noticed, narrowed his eyes when this was mooted. Could these three be amongst his plotters and schemers? My personal opinion was that George and Malc lacked the wit and subtlety, and had too recently renounced strong drink, for anyone to trust them in any great matter. Benjy was sharper. And fast on his feet. If you wanted someone to carry messages from one place to another, such as plotters must surely employ, then Benjy would be a good choice. Young lads can be easily persuaded by the lure of adventure, and secret and dangerous enterprises. I should know. I was such a one myself, and somewhat older than Benjy, when I enlisted under Tom Fairfax. Ben's obvious disapproval when he first encountered Gervase in Cavalier garb didn't chime with Royalist sympathies, and though quick witted in a way his brothers were not, I'd seen nothing that made me suspect him of a talent for dissimulation. There had, however, been something unexpected about his reaction to Lemuel's killing.

As we approached the church once more, Gervase giving Mother his arm and walking a little way ahead, I asked Josiah if Lemuel had offended his family.

'A whited sepulchre!' he grunted, 'The Lord is not mocked!' What this curious utterance meant I couldn't fathom, and as we were soon mingling with other parishioners, I couldn't question him further.

The service was taken by the young curate from Barbondale, and I cannot say that he delivered Lemuel's eulogy with anything approaching enthusiasm, although, since Colonel Moreland and his household were present, he was careful and correct at every point. We buried our priest in the Eastern corner of the churchyard, a bare, open piece of ground, as far as was possible from where Loveday lay.

I was standing with Mother, watching Luke Proctor earning a no doubt welcome bonus as he filled the second grave he'd dug this week, when Lady Brilliana approached us.

'Mistress Haddon, a word!' Lady Brilliana was splendid in black, silk I would hazard, her face partially obscured by a mourning veil of fine lace. As she spoke, her fine eyes flashed in my direction, conveying her wish to speak to Mother alone. Politely, I drew aside. Mother didn't need me to handle Lady Brilliana. My parent is not easily cowed by those who consider themselves her social superiors. However, I didn't see any reason to move too far off.

'My daughter, Judith,' she began.

Mother said nothing, but raised her brows in polite enquiry. I think she knew what was coming

'My girl is impetuous,' Lady Brilliana stated, 'and too forward in her behaviour. Much of the fault lies with us, her parents, far be it from me to deny it! We have, of late, allowed her too much freedom,' she gave a false little laugh that contained no amusement, 'to go careering up and down the dale like a complete hoyden!'

I had no difficulty at all in overhearing any of this, since Lady Brilliana is one of those aristocratic persons who speak loudly and clearly when addressing the peasantry, perhaps under the impression that we are all weak of hearing as well as understanding.

'All the fault of this stupid war,' she continued. 'I wanted from the beginning to send her to Antwerp with her brothers, but the Colonel wouldn't hear of it. Now it seems that hostilities might be coming to an end at last, I feel I must place some curbs on Judith. Make her see that she must now begin to behave as a young lady should, or she will never achieve a respectable marriage. Now you, my dear Mistress Haddon, have been extremely kind to my girl, and made her more than welcome at Lowflatts, but I'm going to ask you not to receive her anymore. I'm afraid it won't do. Judith must marry suitably. She wasn't born to be a farmer's wife, or to go running around with the soldiery. I am, naturally, extremely sorry that your daughter and her friend are missing, and hope they'll be found safe and well, but I can't have Judith scouring the hills unchaperoned, with a raggle-taggle band of young men.'

Well, I wasn't astonished. Only puzzled that Mistress Judith had been allowed so much liberty for so long. But why now? True, Civil War hostilities seemed to be dying out at last, but there were still strong pockets of resistance, and all could suddenly flare up again at any moment. Already there were rumours of a build-up of Royalist supporters in the West Country, eager to continue the fight. Rumours that if the late King's son was triumphant in Scotland, he would come and lead them.

So, where was this errant daughter whilst her Mama was accosting mine? She had been seated with her mother during the service, and I could see her father now, conferring with the curate, but a quick survey of the churchyard confirmed that she was absent. Well, your Ladyship, I thought, she is not 'running around with the soldiery' by whom I supposed I was meant. I strained my ears, interested to hear what Mother would say in reply. Mother doesn't lose her temper when condescended to, but neither is she cowed by arrogance. She inclined her head with a slight smile.

'I understand your concerns, Lady Brilliana. Judith is a delightful child, and we're all very fond of her. I assure you she will never come to any harm from anyone in *my* household.' With this speech, which did not convey any promise that our door would henceforth be barred to Judith Moreland, Mother bowed politely, and turned to give her attention to the Widow Snaith, who was calling everyone to the repast awaiting us in the late Lemuel Drysdale's parlour. Lady Brilliana stalked away, tight lipped.

Walking back to the farm, I said something to Mother about Lady Brilliana's presumption. She shook her head, smiling.

'She cannot help it. Born to the nobility, I suppose her life has been a great disappointment to her. She may be cherishing dreams of taking Judith to London and launching her in society, although I cannot imagine what society she'll find there to meet her nice notions! They're saying Oliver Cromwell is to be offered the post of Lord Protector, or even the crown, but I don't suppose he'll see it as a pressing duty to preside over a marriage mart! Besides, Judith is her father's daughter, strong for Parliament. Brilliana would do better to leave well alone and let Benson Moreland find a husband for their girl!'

I nodded towards Gervase, walking some way in front of us, trying, somewhat fruitlessly, to engage Josiah Postlethwaite in conversation. 'I would have thought my friend here — when he's not dressed as a farm labourer! — might suit Colonel Moreland's ideas. His family have lands in Huntingdonshire and,' I lowered my voice still further, 'I understand him to be the heir. Once this war is over his father will be expecting him to settle down and take over the management of their estate. Judith could be just the wife for him.'

Privately I doubted Gervase's, or Judith's, willingness to go along with such a scheme, but I could see it pleased Mother's idea of what was fitting, and took her mind, for a moment, from her worries about Ann. She liked Gervase, and was truly fond of Judith. I forbore to mention that Gervase had told me that he and his father were frequently at odds — not in the matter of politics, as so many fathers and sons had been these last years — but because he had always, from a boy, as far as I could gather, had a wild adventurous streak. He'd freely admitted seeking excuses, even in times of peace, to be away from home. This War, he'd confessed (camp fire confidences) had been a huge and satisfying adventure for him, an escape from all he found dull and tedious. I doubted whether he would, or even could, settle down to the repetitive life of running a country estate. But Mother and I walked home in charity with one another, pleased with our matchmaking scheme.

Our comfort was quickly at an end. No sooner had we stepped into the kitchen than we were met by a wild, unkempt figure. Miles, in his night shirt, staggering on thin, wasted legs, arms flailing, eyes burning with fever and rage, lurched at me, yelling curses. Cousin Zeke came lolloping after him, bleating in a manner reminiscent of Tabitha, and making fruitless grabs at the tail of his nightshirt.

'Murderer!' My brother yelled, 'you killed her, you killed my girl, my Loveday!'

'Miles, I assure you...'

He lunged at me, thumping me in the chest and jarring my tender shoulder. Mother darted forward, seizing his wrist. 'No, dear, no! Robert had nothing to do with it!' Her gentle voice was conciliatory, seeking to calm him, as she had often done when we sparred too fiercely as boys. Zeke, catching up with him, seized his arms, and between them they pulled him away. He stood, swaying on unsteady legs, many days unshaven, dishevelled and panting, spittle running down his chin.

'I 'ad to tell 'im!' Zeke gasped, 'E made me say. 'E come to and 'e askt where wus she? I couldn't tell 'im no lie, could I?' he added, eyeing me imploringly.

I thought why could you not? Why couldn't you fob him off, saying you knew nothing of Loveday? As indeed would have been partly true, since you never saw her, alive or dead. Mother took Miles' elbow, assisted by Zeke, who was certainly strong in t'arm, as we say around here (though in my opinion, also thick in t'head). No doubt this strength came from his former occupation amongst the mizzens and topsails. As they began to lead Miles back to his makeshift bed, she looked back at me, mouthing, quietly, 'Let me settle him, Rob. When he's calm I'll explain how it was…'

I stood, shaken; pain pounding through my shoulder, though the pain in my heart was greater. Miles and I, born just a year apart, had always been rivals. Rivals in sport and play, and love. For reasons I've never been able to fathom, he resented me. As the eldest son, he was our father's heir; the farm had passed to him. He had won the girl. Yet he still seemed to believe I might snatch these things from him; that in a fit of spite I might have killed Loveday. The girl I'd once so fondly loved.

'Are you hurt, Soldier Rob? Did he catch your shoulder? Shall I make you a soothing posset?' The quiet voice behind me in the kitchen made me jump.

'Judith! What are you doing here? Surely you know your mother doesn't wish …she asked my mother, just now, at the funeral, not to receive you.'

'Did she now? Well, how fortunate that I wasn't there to hear her!' Her tone was dry. Judith Moreland was standing at the kitchen hearth, stirring something in a pot. She was wrapped in one of Mother's aprons, which went around her twice, and looked entirely at home, as though she had spent the morning cooking. Her tall crowned hat, the one without the feather, was hanging on the hook behind the door, where until yesterday my father's old coat had been.

'Funerals are so dreary, I slipped away as soon as they carried the coffin out,' she remarked. 'I thought your mother could probably do with an extra pair of hands, with your brother so ill, and guests in the house. I suppose, once you've eaten, we'll all go up into the fells to search. Or should you rest with your injured shoulder?'

'Judith,' I began, through gritted teeth, but realised I hadn't the strength for another quarrel, and turned to walk away.

'Don't mind Miles!' she called after me, 'he'll come around. We all know 'twas no fault of yours.'

Of course I knew she was right; Miles was always hot tempered, flaring up to anger before he half understood the case, or with whom his quarrel lay, but it infuriated me to hear this young woman speak as though she knew my brother better than I did. I spun on my heel. I've never yet slapped a woman, but Mistress Judith Moreland might have been the first, had not Gervase and Benjy surged into the kitchen at that moment, themselves both in hot dispute.

'Well, here he is!' declared Gervase, 'and can settle the matter himself. Young Benjamin thinks you should rest up this afternoon, while your shoulder heals, but I say you'll want to ride with us, to show us the most likely routes, and where best to search. You must surely know these hills almost as well as this Luke Procter fellow?'

'I'll come, of course,' I said, stiffly, although I might have been sorely tempted to follow Benjy's advice if it had not been for Miles' accusations, and my wrath at Judith's presumption. 'Though I'll need a horse. Caesar must be rested while his wound heals.'

'Tha canst have t'old bedstead tha gave me!' grinned Benjy. 'Then tha'll likely think tha's lying down on t'settle in t' parlour, when tha's half way up t'fell!'

'I'll take the cob,' I said, firmly. 'Mother won't be needing it.' I hoped and prayed she would stay here this afternoon, 'calming' Miles. 'Does Luke Procter come with us to show us these caves 'where the Devil bides?' Is he not so afeared as young Timmy thought?'

'He is afeared all right,' grinned Gervase, 'of his wife! Martha was by when I asked him, and offered him money to go with us. With her and six young 'uns to feed, he dared not refuse!

# Chapter 13

Despite our good intentions, it was already later in the afternoon than I would have wished when we set out. It was the loveliest of days, the kind that, in our boyhood, would have seen Miles and myself running naked down through the meadow to while away the afternoon, splashing in the shallows of the Lune, heedless and happy. Today, accompanied by a sombre band, I forded it on horseback. The river was now running low after several days of fine weather. Ox-eyed daisies and cow parsley nodded on the brim, warblers flitted and chirruped in the bushes, and dippers darted about us, skimming the river's surface as they snatched up insects. Our search party consisted of myself, mounted on the cob, George Postlethwaite and Gervase on their own mounts, and Benjy on the pony (which, newly shod, a neighbour had been kind enough to return to us). Luke Procter rode one of the big carthorses which Benjy had christened 'the four-posters' and Sam Woodley the other.

Sam had arrived to check on Caesar's welfare, but deciding at a glance that all was going well with him, then claimed he also had permission from his employer to join the search. Caesar, seeming to remember that this fellow was the one who had forced physic down his reluctant throat, had taken himself off to the far corner of the garth in high dudgeon. He was mending fast, faster than I was. His gait was even, and his coat retained a good gloss. My opinion regarding Sam was that he was an idle rogue, though a good natured one, and I was glad I wasn't the one paying his wages.

Malachi elected to remain behind, saying he would teach Cousin Zeke to turn hay, a sight I would have liked to witness. Rather to my surprise, though I was careful not to question it, Judith Moreland did not accompany us. Mother must have urged her to return home.

Once across the stream we found Colonel Moreland's steward, Jem, waiting astride his master's big bay. He brought word that the Colonel couldn't go with us this afternoon, a Parliamentary dispatch rider having arrived at Lings whilst we were in church, with urgent business he must attend to. This intrigued me, as I'd assumed the Colonel, having retired from active service, was no longer intimately involved in Parliament's affairs. I stole a glance at Gervase to see what he made of this, but his expression told me nothing.

Jem seemed no better pleased to have been sent to take part in today's search than he had previously. It crossed my mind that he must have made advances to Loveday, or perhaps even tried to pay court to Ann, and been rebuffed. Mother might know. I could imagine no other reason why he should resent his duty as a neighbour to help us search for our missing girls.

We took the route where Timmy Procter had found, on the previous day, those small evidences of cart tracks and the piece of torn lace (Was it only yesterday? My throbbing shoulder kept reminding me of that day's disastrous doings). The horses, fresh now, took the steep slope easily enough until we reached the shale bank, where their iron-shod hooves could get no purchase on the loose slate, and we were forced to dismount.

'This is no better in full daylight,' said Gervase. 'We need to find another route.'

'And if we are obliged to,' I said, 'then surely whoever brought a cart this way must also have done so. No one could safely drive up here, with three people or more aboard. I reckon we should turn back as far as that clump of thorn bushes, there, on the ridge below us, and try if we can go another way. What say you, Jem? We're still on the Colonel's land, are we not?'

'Haven't been this way this season. I doubt anyone brought a cart up here, or if they ever found reason to, they went no further than this.' Jem seemed determined to be surly and unhelpful. Why? Was it possible he knew, or suspected, more than he was prepared to say about the girls' disappearance? Yet I remembered him as an honest, upright fellow. Dull and over-righteous even. He was a church warden after all, and Colonel Moreland's trusted man. Dimly, I recalled some tale about a relative of his, living down towards Crook o' Lune, who had killed a man in a tavern brawl, but that was years ago, and no one ever held it against Jem. As folks had remarked sagely at the time, "Twas some cousin on his mother's side, and she's dead these fifteen year. No blame to Jem. Likely he never set eyes on the man.'

George and Sam, questioned about our route, claimed ignorance. The lie of the land on this side of the river was, to them, as 'far off Bohemia'. Luke Procter, who had been rendered largely speechless by the need to stay astride the big cart horse, his fingers so tightly knotted in its mane that I feared we might have to cut them free, merely nodded at my suggestion of retreating to the thorn bushes, and trying a sideways thrust.

'Ah've niver bin this far into t'hills,' he mumbled, 'Ah'm goon on what me grandfather telled me. He said as there's caves and pot holes up here. But he told us lile 'uns, niver go there, or t'Devil'll drag thee down in t'belly of t'earth! An' Ah tell mine the same!'

We descended to the stand of thorn bushes and cast to the right. This led us into a steep sided ghyll, its sides sparsely dotted with yellow flowering gorse, and with a stream gushing amongst ferns in the bottom of it. However, we were clear of the shale bank, and with some effort our horses breasted the next ridge, where we found a sheep track running along it and swerving out onto a stretch of open moorland.

'No beggar could have taken a cart that road!' grumbled Jem, looking back to the ghyll we'd just left.

'I don't suppose it!' I snapped, 'I'm sure there are other ways. I just happened to choose that one.' I'd been in the army too long, I reflected, and had grown unused to men questioning my decisions. Jem had a point, though it would have been more useful if he'd mentioned it sooner. As we proceeded to climb the shoulder of the fell, I saw that if we'd cast to the left, rather than the right, the way would have been longer, but less steep, and the end result, avoiding the perilous shale bank, would have brought us to the same place.

Seeing open country before us, our horses threw their heads up, eager to break into a canter, but we held them to walking the sheep track, and proceeded in single file. Sheep are foolish creatures, but wise in the ways of the fells. Notwithstanding unseen hazards like rabbit burrows, ground-nesting birds, and occasional patches of treacherous marsh, in this limestone country the earth's crust is shallow. The higher you climb, the more the rock pavement breaks through the surface, exposing itself in jagged irregular blocks. These are divided by deep fissures liable to trap the feet or hooves of the unwary.

As we climbed slowly to the next ridge, I could hear Jem, in the rear, still muttering that this was a waste of time, no horse and cart could have followed this narrow track. He was right, curse him. There was no evidence of wheel ruts, and despite a few dry days, we might have expected to see some sign of the passing of a vehicle with at least three people aboard.

'Jem's right, Beelzebub take him!' I turned to murmur to Gervase, immediately behind me in the file 'No one drove a cart beyond the shale bank.' I wondered, further, whether Jem had known that already, or had simply formed that conclusion today, as I had.

'Perhaps they walked beyond this point? Two men driving our girls before them?' Gervase answered.

Two men. Or more? Colonel Moreland's ragged band of Scots' deserters? Driving Ann and Rachel. Cold gripped my heart at the thought. Would we find their bodies, defiled and murdered, lying beyond the next ridge. Or the next?

But we didn't. We rode on, through the heat of the afternoon, crossing grey green moorland, lightened here and there with tufts of white bog cotton and pink flowering ling. We skirted patches of exposed limestone. We startled peewits and grouse from their nests, and sent them bounding and calling their alarm up into the milky blue heavens At last we reached a high cliff-like 'scar' of rock with a great cleft running down it.

'It'll take some diversion to pass beyond here,' said Gervase, dryly, 'on horse or on foot.'

'Happen this be it!' croaked Luke.' He was shaking, wide-eyed and fearful, atop his placid mount. 'This must be t'Devil's rock, like me grandfather told me.' He pointed to the top of the outcrop, where the jagged tip of some harder rock, weathered almost to a point, stood outlined against the sky. 'He said as t'Devil perches up there, looking down over t'dale, and devises his wickedness.'

'Well, he's not there at the moment,' said Gervase, 'unless he has made himself invisible. So how did your grandfather proceed? How did he find these caves and potholes? Are they still further up?'

'Must be,' interrupted Jem, 'and no way can we go further today, looking for them! The light will begin to go in just over an hour, and retracing the way we've come would be mighty dangerous in the twilight.'

'Aye, tha's right there,' conceded George, indicating the height of the sun, now well below its zenith in the western sky. Sam Woodley, however, slid down from his horse and walked forward, peering into the cleft in the rock face.

'Happen one of t'caves might be here, set back aways? Did tha grandfather say owt about it?' he asked of Luke, but Luke, lacking his redoubtable ancestor's adventurous spirit, simply shook his head and looked glum.

'Aye, could be a cave or summat in there!' Benjy, suddenly excited and not to be left out, jumped from the saddle and followed Sam into the crevasse. The rest of us dismounted but stood around, allowing the horses to crop the short grass at our feet, whilst the two explorers vanished from view. Evidently the split in the rock went back some considerable distance, and a base of rock and soil had built up, flat enough to walk on. We could hear their voices and the crack and rustle of disturbed vegetation as they pushed their way through.

'Waste of good haytiming weather,' muttered Jem, and then flushed darkly, seeing my eye on him. 'Ah'm right sorry your sister's missing,' he continued, 'but Ah don't believe we'll find her up here. Wasn't there talk she and Rachel set out for Lancaster? Isn't it more likely something went amiss with them along the road?'

'The Lord has shown us no more signs.' conceded George. 'No bits o' ribbon or lace beyond the river meadow.'

At this moment a great shadow fell across us, and we looked up, startled, to see what was blotting out the sun. A giant bird was hovering above the rock face. It landed on the jagged point of rock which Luke's grandfather had named as the Devil's look-out post, carefully folded its wings, and withdrew its long neck down between its shoulders. It reminded me of an old fellow hunched over in his favourite chair.

'A golden eagle!' hissed Gervase, who delights in the habits of birds. 'Very likely that's what your Granddad saw, Luke. With the sun behind him, and those great talons, he looks like a devil, perched up there!'

'Aye, and a devil is what he is,' grunted George. 'Ah've been blaming t'foxes for teking our lambs, but chance is, he did!'

The eagle looked down on us disdainfully, as though he knew we had not a weapon between us. Then there was sudden sound from within the rock fissure and Sam burst forth, yelling. The eagle, annoyed, spread its enormous wings and flew off again.

'Young Benjy!' Sam gasped, 'He's gone, I can't find him!'

'But... he f-followed you. He was right behind you,' I stammered.

'Aye, and we spoke as we went along... Then, just now, a cloud must have come across the sun... it went dark as night in there. And then I realised he wasn't following me. I turned back, thinking he must have stopped to look at something, but there was no sign of him!'

'He said nothing? You heard no sound?'

'Can he have fallen into one of these pot holes you people talk about,' demanded Gervase. 'Or into a cave that slants down under the rock?'

'Be a mighty deep hole, if you can't hear him calling,' rumbled George. 'He could have hit his head, knocked himself out of his senses.'

I told Sam about the eagle. 'Can you remember where you were when its shadow blocked out the sun? Benjy must have lost his footing in the darkness, then fallen into this cave. If you show us whereabouts you were, perhaps we can find him.'

'Go ahead. Luke and I'll hold the horses,' Gervase said, immediately. 'You people know this kind of terrain better than I.'

'Ah've a flint,' said George, producing it from within his jerkin, 'if we can find where he went down, Ah can strike a light, mebbe enough to see where he's lying.'

'Very well, let's go in.' I eased my aching shoulder, worrying about how we could raise the unconscious boy when we found him. I turned to ask Jem if he'd fetch a rope if we needed it, Lings being closer than Lowflatts.

He was gone. The wretch had silently mounted his horse and slipped away.

# Chapter 14

'What did he do that for?' demanded Sam, enraged. 'I call that right un-neighbourly!'

'If his conscience wasn't troubling him already, it surely will,' I said, 'but let's waste no more time. We must find Benjy before the light goes.'

We soon discovered that the sun had already dropped low enough that its rays no longer penetrated the cleft. Once inside, it was as if dusk had fallen. Walking was easy enough, the floor seemed smooth and even, as though it had been trodden down, but layers of millstone grit, harder than the limestone, bulged out at the height of our shoulders, making it sometimes necessary to turn sideways to pass. This rough ledge blocked what light was left in the narrow gorge, so that everything at ground level was in darkness. Sam proceeded slowly, trying to identify the spot where he had last spoken to Benjy and received an answer.

'I'd say 'twas hereabouts,' he decided, after we had gone some thirty feet into the cleft. We stopped, George struck the flint, and we crouched to peer under the gritstone ledge. Sure enough, there was a dark hole sloping away into the ground, and signs that earth from the pathway had broken away. The spark from the flint died.

'Benjamin!' bellowed George, 'Is thee down there?' His voice echoed in the void, 'down there, down there', but no answer came. He struck the flint again, but all we could see was a deep funnel dropping away into the rock, and hear, very distantly, the sound of water dripping.

'Luke's grandfather did right to warn his grandchildren agin this place!' Sam remarked. 'Whether the Devil be in it or no!'

'Amen!' said George, his voice unsteady. 'What'll us do?'

'Unless there's more than one of these caves here,' I said, 'then Benjy must have fallen into this one. I'd say he did, judging by this earth that's broken away from the lip. Perhaps he's lying hurt at the bottom of it. If we had a rope and a lantern...' I paused, as we heard a faint sound coming from below.

'Benjamin!' George roared, striking the flint again. We saw nothing, but heard another slight sound. 'By God's mercy, is thee down there?'

This time Benjy's voice came up to us, sounding surprisingly cheerful. 'Aye, Ah'm down here! Great dint in me head, and Ah've twisted me ankle. Thought 'twere broke to start, but 'tis bearing. 'Tis an amazing great place! Tunnels and great strange rocks shaped like... Ah dunno. But Ah can't see ony way to climb out!'

I crouched lower over the hole, cupping my hands to call down. 'There's light down there, Ben?' If he could see the tunnels and strange rock formations, light must surely be getting in from somewhere lower down the fell — which meant there must be another entrance. If it was close enough we might be able to get to him. If he walked or crawled to it he might even be able to get out himself.

'Aye, Ah can see light, away towards the way we came... towards t'dale, Ah think... but Ah dunno as Ah can get there...'

George looked at me. 'Tha's t'man of action. What'll us best do?'

I wished he hadn't asked. No comparable experience in the army had involved anything more difficult than hauling a panic stricken and disobliging mule out of a cess pit in broad daylight — though that had been an experience I wouldn't want to go through again. Ropes would be needed, and men to haul them.

'We'd best take council with Gervase,' I hedged, and called down to Benjy, 'We're going to speak with Gervase and Luke! If we're to pull you up this way we need someone to go for ropes and lanterns. The sun will be very low in an hour. Meanwhile, if your ankle will hold, try if you can find where the light is coming in. But keep returning here, so that we can speak to you.'

'Ah'll do that, the Lord being willing!' replied Benjy, his voice echoing from the depths.

'Amen to that! The Lord be with thee and keep thee.' replied his brother.

'You and Sam stay here, George,' I decided, 'and keep talking to him. I'll go back to Gervase. Even if Benjy finds another exit, ropes and lanterns may be needed.'

'I'll go.' Gervase offered when I told him what had happened. You stop here and rest that shoulder of yours. I'll fetch what's-his-name, Malachi, back with me if I can. Where do you keep your ropes? Lanterns? I suppose your mother can tell me.'

'There's plenty o' rope stored in t'church vestry, as we use for lowering coffins. I could come with thee and show thee,' quavered Luke Proctor. He was clearly desperate to get away from this ill-omened place.

'Yes, go with Gervase,' I agreed. You may be needed at home, and Malachi will certainly come in your place.'

Aside, I muttered to Gervase, 'The Widow Snaith will have gone by the time you get there. She was coming up to the farm this afternoon to help my mother with the dairying.'

'And the hay did, I'm sure, need turning, urgently,' responded Gervase, solemnly. Luke, catching the meaning behind our words, gave a bark of laughter. 'Old man Postlethwaite won't have it! Malc and the widow. He's heard as they was havey-cavey afore t'old miller died, an' that maks her the whore of Babylon!'

'So what does it make him?' asked Gervase, interested.

'An adulterer before the Lord?' I suggested. 'I'll warrant the way Josiah

*84*

Postlethwaite, in his new mood of righteousness, got wind of this sinful behaviour was through something my sister-in-law said in one of her prophesying fits.'

'Amen to that,' agreed Gervase, echoing George. 'The lovely Loveday was playing a dangerous game. I begin to see why someone might have wished her dead.'

Once Gervase and Luke were gone, I tethered the remaining horses to a couple of wind-blasted hawthorns, and went back into the cleft to report to George and Sam. I found them exploring beyond the point where Benjy had fallen into the cave. Benjy, they told me, was insisting that he was 'fair to middling', and doing his own exploring, below.

The fissure we were in widened towards the back, ending in a sheer rock face, at the base of which they were examining signs of human activity; an old tin drinking mug, a broken earthenware plate, the charred remains of a fire, a pile of animal bones.

'Likely this was where them Scotch soldiers camped,' said Sam, pointing out a piece of ragged canvas which still clung, though torn, between two jagged boulders. Behind it, in the gloom, it was possible to make out a low-roofed shallow cave, going back only five or six feet into the rock. This one had a solid sandy floor.

'Two men, three even, could have slept in there, out of the wet. I've slept in worse places myself,' I said. 'Even a shepherd climbing higher to see to his flock would hardly see the smoke from their cooking fire.'

'If he did,' said George, uneasily, gazing up at the cliff face towering above us, 'he'd not come looking, thinking 'twas the Devil roasting the evil doer down below!'

This reminded me of our immediate business here. 'What's Benjy doing? I take it he hasn't found any fires down there? Or the Devil for that matter?'

'No, he sez 'tis cold. Cold and wet. There's a beck running through it, and a waterfall. But he's dry for the present, and t'light's good enough. Now his ankle's eased from paining him, he's trying to see if there's some other way out. He said he'll come back and give us a shout if he finds it.'

I was sorely tempted to engage George, who was clearly even more uncomfortable than I was in this place, in a theological discussion on the whereabouts of hell, such I'd many times heard in the New Model. But I concluded it would probably take George so long to marshal his opinions that we might be here all night.

I'm not of a superstitious turn of mind, an army major with men to lead soon learns to disregard such fancies, but I'd no wish to stay in this gloomy place any longer than I had to. However, we ought to stay close for the present to hear what Benjy might have discovered. I suppose Sam's thoughts must have been travelling a similar path, for as we walked back along the defile he said, 'Ah've alus known there was caves up here in t'fells. T'old timers talk about them. Some claim there's caverns like great feasting halls down below, big enough for King Arthur and his knights to dwell in. Great waterfalls too, and lakes as tha could sail a boat on. Sheep fall into them now and then, but most are afraid to go after them, saying t'Devil's roasting 'em for his dinner!'

I nodded, recalling some of these tales myself, told around the fire on winter evenings. 'But no one's caught sight of the Devil — or King Arthur for that matter?'

'No, but they do say there's strange rocks that look like men turned to stone.'

''Tis the Devil's work all right,' rumbled George, chewing his inner cheek unhappily, 'and Ah've heard that across the sea in Norraway they speak of Hell as a cold place. Howsoever, it's not for us to know these things, but to await God's truth in the silence of our hearts.'

These last sounded like someone else's words, and I glanced at George wondering about the source. Dick Hardcastle perhaps? I didn't know much of the Westmoreland Seekers, but such as I did know made me think of them. I was relieved that Gervase had gone for lanterns and didn't hear George. Gervase seemed to be imagining treason everywhere, and looking to find strange meanings in the most innocent of words. This may be, as some might say, the curse of our age. We're leaving the old ways, the old superstitions, behind, but as we might kick over a stone in our pathway, we reveal new wonders, new horrors, creatures of fancy, as frightening as the old.

We took it in turns to remain by the hole in the rock cleft and converse with Ben — at least that was our agreement, but I'm ashamed to say, that after my painful night and lack of rest, I failed to do my share. Outside on the hill the sun still shone, though it was evening now, and it was sinking low. I sat for a time leaning against an outcrop of rock, allowing the warmth of the late rays to ease my shoulder. The dale lay green and peaceful below me. On the far side, shadows were already lengthening as the sun dropped in the West. Lowflatts was invisible from this vantage point, hidden by the swell of the ground below me, but I could see the farmhouse and barns of Highbiggens, grey against the bright green stand of larch trees. I believed myself to be keeping watch for horses and riders moving up the slope, but I suspect I slept. Presently I roused myself, perhaps as a result of some distant sound, and saw that the rescuers were on their way. To begin with they appeared as blackish, lumpen dots against the green and grey of the moor. Then, as they came closer, I made out Malachi, ropes coiled around his shoulder, lanterns bundled up in a sack tied behind his saddle, and Gervase with someone, also coiled about with rope, and carrying, to my puzzlement, a bundle of farm implements, rakes and hoes, clinging on behind him.

'Thought as you'd need me,' Cousin Zeke gasped, breathless, as he scrambled clumsily down from the horse's back and untangled himself from his bundles. 'Never bin on a horse afore, but a sailor knows ropes! We'll have the lad out in two shakes of the main sail!'

'I thought you fellows' only spliced main braces,' I grumbled. Zeke flashed me a pained look. We followed him into the cleft, struggling to drag the coils of rope after him.

Much time was wasted attempting to light the lanterns with George's flint, and still more in finding places to lodge them so that they shone into the hole and we could see what we were doing. There were too many of us in too narrow a space, and we got in one another's way. Tempers frayed. Cousin Zeke, in the midst, was in his element. First he had us place our coats around the rim of the cavity, to prevent it crumbling further. Then he re-tied his bundle of farm implements securely, and placed them across the mouth of the hole to form a makeshift beam. This, he assured us, would assist in lowering and raising a rope sling. He joined the ropes with complicated seafarers' knots. Then, when he had the resulting long run arranged to his satisfaction, one end looped in some fantastical way around a spiked column of rock, so that, he assured us, it could not slip, he announced that we were ready. All this took an age, and Benjy, whom we had summonsed to stand by below, had grown bored, and wandered away. We spent what felt like many minutes fruitlessly calling his name. Eventually, we heard him reply.

'Can yer get me out now?' he called, and it seemed that the cheerful confidence he had exhibited not an hour before, had evaporated. Either his ankle was now paining him unbearably, or something he'd discovered in the depths of the earth had disturbed him. His voice sounded weak and shaky. His brothers roared back reassurances, and Zeke, determined to show us all how it should be done, solemnly lowered the rope cradle. I did not, and do not, understand what was so particular about the loops, knots and runs that Cousin Zeke had manufactured. Evidently they worked, for after much pulling and heaving by my comrades — I was reduced to lamp-holder duty on account of my shoulder — Benjy was hauled to the surface, seated in a loop of rope as though in his favourite chair. His brothers greeted him with loud praises to God and smart thumps between the shoulder blades. Sam and Gervase engaged Zeke in complementary exchanges about his seaman's skills. I, as the man-with-the-lamp, was, I think, the only person to notice how white and strained Benjy appeared.

'What ails you, Ben?' I enquired. 'Your ankle? Or were you banged against the rocks coming up?'

'Nay,' he replied, shortly. 'Tis a strange place, yon. Ah kept hearing things. But Ah couldn't be sure whether 'twas real or not.' He seemed uneasy; unwilling to say more, and the opportunity was lost. Zeke set us all to the dismantling and coiling of his precious ropes, and we fell to the task of packing up and distributing ropes, tools, and lanterns amongst our horses.

'We can do no more today, Rob,' said Gervase, ruefully. 'The light really has gone. I'm sorry. We don't seem to have achieved much. No sign of Ann and Rachel. No proof that they were ever here.'

'No. We need to get back to the farm, the milking won't wait.' I said no more.

I've stated that I'm not a superstitious man, but it has been my experience that the most practical and down to earth of men can be prey to strong feelings — to impressions that they cannot describe or explain. Some declare it to be something we share with the animals. Others attribute it to the guidance of God. I recalled a number of times during campaigns, when both I and others had been visited with a sudden sense of danger which proved to be only too real. Or even a feeling, unexplained by evident facts, that a certain course of action would bring a desired result. Sometimes it had been as mundane as finding myself convinced that we should turn right instead of left at the junction of a rough track in previously unknown countryside. I'd found myself certain it would bring my battle weary troop to a barn full of dry hay, where we could spend the night, unmolested. Then finding, to my relief, that it was so.

That evening, as we rode down the fellside in the gathering dusk, I knew I had no evidence at all that my sister and Rachel Postlethwaite had been anywhere near the cleft in the rock we'd just left. Yet I also knew that *something* had happened there. Had the girls been brought to this place? And if so, what had then become of them?

# Chapter 15

Mother met us at the farm house door, her anxious face softening into a smile as she counted heads and saw that all who had set out that day were returning.

'No luck in the search, though,' I told her, once she'd heard all the details of Zeke's heroic rescue of Benjy, and our neighbours had taken themselves off to their own homes. 'There was no sign of the girls. Still, I suppose we may hope and pray that they are alive in some other place. Those rocks and caves have a strange atmosphere. *Eerie.* To begin with, once he'd got over the fall, I think Ben was excited by what he saw down there, but then it began to affect him. He was mightily relieved, when Zeke and the others finally hauled him up to the surface.'

'Yes,' said Mother, thoughtfully, 'your father always spoke of those caves in the hills as being outlandish places. He only went near a handful of times in his life as I recall, and only then if he'd a good many sheep astray. The injury to Benjamin's ankle is slight, but the blow to his head has probably affected him more than he thought,' she added, ladling out plates of stew prior to calling us all to the table. 'After a while he was most likely visited with a fierce headache, which would make exploring underground a good deal less agreeable. Once supper is over I'll fix him up with a dose of my willow bark remedy and a compress.'

Seated, we both glanced down the length of the kitchen table at Ben, who was toying listlessly with his plateful. Since in the days previously he had been eating the cupboards bare, it was obvious that something was amiss, and I doubted it was only a headache. Gervase, who together with Zeke, was tucking into the stew with well-deserved zest, noticed, and made a playful snatch at the crust of bread on the rim of Ben's plate. Ben shrugged and let him take it. Gervase caught my eye and raised his eyebrows, feigning alarm.

After we had eaten and gone out to the byres to deal with our indignant livestock (who let us know in their several ways that we had offended them by putting our hunger and comfort before theirs) I looked round for Ben, determined to speak to him on his own. I found him in the lane beyond the garth; a shadowy figure in the midsummer gloaming, a compress bound about his brow. He was intent on plucking greenery for the sheep.

'Leave that, Ben. I'll do it, or Zeke can. That was a nasty knock to your head you took when you fell into the cave, you should rest up.'

'Nay,' replied Benjy, pulling a wry face. 'Ah'm all right. Happen Mistress Haddon has either fixed it, or poisoned me to death with yon dose! She's got Zeke on scouring pots. Women's work! Ah'd rather do this.'

I regarded him narrowly. 'It wasn't just the knock to your noggin, was it? Something about that place gave you a fright.' When he didn't answer I continued, 'and you're not a lad who starts at shadows. What happened?'

Benjy heaved a gusty sigh. 'Ah dunno. 'Twas a strange place. There was a great waterfall running through it, made a noise like thunder crashing down into a washpot it had made for itself — so as yer couldn't hardly mek out ony other sound. But, Ah kept thinking Ah could hear music.'

'*Music?*'

'Aye. Like as if someone were playing on t'fife and drum!' He saw my expression and added, 'Ah thought 'twere just some echo made by the water on the rocks, or mebbe the wind blowing through them caverns. There's great long thin pillars in there made outa rock, hanging from t'ceiling, that looks like organ pipes, and Ah thought could it be them? But when Ah stood agin 'em, Ah could only hear water dripping. Most of the time yer couldn't hear — *it* — above the waterfall, but now and agin it sounded plain.'

I didn't doubt him. Older heads than his had found exploring the caves a disturbing experience.

'But Ben, who'd be playing the fife and drum down there?'

'Ah know, 'tis daft,' he acknowledged. 'Ah don't believe the Devil bides down there neither, no matter what Luke Procter's old granfer said. And Ah never seen onybody, for all Ah looked around. But then Ah thought, mebbe them Scotch soldiers? Could be they're living down there still? Or could be they're dead? 'Twas cold enough to kill a body — and what Ah heard was their ghosts? Ah didn't believe it above half, but it give me a right dose of the collywobbles!'

'I'm not surprised, Ben! It doesn't seem possible they could still be living there, and yet, like you, I'm not inclined to believe in ghosts. This playing of the fife and drum? Could you make out any kind of tune?'

Despite having just dismissed the idea, I found myself seriously considering whether those renegade mercenaries really could have set up camp in the depths of the earth. One might think that they'd have made for the Scottish border and home long ago, but experience had taught me that mercenary soldiers often continue in that trade because they have no homes to go to. Would Ben recognise a Scotch marching tune if he heard one? I asked him, but he grinned and shook his head.

'Our Hannah and our Rachel, they're the ones can put a name to tunes and such. They say Ah've a tin ear!'

The whole thing sounded improbable, yet Benjy had never struck me as a lad with too vivid an imagination. On the other hand, the caves were acknowledged to be peculiar places, and who knew what sound effects might be caused by a combination of wind and water passing through tunnels within the rock? I cast my mind around the district. Were there farmers and shepherds within hailing distance who'd been into the caves, and could tell me what sounds they'd heard there?

My thoughts on whom I might ask were interrupted by the rattle of cart wheels in the lane, and the glow of a swinging lantern. Jem Robinson drew up alongside us, driving Colonel Moreland's gig.

'I'm right sorry I had to leave this afternoon,' he said, sounding sulky, rather than remorseful, 'but I'd things to see to for the Colonel, and couldn't spare more time. We're shorthanded, and I've been that overstretched that I've only just got around to your fellow here.'

He jerked his thumb over his shoulder, and I saw that there was someone, wrapped in sacking, seated in the gig. A weak but delighted, 'Rah! Rah!' soon told me who it was.

'Lanty!' I was genuinely glad to see our old shepherd, set free at last, and hurried to help him down. 'Mother will be so pleased!' I told him. 'Go you on in, and she'll warm up some stew, I know there is some left. Benjy here was off his food at supper, and didn't take a second helping!' Lanty, unable, of course, to hear my words, looked puzzled but pleased, sensing friendly intentions.

Jem, turning the gig to be off, now affected to notice Benjy for the first time, standing by the hedgerow with a bundle of greens in his arms. He nodded to me.

'So, you found Ben Postlethwaite, and brought him back safe?'

'We did,' I replied shortly.

'Fell into one o'them pot holes, did yer?' Jem reigned in and peered down at Ben

'Yeah, but tha sees Ah'm come out from it, safe and sound. With no help from thee, Jem Robinson!' he added, not entirely under his breath.

'Tha was lucky then!' Jem chose to ignore Ben's thrust. 'Can be a nasty fall, into one o'them! Reckon tha'd see a few stars, hear a few angels singing, in a fall like that?'

'Well, Ah never,' replied Ben, glaring at him.

'Pleased to hear it!' the Colonel's steward replied, and signalled to his horse to trot on.

Benjy went off to take the fodder to the sheep, and I escorted Lanty to the kitchen door, a less than pleasant experience, as no one had thought to give the old fellow any fresh clothing since his arrest, and as a result of his fit at the time, and his continuing terror during his imprisonment, he smelt as though he had pissed and soiled himself several times over. Mother was, as I expected, delighted to have him back, but less delighted to smell him, and soon banished him to the barn with a cloth, a bucket of soap suds and fresh garments, telling him, with her series of quick hand signs, to clean himself up and dress, and then come indoors again to eat.

Bone weary, I folded myself into the old wooden chair by the kitchen range, just as I remembered Father doing, so many years ago, able at last to sit idle, if only for a while. To my surprise I found my shoulder much easier, and moreover, realised that despite the exertions of the day, I'd hardly thought of my thigh wound at all.

How's Miles faring?' I asked Mother as she pottered at the range, dividing lumps of dough and setting them to rise again.

'Asleep, praise be!' She gave me a tremulous smile. 'The fever comes and goes with him. I fear it could be a while before he is fit for the work of the farm, and it worries me that his senses are so disturbed. How could he suppose that you would kill Loveday? In his right mind he'd never think such a thing of you! 'Tis fortunate you came when you did, and your friend Gervase too — and the Postlethwaite lads being so helpful. Otherwise, with Loveday gone, and the girls missing, I don't know how I could manage!'

She was silent for a while, arranging muslin cloths over her dough pans. Then she said, 'Will you be able to stay awhile longer, Robert? It won't put you into Oliver Cromwell's black books, if you stay away a month or two?'

This was a conundrum that I'd tried to banish to the back of my mind. Not that I supposed for a moment that Cromwell himself would even recognise my name, let alone miss my presence, but I'd left my troop behind in Scotland under another man's care, and at the time of my leaving I'd told him that I'd be gone for as short a time as possible. Now it was looking as though I would have to break my word.

'I'll write to Andrew Leyburn,' I told her. 'He is my Captain, and has charge of my men in my absence. At the time I left there was no great amount of skirmishing going forward. Edinburgh was reasonably quiet.'

Reasonably, and might have been more so, if the men's pay had arrived on time, and when it did, if the pesky Scots had not persisted in selling their whisky to them. The entire population seemed to take great delight in seeing the effect this strong spirit had on our callow youths, who'd never before drunk anything stronger than small beer.

'As I think I told you, Mother, Cromwell himself has been sick with some low burning fever, and not inclined to mount any new campaigns north of the border. I fancy I can be spared for a month or two. However, if the Royalists succeed in rallying the Clansmen to fight again, as they vow, things could change.' Even so, it would surely take several weeks for that to happen. 'Gervase, I cannot speak for, but you can count on me for the present,' I assured her.

'Robert,' she paused for a long moment, and I guessed what she was about to say. 'I understand that you may not be free to tell me, but what *is* Gervase doing here?'

'I can't tell you, Mother, because I don't know. I understand he has some information — or believes he has — about some plot. Or suspicion of a plot. Some evidence must have been laid before the Parliamentary

Council about someone in this neighbourhood. But whether it has any basis in truth, I know not. There have been instances of over eager busybodies laying information against a neighbour as the result of a misunderstanding, or worse, out of spite, hoping to gain from someone else's downfall.' I didn't want to distress her by mentioning that prayer meetings in individual's houses were one of the sources of suspicion.

Mother stood at the kitchen table, a cloth dangling from her fingers, troubled. 'For spite? That's wicked,' she said. 'Who, amongst our neighbours would do a cruel thing like that?'

'Mason Hardcastle? He's a spiteful fellow. He's always in dispute with someone over a boundary fence, or animals straying onto his land, and didn't he, last summer, accuse someone of firing his hayrick?'

'And went and laid information against them with *Parliament*? Surely not? He is spiteful, I'll grant you, but he can hardly write his name, and Nell and the girls would never… and Richard, the son, is as honest a young fellow as you'd meet in a month of Sundays. If he thought his father was playing a nasty trick like that, he'd soon put in a word with Colonel Moreland!'

'In my opinion, Mother, the whole thing is a mare's nest, but Gervase no doubt has his orders from the Council of State, and must follow them. Colonel Moreland is aware of his commission, of that I'm certain. Gervase would never start investigating in the neighbourhood without letting him know what he was about.'

Mother rubbed the bridge of her nose with her floured thumb, a habit she has, when perplexed. 'It may be just my fancy,' she said slowly, 'but when I've seen the Colonel of late, such as when he came over here the other day, to question folks about poor Lemuel, he's seemed… troubled? No, not that exactly. Not his usual easy self.'

'Well, he can't be happy to know that Parliament believes someone in this district may be guilty of plotting against the state, even if he considers the accusation to be unfounded. He's a Magistrate, after all. No one in his position likes to think there might be things going on under his nose about which he knows nothing.'

'And with Lady Brilliana's family known to have supported the late King. Despite all the loyalty he's shown to Parliament, I can see he's in a difficult position, poor man.'

'That murder — *Lemuel's* murder, was nasty, Mother. There was viciousness in that, in the way it was done. Enough to make any Magistrate uneasy, to think that there's someone in his jurisdiction who could think up such a beastly way to kill a man. Loveday's killing was cruel, I don't deny, but surely the way of it suggested a sudden angry outburst? Perhaps the slayer didn't even mean to hurt her, just to knock her out of his way?'

'Yes, I suppose it could have happened that way' Mother responded, her brow creased in thought. 'If strangers set upon Ann and Rachel, and were making off with them in a cart, when along comes Loveday (perhaps they hadn't even known she was about. Mayhap she was over in the barn or the cow byre, when they came). When she realised what was happening, she'd run down the lane after them, screaming her head off,' said Mother, obviously picturing the scene. 'Heaven knows she was a selfish creature, but she wouldn't stand by and let strange men abduct those girls.'

'Yes,' I said, slowly. 'It could have happened like that. The cart is ready to drive away. One man driving, the other man — or perhaps there were three of them altogether — forcing Ann and Rachel on board. They would certainly both be screaming. Loveday hears the commotion and comes running, and one of the men, perhaps he had a whip or a blackthorn stick, strikes down at her, and accidently kills her. She falls back into the ditch, and there they leave her. The only things that don't fit that notion are, firstly, that they were so far down the lane when Loveday caught up with them — although one of the girls might have tried to escape, and they'd stopped to restrain her — and secondly that no one in Beckside heard anything, although they were close. Even if the girls were gagged by this time, Loveday wasn't, though she might have been too out of breath from running to make much noise. And if they did bind and gag Ann and Rachel, it would explain why they drove across the river rather than going by the road. The boldest raiders would hardly drive through the village with two girls clearly being held prisoner.'

By now, listening to me expound, Mother's hands were clasped in prayer, eyes closed, tears rolling down, making rivulets in the flour dust that powdered her cheeks. 'Oh, those poor dear girls!' was all she said.

'We must not despair, Mother.' (although I was despairing) 'We may be quite wrong about what happened. And the girls had their hands free once they got cross the Lune, because we know they tore the ribbon and lace and threw them down.'

'Gagged but not bound. An interesting point,' said a voice in the doorway. 'I wonder why?'

I wondered how long Gervase had been standing there. Listening to Mother and I, talking about him.

'Just a notion,' I shrugged, 'of how it happened that Ann and Rachel were taken, but Loveday killed. Mother thinks the raiders took the two girls whilst Loveday was elsewhere about the farm, and she ran to try and save them when she heard their screams. It would fit with what we know, except for small details.'

'We ought to ask Colonel Moreland if anyone might know more about those Scots mercenaries he mentioned,' said Gervase. 'Men of that stamp might do a thing like that. Does he know for certain that they've left the district? Which of his farm tenants actually saw them, and where? Has anyone lost a horse — and a cart?'

'I'll ride over to Lings tomorrow,' I said, 'and ask him. There's no point in our wasting time and energy searching anywhere further until we have more particulars.'

I didn't tell Mother and Gervase what Benjy had said about hearing music in the caves, and how he and I had wondered if the Scottish soldiers might be hiding there. The sounds he'd heard were surely more likely to have been made by wind and water rather than fife and drum, and, I admitted, if only to myself, I didn't want to go and search the caves unless I had to. Now, too, thinking of Benjy, and having just been speaking of the manner of Lemuel's death, I remembered his strange (guilty?) reaction to it. I'd never questioned him about that. I must.

# Chapter 16

Not entirely to my surprise, on the following morning Gervase elected to ride with me to Lings Hall. I imagined he saw it as an opportunity to report to Colonel Moreland without arousing curiosity. He must have made his mind up overnight, for he appeared in the kitchen no longer disguised as a farm hand, but as a modest youth of limited means, intending to make a morning call on his magistrate neighbour. Quite how he effects these changes of personality with the small amounts of clothing he must carry in his pack roll, I don't know.

We did not, in fact, set out as early as I had intended, due to a commotion in the farmyard when Saul and Timmy Proctor arrived to take the sheep to the grazing grounds and found Lanty returned, and by no means willing to let them. We hadn't thought to send word the night before than they would not be needed, and the boys were tearful with indignation. Mother went out and tried to persuade Lanty to rest up for the day, and let the lads go for one last time, but the old shepherd was obdurate. The fact that these two little boys had successfully guarded our flock for best part of a week without losing even one, did not weigh with him. To his mind they were his sheep, and no one else had any right to deal with them. At this, Mother threw up her hands in despair, and everyone else turned and looked at me. This happens all the time on campaign, and I've become used to making snap decisions in the hope of soothing wounded feelings. It rarely works.

'Saul and Timmy could help in the hayfield?' I suggested. Malachi Postlethwaite, who had just arrived to finish turning and stooking the meadow started yesterday, looked less than delighted. I took him aside and pointed out that they could hardly be of less help than Zeke, and my mother had need of him for what he himself called 'galley work,' and to help with nursing Miles. Malachi reluctantly agreed to take the boys on.

So Lanty went off, triumphant, with the sheep, and the Procter boys disappeared through the gate into the meadow, executing imaginary pike thrusts with their pitchforks, and yelling like banshees. If I felt some guilt at leaving Malachi with these young rascals in his charge, it was no more than I'd often felt at leaving one of my sergeants to supervise a bunch of raw recruits. If people look to me to give the orders, they must swallow their displeasure at what orders I give.

'It must be a drain on your resources, Mistress Haddon, to be feeding so many extra mouths,' Gervase commented to Mother. 'You know I'd be glad to make a contribution to my bed and board. The army doesn't expect you to quarter me indefinitely.'

Mother, of course, refused, pretending to be affronted that anyone should question her unlimited hospitality, particularly towards her son's comrade, but I decided, privately, that if he offered me money I would take it for Miles' sake. After all, it appeared Gervase had been coming here on and off for months, and filling his belly at Lowflatts' expense. Feeding him was a drain on the farm's resources. One of the things that has weighed well with the general population in favour of the New Model Army, is that funds have been made available to recompense them for giving soldiers food and shelter. Mind you, I do not say that this has always been done. I'm sure there are many people up and down the country who have been given one of the famous 'tickets' which supposedly proved their entitlement, but have never received a penny. However, it was more likely to have been done by them, than by one of the Royalist regiments, whose aristocratic leaders had never suffered poverty themselves, and had little understanding of the hardship they were inflicting on ordinary people by requisitioning their food, their firewood, and the fodder intended for their livestock. Then again, having lost so many battles, the Royalists probably lack the means.

I didn't speak of this to Gervase as we rode through Beckside and made our way to Lings Hall. I remembered him telling me once that it had come as a shock to him to discover, as he rode around the country, how many folk lived in dire poverty. He'd confessed that he had never thought his own parent to be overly generous in the matter of repairs, but now saw that his father was a paragon, when he compared the state of his tenants' cottages with the tumble-down hovels he'd seen at the gates of some of the wealthiest landowners in the Kingdom. Then he hastily corrected himself saying, 'I mean, of course, the Commonwealth.' Gervase has espoused the Parliamentary cause, but some of the ideas that the men of the New Model have put forward are hard for him to assimilate.

Instead, we spoke of horses. I was riding the cob, although Caesar had been waiting at the gate to the garth, ears pricked. 'Not today, old fellow, I told him. 'A day or two more to be sure of that flank of yours.' Hearing, from the tone of my voice that I was going to ride out on some inferior nag, he retired to sulk by the kitchen gate, favouring his left hind, as though to remind me that he was wounded in body and spirit. In truth he was healing well. As Sam Woodley had predicted, though a scar might mar the perfection of his glossy coat, he would soon be fit for service. I said as much to Gervase, astride his pretty Venus, and he chaffed me, as we rode along, on the wilful disposition of my horse.

'That animal rules you!' he declared. 'If Cromwell gave the order to charge and your Caesar disagreed with his decision, where would you be?

'Probably head down in a duck pond!' I laughed. 'Although Caesar is generally more enthusiastic about the charge than I am. That's how he got us into difficulties at Withins. I was for circumspection, but he wanted to join the fray.'

'That reminds me. That man, Hardcastle, is he in his right mind?' Naturally, given the conversation I had recently had with Mother, I wondered why Gervase wanted to know.

'Eccentric, as you have noted many are in these parts,' I answered. 'He's honest enough in his way, but he thinks everyone is against him, and imagines they are ganging up to do him harm. Destroying his fences, letting their cattle break through onto his land, impregnating his daughter! He always has some complaint against someone,' I added, choosing my words carefully. Gervase made no further comment.

We found Colonel Moreland absent from home, ridden out, we were informed, with Jem, to look over some sheep that had been showing signs of the staggers. We were met with the news in the entrance hall at Lings, but no sooner had the elderly manservant explained, than Lady Brilliana, hearing our voices, emerged from her parlour and invited us to come in and take some refreshment.

'I'm sure my husband won't be long gone,' she assured us, turning her fine eyes, and her smile, I thought, particularly upon Gervase. 'Judith and I are very dull here, with nothing but darning to fill our morning! Do come and tell us some stirring tale of gallantry on the battlefield! I am sure,' she said, archly, 'that there have been many brave fighters on both sides of this conflict. You young men must have taken part in some thrilling engagements!'

We wiped our boots, and deposited our hats on the hall table. I hoped Gervase would feel able to meet her ladyship's requirements, for I was sure there was nothing I had experienced on a battlefield that I wanted to talk about in a lady's withdrawing room. Blood and entrails and the screams of dying men and horses don't strike me as suitable subjects for small talk.

Judith looked as though she agreed with me. Huddled in a chair by the window, she barely raised her eyes from the stocking she was darning to acknowledge our arrival.

'Do sit down, and make yourselves comfortable,' said our hostess, ringing a tiny silver bell for the servant, and when he came, asking whether we would prefer small beer or wine. The old man had perhaps once been a servant in a superior household to this one, and his expression suggested that carrying out such menial tasks was beneath him, but he bowed politely and complied. Although he obviously considered himself to be a superior person (superior to me at any rate) I noticed about this old fellow, a curious and rather unpleasant smell, but if Lady Brilliana was aware of it she said nothing. Perhaps he'd come with her from her father's establishment when she married, and was excused and indulged on that account.

'I'm sure the Colonel will be back presently,' she told us. 'As I understand it, the livestock they have gone to look at are in one of the nearer fields.'

'The twelve acre,' muttered Judith. 'It's two miles or more.' Her mother ignored this intervention. Clearly mother and daughter were at odds this morning, but Lady Brilliana was determined to ignore her graceless child.

She proceeded to canter gently, not onto the battlefield, but into small talk about her relatives, a cadet branch of her family, some of whom lived in the same midland county as Gervase's people. Did he know them? Had they perhaps been on visiting terms before this foolish war began?

'I think,' she said, with a tinkling laugh that echoed her little bell, 'that my cousins have been very reluctant to take sides, and have kept to themselves these last few years. Very wise of them, and I wish that the Earl and my brothers might have done the same.'

Gervase answered her politely, admitting that he thought he'd at some time met these cousins, and that his father certainly knew them through a shared love of hunting. This led her Ladyship to sigh over the present situation, when opportunities for what she called a 'real day out with the hounds,' of which she was herself passionately fond, were not to be thought of. Indeed her husband had been forced to let their hunting dogs go because of the expense of feeding them through a time of war. She supposed Gervase's family had made similar sacrifices? Gervase began to look discomforted, guessing, I think, that this social chit-chat was leading up to something. He glanced in my direction, hoping perhaps that I'd join the conversation, but I saw no way of doing this, since the men of my family have never hunted more than a rabbit or a pheasant for the cooking pot. Furthermore, I suspected, perhaps unjustifiably, that Lady Brilliana had deliberately seized on the topic as a way of emphasising the social distinction between Gervase and myself. The army had thrown us together, but once the fighting came to an end, Gervase would be returning to his own sphere, and I to mine. Mother and I had speculated that Colonel Moreland might view Gervase as a suitable match for Judith. I now thought I perceived that Lady Brilliana had decided he would 'do'. Perhaps she'd already made enquiries of her cousins, and received a favourable report?

A fleeting look in Judith's direction told me that if this was the case, it did not meet with her approval. Thunderclouds hovered on her brow, and her lips parted as though she might make some fierce interjection. However, before she could do so, there was a sudden hubbub in the hallway, and Lady Brilliana rose, startled as a pheasant herself. Young men's voices could be heard, loudly calling to the serving man, 'Come Joseph, help us off with our boots!'

'Edwin? Nicholas? It *cannot* be!' With a swish of her silken skirts, she darted from the room. Judith sat up straight in her chair at the din, but made no attempt to follow. Instead she shrugged her shoulders, smiled, and went back to plying her darning needle.

'I'm sorry, gentlemen,' she said, 'I'm afraid this means your audience with Mama is at an end. It sounds as though my scape-grace brothers have ignored Papa's instructions and come home.'

Gervase extricated us very neatly from Lings Hall, I thought. There is no doubt that he has skills which I have yet to acquire. One of them seems to be that of quietly fading away without causing offence. In his work as a Parliamentary agent he has probably had many occasions to practise it. Leaving Lady Brilliana to find a welcome for her prodigal sons, we collected our horses, consulted the lone stable lad we found sweeping the yard, and set out in the direction of the 'twelve acre'. We'd come to see Colonel Moreland, and see him we would.

Riding along the river, skirting hay meadows as yet uncut and in danger of running to seed, it struck me that Lings' farmland was not so well cared for as I would have expected. I noted hedges where cattle had pushed through and no repairs had been made. Where the ride followed the river bank, thorn bushes, bracken, and trailing blackberry runners had not been trimmed back, making passage for our horses difficult. Jem Robinson had complained of being over-stretched, but I'd dismissed him as merely churlish and unhelpful. Now I began to think that Colonel Moreland must be in deeper financial straits than I'd imagined. These neglected fields shouted that aloud. I recalled that we had found but one youth visible at work in the stable yard, where formally I'd have hazarded there would be three or four grooms. I'd been mildly surprised too, now I thought of it, that we had been greeted and served by a doddering manservant. I would have expected Lady Brilliana to employ several smart indoor maids to do her bidding. Perhaps Judith's talk of ruin was not just girlish exaggeration? Most of the Morelands' servants must have been let go, and no new ones taken on at the Whitsun hiring fair just past. I wondered what Gervase made of this, but some feeling of constraint held me back for raising the subject. For all the talk of equality between men that I'd heard whilst serving in the army, I'd been reminded this morning that our status in life was very different. Gervase and the Morelands were of a higher social class, and I feared he would think me insolent (although he would not say so) if I drew attention to the Colonel's difficulties. It was no wonder (though I hesitated to mention this too) that Lady Brilliana was on the lookout for a wealthy husband for Judith.

We found the Colonel leaning on a gate, watching Jem, who had ridden up the field to look over some sheep huddled in the furthest corner in the unhelpful way that sheep do.

'Good morning! You have some problems with sick animals, Sir?' Gervase greeted him.

'Fortunately not, it now appears,' he replied. 'Jem was being unnecessarily cautious. What brings you riding out this way? You have news of those girls?'

I thought how tired he looked, the skin of his face grey and drained. Mother was right, he did not seem his usual easy, confident self. Seeing his estate in such poor heart, and now seemingly having so few men to work it, must be taking a toll. It seemed cruel of us to bring him more worries. I looked enquiringly at Gervase. Which matter should we raise first, the Scottish mercenaries or the return of his spendthrift sons?

'Alas, no news,' I said, taking the initiative, since he'd asked about my sister, 'but we've given some thought to how they could have been taken and Loveday killed.'

I described the sequence of events that Mother, Gervase, and I had discussed. 'It seemed to us that the kind of men who might do that would most likely be renegades from some mercenary band. You, Sir, mentioned that there had been sightings, some time ago, supposedly of Scots soldiers camping out in the hills. Yesterday when we searched the fellside, we found traces of an old encampment. Can you recall which local people saw these men, and whether they had definite knowledge that they'd left the district?'

Colonel Moreland drew his hand down his tired face. 'I can't say I do. Perhaps Jem? No, it wasn't he. Lemuel Drysdale mentioned seeing them as he rode around the neighbourhood, and... Mason Hardcastle. Yes, Hardcastle told me that he'd seen rough, wild looking characters collecting firewood on the boundary of his land and mine, and feared they would come at night and steal his poultry. Highly incensed he was, demanding that I exercise my powers as Justice of the Peace to arrest them, or at least drive them from the district. I heard no more, and concluded that they'd left of their own accord, and without the chickens. Here's Jem, and we can ask if he knows anything.'

Jem shrugged, and claimed to know nothing further. 'And them that saw them. It was mebbe a month back,' he told us, shortly.

'A month back?' queried the Colonel, 'I hadn't thought it was so long, but then my mind's been taken up with other matters.'

'A month, easy,' reiterated Jem, and began to report on the sheep, as though our questioning was an intrusion on the day's serious business. I wondered that Colonel Moreland should tolerate this rudeness in an employee. I had also observed that Jem's eyes slid away from mine as he spoke. I've become something of an expert on liars, having interrogated more than a few. Jem Robinson was lying, but why he should do so, I couldn't guess.

Gervase and I rode away without mentioning the return of Edwin and Nicholas. It was not our responsibility we decided, cravenly, to break the news to Benson Moreland that he had another headache to contend with. Whatever Gervase had intended to say to him also remained unsaid. Perhaps it was not necessary to say anything, merely, by his appearance, to signal to the magistrate that he was still here in his official role; still striving to find what needed to be discovered.

'Lemuel Drysdale is dead,' he remarked, as we rode back along the river.

'Unfortunately he is,' I replied, 'and can therefore tell us nothing.'

Gervase chuckled. 'So, now, should you not interview Mason Hardcastle once again? Shall I come with you and form an armed guard, lest he shoot you on purpose this time?'

I steered the cob away from a place where the river bank was crumbling, and through girth high ragwort and stinging nettles before I replied.

'I suppose I must, and certainly you may come. You could drop hints, in the name of Parliament, that you'll be obliged to run him through if he refuses to answer! As he very likely will. He is the most awkward old termagant that ever lived! He knows the girls are missing. He knew that was the purpose of our search, and the reason I rode up to the farm. Colonel Moreland had explained it all to him. So, if he knew that these doubtful characters were about, why didn't he mention it?'

'Because it really was a month back, as the steward said, and he didn't think it relevant? Or because he has a one track mind, and two days ago it was fixed on his daughter and Sam Woodley?'

'Quite likely the latter,' I agreed, musing, as the cob breasted his way through dense vegetation. 'If Jem is lying, and I'm certain he is, then these wild men have been seen much more recently than a month back. But *why* does he lie?'

Gervase, riding behind me, because the track was too overgrown for us to ride side by side, remained silent for some time. Then he said, 'He could have a hundred reasons. Perhaps he knows one of these men? Did you not say he had some relative who murdered someone? Perchance these people are escaped felons rather than mercenaries?'

'His relative was hanged.'

'But mayhap he has others, also with criminal tendencies?'

'Not that I ever heard. Mother may know if there are other relations. Jem himself has always lived an exemplary life. He's a pillar of the church. I can't understand why he's turned so surly.'

'He has information, but someone else has a hold over him, so he dare not reveal it?'

We'd come to a place, beneath a stand of beeches, where the ride was clear of undergrowth, and Gervase was able to bring his horse alongside mine. We halted and sat a while, considering. Our war experience had brought both of us into contact with people who regarded us as 'the enemy', not necessarily because they were supporters of the late king, but because they feared anyone in authority; anyone who turned up smelling of 'officialdom' and demanded that they answer questions.

'Yes. Now you say it, it was that kind of response,' I said. 'I wouldn't have thought Jem a secret Royalist. He's loyal to the Colonel, of that I'm sure.'

'But perhaps to Lady Brilliana too? A man split down the middle by divided loyalties? Or fear, of what one might reveal to the other?'

'You think so?'

'I think the lady has been far from loyal to her husband's *cause*. Also, she is an attractive woman, even if no longer young, and is not afraid to use her female wiles. She has no doubt had Jem doing her bidding for months on end whilst her husband was away campaigning. Could she have put him in some compromising position which he fears to have Colonel Moreland discover?'

I found myself taking a startled inbreath. 'You mean she may have… seduced him?'

'I know not. But I suspect she could, if a man was at all susceptible. You noticed how she turned those glorious eyes on me this morning? All that talk of her relatives? Hinting that if she wished she might discover more about me from them? All my youthful peccadillos perhaps, so that she might have some kind of hold over me?'

I burst out laughing. 'Gervase, you've been too long a spy, you think everyone is up to no good! I believe she was considering whether you might be a suitable husband for Mistress Judith!'

It was Gervase's turn to be startled. He uttered an oath that would have earned him a sharp reprimand from the more puritanical spirits in our regiment.

'Judith is not to your taste?' I teased. 'She's a pretty enough wench, and, I'm told, strong for Parliament like her father. From what we've seen this morning, I doubt she would bring you much of a dowry, but that need not be a consideration for a man like yourself.'

Gervase favoured me with a sour look. 'Marrying is not something I have a mind to do just yet. Oh, I shall do so one day, so that I may have a son to quarrel with me whilst I live, and inherit the estate when I die — but for the present it is easier to remain single. In my current line of work there is little time for married life. A wife would never see me, and when she did, I would have little time for tender exchanges. However, I doubt Lady Brilliana is seriously considering me for her daughter.' He grinned suddenly. 'No, 'tis all a game with her. She likes to think what she *might* do, perhaps even raise my hopes if I were hanging out for a bride. And to make it clear to you, that you are not under consideration!'

At this I laughed too. 'I understood that well enough! She'd no need to remind me, and need have no fear that I'll make up to the lass.'

'But will Judith pay attention to her mother? She has shown a marked partiality for members of your family, and somewhat, I would say, for yourself, Rob.'

'Her Ladyship has forbidden Judith to visit Lowflatts, and told my mother she must not receive her. I imagine, with the Colonel coming home, and now the sons, she's suddenly become aware that Judith has been running wild.'

'I wonder,' said Gervase, as we began to walk our horses forward once more, 'what has so claimed Lady Brilliana's attention until now, that it has prevented her from noticing what her daughter was doing?'

# Chapter 17

Back at the farm we found Mother in a rare state of exasperation. Pots and pans were being clashed about, a sure and certain sign. Zeke was nowhere to be seen, and it seemed doubtful that anyone was going to get a midday meal.

'What is it, Mother?' I asked. 'Has Zeke broken the best china?'

'No, but he was getting under my feet, and telling me how they cook aboard ship, and singing those tiresome sea chanties! Listening to his tarradiddles, I let the crust burn on the rabbit pies!'

'Foolish Ezekiel! Are the pies burned beyond eating?'

'No, but they're not my best. However they must do, for I've nothing else. I sent him to sit with Miles. I'm that put about!' she stormed, snatching up a pan of greens from the hob. His fever is up again, and *your* horse has eaten my marigolds!'

Gervase went and put an arm around her and laid his head on top of hers. 'Mistress Haddon, you are a woman in ten thousand, and mightily hard done to. How came it that Caesar ate your flowers? I'd understood that the goat was the most likely culprit around here? I'm sure I had a most severe telling off from one of the girls one time, for leaving the gate to the field unlatched, so that Tabitha could get out and wage destruction.'

'So she does, and so she would,' agreed Mother hovering between smiles and exasperation at Gervase's compliments. 'But Zeke was milking her out in the garth, and left the gate ajar while he did so, and I saw that Caesar with my own eyes, pushing his head around the wicket, and snatching up my marigolds by the roots with his great teeth!'

'I apologise on behalf of my horse,' I said, trying to keep my face straight. ''Twill serve him right if he gets colic. He's not in charity with me because I rode out on the cob. Obviously Tabitha is teaching him bad habits.'

'I was cherishing those marigolds,' said Mother, partly mollified, 'to make a cream the girls like to use on their complexions.' Then, realising what she'd said, her face fell again, and she sighed. 'Still, chances are 'twill never be needed, will it?' We stood a moment, sombre, acknowledging the truth of this.

'We got a little more information from Colonel Moreland,' I said, hoping to raise her spirits, 'although one of the people who saw these deserters, or wild men or whatever they were, seems to have been Parson Drysdale. The other, according to the Colonel, was Mason Hardcastle, who thought they were after his poultry. Jem Robinson however, insists that this was at least a month ago.'

'Jem Robinson said that?' said Mother, surprised. 'Well, he's wrong.

Nell Hardcastle told me some ragged fellows had been gathering kindling from Lings Wood not above a week past! She and Nan were in Beckside selling eggs from door to door, and we spoke of it. 'Twas just before we had word of Miles' misfortune. I'm sure of it. I set out for Lancaster the next day.'

'I'll go this afternoon, and question Mason,' I promised. 'Mother Hardcastle and the girls will tell me what happened, even if the old man proves obdurate. I'll take Caesar. That will keep him from doing any more damage to your flowerbeds, and at the same time remind Mason that I'm being charitable in not having him taken up for wounding my horse.'

'And I'll go with him,' said Gervase, his eyes twinkling, 'to make sure that this Farmer Hardcastle does not shoot at Robert again. But not before I taste your rabbit pie!'

'The pies!' she cried, flapping her apron at us. 'I set them to keep warm and the pastry will be quite dried out! Will one of you great lummoxes go quickly and call them in from the hayfield? They must be starved and parched!'

It was true that the crust on the pies was a little blackened along their edges, but nobody failed to eat his share, and the eyes of Saul and Timmy Proctor grew round with bliss as their helpings were placed before them.

I looked in on Miles before I left for Withins. He was awake, and permitting Zeke to spoon rabbit broth into his mouth. Seeing me in the doorway he closed his lips against the next spoonful, and then said, his eyes still hollow, his voice croaky with disuse over so many days, 'I did it for you, brother. Claimed your inheritance, which you will no doubt squander…and now…my wife is dead… and I am reduced to this.'

'I am sorry,' I said. 'Truly, I am. To come home, and find Loveday dead, and the farm deserted. It was more terrible than anything I have seen away at the wars, believe me! I thought you all dead.'

'So you say,' he mumbled, 'and Mother takes your side. You were always her favourite.' He closed his eyes, weary and bitter with sickness and jealousy.

Zeke looked at me, and raised his index finger to his forehead. Then he twisted it to and fro and shrugged.

'Tek no notice,' he mouthed, getting to his feet. He followed me out of the parlour, closing the door behind us. ''Twas never your fault he caught this fever! He ain't seeing things clear… and the girl, Loveday, it seems to me from what he says when he rambles, talks in his sleep like, that she goaded him. Always hinting to him you were the better man! Hinting maybe that you'd known her better than you should?'

I stared at him, mystified.

'*Known* her, like unto in the manner it says in the Bible?' Zeke studied me, head on one side, his bright gypsy eyes trying to read my face.

'Never! I never touched my brother's wife!'

'Ne'er so much as a kiss under the apple tree?'

I charged out of the house, in a fury. Of course I had kissed her under the apple tree! I was seventeen years old, Miles eighteen, and Loveday, aged fourteen, was then promised to neither of us. How like Loveday to have used that one kiss, years later, to taunt Miles, to use hints of more, to stir up his jealousy. When he must have been worried about the farm, the livestock, the weather, the state of our poor war torn country. Could my brother and I ever live together in peace? Would he ever believe that I'd loved and lost, and gone to the wars, and never afterwards tried to steal his wife's affections?

I thought, as I made my way to saddle Caesar and take myself off to Withins, that I'd better try and find a spice merchant and get him to teach me his trade. I felt no particular desire to turn shopkeeper once my soldiering days were over, but it might be all that was open to me, if Miles' resentment made returning to live at Lowflatts impossible.

At Withins we found Mason Hardcastle in, what for him, passed for a conciliatory mood. From the darkling looks he gave his wife and eldest daughter, who were present when we arrived, I concluded that they'd forbidden him to quarrel with me.

Had he seen these wild men, as Colonel Moreland reported? Indeed he had, and he launched into a tirade against all 'foreigners and ne'er do wells' and against our magistrate, who had not immediately sent a convoy of men to arrest them, or at least drive them into the next parish. Could he say exactly when he had seen these men? Of this he was less certain, and called Nan, who was chopping vegetables at the kitchen table, for her opinion. At this passage of time Nan was not sure to the day, but named, without prompting, as likely, the day before Mother had gone to Lancaster. Not as much as a month ago? No. She recalled their meeting in Beckside and speaking of these men. Nan was positive it had been within a day or two. She was sorry she could not tell us more. I asked what had it been about them that had suggested that they were Scottish soldiers? I was thinking, of course, of Ben's experience in the caves, and puzzling as to why, if there were such people living up there, they had come so far, clear across the river, to look for firewood.

Nan looked startled, and Mason was adamant. Scottish? Who said they were Scottish? He'd never said anything of the kind. Mercenaries then? Deserters from some foreign troop imported by the defeated Royalist army, and now abandoned, having spent their pay? Separated from whomever their leaders had been, and left without the means to return to their own land?

Again this provoked a furious tirade. These men were not mercenaries! Could never have been soldiers! Lawless layabouts was what they were!

Gypsies, Irishmen, Chicken thieves! Was I forgetting that Mason had been a mercenary himself, and knew fighting men from common rogues? (I didn't tell him that my own experience of mercenaries was that they were much the same thing). I looked at Gervase and raised a brow. We had often worked together in the army in this way. One will act as the hard man, demanding answers to difficult questions. The other will appear milder, less threatening, and distract the suspect by introducing a quite different topic. Gervase smoothly picked up the questioning.

Did these men have a horse? A mule? A cart or wagon of some kind? This effectively stopped the old farmer in his tracks. A cart? No, he had not seen one. Nan and her sisters were the ones who had seen them close up. Did they have a horse? 'No', said Nan, casting her eyes up to the smoke-blackened ceiling to aid thought. At least none had been visible, but it could be that they had some pack animal tied amongst the trees. They had been collecting great armfuls of kindling, perhaps more than they could easily carry off, unless their camp was close by.

This incited Mason to a further rant, maintaining that any camp they had was certainly not on his land, and must therefore have been on the Colonel's. If Benson Moreland could not bestir himself to do anything when a neighbour took the trouble to warn him, then he deserved the consequences! We thanked him solemnly, and took our leave.

We found Mother Hardcastle and Joan in the yard, resting from the labour of cleaning out the byre, and making much of Caesar. Caesar, I have to say, had seemed unconcerned at being brought back to Withins. What had happened here had either faded from his equine mind, or he supposed I had come back to arrest the enemy. Now he was basking in Nell and Joan's admiration, and permitting Joan to feed him stubs of carrot.

'He's a right handsome fellow!' she said, patting his gleaming neck. 'I can't tell tha how relieved we are that Father's shooting him has done no great harm.'

'He is mending well, as you see' I confirmed, 'but he does not deserve your treats!' I described Caesar's infamy in eating Mother's marigolds. This had Nell and Joan cackling with laughter, whilst Caesar threw up his head, and rolled his eyes. I could almost swear he was proud of his bad behaviour.

'Take note of Venus!' I chided him, as I swung myself up into the saddle. 'She is a model of decorum. Gervase never has to apologise for her!'

We were riding out of the gate when we met with Prudence and her small son Christopher, returning with pails from some errand in the fields. Nan, sighting her from the kitchen door, came running out, calling her name.

'Prue! Robert Haddon and his friend here have been asking about them fellows we saw picking up kindling in the woods. Canst tha recall owt about them? Was there two of 'em or three? Did tha notice, had they a horse or a mule?'

Prudence, out of breath from whatever she had been doing about the farm, in addition to being heavy with child, paused, puffing and blowing, unable to respond immediately.

'Them men as come after Grandpa's chooks?' squeaked small Christopher. 'They niver when they was apickin' up sticks, but I seen 'em talking to the Colonel's man, and *then* they had a hoss!'

'That's right!' gasped his mother, finding her voice. 'Us went down to t'beck for watercress, a day or two after that time we saw them in the wood, and there were three of 'em, speaking to Jem Robinson. I'd suppose he was warning them to be off out of the district! One of 'em was leading a skinny grey nag on a rope.'

Gervase and I rode most of the way home in silence, prey to our seething thoughts. It would seem we had identified the men who had taken the girls. Jem Robinson had a great deal of explaining to do. Prue Hardcastle had assumed he was warning the men off the Colonel's land, and we might have believed that, had he not denied all knowledge of them.

'This fellow Jem Robinson?' Gervase eventually asked, as we rode into the yard at Lowflatts. 'Does he live within the servants' quarters at Lings?'

'No. He lives alone in a cottage by the gates. We'll go there.'

'Aye, and jab some sharp implement into his dastardly throat until he talks!'

'He's the Colonel's steward,' I pondered. 'Military etiquette says we should inform his master before we skewer the wretch to his bedpost.'

'Military etiquette be damned! That beauteous Loveday murdered; those two innocent girls taken! If they still live, in what state must they be? This doesn't merit the rules of war, this is damned wickedness, and no occasion for gentlemanly behaviour!'

I don't think I'd ever heard Gervase so angry. Even in the heat of battle I'd hardly ever seen him anything but sanguine. Fellow officers had joked that he seemed to have enlisted on the wrong side. The lower ranks even speculated that he was spying on us for the Royalists. With his charm and ease of manner, it was no surprise that he found no difficulty in impersonating some nobly born cavalier.

I wondered, for a fleeting moment, what he'd felt for Loveday? He'd flirted with her when he came to the farm, or so Mother had indicated, perhaps to rouse Miles, perhaps simply to idle away the time in the company of a pretty wench. But had he too, as I once had, fallen under her spell?

The evenings are long and light in the north of England at this time of year, so we made our apologies to Malachi, who'd borne the brunt of the day's farm work, and went out after supper and worked ourselves, together with the inexhaustible Benjy, carting the dry hay to the barn, and scything the last field ready to be turned the following day.

Malachi swore that George and Hannah, together with their father, were managing well enough without him, but I insisted in my turn that he should go home and sleep in his own bed. I cannot, however, confirm that he did so, because when he left, to take the two Proctor boys home to Beckside, sodden with slumber after their long day in the hayfield, he was going in the opposite direction to Highbiggens. I never, throughout that long evening amongst the hay, saw or heard his horse pass by again, so I imagine he spent the night with Widow Snaith. Little wonder Loveday had ammunition for her so-called prophesies.

Gervase and I had plenty of time, as we scythed and turned and stooked in the twilight, and Gervase grumbled about his blistered palms, to discuss how and when we should tackle Jem Robinson. I was for going as soon as it was fully dark.

'He must be abed early, to be up betimes and ready at the Colonel's command. If we wake him from his first sleep he'll be confused, and less likely to come up with lies and evasions.'

'No. We go at dawn. Or I will, if you're still feeling the effects of your fall?' said Gervase. I assured him I fully recovered.

'You must know that just before first light is the best time for a serious interrogation,' he went on. 'Then, the human body is at its lowest ebb, and the suspect cannot find the strength to resist. Believe me, I know. We'll break him.'

I believed him. I'd done my share of interrogating suspects for the New Model, but only when captured prisoners had been brought to me, or when I'd surprised the man I wanted to question at home, with his family and servants about him. Gervase had undertaken the questioning of far more significant prisoners than those who had fallen into my hands. It's an interesting fact that, although the New Model Army prides itself on offering equality to all, and promoting men on merit rather than by social class, our generals still feel they must, where possible, match like with like. If Earl Tarradiddle or Lord Farafiddle is to be interrogated, someone from his own level of society is usually found to do it. Back in '48, there were, I believe, as many men on our own side who were shocked that Cornet Joyce, a mere cornet should have taken it upon himself to arrest the King, as there were amongst the Royalists.

As we led the last load into the barn, I said, 'Very well. We'll go just before first light. But I'm weary enough to sleep 'til noon. How shall we wake in time?'

'Don't worry,' replied Gervase. 'I'll rouse you.'

I admit I wasn't comfortable. Gervase had always been an easy going comrade, but his animosity towards Jem Robinson was showing me a more cold-blooded side of him than I'd previously known. I'm no weakling, the war has hardened me, as it has all of us who have fought in it. I felt righteous anger towards Jem, who had either caused or allowed my sister to be stolen away. I was prepared to break into his home, hold him at the point of a sword, and attempt to frighten the truth out of him. Was I prepared to do more? Gervase had spoken of 'breaking' him. By torture, I supposed. Why should I have any qualms about torturing, in his turn, a man who had connived in the abduction, and very likely the rape and killing of those two sweet girls? Because I had known Jem from boyhood, as Gervase had not, and had always believed him essentially a 'good man?' Because part of me wanted to believe that Jem, too, was a victim, that someone must have put intolerable pressure on him to have involved him in this? Yes, I wanted to scare him, to catch him off guard and get the truth. I didn't want to end up killing him in cold blood. Gervase, I was beginning to fear, might not scruple to do so.

I was as much afraid I wouldn't be able to sleep, as that I would oversleep, with this hanging over me, but I was exhausted, and I slept, as exhausted men do, even when they know they will be pitched into battle at daybreak. A small corner of my mind perhaps hoped that Gervase wouldn't wake me, and would go alone, to do what I need never fully know. But he roused me, as he'd promised, when the fingers of Mother's clock in the hall stood at three, and together we slipped out into the grey light that precedes a summer dawn.

'Horses?' I whispered.

'No, a man with a conscience as black as his sleeps lightly. He'll hear the hoof beats on the road. We'll walk.'

'Then I suggest we take a short cut across the meadow. The Lune is running low. We can wade across, cut a mile or more off the journey, and avoid Beckside. It's unlikely anyone there would be awake to see or hear us, but I'd rather not take the risk.'

Halfway across the meadow two dark shapes loomed up. Caesar and Venus, asleep on their feet, knees locked, heads down. Caesar, ever alert for the bugle call, twitched his ears and lifted his head as we approached.

'Rest on, old fellow,' I told him, slapping his rump in passing. 'This is an infantry exercise.'

Gervase, snorted. 'That horse of yours! Anyone would think he was your master, rather than you his! I never feel the need to explain where I am going to any steed of mine.'

'And have had six horses shot from under you,' I remarked, stung. 'Whereas Caesar and I have come safely through four major encounters. Until the most recent one,' I acknowledged, grinning at my own pretension. 'In Mason Hardcastle, I admit we met our match!'

'*He* did not seem quite so crazy yesterday. Perhaps he is affected by the phases of the moon?'

I merely grunted at this. I had no opinion on the cause of Mason's varying moods, but I thought what we had learned from his womenfolk and his little grandson was reliable.

We forded the river at one of the places where Lanty was wont to bring the sheep across, and then walked on through the cropped meadow grass carrying our boots and stockings. The drive that led to Lings Hall was directly ahead, and now we were close, we wanted our approach to be as quiet as possible. The night, now close to dawn, was so still that a cow coughing three fields further on sounded loud enough to be the last trump. The birds were waking and beginning small twitterings in the bushes, but June being now advanced, they were quieter than they would have been earlier in the year.

Our approach was not destined to be as stealthy as we hoped. Having crossed the last open field, and made for a gate amongst the trees that led into the lane, Gervase stumbled on a mound of straw and hedge pullings, and went sprawling over a man's supine body.

The man was not dead. Far from it. He rose up with a yell, thrusting Gervase aside, and sat up blinking in the pale grey light.

'Oh, 'tis thee,' he said, recognising me. 'The Lord be praised. I thought I was set upon by thieves.'

'Richard Hardcastle? What are you doing sleeping in the fields?'

'Yes, what indeed?' demanded Gervase, annoyed, scrambling to his feet and trying to detach swatches of goose grass from his coat. 'Why are you trespassing on Colonel Moreland's land? From what I hear, your father takes a dim view of others trespassing on his!'

I hadn't seen old Mason's son in several years. I had always thought of him as a puny fellow, lacking his father's undeniable vigour, but now, as he rose to his feet, I saw that he had broadened across the shoulders, and his previously spindly legs looked sturdy in leather breeches.

He shook himself and stretched, much like a dog who has been roused from a comfortable sleep before the fire.

'I came last evening, over from Westmorland. I had to return the horse I'd the loan of to a man in Barbondale.' He yawned prodigiously. 'I stayed talking with him, of certain contradictions within Bible passages which perplex him. Then I set forth to walk back to Withins, but it came to me that it was now very late, and my father would be angry if I woke them all. I took council with the Lord Jesus Christ, and He made me to understand that He had set before me a place to sleep.' He indicated the pile of straw and hedge trimmings. 'So, I slept.'

'On Colonel Moreland's land,' grunted Gervase, who was huffily hunting about for his dropped boots and stockings.

Richard yawned. 'The Colonel is a Godly man,' he remarked. 'He would pardon my trespass. I'm not in fellowship with my father on this matter. I would deny no weary man a place to rest.' He yawned again. 'You have some purpose in walking out at this hour?'

'We do,' I said, trying frantically to think of an explanation that would satisfy this young disciple of the Lord. He might sit up half the night disputing about obscure verses in the Bible, and leave it too late to go home, but Richard Hardcastle was no fool. I didn't want him to know that we planned to beat the truth out of Jem Robinson — in part because I was ashamed.

'You've heard that my sister and Rachel Postlethwaite have disappeared, we believe kidnapped by wicked men?'

He shook his head. 'No, I have not been at home these past weeks. The Lord's work took me into Westmorland, where I met with many who seek to live in the Light. I'm right sorry to hear this news. Rachel is a pure soul, and dear to me. You're going to search for them?'

'Acting on information received,' said Gervase, tight lipped. This is the standard phrase the army uses (undoubtedly both armies use) when they wish to search someone's premises without written authority, and don't relish any questions about their right to do so. I doubted it would content Richard, but in this I was wrong. Even a man busy about the Lord's work must rest and sleep. He yawned again, hugely.

'Then I'll pray for your success in this Godly endeavour,' he said, and lay down again on his bed of weeds. 'Presently the sun will wake me, and I'll go home and help my sisters with the milking.'

Gervase and I walked on. Reaching the lane we sat on the verge and donned stockings and boots once more. 'We've made so much noise already,' muttered Gervase, tugging his on, 'that we may as well. I've a thorn in my toe, and I don't want grit from this lane in addition. There are no lights showing in this cot of Robinson's. Can he really have slept through the racket we made back there?'

The cottage, one storey high, huddled on the lane's edge, no path or garden before it. We stood awhile, under the slate eaves, looking and listening for any sign that Jem was awake and moving about, but hearing none.

'There's a window open a crack,' he whispered. 'I'd best attempt it. Your shoulder may be mending, but scrambling through will be awkward. I'll go as quietly as I may, and let you in by the door.'

I was glad to let him, mildly puzzled that Jem should have left a window ajar. It was a quiet road, and very little frequented during the night hours. I doubted Jem kept money in his house, but he would have stout boots and tools that could attract a thief. Besides, though the weather was warm, country folk are generally suspicious of the night air, and keep their casements closed.

'Beware he doesn't sleep immediately below this window!' I hissed back. 'You've already woken one sleeper!'

I waited for what seemed a long while. Through the part opened window I could hear Gervase creeping about. Floor boards creaked, and a door squeaked on its hinges. Since there was no upper floor, I could not understand why Gervase had not found him, or why it was taking him so long to summons me.

Just as I was beginning to fear that the sun would be up, and my presence, lurking under the eaves would be only too visible to farm labourers passing on their way to work, the front door of the cottage opened. Gervase stood silhouetted on the step against the dim glow of a lantern.

'He's not here,' he said. 'You'd better come and take a look.'

'You think he heard us, guessed our intentions …?' I began to say, as I followed him over the threshold, but the words died on my lips as I saw what the lantern revealed. Either there had been a fight, or someone had turned the place upside down, searching for something.

'Gervase nodded to the lantern standing on the sideboard. 'I found that on the floor. The glass is smashed and the metal bent as though someone has trodden on it, but I managed to light it. It took me a while to find out was he here, dead or injured, underneath some of this. He isn't.'

'It doesn't look as though he left willingly,' I said, taking in the broken bed frame, torn bedclothes and upended chairs. The thought passed through my mind that Jem's possessions, even allowing for the fact that they had been smashed, were poor sticks of things. Dirty food bowls crowded the sideboard. His bed linen, now strewn across the floor, was torn and filthy. The whole place smelled of unwashed human flesh and stale rotting food. A further irrelevant thought followed; that if this was how he kept house, and if I ever found her alive, I would never let my sister marry a man who lived worse than a pig in its sty. Then I wondered if Ann knew how he lived, and had refused him on account of it, and this was at the bottom of his recent animosity towards our family?

Gervase stood by, considering the situation. 'He's been gone since soon after dark.' He pointed to a burned out candle stub standing in a cracked saucer next to the lantern on the sideboard (the only piece of furniture that was still upright). 'Someone came after he lit that. It burnt right down, but the wax is still warm. He put up a fight, or perhaps he fled? And the attacker, or I'd guess there was more than one, did this, either during the fight, or afterwards. From malice, if Jem managed to flee. The front door was unlocked. The attackers are gone.'

'Possibly taking Jem with them?'

'Unless he managed to escape. I doubt it. I don't see much blood, but they meant serious harm.'

'Is there a back door?' I asked, suddenly uneasy, though I couldn't have said why. We found it, through a tiny hovel of a scullery. It led out into a small yard where we found a rust coloured pig in a pen, asleep. The pen was solidly built and the straw, in the light of the first rays of the rising sun, looked clean.

'The pig lives more luxuriously than Jem!' I commented.

'The pig lives!' replied Gervase, who had wandered over to examine something in the shadowy corner of the yard. 'Jem, poor fellow…' he bent down to examine what he had found. 'This must be his.'

Jem Robinson had tried to escape. Gervase held up a blood stained shirt, slashed to ribbons by a knife.

# Chapter 18

Colonel Moreland saw us in his study. It was scarce five in the morning when we roused him from his bed. When he heard what we had to say, he dropped his face into his hands, and sat there awhile, seeming unable to assimilate this latest blow.

'We are not reproaching you, Sir,' said Gervase, gently. 'Whatever your steward has got himself involved with, we don't suppose you knew, or condoned it. From the eye witness accounts we had from Prudence Hardcastle and her son, we discovered Jem had spoken to these ruffians. Yet he denied it in your presence, and tried to divert us with false information, saying that the men had left the district over a month ago. Clearly they had been seen much more recently. Rob and I were busy with the hay at Lowflatts until late last night, and so decided to go and see Jem early this morning.' He held up the blood soaked shirt. 'We found his cottage wrecked, and this lying in the backyard.'

'So, in all likelihood he is dead.' the Colonel sighed, raising his eyes, and looking over our heads at some thought or vision that his mind had conjured up. 'Jem is, was, a good man. I have always found him so, and trusted him with…with everything. Of late I've known he was troubled. Angry? Unhappy? Perplexed? I know not, and he has not confided in me. But which of us has not experienced those emotions these last few years? As you probably realise, the war has left me short of resources, and I've had to let most of my farm hands go. That placed a heavy burden on Jem. He is a perfectionist, and it's been hard for him to see Lings in poor shape through lack of men to work the land. Also, it has troubled him that I took Parliament's part, whilst my wife supported the late King. He said something to me once — all wrapped about in Biblical language, and nothing said clear — to the effect that he believed a wife should always be of the same mind as her husband, and if she would not accept his authority, the husband should put her from him. At the time I didn't entirely understand his meaning, and didn't take it as a criticism of myself, as he perhaps intended. He was not normally insolent, if sometimes overly blunt. I assumed it was a concern of his own. You know, perhaps, Major Haddon, that he had some thought of asking your sister Ann to be his wife? But she, though a shy little maid, made no secret of her vigorous support for you and for Parliament.'

'You are saying, Sir, that Jem supports the King's party?' Gervase asked.

'No, I don't say that. Not essentially. Jem inclines to Puritanism. Many of the reforms to the church that Parliament has been proposing are to his liking. The regicide however, was a step too far. Something many of us found difficult to accept. No, Jem wanted Puritanism, the reform of the church, and the old order back again.'

I nodded sympathetically. Gervase I noticed, did not. This is a topic he and I generally avoid. He says the regicide was necessary. I disagree. King Charles had to be deposed, I accept, but we could have sent him into exile in the Low Countries. Yes, the Royalists would have gathered around him there, and plotted for his return at the head of an invading army, but it would have taken them time to raise sufficient funds. Meanwhile, Parliament could have dealt with them. Negotiated. Suggested that he might return without the expense of mounting an invasion. Put off the hour of his homecoming until the planned reforms were complete, and tied up so tightly in law that treaties could not be broken, as they had been so many times in the past. Held off, some suggested, until they could offer the throne to his son in his place. Now, three years on, the son was trying to win the throne himself.

'Jem is thoroughly confused,' continued Benson Moreland, 'and I don't blame him for that. We live in frightening and confusing times. Some have even proclaimed that we are living in the End Times, and that the Day of Judgement is at hand. I cannot say that I believe that, but I understand the fears of ordinary people.' He sat silent for some minutes, and then roused himself. 'What can have happened? Who were these people who attacked Jem in his own home, and have now abducted him, dead or alive? You consider that they were the three ruffians who were stealing firewood on my land? And who probably took Ann and Rachel?'

'Who else?' I asked. 'I spoke with Mason Hardcastle and his family yesterday. I had the notion from you, Sir, that they were renegade mercenaries who had been left behind when the late hostilities ceased, but Hardcastle insists they were just common vagabonds. Young Christopher, his grandson, told us he saw them talking to Jem. At that time they had a horse. His mother described it as a skinny grey nag What Jem was speaking to them about, and why he then denied having done so, we don't know.'

'Clearly they had some kind of a hold over him' put in Gervase. 'Some secret matter that bound him to them against his will. Mistress Haddon told us Jem had some relative on his late mother's side who was hanged for killing a man. Mayhap, though an honest fellow himself, he has other relatives who live outside the law?'

'Not that I know of,' replied Benson Moreland. 'I knew of the cousin. I was told of it by one of the Lancaster magistrates. But, as you say, he was hanged, ten years ago. So far as I am aware he'd no siblings. Jem has always been a man very much alone in the world. He's worked for me for twelve years, and I've never had reason to doubt his decency, or his loyalty to me and mine.'

Gervase and I glanced at one another. Would either of us dare to raise that matter we had speculated upon — the supposed wiles of Lady Brilliana? Neither of us had a crumb of evidence, beyond the lady's use of her fine eyes, and her daughter's tale of jewellery sold for the Royalist cause. We said nothing.

Colonel Moreland roused himself. 'The shirt. You'll have heard that my young sons have returned home?' We nodded, unsure what this had to do with anything. 'I didn't wish it, but now they're here it occurs to me... Edwin and Nicholas are wild scamps, who spend money heedlessly. They've brought back with them two hounds, some breed of Flemish hunting dog, that friends they made in Antwerp urged them to buy. I've never seen dogs of this breed before, and have no idea of their capabilities, but I'd like to keep Jem's shirt if I may, and set these dogs on. If they can follow the scent, at least sufficiently to show us the direction in which the villains went, we might find Jem.' He smiled, bitterly. 'It would provide useful employment for Edwin and Nicholas, and give me an excuse to lug them from their beds before noon.'

The old serving man, Joseph, brought coffee, and we spoke of general subjects whilst he served us. Benson Moreland invited us to wait and break our fast with the rest of his household, but he looked so stricken and weary that we politely declined. Walking back to Lowflatts through Beckside, in the beauty of an early June morning, Gervase and I were silent for a good way, mulling over what we'd found in Jem's cottage and the outcome of our discussion with the Colonel.

'Are you satisfied that Moreland and his sons should organise this hunt for Jem's attackers? Should we have insisted on taking part?' Gervase wondered, as we began the ascent of the grassy lane leading to the farm.

'I'd have liked to be there,' I agreed, 'but didn't see how we could insist. The Colonel is Jem's master, and so has more right than anyone to discover what happened to him. If these hounds his sons have are able to pick up the scent, then perhaps they'll succeed They might even lead them to Ann and Rachel. We must hope they will.'

I was low in spirits. So far I'd achieved nothing. We were no nearer knowing who had killed Loveday and Parson Drysdale. Ann, Rachel, and now Jem, were probably dead too. It might be better if I left off searching. If I did nothing but follow my mother's example; left it all in the hands of the Almighty and minded the farm. Then perhaps no one else would be killed?

Gervase, however, was fascinated by the Flemish hunting dogs, and began to talk of them. This is another instance of the difference between our two estates. My brother had a dog, Bess, who went with him whenever he rode out; who would go in the evening on her own and bring the cattle in for milking, would round up the sheep too, if Lanty had had one of his 'turns' and was confined to bed. Lanty never used a dog, preferring to signal the sheep with his own peculiar caws and cries, which strangely they seemed to understand perfectly, and obey without question. Good dog Bess had died, in her thirteenth year, last Autumn, and Miles, who had raised her from a pup, hadn't yet had the heart to replace her. But Gervase, whose father has a prosperous estate, knew dogs, and liked to talk of the differing breeds and their aptitudes.

'They sound to be extraordinary animals! Flemish Bouviers, the Colonel called them. I've heard of them once or twice before. They're not the sleek hounds we know, Rob, but great hairy creatures, more resembling small bears than hunting dogs! I own I should like to see them in action. I believe they were originally bred by the monks in the Low Countries to fetch rabbits and partridges for the monastery tables. Flemish farmers use them to herd sheep and cattle, but also to find and retrieve game.'

'Edwin and Nicholas have no doubt assured their father that they are the very thing that Lings needs!' I was amused by this thought in spite of my dismal mood. 'Quite regardless of the fact that they probably eat twice as much as the Colonel's own farm dogs. They'll be trained, if they've been trained at all, for the hunt. Very likely they'll chase his sheep over the rocks and devour his poultry!'

'All too probable!' chuckled my friend. 'I've yet to make the acquaintance of Edwin and Nicholas, but something tells me any dogs these two youngsters own are unlikely to prove obedient! Well, I suppose we must get back to the hayfield, and wait to hear what luck they have.'

Mother gave us a hearty breakfast. She didn't ask why we had been up and out so early, guessing that if we had made any progress we'd have told her. Also, Timmy and Saul Proctor were at the table before us, and speaking of where we'd been and what we'd seen was not for their ears.

'Have you adopted these two?' Gervase joked, eyeing the food disappearing into the mouths of those two urchins. 'Their parents have sold them to you?'

'Goodness no!' replied Mother, pretending indignation at the idea. 'Their mother is come to help me with the wash, and the boys are to help you men with the last of the hay. Are you not, Saul and Timmy?' The two children nodded, their mouths too full to speak.

I forbore to mention my suspicion that although Luke and Martha Proctor were carelessly fond of their large brood, they might well consider selling one or two if the offer was a good one.

Malachi and Benjy were already at work when we joined them in the hay. We told them Jem Robinson had been attacked and was missing, but didn't burden them with the reason we had gone to see him. Hay is master of all at this time of the year. The last meadow was already cut and part turned, and there was a strong likelihood, God willing, that all our crop could be in the barn by nightfall.

'We owe your family a debt,' I said to Benjy, when I found myself beside him, raking up the last few rows of sweetly perfumed grass. 'Your father must tell us how we can repay it.'

'The Bible bids us be good neighbours,' he replied, piously. I looked around. This seemed as good a moment as any to tackle him. The others were piling the hay into stooks. It was almost dry enough for carting. Saul and Timmy, swinging sharp tined forks in a manner that did not bode well for anyone's eyesight, were attempting to fling some of it up onto the wagon.

'Benjy, tell me something?'

'Tell thee what?'

'Something that's been puzzling me. Lemuel Drysdale. Someone put burrs beneath his horse's saddle which so maddened the beast that it threw him. It seemed to me that you were surprised and alarmed by that? It had the air of a boy's trick, and I wondered — I'm not accusing you — if you knew something of it? Or who might have done it?'

Benjy scowled, and raked hay in silence for a while. I waited.

'Ah know not who did it,' he said, eventually. 'Only, Ah heard them speak of it, how it could be done.'

'Some lads discussed it? Whether it could be done, and might cause the horse to throw the rider?'

"Twas not lads, but them as had been lads. Grown men.'

'You overheard grown men discussing something they'd done, or had tried to do as boys?' Getting information out of Benjy was like drawing teeth, but I'd met with many up and down the land who were equally unwilling to part with what they knew, and I'd learned patience to wait them out.

"Twas in the tavern in Sedbergh one market day back in t'spring,' Benjy grudgingly confided. 'Ah was there with our George and Malc, and a few from round here. They were talking of tricks they'd played as lads. Some said t'would work if the beast had a thin coat to feel the pricks and the rider sat heavy. Others gave the opinion that the hoss would feel it and be skittish, but no more. Ah don't know as ony of them had done it.'

'And you were alarmed because you thought someone might think you'd done it with Drysdale's pony?'

'Aye. There was a few of them present when the priest was thrown that had been in the tavern that time, and Ah was afeared they've say, *he* was there, Benjamin Postlethwaite. Like as not he did it, jesting. Bein' nobbut a lad and heedless. 'Twas only for a minute, Ah knew our George would stand my corner.'

'I see,' I said, remembering irresponsible things I'd done as a boy, and other times when I'd feared I'd be blamed for what others had done. I took note, also, that Benjy did not mention Malachi, who had been in the priest's black books over his affair with Deb Snaith.

'I would have 'stood your corner' as you put it Benjy, since I knew you'd been with me, here at Lowflatts, until we left for the service. Who else was present at this conversation in the tavern — and present also at Loveday's burial?'

Benjy seemed surprised that I wanted to know this. 'Them was all men grown! Ah was t'only lad.'

'Never the less, someone used that trick to murder Lemuel Drysdale. You realise that, knowing that you'd heard it described, the killer may have chosen that method so that the blame would fall on you? Whether he or they actually intended to kill Drysdale, or merely give him a fright, we cannot know.'

Benjy lowered his hayrake and stood scratching his thatch of dark hair. 'Happen so. All Ah can tell thee is,' he began to reel off the names of the men who had been present in the tavern. George, Malachi, Sam Woodley, Jem Robinson, my brother Miles, Richard Hardcastle and his father, and two or three other farmers from up the dale who had come to Loveday's funeral out of respect for our family.

'Jem Robinson was there?'

'Aye, and all them others. And happen there was yet more there that heard what was said. T'tavern was full to bustin', it being market day, and they wus laughing and talking loud, of the tricks they tried when they wus young.'

'But those other men were not at the funeral?'

'Some might have been, but Ah disremember which.'

I raked hay, thinking it through. Benjy, relieved to escape my questioning, moved down the row, away from me. Was the most likely person to have done it Jem Robinson? As church warden he probably came early to the church, to confer with Parson Drysdale. Almost certainly, Lemuel would have told him he was going to Lancaster immediately after the service. He would have asked him to see the church was left in order. Few besides Jem and myself would have known of the Parson's intended trip. But where would Jem get burrs at such short notice? He'd hardly have had time to hunt the hedgerows. When did he apply them to the saddle? And even if he had done it (now I looked back I recalled how disconcerted he'd been at being asked to read the prayers for the dead over Lemuel's corpse) why had he in his turn been attacked?

Who else amongst the crowd Benjy had named as being in the tavern that time could possibly be behind all this? Malachi Postlethwaite, who had been denounced by the priest as an adulterer? Sam Woodley, likewise? Malachi, a fretful sort, might resort to something desperate if he were pushed to an extremity. But murder a man? Sam, I judged to be a sharper fellow, with more guile about him, but unabashed by his sin in fathering

Prue's children. One day he hoped to make an honest woman of her. Murdering the village priest wouldn't further that aim. Now, someone had attacked Jem — because Jem knew who'd killed Loveday and the priest? Because Jem knew who'd taken the girls, or was that a different matter? Could all this be the work of the three ruffians the Hardcastles had seen?

At last, the final wagon, piled high, pulled by those great dray horses we had not yet returned to their rightful owner, and with Saul and Timmy seated triumphantly on top of the load, made its way slowly to the barn.

Malachi, collecting rakes and hayforks, looked up at the sky. ' Just in time, praise the Lord. Weather's on the turn,' he remarked, the most I'd heard him say all day. I looked over into Westmorland, and saw that he was right. Fat white clouds, bellying like wind-filled sails, were sailing in from the Atlantic ocean. Tomorrow could well see rain.

# Chapter 19

We were seated, sated and exhausted, supper over, around the kitchen table once more, when the message came from Lings. Colonel Moreland had sent his stable lad, Abel, hot foot with it. In truth, so hot of foot that the boy nearly collapsed, breathless, on the doorstep, trying to speak and catch his breath at the same time. I took the missive through to the kitchen and read it aloud to the assembled company.

*Major Haddon*, (Moreland had written)

*I write to inform you that Jem Robinson is found, though grievously injured. He hath a number of stab wounds, including one to the throat, and cannot speak to say who did this. We went out with my sons' dogs, and they led us to a ghyll or gully on the fellside, somewhat in the direction in which you and yours first searched, (as I understood it from Jem at the time) for the missing girls. The malefactors had left Jem, probably supposing him dead or dying, under a rocky overhang amongst gorse bushes. We should not have found him, for he was lost to consciousness, but for the dogs, which, although I regret to say they are ill-disciplined, never the less proved effective in following the scent. My sons are delighted with their dogs' success, and bid me offer them to help you search further for Ann and Rachel. I am doubtful that they would be easily able to do this, as the weather is on the turn, and the scent from any garments belonging to the girls will be less strong after such a length of time, but send me word with Abel if they are to wait on you on the morrow.*

*Thine, by the grace of our Lord Jesus Christ, Benson Moreland.*

'So send, brother!' said a harsh voice from the fireside. 'Nothing else useful has been done to find my sister. Send for Moreland's dogs, and go tomorrow before the weather breaks. I would that I could go. If I were not sick I would have found her before now.'

'Miles, dear son, you do Robert an injustice,' said Mother, unhappily. 'Truly he has done all he could, and Gervase and Benjamin here, and even your cousin Ezekiel, have done everything possible. But we'd no scent hounds. And besides that they have brought in all the hay…'

Miles huddled in Father's old chair by the hearth. He was still in his nightshirt, with a blanket wrapped about him for decency. His eyes looked clearer then I had seen them since Mother brought him home. His fever seemed abated, but his mood was sour.

'So you say. But how much of it will rot in the barn?'

'It'll not rot, the Lord being ever merciful,' said Malachi, rising from the table and signalling to Saul and Timmy that he would take them home. The boys rose and scampered after him. Timmy, however, turned when he reached the door and caught my gaze.

'If tha goes out with t'dogs, can Ah come?' he pleaded. 'Ah've sharp eyes. Tha said so tha self!'

'We'll see. Much depends on how quickly the weather changes,' I prevaricated.

'I'm no weather sage, away from the sea,' offered Zeke, who was engaged in noisily washing pots. 'I'd say '

'tis due to change, but the rain could hold off until the middle of the day.'

'I've been thinking,' Mother said, hesitantly. 'There's a woollen gown of Ann's that she wore a good deal of late, until the weather grew too warm. I'd been intending to wash it, and while Martha was here today I thought to fetch it out, but then it came to me that it might still hold the scent of her. Would these dogs be able to find her from that?'

'Hardly,' grunted Miles. ''Tis not the gown would be the problem, but the scent of her passing being gone from the air and the places where she was, after what is it? Six days? The trail will be cold. I doubt any dog could trace where they took her from here.'

'But we know where they took Jem,' I said, slowly. 'So we could start from there. I think it's worth our searching that ghyll. We didn't do so before, seeing no signs of disturbance. We assumed they had gone on, higher up the fell.'

'We should have searched those bushes,' agreed Gervase. 'As you say, there was no sign of disturbance, no broken branches, no sign of earth scuffed aside. Jem distracted us at the time, grumbling that you had chosen that route, when if we'd cast to the right, the way would have been easier. We were so busy urging the horses up the steep sides of the place that we didn't look closely. We should have searched the top of the gully where that stream disgorges. Even if it rains it must be somewhat sheltered by the rocks and bushes. We should try. With or without dogs.'

'I'll stay here and be of assistance to Auntie Sarah and Cousin Miles,' said Zeke, firmly. 'Dogs and myself are not congenial. If it comes to needing ropes however, send and I will risk my life agin on one of them hosses.'

'Face the truth. You'll be finding bodies. Take hurdles or canvases. And keep the dogs away from them!' said Miles. He was right, of course. A sick man of whom much must be excused, but a glance at Mother's stricken face made me long to fetch my brother a hefty clout.

The decision seemed to have been made. I nodded to Abel, who had followed me into the kitchen and hunkered himself down in a corner. 'Thank Colonel Moreland for me, and tell him we'd be pleased to have the dogs. In view of the change coming in the weather we'll need to start as early as possible.' I named the hour, wondering what chance there was that Edwin and Nicholas could be persuaded to rise so early.

'So, on whom do we rely to carry out this search?' Gervase enquired once I'd sent the boy on his way. 'I have to tell you that tomorrow may be the last day I can devote to your affairs, and it's possible I may be called away even as the day progresses. I hope otherwise. I would want to see this business through for the sake of our comradeship, and the kindness your family have shown me.'

I thanked him, saying that I would have Benjy, and with help from the Morelands, I wouldn't need many people to assist me.

'I'll come if I can,' Gervase vowed, adding thoughtfully, 'As you know, I still harbour suspicions that there is some connection between the matter I was sent here to investigate, and what happened to Loveday and the girls. Although it is hard to fathom what it might be. It frustrates me! Surely there must be a connection? This is a peaceful valley, yet this great wave of carnage has broken out, two, perhaps four people dead, and one grievously injured.'

We left soon after sunrise next morning, following Lanty and the sheep as they streamed across the river. There we found Colonel Moreland himself, on horseback, and the unfortunate Abel once again, on foot, struggling to hold, on a double ended leash, two black dogs with thick woolly coats. As Gervase had intimated, they did somewhat resemble bear cubs, or how I imagine a bear cub to be, having seen only an adult dancing bear, once, at the fair.

The Lowflatts contingent consisted of myself, Gervase, and Benjy, who insisted that his family could continue to manage without him. Seeing the Colonel himself waiting, I feared for a moment that he had received some message from the Council of State in London, and had come to give Gervase his marching orders. However, it was nothing more than the fact that, despite the promise of the hunt, and the opportunity to show off their hounds' prowess, he'd not succeeded in rousing Edwin and Nicholas from their beds.

'I told Joseph to rouse them again in another hour,' he said, 'and have them follow us. I explained to them last night that we're to search in the same place as before, so it is up to them to find us.'

I enquired of Jem, and was told that he had spent a reasonable night, and that a woman who had once been nursemaid to the Moreland children, a widow who lived with her elderly mother, had taken him in, and was nursing him.

We rode by the same route we'd taken three days back, came to the same shale bank, the same thorn bushes, and took that same diversion to the left, bringing us abruptly to the steep sided ghyll. Here, on the rim, we waited for Abel to catch up with us. Benjy was scornful.

'Tha'll niver win fell races, Abel Haythornethwaite! Tha creeps no better than a snail! With them powerful dogs to pull thee along, tha should have been here afore us!' he jeered.

'Lord save us,' murmured Gervase to me, 'is this Abel a lad with an even longer name than Postlethwaite?'

As the dogs approached however, Venus began to sidle away skittishly, and he was forced to rein her in and walk her about. 'It would seem,' he said, between clenched teeth, 'that Zeke is not the only one who is not congenial with dogs! I think I must tether her well away from the scene of action.'

This was the first time I had observed the mare, Venus, to be anything but perfectly mannered and collected. 'I'm pleased to note she has some faults,' I said, grinning. 'I was beginning to have feelings of inferiority on Caesar's behalf, but he is perfectly congenial with dogs!'

'Aye, and were he not so big would probably dive down rabbit holes after them!' Gervase replied, dismounting and leading Venus to a tree some way distant from our party.

The Colonel pointed with his whip to a slight overhang of rock half way up the right hand side of the ghyll. 'That's where we found Jem,' he told us, 'but there was no sign of any other... bodies, and I imagine the dogs would have shown interest if there had been. So I envisage we may end up searching amongst those gorse and rowan bushes, where the rocks come together at the head? How do you want us deployed, Major Haddon?'

I admit I experienced a slight jolt of surprise. Usually someone who has attained the rank of Colonel has very decided ideas about how men should be deployed, and mere Majors must just make the best of it. It hadn't occurred to me that Benson Moreland was expecting me to take command here, but after all it was my sister we were looking for. I snapped to attention, and led our party down into the level base of the ghyll. Gervase, having tethered Venus, now followed us on foot, holding the two dogs he'd taken from Abel.

'The boy is reluctant,' he told me, 'fearing to see dead bodies. He intends to stay up there with the horses, unless we order otherwise. Finding Jem in such a poor way has badly upset him.' He moved closer, and muttered in my ear, 'I must warn you. Someone is just starting up the fell to our rear. I'm not sure, because I think there might be two people on the horse, one perhaps a child, but I'd guess by the set of her hat it's Mistress Judith. Evidently *she* rises early, and is not afraid to encounter dead bodies.'

'Well, if it is, her father must send her away,' I replied. I turned my attention to the dogs, panting eagerly at Gervase's feet. 'Did the boy give you their names?'

'He did. This one is Claes, and this is Piet, but he tells me it's of no use to call them by their names, since they pay no heed to calling or whistling until such time as either they find what they are casting for, or they grow tired and lose interest.'

'So, Sir, if we let them loose, we may never catch them again?' I asked of Benson Moreland.

'But for the fact that they would probably savage someone else's sheep, I would be happy to see them go,' he replied. 'My sons are too much ruled by impulse. They've wished these animals upon us, and will conveniently forget this when something new catches their attention. Thus leaving my unlucky servants with the problem of trying to train them to obedience. However, let us try them here!'

I divided my search party into two, the Colonel, and Gervase to the right bank of the little stream, shrunk to a trickle after so many fine days. Benjy and myself would take the left. Starting beyond where Jem had been found, they were to set Claes on, with Gervase hanging on grimly to his collar for the moment. We would take Piet. So far, although the sky was clouded over, white and milky, there was no sign of rain.

First, I produced Ann's gown from my knapsack. Mother had wrapped it in a piece of worn cotton and lace to preserve the scent. Unfolding this, I realised it was a piece of a Christening gown, the very one, passed down through our family, that Ann had been the last of the Haddons to wear. I remembered Mother cutting it up one winter evening soon after Miles and Loveday were married, saying that if and when Loveday should have a child, she would sew a brand new one in honour of her first grandchild. I am not ashamed to say that tears blurred my sight for a moment, at the realisation of those disappointed hopes. With the result that the heavy woollen gown, which was to give the scent to the dogs, tumbled abruptly onto the grass, causing them to leap backwards. Gervase and Benjy staggered to keep their footings. Then, sensing their business was to explore this strange object, the two hounds nosed closer.

'Good dogs,' rumbled the Colonel, 'Take! Take! There must be Flemish words to encourage them, but my sons don't seem to have learned them. Or any others for that matter,' he added. 'It's been too dry for a good spoor to linger on the grass, but by the stream and amongst the bushes, where moisture persists, we may have luck. We'd best start the search while they have the scent fresh in their nostrils.'

We set forth with the dogs for the sides of the miniature valley. Benjy kept Piet on the leash, whilst Gervase had contributed his belt to hold Claes. This proved very necessary because the dogs strained ahead, eager, noses to the ground, though it was impossible to know whether they were following a trail, or merely hoping for rabbits. The Colonel and Gervase took Claes to a starting point above where Jem had been found, in the hope that Claes would not become confused. Benjy and I started lower down.

'Ah hope us finds summat!' gasped Benjy, after a while, 'afore this creature pulls me arm from t'socket!'

Along the sides of the ghyll we found nothing. Twice I took Piet whilst Benjy ran across with Ann's gown to give Claes the opportunity to refresh his familiarity with the scent. Both the dogs continued to plunge ahead, enthusiastic to 'find'. Piet did indeed find the corpse of a long dead hare, its flesh stripped away from its bones by some predator, mayhap the golden eagle we'd seen during our previous search. However, to my surprise, after snorting over it like a tantony pig, he didn't allow it to distract him further, but forged on.

We now came, all four searchers and two hounds, to the point where the ghyll narrowed and the bushes crowded together. We were considering which of us should push through the gorse — the dogs seemed undismayed, and impatient to continue — when we heard hoof beats approaching.

'As I conjectured,' muttered Gervase, as horse and rider breasted the crest of the ghyll and began the descent towards us. 'Mistress Judith Moreland.'

'And with her, Timmy Proctor,' I sighed. 'He begged me, you'll remember, to let him come, but I preferred to forget about it. Dead bodies are no sight for a young boy.'

'Dost tha think he ain't seen bodies?' grunted Benjy, astonished. 'Wi' Luke, 'is Dad havin' the buryin' of 'em? Reckon as soon as his lads is tall enough to reach into t'coffin, he has 'em hold the corpse's jaw shut, whilst he binds the cloth around.'

At this revelation, the jaws of Gervase and myself fell open. It had taken us long months in the Army to accustom ourselves to intimate encounters with the dead. Colonel Moreland too, winced, and murmured something about having it in mind to speak with neighbouring landowners about providing schooling for the children of the poorer families in the dale. Then he stepped forward to greet his daughter.

The twins are coming!' she announced, dismounting from her mare, 'But, for what reason I know not, it takes them a long time to outfit themselves, and dress their hair to their satisfaction. It appears the edicts of fashion in Antwerp are very severe! However, it was fortunate that I came ahead, as I was able to bring Timmy, who is certain you'll need him.'

'Tha forgot to fetch me, Major Rob,' said the child, eyeing me reproachfully. 'Tis a good thing Mistress Judith took me up, or tha'd be spoilin' tha good clothes crawling through yon thicket!'

'I cannot see,' called Gervase, who was walking around the edge of the said thicket, 'how anyone could pass through these thorns with...!' he paused with a grunt. 'Here, against the cliff edge, under this, what is it? A rowan tree? There *is* a pathway of sorts.' At this moment, the hound Claes, whom he was still leading on his improvised leash, bounded forward, dragging Gervase, yelling obscenities, through the lower branches of the rowan. The two of them disappeared from view, although the sound of Gervase swearing, and the dog's excited barking, echoed back to us from the rock face above. Now, Piet set up a howl, and tugging frantically, managed to wrest the leash from Benjy. He dived into the undergrowth after his brother hound, and after him, determined not to left out, hurtled the diminutive figure of Timmy Proctor. The rest of us stood like those characters in the Bible who were turned to pillars of salt.

'I suppose there is *something* to be found in there,' said Judith is a small voice, 'but it cannot be good, can it, Major Rob?' She raised her eyes to mine, and I saw tears form and spill onto her cheeks. It was a strange moment for me. I felt as though I suddenly saw inside her mind, as though we were two people alone in this place, sharing our dread and our sorrow. I wanted to put my arms around her and comfort her, and tell her we'd face this thing together, and try to be strong. But what could I say of comfort? And how could I, a man making his way from lowly beginnings, embrace a fine young lady in her fashionable riding habit, in front of a Colonel and a Magistrate, her esteemed father?

'Alas, I fear this cannot have a good outcome…' I began, but was interrupted by shouts from Gervase. Both dogs were barking hysterically, and we could hear Timmy Proctor's squeaky tones, questioning something.

'Coming back out to report!' Gervase yelled, and presently he emerged, without his hat, and covered in thorny twigs and strands of foliage He was breathing hard, and rolling a painful shoulder from the tugging it had received from the frantic Claes.

'No bodies…' he panted, 'but another of those caves like the one we found higher up. This one goes back rather than down… goes back a long way, I'd warrant. The stream flows out of one side of it, leaving a ledge along which it would be possible for a man to walk at a crouch. The dogs want to go in. They obviously think there is something in there. I've tied them to a sapling, which I pray will hold. There were small signs that the earth has been worn away by the passage of people or a large animal. You don't have bears in these hills do you? Foxes? They don't live in caves. I have to say it looks as though someone has been using the entrance, regularly. Of course, in stormy weather I suppose the stream must rise and wash soil away, but this looks like recent wear. Timmy offered to go in and see how far back it goes.'

'No, we can't let the boy go, not alone. These caves are dangerous,' said Benson Moreland. 'I explored one or two myself as a youth, but more Benjamin's age than Timmy's. He could come to a sudden drop and fall. We'd never get him out.'

Benjy, who had been standing unhappily by, obviously angry with himself for losing control of Piet, suddenly burst into speech.

'Reckon 'tis where Ah could see the light comin' in, when Ah fell in that time, up above. 'Tis one of the openings where t'beck comes out onto t'fell.'

'One of them,' I agreed. 'There must be others. This stream cannot be carrying all the water that flows through after heavy rain. Despite what you and I said at the time, Benjy, I'm coming round to believing there may be people living in these caves. Will you tell Colonel Moreland and Gervase what you heard there?'

Benjy stepped uneasily from foot to foot, flushing with embarrassment. 'Music,' he muttered uneasily. 'Ah thought Ah could hear music when t'water weren't too loud. Ah thought 'twas someone playing the fife and drum. It were beneath my feet aways, but mebbe 'twas just the wind in the passageways.' He paused, his eyes sliding sideways to see how the Colonel and Gervase were reacting to this, and seeing that they were listening intently, and not inclined to mock him, went on. 'There's great caverns down there. Ah wus afraid to get lost or fall over a drop, like the Colonel says... and anyway they wus getting ready to pull me out. Major Rob's Cousin Zeke and them,' he finished.

We stood awhile, absorbing this information.

'Rachel can play the fife!' Judith burst out. 'We found one in a chest at Lowflatts one time, amongst some things that had come down from Loveday's family. We all tried it, but only Rachel could get a tune out of it.'

We were silent again. Was it possible? The two Bouviers, tied up and bored beside the mouth of the cave, began to whine. We could hear Timmy talking to them, telling them to hold their noise.

'So they could be in there? Ann and Rachel? Kept prisoner in the caves?' demanded Gervase at last

'The dogs seem to think so,' replied Colonel Moreland. 'They led us straight to this cave. Pray God the girls are still alive! Is it *possible*, after so many days?'

Benjy!' I ordered, as though he were my sergeant in the field, 'take the cob and go for Zeke — and anyone else who can be spared! We may need those ropes.'

'Nay, let Abel tek t'cob, and rouse 'em at Lings! Ah'll run! Ah'll fetch back as mony men from our side of t'dale as Ah can find!'

# Chapter 20

We three military men held a council of war, there on the fellside. Colonel Moreland scratched rough sketches in the dirt with a twig, of what he remembered of the cave system from his boyhood explorations.

'Should we not be starting from that cave we found higher up?' asked Gervase. 'Benjy heard the fife and drum there, so they could be a long way up the hill from where we are now?'

'Perhaps, but the dogs seem to be signalling that this is where the girls were taken inside,' argued the Colonel. 'It would take time to climb up higher, and we mustn't waste any. The clouds are thickening, and once the rain comes, all the water courses will quickly turn to torrents. The girls, if they still live, will be trapped and could drown, and we with them. Only the fact that the weather has been set fair this past week may have prevented that from happening.' He paused, his brow creased in thought.

'We have to assume that these villains had the girls walk to where they have imprisoned them. They could not, I believe, have carried two healthy girls for any distance along what are likely to be narrow ledges. From what you say of the upper cave, Benjamin fell as much as twenty feet. If the girls survived, it's fairly certain they were not dropped twenty feet.'

'And Benjy only heard the sounds faintly,' I pointed out, 'which may mean that the place where the girls are is a long way below where he was. Sound rises, does it not? So it could easily be that it resounded up through these lofty caverns you've described.'

'Oh! In the name of Heaven will you stop talking about it and go in, and at least *see* what might be done!' stormed Mistress Judith, emerging from the thicket, where she'd gone to talk to Timmy, and the dogs. 'Those girls may be starving to death, if they haven't already. I swear the Royalists could have been beaten finally and forever, years ago, if you men hadn't spent so much time talking of all the possibilities that could arise!'

We ignored this. Girls know nothing of warfare or politics, nor should they. Her father did explain that we'd probably need men and ropes, and were awaiting our reinforcements, but she continued to argue, saying she was minded to go inside the cave herself and call out, to try to make contact with Ann and Rachel.

'If they heard someone call their names, they'd call out in reply. We would then know that they're alive, and perhaps at what distance. *They* would be heartened to know that we're making some attempt to find them!'

'But if the villains who brought them here are in there too, as they may well be,' warned Gervase, 'they might kill them to silence them, and escape by one of the other routes your father believes exist.'

At this Judith stamped her booted foot in frustration, but before she could let fly with a further instalment of her opinion of Parliament men and their feebleness, her brothers, mounted on a neat pair of bay geldings, to all appearances twins like themselves, cantered gently down the slope. As their sister had intimated, they'd taken time to dress themselves finely, completing their outfits with hats so begirt with feathers that I feared for the bird population of the Low Countries. Caesar, who had been cropping at the grass at the top of the slope, and thus keeping company with the tethered Venus, raised his head at the sight of the new arrivals, decided they merited closer inspection, and ambled down into the grassy bowl at the base of the ghyll to join them. We now had six adults and five horses churning about in a comparatively small space.

'We met Abel, Papa, so we know the dogs have found!' said Edwin, vaulting from his horse. Edwin and Nicholas are almost identical in appearance, but Edwin had a more pronounced version of the Moreland jaw, and, I think, the sharper intellect. Certainly he was the leader in most things, particularly the pranks these two had played when they were younger.

'Did I not tell you, Father? These dogs are unbeatable. A cave! Famous! Where is this cave?' he went on.

Myself, I think I would have been inclined to deny the cave, or insist that it was much further up the fell, and we were merely waiting here for reinforcements. However, Colonel Moreland was their parent, and if he chose to tell them, and was then quite unable, despite his express orders, to prevent them from crashing through the thicket to examine it, that was his look out. Ignoring all warnings, these tiresome youths disappeared inside the cave mouth.

'Papa! How could you! You wouldn't even let me step inside to call out! Now, if the villains are there, they cannot fail to hear those two jabbering, and will very likely kill Ann and Rachel!' Judith was in tears of fury. 'My brothers are become the most *disobedient, headstrong...*! Even if they don't alert the girls' captors, most probably they'll fall into a pot hole and break their idiotish necks!'

'The dogs will very likely alert us to that,' said her father, sadly. He seemed stunned and shaken by his sons' careless defiance. 'I'm sorry, Judith. I paid a good man, a Divine, to tutor them in Antwerp, and I'd good reports from him of their improved conduct. I see now that it was not enough to steady their characters.' He placed his arm about her shoulders, sighing. 'My daughter, I must thank God I have thee.'

Gervase and I were forced to stand by, uncomfortable witnesses to this private trouble. Clearly there had been more to the twins' banishment to Antwerp than just 'keeping them away from the war.' Benson Moreland was a good man and a fine soldier. No one who had served under him these past years would have exhibited the disdain for his orders his sons had just shown.

Gervase stepped some way apart, and I followed, guessing from his expression that he had something he wished to say to me privately.

'I begin to see something,' he murmured. 'Those boys are worse than spoiled. How old are they? Sixteen? Someone has taught them to disregard their father. I cannot otherwise think that they would so blithely flout his authority. Can it be that they have been won for the Royalist cause, and have all the while been serving that cause abroad? For money, I suppose,' he added, bitterly, 'to buy feathered hats and hunting dogs! The treachery I suspected had its roots here has spread further than I feared.'

'It's not just a matter of people holding private prayer meetings, perhaps using Bible verses to pass information? You know…?' I began.

'No, no, Rob! That's innocent stuff. I quickly saw that there was nothing to that but what some of our leaders in Parliament might consider misguided religious zeal…' He stopped short.

People were arriving, streaming up to and over the rim of the ghyll, some on foot, some on horseback. All three of the Postlethwaite brothers, and Cousin Zeke, swaddled in rope, clinging on behind Malachi once again; Abel, with two of the Lings' farm hands. Sam Woodley, and the elderly relative who was his employer. Luke Procter, Richard Hardcastle… even some of the women. Deb Snaith. Martha Procter, and several of her children.

'Father's walking up, and Hannah!' said Benjy, sliding down the bank to report, 'and tha mother had difficulty in persuading Miles not to come. Hast tha found where they are, spoken to them?' He carried a string of lanterns, which I had forgotten to mention, but which Mother had never the less provided. It seemed, once again, incredible to me that he could have run so far in such a short time, but then Benjy *did* win fell races.

This assembly crowded together on the slope above Benson Moreland, adopting solemn faces, as though to listen to an outdoor preacher. The Colonel was a major landowner in the dale, and their Justice of the Peace. He had served as a distinguished soldier in the recent wars. They also knew him to be a trusted confidant of General Fairfax, and often consulted by the Council of State in Westminster. They might, or might not, agree with his politics, but in this situation they looked to him to tell them what was to be done. It must therefore have been a bitter moment for him, having to confess that his two graceless sons had gone ahead (they had not emerged from the cave) and might well have ruined the rescue attempt before it began.

Having no choice, he began by honestly stating the case. 'My sons are at this moment inside the cave with their dogs. I advised against this, but as many of you will know, Edwin and Nicholas are… impulsive. I hope they'll make an initial survey of the conditions and return to report.'

Trying not to grind my teeth audibly, I hoped so too. But I feared they would only clamber about in there, make a great deal of cheerful noise, alert the rogues we hoped to catch, and befoul our plans. I was recalling half a dozen incidents during the past wars when over eager stupidity had ruined a stealthy approach on an enemy position.

Benson Moreland began to explain the tactics we'd discussed. He spoke briefly but succinctly of his own boyhood expeditions inside the cave system, describing the terrain there, and outlining the dangers. The faces of the assembled dales folk grew still, concentrating on his words. Few, if any, had ever been inside the caves themselves. Probably all of them had been warned away from them as children by old timers like Luke Procter's grandfather. They knew of them only as places of ill-omen, swallowers up of livestock, and if they believed in his literal existence, likely abodes of the Devil himself.

'We need young, active men!' said Benson Moreland, looking around at the faces before him.

If the situation had not been so serious, I'd have got some enjoyment from the reactions to this. Sam Woodley pushed out his chest, ready to take the Commonwealth's coin. George Postlethwaite stood straighter, grim but determined. Benjy took a step forward, an eager volunteer. Malachi's eyes slid sideways to judge his brothers' reactions, then he too straightened up. Richard Hardcastle's hands came together as though he might break into spontaneous prayer, ready for martyrdom if the Lord so willed. Luke Procter shrank back behind his wife, hoping to be overlooked, and Abel retreated to invisibility between the flanks of the two horses he was holding. Gervase caught my eye, and the corner of his mouth twitched in amusement. We'd seen these varied reactions so many times when the New Model called for volunteers.

In the end, with Ling's farm hands and two or three men from other farms in the valley, we were twelve. The Colonel announced that I should lead, and Gervase with me. We would all go forward together for the first fifty paces, just far enough for the man at the back to see, or at the very least if the passage curved, call, to those at the entrance. That man would remain at that point, and the next would be stationed fifty paces ahead of him, and then the next, so that we were strung out along the passage. Colonel Moreland would remain just inside the entrance. I was to pass back information on conditions within, via these men, after covering, if it proved possible, approximately six hundred paces. The Colonel and I would then decide whether it was safe to move forward. Depending what information we found, or failed to find, we would then repeat the exercise.

'I'll stand ready with the ropes' announced Cousin Zeke, 'caves not bein' my element, and play them out or pass them forward as required.' Naval men do not allow themselves to be in any way impressed by what the army does.

I lined my volunteers up, and we struck flints to light the lanterns. Useful, active fellows like Sam and Benjy, I placed towards the front. Men I was less sure of, like the farmhands, towards the rear, and last in line, Richard Hardcastle, whom I judged to be a dreamer. I thought he would be more comfortable offering up prayers for our safety at a distance.

Whilst we were mustering, I noticed that those who remained behind were setting up an encampment. Now that the rescue attempt was beginning, almost a Whitsun Fair atmosphere prevailed. People were still arriving. Old Josiah and Hannah waved to us. The slopes of the little dell were fast filling with people, some of whom had brought baskets of food, and stools to sit on. Abel was herding the horses up the slope out of the way. Luke Procter was assuaging his cowardice by building a fire. Other men and boys hacked at the thorn bushes with knives and sickles, so that the cave mouth was visible from below. The womenfolk seemed to be spreading cloths and preparing plates of food, as though they planned to re-enact the feeding of the five thousand.

At the last moment, before ducking down to enter the cave, I looked up at the sky. The clouds were thicker and darker, and a small breeze was stirring the rowan leaves.

'Pray God we can do this before the rain comes!' I said as I made my way inside.

'Amen!' pronounced Richard at our rear, and his preacher's voice echoed off the rocks ahead, 'Amen! *Amen! Amen… Amen…*' Everyone turned to shush him. We'd agreed not to speak above a whisper, unless we needed to call for help.

We followed the Colonel's orders. The pathway along the side of the stream was reasonably level, and by the time Gervase had counted fifty paces, the ceiling above us was higher, and we no longer had to crouch. Although the walls of the cave bulged out from time to time, we could pass through easily enough. Looking back, when we left him at first post, Richard confirmed he could see the glow of the Colonel's lantern.

'Good enough,' I hissed in reply. 'He'll see yours. Call to him only if you need to, and signal up to the next man, if he sends a message to you.'

We dropped off one of the farm hands at one hundred paces, and Malachi Postlethwaite at one hundred and fifty. The way was becoming rougher. We were beginning to climb, and had to crouch once more, and at the same time watch out for broken places and sudden dips in the floor. The stream ran low, the sound of its rushing muted, but we could hear the drip, drip of water from the roof, and we began to see the strange rock formations Benjy had described. Some even had the appearance, at first glance, of the statues of saints, such as are found on the front of the great cathedrals, and which the Puritans have set about destroying.

At two hundred paces we placed one of the farmers. It was still possible, despite the bulges in the rock wall, to see the glow of the lanterns the men behind were holding. I could even make out that Richard Hardcastle had found a niche in which to lodge his, and was studying a book he'd brought with him.

'Bible?' murmured Gervase, 'I hope he'll not become so engrossed in the fate of Jonah inside the whale, that he fails to heed our signals!'

'Ah feel as how we're in the belly of a whale,' remarked George, gloomily. 'We mun trust in t'Lord that we'll come out of it as well as he did.'

The way was getting steeper, although the ceiling too rose, and we were able to walk upright for a spell. We dropped men off every fifty paces. Then the passage began to bend to the left, and for the first time we could no longer see those behind us, although the glow from the nearest lantern shone faintly on the roof.

'So where's the Colonel's lads?' Sam Woodley hissed, voicing something that had begun to puzzle me. 'Here's us, come three hundred and fifty paces, and neither sight nor sound of 'em! Did they have lanterns?'

'Ah think they'd flints, just,' supplied Benjy.

'And two great unruly dogs,' remarked Gervase, 'who no doubt bounded ahead, with the lads rushing after! We've passed no side turnings. They must be ahead.'

'How well can dogs see in the dark?' I queried.

'Well enough, happen,' replied one of the farmers. 'Better than lads with nobbut flints. 'Tis a wonder they haven't come to grief falling over, or knocking they selves out on these great rock icicles that's hangin' down! Howsoever, we ain't heard any shouts. Though happen we mightn't, above t'sound of t'beck.'

We turned another corner. It was true that the sound of rushing water was getting louder. I wondered if we were getting close to the lower end of Benjy's waterfall. However, at the end of four hundred paces, we did hear something. Childish sniffles and a dog whining. Rounding yet another bend, we found Timmy Procter, forlorn on a rock, his arms wrapped around one of the Bouviers, who was licking his grime encrusted face. I'd completely forgotten Timmy. With all the commotion that had been going on outside in the ghyll, I'd no notion that he'd gone with Edwin and Nicholas into the cave.

'They said Ah should come to help hold t'dogs,' he explained. 'Ah said as tha wouldn't like it, but they paid no heed. And Piet here's gone lame from a thorn in his paw, so they left us.'

'In the dark?' demanded Gervase, shocked. It was an education for him to see how thoughtless those born to privilege can be towards those they see as social inferiors.

Timmy nodded. 'Ah was right frit, but then Ah seed thee coming with t'lanterns, and heard tha footsteps, trampin.'

One of the farmers, the one who was sure that dogs can see in the dark, and who obviously knew them well, lifted Piet's front paw, and with Benjy holding a lantern close, managed to extract the twig of spiny gorse that had lodged itself between the dog's pads. Piet immediately put the paw to the ground, and jumped up to lick his rescuer's face.

'No discipline at all,' Gervase grunted, 'but they're good natured. Take him back outside now, Timmy. You'll find men stationed with lanterns all along the way.'

'Aye, but what about *'im*? Yon man?' demanded the child, nodding his head back over his shoulder towards the stream flowing alongside. 'Happen 'e's been dead awhile, gone stiff like as not. Ah don't know as me Dad could fetch 'im out, even.'

We raised our lanterns and peered down into the stream bed. The body of a man lay half in and half out of the water, his right hand trailing in the current. As Timmy said, he'd been dead sometime. The hand in the stream was already showing signs of what I understand is called calcification, the process by which the elements carried by the water had created those weird rock shapes all around us. By which it can, over time I'm told, turn even a man to solid stone.

'Ah'll tell me Dad, but he won't like it,' said Timmy.

# Chapter 21

We were silent for a beat, then Sam Woodley said, 'Why, 'tis Matthew Garstang.' Others around me peered closer, and agreed.

'Who is he? Was he?' Gervase demanded.

'Jem's cousin from Crook O'Lune.'

'But wasn't he the fellow that was hanged? I know I was told so, and Colonel Moreland confirmed it.'

'Aye,' agreed Sam, 'but some held that t'rope broke, and so he survived and was let go, for they say you can't hang a man twice. Word was he took ship to Ireland, lest the magistrates changed their minds.'

'Word also was, he bribed the hangman to use frayed rope!' rumbled George. 'But the Lord is not mocked! The sinner shall come by his just deserts!'

'Stabbed, rather than hanged this time,' observed Gervase, crouching down to examine the dead man. 'I suppose he was a prime mover amongst these renegades who took the girls? Indeed, he must have been the one who had some hold over Jem. Rob and I thought of him, but were told he was long dead. Did Edwin and Nicholas see this fellow?'

Timmy nodded. 'They said 'twas famous, finding a corpse, and 'twas a good thing, as now there could be only two rogues, not three, and very likely they could overpower them with the dogs to aid them. That was afore they seed Piet had a thorn in his paw.'

'But they still went on?' I asked, 'unfazed that they had only Claes? They carried no swords. Or not that I saw when they dismounted.'

'They'd knives,' said Timmy. 'They drew 'em from out their boots. They'd an argumentation, whether both should hold 'em ready when they went forward, or only Master Edwin, with Master Nicholas holding t'flint. Edwin said very likely, if they stopped sudden, Nicholas would stab 'im in t'back by mistake.'

We too went forward. We placed our next man. The noise of the waterfall grew louder. It was no longer possible to speak in low voices. I judged Edwin and Nicholas would have taken no such precautions, so it wasn't needful anyway. If the villains were within, they'd have had warning enough. At four hundred paces we left George, and at four hundred and fifty, Sam. Reliable men, who would act prudently if we met with violent resistance. At five hundred I placed Benjy, close enough to holler to, if I needed him to run for help.

At five hundred and twenty paces, just short of the mark where Gervase was to take up his position, the passage way divided, two tunnels of equal size running off to the right and left. Gervase uttered another of those blasphemies of which the New Model has failed to cure him. 'Now what, Major Haddon?' he enquired, raising an eyebrow. 'Which do we take?'

We held up our lanterns, examining each tunnel for signs that people had passed one way rather than the other. We found none.

'Unhelpful villains,' Gervase grumbled. 'They might at least have marked the way with an arrow, so we'd guess they were misleading us, and take the other. We should have brought Timmy and Piet. Presumably Claes showed the way to the twins.'

'I'd best send Benjy back down the line to fetch Piet,' I began, but before I could put this into action, frightened yells and pounding footsteps issued from the right hand tunnel, and Nicholas Moreland fell out of it, collapsing at our feet.

He was a sorry sight. His feathered hat was gone, his smart sateen coat and Brussels lace collar were filthy, his breeches torn and soaked.

'Oh, Masters!' cried he, evidently not recognising us in the shadowy lantern light. 'Help me! My brother is lost! The water carried him away!'

'Edwin?' enquired Gervase. The boy was hysterical.

'Oh 'tis horrible! He was climbing... the waterfall divides the way... we couldn't find a bridge... there is one...a plank... but 'twas on the other side... Edwin thought... if we climbed to the top of the spout... 'tis narrow there, where the water pushes through the rock... we could step across.'

'He slipped?'

'The force of the water... carried him down, and I couldn't... I tried to catch hold of his coat but...'

'So he fell into some chasm below this present level? Could you see him? Or has the waterfall carried him yet further?'

'Mayhap further!' Nicholas began to sob, helplessly.

'We need ropes,' I told Gervase. 'Don't bother to pass it on. Send Benjy running to the entrance straight away.'

'A ladder might be useful, if anyone could contrive one!' I called after him as he started back down the passage. 'When you return, the *right hand* passage! I'll go and reconnoitre with Nicholas!' I hauled the lad to his feet.

'Thee is Robert Haddon, from Lowflatts,' he stated. 'Thee should call me Master Nicholas,' he added, churlishly.

I raised the lantern so that it shone on both our faces. 'You are fortunate I'm willing to call you anything but a *stupid, addle pated*...young fool! If you're to be Master Nicholas to me, then I'm Major Haddon to you, who has served with your father the Colonel, and know where respect is due. It is not due to you and your idiotic brother. By your antics you may have already jeopardised our efforts to rescue those two girls. Now, show me to this waterfall. If we can get to your brother we will. But this rescue mission is intended to find two innocent young women who didn't deserve what's happened to them. What became of the dog?'

For a moment he looked so bemused that I thought he was going to say, 'What dog?' but he pulled himself together, and instead said, 'I don't know. He ran on. I think he must have leapt across the stream…or mayhap he was swept down too. I didn't notice.'

'Start noticing now, *Master* Nicholas! That's a valuable animal on which you have spent a good deal of your father's money. 'Tis a shame you then neglected to train him, but he has good instincts, and could be of help to us.'

He trailed after me, sullenly. After several yards he told my back, "Twas not Father's money. He wouldn't send any. My uncle, Mama's brother, kept us in funds. Father didn't care if we starved!'

I didn't bother to turn and look at him. 'I doubt that. I think your father sent sufficient to keep you in comfort, but being silly fellows, you got into debt.'

'Thee wouldn't understand! 'Twas expensive living in Antwerp. The set of men we were friendly with…we had to pay our share.'

'Never mind that!' I stopped him, sharply. We were coming close to the waterfall. 'Let's see if we can find your brother.'

The waterfall was not in full spate. Due to the dry weather which had blessed our hay making it had dwindled, more even since Benjy had seen it nearly a week ago, yet it was still a mighty force, roaring and tumbling over the rocks and disappearing down into the bowels of the earth.

It was obvious what had happened. About six feet above our heads jutted a harder layer of rock, which the constant passage of the torrent had fashioned into a spout, not unlike the lip of a great jug. Here, the water spilled from a narrow channel, and if one could safely climb up there, it would be possible to step across, and climb down the other side. The twins had attempted this, but Edwin, in his haste, had failed to realise how wet and slippery the rocks, drenched in spray, would be, and had lost his footing. He'd fallen into the cascade, which had carried him on down into the abyss.

'I only had a flint, Major Haddon, I couldn't see anything below,' whined Nicholas. Faced with the roaring waterspout, and enormity of what had happened, he was humbled sufficiently to address me civilly.

It would be difficult, even with a lantern. The last thing I needed was for the water either to douse the flame, or worse still, snatch the lamp from me. I chose a spot as far away from the spray as was possible, and crouched. It was awkward, in the confines of the passage opening, to lie full length and peer into the depths. Lowering the lantern without getting it wet was nigh on impossible. Yet, by angling it to and fro, I managed to make out, about fifteen feet below us on a rock just clear of the main thrust of the water, a patch of white that must be Edwin's lace trimmed collar.

I called down to him, using his full name, 'Edwin Moreland? Can you hear me?'

I heard nothing above the water's roar, but had the fleeting impression that the white patch moved. It was possible that Edwin lived, injured, how badly I couldn't guess. I told his brother this.

'Can we get to him?' he demanded, beginning to whimper.

'*We* cannot,' I told him, 'but others are on their way. My cousin Ezekiel is a sailor, and handy with ropes. He got Benjamin Postlethwaite out of a deep hole further up the fell, but I don't know whether he can do anything here.'

I'd never thought there would come a day when the one person that I wanted to see above all would be snaggle toothed, bow legged Cousin Zeke. When he arrived, slung about with Luke's coffin ropes, and accompanied by others carrying more, I made an inner vow that whether he succeeded here or no, I should at least offer to employ him in my shop.

With him, of course, since Benjy had faithfully delivered the message, came Benson Moreland, to see what had befallen to his son and heir. The rest of our carefully spaced line of men had fallen in behind him. This didn't matter any longer, since we knew the way out was passable, and the only rogue to be found along that stretch was dead, but it made for a crowd at the waterfall.

'Is it feasible to reach him?' Colonel Moreland asked; always the quiet professional soldier, no matter what his inner distress might be.

Zeke was weighing up the situation, sucking on those blackened teeth. ''Twill be difficult, Sir. If he lives 'tis worth a try. If not …' he shrugged his shoulders.

I said, 'When I called his name I thought he moved. He may have spoken. It's impossible to hear anything above the noise of the water.'

While we were speaking Zeke's eyes travelled around, looking for rocks to tie ropes around, anything that would help.

'There's good sized plank across on the other side,' he remarked. 'If we could get that to bridge the stream t'would be easier.'

'Ah could climb up, go over the spout, and toss it across,' offered Benjy.

'No! It's too dangerous, Ben,' I said. 'That's what Edwin tried, and fell.'

'And I ain't inclined to pull thee out of a hole twice!' decided Zeke. 'No, I'll try for it with a loop. See, how it's propped agin yon rock? With a good piece standing clear? If I can get a loop of rope around it, and pull tight, I can drag it across. 'Tis risky, but we do it on shipboard, when something falls into the hold, or when there's no one on shore to hitch us to a bollard. Ain't easy mind! You lot'll have to stand back and give me space.' We retreated to the passage while Zeke plied his rope. No one mentioned what might happen to Edwin if the plank fell into the chasm.

*141*

'Your cousin learned his skills on shipboard?' Benson Moreland asked, quietly. 'He seems to know what he is doing.'

'I think he does. I pray so,' I replied.

'Father?' began Nicholas.

'Not now, Nicholas. It's useless for you to tell me that you didn't mean this to happen, just as it's useless for me to remind you that I forbade you both to go into the cave.'

The boy's face crumpled, and he began to weep, choking on his sobs. The rest of us stood in discomfited silence, listening to the water crashing down beyond the tunnel mouth.

Then Zeke called, 'Cousin Rob! Benjamin! Just you two, come through.'

We went. 'Come and lie down and see can you guide this thing into place?' he said, panting. He'd snared the plank with a loop of thick rope, and dragged it across the rocks to the edge of the water channel.

'If I pull it out too far it'll tip into the current, and I'll lose it. I've seen a few gang planks lost that way. Stretch your arms out and grab it when I have it about half way across. Just your arms, don't lean too far and tip yourselves in!'

It was awkward indeed, in such a confined space, for the two of us to lie in the opening of the tunnel alongside Zeke, but we managed. Slowly, as Zeke pulled, the plank began to jut out over the water. Once it slithered and wobbled on a rock, but then I caught hold of the leading edge, and then Benjy caught it too, and we guided it until we had it across, and firmly set in place.

'There,' grunted Zeke, 'as good a gang plank as ever I saw. I'll warrant your rogues have been using this as a bridge. Mayhap they usually leave it in place, and draw it back when they're at home and fear visitors. 'Twould be easy enough to drop it in place from the other side.'

'So, what now?' I asked.

'Send me George and Malachi to sit on either end and keep it secure, and I'll rope myself up, and go down.'

Why George and Malachi? Benjy and I could...'

'No. George and Malachi are heavy set fellows, and not likely to give way to excitement. *You* need to go across to look for your sister, in case you'd forgotten?'

# Chapter 22

I'd been distracted from our original mission, and it discomforted me to be reminded of it by Cousin Zeke. He was, of course, right. If I was to have any hope of finding the girls before the weather broke I should be on my way.

We stayed just long enough, having walked the plank to the other side, to see Zeke, fastened into a rope harness of his own devising, lower himself from the centre of the plank into the gorge — and hear him shout up that Edwin lived, though he feared his legs were broken. We didn't stay to see the elaborate rope cradle he then fashioned to lift him (he told Colonel Moreland this was the way sailors loaded fragile cargo from shore to ship) to the surface.

Instead, Gervase, Benjy, Sam Woodley and I, set forth to complete our original mission. The Colonel gave us his blessing, and a warning that he thought the rains would be upon us in another hour. An hour! What chance was there that we could find the girls and bring them out in that small space of time?

'Can we do it?' Gervase asked.

'Probably not,' I replied. 'And if they're dead, there is no point, but at least we'll know for sure, and turn back and save ourselves.'

'The water rises right quick, as I understand,' said Sam. 'If t'rain comes on heavy we'll stand no chance!' He sounded remarkably cheerful about it.

Gervase produced his weighty round Nuremburg watch from his coat pocket, and peered at it against his lantern. It showed only the hours, but he knew its movement well enough to calculate whereabouts we were in the present hour. 'Half an hour forward, then we beat retreat,' he pronounced.

But only minutes brought us to an opening in the rock wall, and found us staring down into a cavern the size of a great cathedral. We stepped out onto a broad ledge about eight feet above the ground, and looked around. It was a truly amazing place. Huge rock formations grew out of the floor and hung from the ceiling. At one end these rocky growths had met, top and bottom, curving out so they looked like a great stone couch on which a giant might take his ease. The floor of the cavern resembled a shallow bowl, which must in a wetter season hold a lake big enough for a boat to sail on. Now, this had shrunk until it was no more than a pool, and by this pool stood two men. One was a big hefty fellow, the other a scrawny runt. Standing on a jutting rock, just beyond the reach of the big fellow, who was making vicious passes at him with a long-bladed knife, was a black woolly dog.

I would never have expected to find anything comical in that awe inspiring place, but it's a fact that we all four had to clap our hands over our mouths to keep from shouting with mirth. The big man was red in the face with rage and effort, trying to stab Claes, who leapt nimbly out of his reach, and then advanced again, barking and snarling.

More droll still was the behaviour of his skinny companion. He, too, had a knife, but was evidently desperate to pass water, and instead of lunging at the dog, was clutching frantically at the front of his breeks, so that the blade seemed likely to castrate him! Neither of them had noted our arrival. The big man was tiring, but the little man was desperate. He rushed over to a crevasse in the rock below us, threw down his knife, pulled apart his breeks and began to relieve himself. A great jet of piss streamed forth, almost rivalling the waterfall we'd left behind.

Six years in the army sharpens men's responses. I only glanced at Gervase and he at me.

'Take him! Benjy, jump on his back! Sam, we'll take the other!' he hissed.

'Ain't goin' t'jump on his front for certain!' said Benjy, and leapt. I flung myself after him. From the corner of my eye I saw Gervase and Sam run along the ledge and rush at the big man. Surprise is often the winning tactic in battles, great or small. Our little fellow collapsed, winded, to the ground under the shock of Benjy's sudden arrival on his shoulders.

'Ah can sit on 'im,' he said, calmly. 'Tha go after t'other 'un.'

I scooped up the little fellow's knife and ran to aid Gervase and Sam. The big man was giving combat, although he was already outnumbered by two men and a dog. Sam had no weapon, but while Gervase held him off, knife blade clashing against sword, he went behind him, and, quite calmly, as though he was dealing with a recalcitrant ewe at shearing time, put a strangle hold around his neck. Claes, who'd been awaiting his moment, flew down and fastened his teeth into his leg. Our adversary howled with pain, and lashed out wildly, catching my forearm as I lunged for his knife. Luckily for me, the strangle hold had taken the last of his breath, and what might have been a great gash, merely drew a thin trail of blood. Our man collapsed, purple of face, the knife falling harmlessly to the ground.

'Rope?' Gervase panted. He, too, was bleeding from a cut between thumb and forefinger.

'Can't see any.' My eyes skimmed the cavern.

'Tek me belt,' gasped Sam. He pulled it free with one hand and passed it over. Between us, Gervase and I got the man's arms pinioned behind his back.

'There's plenty else we could use,' I panted, looking round whilst trying to avoid our captive's kicks. The men had evidently been doing their laundry. Tattered shirts were draped over rocks. We tore them up, and tied our two villains securely. They used a lot of words we didn't think a young lad like Benjy ought to hear. (It appeared these were the rogues' best shirts).

However, if he was serious about joining the Army, he would soon hear worse. We could have gagged the rogues, but we wanted to know what they'd done with the girls. Sullen silence was our only reward. Time was running out. We'd been gone half an hour or perhaps more, and for all we knew, outside the rain was already falling.

As I have said, I'm uncomfortable about using torture, but there was no time now for persuasion. Gervase was already holding his sword so that the point pricked at the little man's Adam's apple.

Speak! Or I cut your vile throat! Stop snivelling! We know what you did to Jem Robinson! We know you killed the girl at the farm, and the priest! We've seen the body of your comrade, Matthew Garstang! *Where are those two girls?'*

The big man growled, as though, even at this extreme, he was forbidding his companion to tattle, but Gervase had chosen the right man to intimidate.

'Ah niver!' the little fellow gabbled,' Ah niver killed Matthew! 'Twas Zadoc here, and 'twas Matthew killed Jem!'

Then he added, 'And them girls is up on high.'

Up on high. He could only mean they were in Heaven. I felt my heart crack within me. If only we'd found this place sooner. If only I'd taken Benjy's tale of hearing music seriously, and come back next day to search the caves! Looking round now, I saw any number of articles leaning against rocks, piled against one another. My despairing eye noted a trumpet, a fiddle, and a squeeze box such as sailors use. There was other booty too, some tarnished silver plate, a small chest, broken open, a pair of pewter candle sticks, several pairs of good boots in a variety of sizes. These wretches had been stealing whatever they could from the surrounding houses and farms. Somewhere they must have acquired a fife and drum, and in their idle hours perhaps amused themselves, playing them. I stood silent, sorrowfully absorbing how close we had come to finding Ann and Rachel, and how tragically we had failed.

'Anyway,' whined our captive, 'Matthew only meant to lame the priest, to keep 'im from 'is meddlin'... and *we* niver killed that girl at the farm! 'Twas not us did that!'

'Matt Garstang told us we wus to take them two girls after he heard t'other one was dead.' growled Zadoc. 'He said as 'twas our orders to do so.' His comrade having told so much, he evidently wanted to put the record straight. 'Job here, and me, we only did what Matthew told us. And I killed Matthew in a fair fight! 'Twas him or me! He was a devil when he was in drink! He'd spent all our siller on liquor, and brought back no provisions!' he added, indignant at the memory.

'Job, eh?' sighed Gervase, locking eyes with the little fellow. 'Thee is past needing a comforter. Do we try to take these two back with us, Rob?

Then hand them over to the Magistrate, or shall we leave them, and let the rising water do its work?'

'I care not...' I began, when Benjy interrupted me, suddenly saying, 'What didst tha mean, when tha said the girls are up on high? Is tha saying they're dead?'

Both rogues looked outraged.

'Nay! Up yonder! 'squeaked Job 'Well, they may be dead, for since Zadoc fought with Matthew and slew him for bringing us no provender, we haven't dared go out. Like as not they've eaten nowt these past days. We'd only crusts us selves.'

While he spoke his eyes travelled up the side of the rocky chamber to a ledge high above our heads. 'Matthew put 'em up there so we couldn't touch 'em! He said as one was to be wife to Jem, and Jem wouldn't aid him no more, nor keep mum, even if he hung for it, if we tried any love games with those girls. I've a notion Matt was minded to marry t'other one himself!'

'They could've come down, if they wanted to,' supplied Zadoc,' Matt had 'em pull up the ladder, but they could've let it down. We'd 'ave shared with 'em, such fodder as we had. But they wouldn't answer us,' he added. 'So likely they've starved to death. Too niffy-naffy, for the likes of us.'

My wits were so bludgeoned by this turn of events, that I could hardly react sensibly. It was Gervase who ran across the floor of the chamber and began calling up to them. 'Ann! Mistress Ann! Are you there? 'Tis Gervase Fenton, and your brother Robert come to find you!' Then Benjy joined him, bawling Rachel's name. I stumbled across, adding my voice, absorbing my wonder that it was Ann's name alone that Gervase had called. Little Ann, *my baby sister*? Was it possible that it was Ann's shy smile, and not Loveday's beauty that had drawn my friend back to Lowflatts time and again?

The great cavern with its soaring ceiling distorted our voices, altered them, and carried them away. The sound of the waterfall, though muted by the rock wall we had passed through, was ever present. Were the girls alive? Could they hear us? If starvation had rendered them too weak to move from whatever beds they had contrived for themselves, would they be able to respond? Would they realise that we were here?

''Tis pity we've no ladder,' opined Sam, ever matter of fact, 'or we could go up and take a look.'

Our throats became hoarse with shouting. Claes, who had been sniffing disdainfully at our prisoners, began to whine and bark. Perhaps he already sensed, as we later discovered, that outside rain had begun to fall, and time was running out.

Then, just as hope was beginning to change to despair, a thin white face, just visible by the light of our upheld lanterns, hovered above the edge of the rock ledge. Rachel Postlethwaite peered down at us.

'Our Rachel!' yelled Benjy. 'Canst get t'ladder? We've no ladder to get thee down!'

The face disappeared. We stood, helpless. Perhaps she was too weak to speak, too ill from starvation and neglect to understand? Then we could just make out scraping sounds, as a ladder was, with great difficulty, dragged across rocks. Two sets of heads and shoulders appeared, bowed with effort, pushing something before them. We jumped back several feet as the ladder came crashing down.

Both girls were alive! Alive but weak from three days living on sips of water, from a meagre pool in their cave. The refuge Jem's cousin Matthew had placed them in was, we were to learn, a cave within a cave, too high up in the smooth wall of the great cavern to be reached by climbing. In doing so, he'd defended them from ravishment, that much we understood. Why he'd felt compelled to do so, we did not then enquire. Getting the girls down the ladder was hazardous enough. Rachel, perhaps the sturdier of the two to begin with, managed to creep down, rung by rung, clinging on desperately until the willing hands of Benjy and Sam took her weight and lifted her clear. Ann managed to turn and step onto the top rung and begin the descent, but then her strength failed, and she slipped and fell. Gervase and I caught her between us, and held her, before she dropped to the floor.

'We must get out of here!' I muttered. Little daylight had seemed to penetrate the great cavern when we first arrived, but the darkness had imperceptibly thickened. The waterfall had acquired, I thought, a new, deeper throated boom.

'What of these fellows?' asked Sam, indicating our two rogues.

'Let them go,' I answered, and to Zadoc and Job I said, 'Stay and drown, or go and hang! We've no time for you.' Freed of their bonds by my clasp knife they made off through the opening in the rock, like rabbits fleeing their burrow. Claes, seeing his enemies escaping, bounded after them.

'You were hasty there, Rob,' said Gervase grimly, 'I fancy those rogues won't stop until they reach the open air. God help us if they pull that plank away. And it's likely they will run into the other rescue party. We should have tried to keep them with us.'

'How?' I asked.

'Why let 'em go?' chimed in Sam. 'I'd have left them to drown.'

The girls, weakened by their ordeal, struggled to walk. We had to lift them up onto the rock ledge by which we had first entered the cavern. Thereafter Rachel, supported by her brother, managed to make headway. Ann however, wavered and stumbled, and seemed likely to faint, until Gervase lifted her bodily and placed her over his shoulder, as I've seen men carry the injured from burning houses. Sam strode ahead, lighting our way.

I brought up the rear, anxious now, about the two thieves I'd let go. Oft times a decision, made in the heat of a skirmish, has haunted me for days. I'd made a snap decision on what seemed best at the time, but had I in fact made things worse, brought further harm or death to others? I knew that there was no way we could have brought the men out as prisoners, but now I was afraid of what they might do, in their desperation, to the other rescue party. If successful in rescuing Edwin, they must, surely, be ahead of us, carrying the boy to safety and medical attention? Zadoc and Job had lost their weapons, but their frantic bodies, charging into a line of people transporting a gravely wounded youth, could kill him, and injure several others.

We reached the plank bridge without incident. It stood slightly askew, as though someone had run across it in haste and half kicked it aside, but Sam straightened it, and we crossed over. I offered to help Gervase carry Ann, but he said it would be easier to do it alone, and indeed her weight seemed so slight that the plank bent no more under their combined weight than it had when Sam alone tramped across.

Everyone was gone from that place. Either Zeke had succeeded in raising Edwin from the waterfall, or the attempt had been abandoned. I didn't allow myself to look down. If either Edwin or Zeke had perished here, I could do nothing. Already, as I'd feared, there was more water pouring down from above. The weight and volume of it had spread beyond the narrow lip in the rock, and great waves of spray lashed us as we hurried across the plank bridge. The tunnel we were now walking through had, after all, been created not by human endeavour, but by the water itself, boring through the rock to its outlet on the fellside. Already I could see that the bed of the stream was filling up. Soon the water would be flowing over our feet, and we'd six hundred paces still to travel, with two frail girls. The passageway was too narrow for Benjy to walk beside Rachel, so now he put her before him, holding her shoulders and guiding her forward. I could hear him speaking to his sister, encouraging her to move quickly, and she seemed to make some reply, but their progress was stumbling and slow. When we reached the place where the floor of the passage was uneven, she staggered and fell. Gervase was labouring too, despite Ann's meagre weight. It was time for another decision.

'Sam, take Rachel on your back for a spell. Benjy, walk behind in case she slips. It will be awkward for you, but there's no time to stop. I'll come past you and hold two lanterns. I'll try to hold one high and one low, so that you can judge where to crouch, and what lies underfoot. We must keep going. The water's rising!'

So far, I was relieved to note, we'd seen no sign of the other rescue team, (or indeed of Zadoc and Job). I prayed this meant they were already out of the caves, out of the ghyll, and conveying the injured Edwin home.

We turned a corner, and then another. Sam was tiring, carrying Rachel, and began to stumble. She whispered that she thought she could walk again, and between them Sam and Benjy set her down. Gervase took the opportunity to transfer Ann from his shoulder to carrying her in his arms. We set forth again, and turned another corner. Now I could make out a slice of daylight, though it was blocked by a slow moving procession before us. We were about to catch up with the others.

There was no way we could pass them, the walkway beside the stream was far too narrow, and walking in the rock strewn stream bed was far too difficult for the girls. They were moving very gradually, and now came to a halt. I signalled to my party to wait, catching up with George, who was their lantern bearer. I soon saw why they had halted. Across the open mouth of the cave rain fell in great slanting sheets. Thunder growled, and lightening flared. The weather had broken with a vengeance.

'We can't go 'til they raise t'canvas,' George called back to us. 'Can't tek t'lad out in this.'

'Zeke got him?'

'Aye, but he's mortal bad. T'surgeon's sent for, and they're raising a canvas on t'high ground.'

'We got your sister and Ann. They're here, behind me. No great harm has come to them… just lack of food.'

George peered back, glimpsed his sister, and intoned, 'The Lord God be praised, for He is merciful!'

I returned to tell my party what the holdup was. 'You can see the extent of the rain! They're afraid to take Edwin out in it. He must already be suffering from the effects of cold and wet. Someone's gone to fetch a surgeon, and they'll raise the canvas to make a tent. We must wait.'

'I trust not long!' said Gervase. He seated Ann gently on a ledge, holding her upright. I saw what he meant. The stream, rushing alongside us, was becoming a churning torrent. Already it reached the rim of the walkway, and was lapping at our boot soles.

# Chapter 23

The waiting seemed endless. The water rose; slowly at first, covering our insteps, then our calves, then creeping towards our boot tops. Rachel was shivering with cold and exhaustion, and Benjy and I managed to lift her onto the ledge alongside Ann, where they sat, crammed together, arms around one another, for warmth, and to keep from falling.

'We can't stay here much longer,' observed Gervase, and staggering even as he spoke. The water swirled around his knees, nearly dragging him into the stream.

Then George, ahead of us, raised his arm, signalling that his party were moving forward. Squinting at the tiny section of sky visible beyond the cave mouth, I saw the rain was slackening. Edwin's rescuers must have decided it was now or never. The current swirled about our legs so strongly now, that it was as much as we could do to remain upright. When we moved, the water spilled into our boots, dragging us down. The torrent had risen well above the walkway. We could no longer see the divide between it and the stream, and were in danger at every step of plunging in up to our waists.

'The girls..' I began. The two of them sat huddled together in their rock niche, eyes huge above their sunken cheeks, reminding me of two fledgling birds nesting in the wall of a barn, stiff with terror whilst the barn cats prowled below. There was no way, I believed, that weakened by lack of nourishment, they'd be able walk through this raging flood. And no way we could carry them to safely.

'Happen us needs help,' said Benjy. He spoke for us all.

'Rope,' said Sam. 'If us had a rope we could tie it to yon pillar, aye and yon too, and mek summat to hold onto. Get closer to t'entrance.'

A useful idea. If we had rope. The rock columns growing up from the floor at intervals along the tunnel would make sturdy hitching posts, and a rope stretching between them a valuable handrail. Clinging to it, we might keep our balance and wade forward without being swept away. Ann and Rachel might not be strong enough to maintain a grip, but if a *secondary* rope were tied around their waists and looped around this handrail…

'Can you run through this water, Ben?'

In any other circumstances I'd have already dispatched Benjy for Cousin Zeke. He replied now by pulling off his boots and tossing them into the churning brown torrent. He watched them, borne on the flood, bobbing towards the mouth of the cave, and sighed hugely.

'They'd only weigh me down, full o' water.' He set off, slipping and sloshing, sliding off the relatively smooth walkway onto the stony base of the flooding stream, scrambling out, and stumbling forward again. We saw him duck out through the cave entrance, a black shape against the oval of

*150*

light.

We waited another age. At least the water rose no further. The brief storm, though violent, had for the moment passed.

Of course, I should have warned Ben to be circumspect. Hadn't I, after all, spent the last six years in the company of excitable youths? But I hadn't, and so he must have burst from the cave mouth, soaked to the skin, and dripping like some monster risen from the deep, carolling forth his news. The rest of what he'd said was probably drowned by the happy cheers of his hearers. Inside the cave we heard nothing but the rushing of water, but outside he must have started a small riot.

As we were later to discover, the main wrath of the storm had passed, but not before the gathering in the ghyll had been forced to abandon their feast. A rough canvas tent had been erected, under which the womenfolk had retreated, and where they were able to receive the gravely injured Edwin. The boys and men had taken what cover they could beneath a couple of carts left at the top of the slope, from which inadequate shelter they were eager enough to come forth, never staying to listen to Benjy's request for ropes.

So, half a dozen likely lads shoved and pushed their way into the mouth of our cave, capsizing the lantern Colonel Moreland had left at the entrance, and plunging themselves into darkness. Their yells and curses reverberated off the walls and roof of the passage. Fortunately for them, and ultimately for us, I had ours still, which enabled them to see where we were, although they remained a confusion of dark shapes to us, against the brightening sky.

As they plunged forward, splashing, cursing, falling down and scrambling up again, I tried to take control of the situation, by barking out the order to 'Halt!' It was a waste of my breath. I can only say that what works on the battlefield (although, if I'm honest, not always there) had no effect on these excitable farmhands.

They hurtled towards us, yelling, and elbowing one another aside in their attempts to seize hold of the girls and drag them from their niche. Ann's and Rachel's cries of alarm rose above the shouts of excitement (theirs) and orders to desist (ours). Someone knocked one of the lanterns from my hand, and I heard the glass shatter against the wall of the tunnel. Now we had broken glass in the bed of the stream to add to the hazards. Gervase, infuriated, lashed out with his fists. Sam added his brawn to the fray, kicking at shins and private parts, wherever he could make contact, and trying to shove our would-be rescuers back. I was hampered by the necessity to hold onto our remaining lantern. All I could do was bellow above the fracas.

'Stop! In the name of God!'

I was surprised as well relieved when they did. It could all so easily have ended in tragedy — a mob of well-intentioned idiots, determined to be heroes, accidently killing the people they'd come to save.

'That's why they made this man a Major,' Gervase growled at them in the sudden silence. 'A good pair of lungs and a loud voice. Now listen to him, you beef wits!'

'Don't come any nearer,' I warned. 'Apart from nearly killing us and frightening the young women, those of you who are barefooted are going to cut your feet to ribbons on the glass that's just been broken when some lunatic knocked the lantern out of my hand.'

There were the expected mutters of 'only trying to help,' and 'couldn't see what us was doing, could us?'

By holding a lamp aloft I could now see that what had seemed an incalculable mob was in fact only four or five youths, all now extremely wet, the water swirling around their thighs.

'Along the edge of this tunnel,' I explained, measuring out my words, 'there's a ledge, currently under a few inches of water, along which it's possible to walk. Since you're already wet to your skins, there's no point in your using it. However, if you turn and walk back the way you came, with two or three of you each supporting one of the young women, who will walk on the ledge, we may all get out safely. As you've already discovered, there are hollows and rocks on the bed of the stream, which will cause you to stumble and perhaps fall. When that happens, I want you to drop the hand or arm of the girl you are helping, so that she isn't dragged into the water with you. It's to be hoped one of your comrades can hold her in place. Gervase and Sam here, will space themselves between the girls so that they too can give them support and guide them forward. We'll proceed slowly and cautiously. If either of the girls stumbles or seems likely to faint, we'll stop immediately while she recovers. I'll lead the way, as I have the only source of light.'

'I won't faint. I won't! I can walk without anyone holding me,' said a voice. They were the first words I had heard Ann say since we found her.

She did too, although where she found the strength after days of fear and starvation, I know not. So, too, did Rachel. Now that their ordeal was nearly over, hope must have given them new fortitude, and they waded through the water, skirts kirtled up, as though taking a stroll through the garth in the dew of morning.

It was we men who felt like sinking to the ground in relief when at last we emerged into the watery sunlight of the ghyll, and saw the two girls swept into the arms of Hannah, Martha and Deb, all of them weeping tears of joy. I could have lain down there and then, on the sodden grass, and Gervase summed up how we all felt, saying, 'I must be growing old, Rob. I felt better after a whole day's fighting at Edgehill, and on that day we lost!'

Today we'd won. Our girls were safe. What had become of their kidnappers we didn't know, nor were any of us in a mood to wonder. There was rejoicing, but also concern for the injured Edwin, and presently such joy as there was, was cut short. I was just beginning an explanation to Benson Moreland, of how we had found Ann and Rachel, when a figure on a chestnut mare rode over the rim of the ghyll. Even as she approached it could be seen that Lady Brilliana's spine was rigid, her eyes furious. She'd brought with her, in lieu of a groom, and looking surprisingly at home bestride a rough coated pony, the smelly old servant, Joseph.

'What has become of my son, husband?' demanded the Lady.

'Edwin is injured my dear. He met with an accident…' the Colonel began. 'You may see for yourself. He's yonder, beneath the canvas. The surgeon has been sent for, but in the meanwhile our neighbours are doing their best to make him comfortable.'

'I already know he met with an accident!' she snapped. 'Have not all our servants deserted their work to come rushing here? Do you not think I asked them why?' Her angry gaze swept the assembled company. 'How is it, husband, that you can command a regiment but cannot keep your own sons out of danger? I suppose you *encouraged* them to go exploring these caves?'

'No, Mama, he did not. Truly. Tell her, Nicholas, how it was. How you disobeyed Papa!' Judith, tugging roughly at her brother's elbow, stepped forward to give her father support.

"Twas an accident, as Father said,' the lad mumbled, flushed and miserable. 'We thought… that is… Edwin thought, t'would be a f-famous adventure if we could be the f-first to f-find the missing girls. The dogs were hot on the scent! But Edwin missed his f-footing and slipped…' His voice quavered and died away.

It seemed that, until that moment, Lady Brilliana had not registered that Ann and Rachel were found. Her expression changed as she spotted them now, sitting, wrapped in blankets, under the shelter of an overhanging rock. I could almost swear she was disconcerted. Had she not realised that this was the whole purpose of the expedition? Was she embarrassed to have upbraided her husband so publically, and never asked after the girls' welfare?

'I'm glad your sister is found,' she said, turning to me. 'Your mother will be relieved. It's only a pity to me that a way could not have been discovered to find them without involving Edwin.' With no word of thanks that we'd saved Edwin from his folly, she touched her mare's flank with her whip, and rode across to where her injured son lay.

'My wife resembles the tigress when her young are endangered,' murmured Colonel Moreland. He didn't appear embarrassed at his wife's public outburst, merely sombre. Perhaps he knew there would be more to come when the extent of Edwin's injuries became clear.

'What we must now do, Major Haddon,' he went on, dismissing his children, 'is work out how to get your sister and the Postlethwaite girl, as well as my son, away from here. It's plain that the girls are exhausted. They did well to achieve what they did inside that fearful place. And, if we can transport him without adding to his hurts, we must get Edwin home. I can leave word at the tavern in Beckside that the surgeon, when he comes, should ride on to Lings.'

It wasn't an order, but of course Gervase and I took it as one. Planning a withdrawal from the field is as much a part of warfare as a sortie or a charge. We'd both done it many times, and with more wounded to escort to safety than we had here today. These past years it had become almost as normal to us as breathing. We rallied the men. Had them lift Edwin onto one of the carts. Commandeered the other, which belonged to a farmer who would have preferred to go straight home to his milking now the excitement was over. The whole could have been organised in a trice, but for the women. Although every army has its camp followers, they, as well as their menfolk, know the rules. These independently minded dales women however, were not inclined to pay much heed to mere men giving orders. First they must fuss around Edwin, tucking shawls about him. Then they must load up the baskets with the left over provisions (which would 'come in'). Then it was decided that Martha's children must also be put into the cart with Ann and Rachel. Then it was discovered that several people's belongings had been mislaid, and must be sought and retrieved. Amongst them, Benjy's sodden boots, which I suppose he was glad to have, although I doubted they would be anything but misshapen, once they dried out.

The last straw for me was that one of the carthorses stood on my foot, bruising my instep. A minor matter, but it seemed to me that I was doomed to receive as many injuries off the battlefield as I ever had on it. However, we got down from the fell at last, and it was all worth it, to see Mother's beaming face as she opened the door and saw Ann being helped from the cart to run into her arms.

# Chapter 24

'Twas not that I was expecting a reward,' Cousin Zeke was remarking, next morning, as I hobbled into the kitchen from the cow byre, favouring my bruised foot. He was standing at one end of the table, engaged in chopping onions. 'But a word or two of thanks for rescuing the boy would not have come amiss.'

'I'm sure Colonel Moreland *will* thank thee, Zeke,' Mother soothed. She was rolling out pastry at the other end of the table. 'It's been a bad shock for them. Edwin is the heir, and a favourite with his grandfather, the Earl, or so Lady Brilliana says.'

'What of that, since he's not heir to the Earldom, and that family has no money anyway?' drawled Gervase, who was sitting on the window ledge, paring his nails. Benjy was perched beside him, eating a crust liberally spread with Mother's gooseberry preserve. 'Though I suppose he's less of a clodpoll than Nicholas,' Gervase went on. 'He'll probably learn to run the Lings estate well enough if his legs mend.'

'Judith could manage Lings better than either of her brothers!' a husky little voice chimed in. Ann was seated, huddled in layers of rugs and shawls, in a chair by the fire. Mother had only permitted her baby to rise if she consented to be treated as an invalid. I was puzzled, for a moment, to account for the black rug covering her feet. Then it sat up and yawned, and I saw it was one of the Flemish Bouviers.

'Claes,' said Gervase, with a shrug. 'Well, we think it is. Abel took Piet home. This one was whining on the doorstep this morning when Benjy here first went out to see to the rabbit snares. We set him to find Ann, and he carried on until he found her!'

'He did...' Ann said, her lip beginning to tremble. 'Those terrible men! He's a brave dog, he tried and tried to bite them! The big one, Zadoc, would have killed him. He kept dashing at him with a knife!' She turned to me. 'Rob, I don't have to marry Jem Robinson do I? Not now? He made me promise. But I only agreed so that he'd make those men take an oath they wouldn't touch us! Rachel and me.'

'I was sorry for Jem, in a way,' she went on, 'because he was afraid of them. Especially the man he called his cousin, Matthew. But Matthew must have been beholden to Jem too, because he put us up in that high place. And they *didn't* touch us, or only a little at first.' She looked at Mother, and tears began to trickle down her cheeks. "Twas only touching, Mama, through our clothes. We aren't ruined, are we? And... I don't have to marry Jem to save my good name?'

Mother fairly flew across the kitchen in a cloud of flour dust to envelope Ann in her arms. 'There, there! Hush, my sweeting! You don't

*155*

have to marry anyone! You are safe now from those wicked men!'

'You cannot marry Jem Robinson,' said Gervase, firmly, 'firstly because he is gravely injured and may die, and secondly because you are going to marry me. Not yet!' he added, grinning round the room at our gape-mouthed faces. 'But let a year or two pass. Let this wretched war be finally over…whilst you grow into a young lady, and learn to cook as well as your mother.'

There was silence in our kitchen whilst our minds scurried about, trying to assimilate this startling proposal.

'You're jesting with me?'

'No, I'm quite serious.'

'Well then, I thank you for your offer, Master Gervase,' said my sister, solemnly. 'Mama says I have a light hand with pastry… and I always liked you for noticing I existed as well as Loveday…but… I should like to wait a little longer to be wed.'

'So you shall.'

'So you shall indeed, and not to this fellow, if I, as your brother, and head of this household, have any say in the matter!' Miles strode into the kitchen, his step firmer than I had seen it since he'd first risen from his sick bed. Today he was dressed in shirt and breeches, and seemed ready for a quarrel. A sure sign that my brother was recovering his health. 'This Gervase Fenton has been forever hanging around this farm, speaking sweet nothings to the girls,' he added, glaring at me. 'He may be a good soldier. Parliament may trust him, but I don't. Not enough to let him marry my sister! Very like he has a wife already?'

'Not that I ever heard of,' I replied, surprised by his hostility. In truth, I was confused. I wouldn't have believed Gervase's declaration to Ann was serious; yet I'd seen him race across the floor of the cavern yesterday, calling out her name in anguish lest we'd come too late for rescue. 'In my hearing he has always spoken against marriage…'

'Until this war is over, and the peace secure,' Gervase interrupted, folding his clasp knife deliberately and stowing it in his pocket, signalling he didn't intend to quarrel with Miles. 'Which I fear 'tis not. Meanwhile, Mistress Ann may have space to decide for herself.'

'I shall,' said Ann, setting her jaw, and I suddenly saw how like my mother my sister was, and how much she would come to resemble her, both in looks and character, in the years ahead. 'People will talk, won't they? 'she added, turning to look at Mother, whose hands still lay on her shoulders. 'They'll say we were alone with those men, and no matter what Rachel and I insist, some will believe they *did* ravish us. So, if we put it about that I'm to be betrothed…and perhaps Rob, you might be kind enough to offer for Rachel? Then, we will not be pariahs. We can always decide that we don't suit, when all is forgotten.'

'Tha needn't, Major Rob!' said Benjy, grinning at my dismayed expression, 'Our Rachel is spoken for. Richard Hardcastle has expectations from some old relative that quarrelled with his father, and is like to die soon. He thinks to rent a small holding in a year or two, and start a community of True Believers. He wants Rachel to be his helpmeet.'

'Has Rachel agreed?' I asked, as much to cover my own discomfort, as because I wanted to know. Why had so much heat rushed to infuse my face and neck? Why was I fighting to clear my mind of a vision of Judith Moreland's tear filled eyes meeting mine, as we'd stood outside the entrance to the cave?

'She's thinking on't,' said Benjy, laconically. 'Richard's a great believer in t'Truth. Being at all times a truthful man himself, as he says, both before the Lord God and before his fellows. If Rachel tells him she received no hurt from yon rogues, he'll know she speaks Truth. He'll not turn against her.'

'Well, then. We need not fear that our girls' characters will be defamed.' I was relieved.

'We must thank the Lord God for His mercy,' said Mother, stroking Ann's hair. ''Twill do no harm for folks to think you and Master Fenton may be betrothed, dear. Indeed, I hope you will think of it.' Mother might know little of Gervase's true background, but she knew enough to sense that if he were serious, it must be a splendid match for Ann. Having a fount of common sense, I thought she'd also guess that his family might not welcome it.

'So, all's well eh? My wishes, my authority, are of no account! My poor Loveday is dead, murdered. These villains who held Ann captive deny they killed her — and all you people can think of is betrothals!' My brother was furious, as red in the face with anger now, as mine must have been with embarrassment. 'Well, I'll have you know, Master Fenton, my sister'll have no dowry. Lowflatts cannot afford it!'

Miles turned on his heel and marched out. We sat in silence for a few moments.

'He's every right to be angry,' Gervase said, shrugging. 'We still have no idea what happened to Loveday. We know that Zadoc and Job took Ann and Rachel on the orders of Matthew Garstang. We know that Jem Robinson was forced to aid Matthew out of fear, although he did what he could to protect the girls. We know that he's been gravely injured, left for dead, by Matthew and his band, and that Matthew in his turn was killed in a fight with Zadoc. Matthew was also responsible for what happened to Lemuel Drysdale, they told us as much. But they denied that they killed 'that girl at the farm', by whom they surely meant Loveday? Were they lying, Rob?'

'I didn't think so, at the time,' I said, 'but who else could, or would,

*157*

have done so? Matthew? But why? Why not capture her along with Ann and Rachel?'

'Loveday wasn't with us when... when those men came,' said Ann, shuddering at the memory. 'She'd been gone all morning, and we were thinking, where could she be? She went down to Beckside to ask if any of the carters were going to Lancaster, and would give her a ride. Because of Miles being in gaol, you see? She had a dream that he was dying. She went straight after milking, and when midday came and she hadn't returned, and had sent no message, Rachel and I began to fret a little. We thought maybe someone had offered her a lift straight away — but then surely she'd have sent one of the Proctor boys to let us know? Then we thought, being children, they might have stopped to play some game along the way, and forgotten. When we heard the cart draw up, we ran outside, thinking she had found a lift, and had come to see if we'd go with her.'

She choked back sobs. Mother, who had gone back to preparing her pudding cloths, moved to go to her, but Gervase reached across to take her hand and squeezed it, and she rewarded him with a wavering smile.

This was all much as we had thought. We now knew why Loveday had not been present when Zadoc and Job abducted the other two. Perhaps she had been returning on foot, not having found her lift, when she was struck down. It was perfectly possible that Ann and Rachel had not seen her lying in the ditch when they were driven past. Ann insisted that they hadn't, but agreed that they'd both been so terrified, and had been struggling so hard to get free of the gags over their mouths (It appeared the rogues were more concerned about their screams being heard than that they might escape) that they'd hardly been aware of anything else.

'Others must have been behind all this,' I fretted. Matthew Garstang and his band of thieves may have lusted after female companionship, and pretty, smart young girls like Ann and Rachel would have appealed to their base desires, but how did they know where to find them? Would that we could question Jem — he must know what it's all about!'

'That we may never be able to do,' said Gervase. 'Even if he lives, that wound to his throat sounds like to render him mute.' He rose from his seat on the window ledge with a groan. 'To appease Miles I suppose we'd better turn our hands to farm work.'

'I'd certainly be glad of the space in my kitchen!' said Mother.

'And t'would give me chance to get these onions softened for the puddings!' grunted Zeke, leaping up and seizing the skillet. 'Mysteries and the solving of 'em is all very well, but someone's gotta think about victuals!'

Gervase turned at the door and smiled at Ann, then put two fingers to his lips and released a sharp whistle. Claes rose to his feet, stretched, and padded after him. Benjy and I brought up the rear. There is always work to be done around a farm. It seemed this morning, that our troubles were over. So, apart from the bad feeling Miles had engendered — and what was new about that? — why did I feel so uneasy?

*Because Loveday was dead, and we didn't know why.* Almost certainly, she was killed before Ann and Rachel were taken. The person who killed her wanted the girls out of the way, so that they wouldn't raise the alarm when she didn't return. Matthew Garstang and his men, I now believed, were sent to remove them before they raised hue and cry. Perhaps even with instructions to dispose of them? Or at any rate keep them prisoner for a time. Sooner or later someone *would* find Loveday's corpse, but once sufficient time had elapsed no one would be able to say exactly when she died, or pinpoint the murderer's presence in the lane that day. Something Loveday had said or done had aroused the killer to fury, but her dying was inconvenient. Discovery would prevent her murderer from carrying out some secret deed or plan. Something he regarded as being of vital importance. Could this be the man Gervase was searching for?

# Chapter 25

I found Miles in the yard, leaning on the gate to the meadow, gazing glumly out towards the fells. They appeared flattened down, dull and grey today, sulking under cloudy skies. Our halcyon haytiming weather was over.

'I think you'll find all in good order,' I had to say something, yet knew it probable that nothing I said would find favour with my brother.

'So it should be,' he growled, 'with all the help you've had. I mun do it all with just Lanty, Mother, and the girls. And now Loveday's gone…' He laid his head in his arms atop the gate. I hadn't seen my brother weep since he was eight years old. He didn't want me to see him weep now.

'Our neighbours have been good to us,' I said, to fill the moment whilst he regained composure, 'and Benjy Postlethwaite tells me he can be spared from Highbiggens … now that they're all sober up there.'

'I can't pay him,' said Miles, bleakly. 'Lowflatts is bringing in little money. I meant it when I said there'll be no dowry for Ann, whether your Parliamentary Agent friend is serious or not.'

'I think perhaps he is. Or thinks he is. It was a wondrous moment, finding the girls alive in that cave. I imagine he's always had a fondness for Ann, and it made him realise how near we'd come to losing her… but he said he'll give her time to decide, and I'm sure he meant that — and rest assured, lack of a dowry wouldn't weigh with him. He's money enough.'

'And so do you,' snarled my brother. 'A soldier's pay, and Uncle William's shop besides.' Useless to point out to him that the New Model Army wouldn't be paying me for this time I'd spent at home, and if this uneasy peace prevailed, might soon cease to pay me at all.

'Does… did you gather whether Uncle William's shop is profitable?' If it was, I could offer to help Miles. Whether he would accept my help was another matter.

'I've no notion,' he replied. 'It must make something, or Uncle would have closed up. Nothing prospers while this stupid war of yours continues!'

'Not my war, our country's war,' I said, mildly.

'You could sell out and come home…now.'

'I could… but would you want me here?'

'Why not? She's gone.'

'Yes. She's gone.' I heaved a sigh clear down to my boots. 'You don't really believe I'd anything to do with her death?'

'Oh, I suppose not. When that barmpot Cousin Ezekiel first told me, I thought… I thought you and Gervase Fenton must have been working on some damned fool plan together. Spying, gathering information to prove that someone was planning something Parliament didn't like. Sparring with shadows! Poking at a wasps' nest! And somehow the pair of you'd got Loveday caught up in it.'

'I didn't. I don't believe Gervase did.'

'*He's* been spying. Don't deny it!'

'True enough, but he wouldn't involve Loveday.'

'She might have involved herself,' he said, slowly. 'To please him. Oh, I can't say otherwise. She liked to have men notice her, pay court to her! 'Twas all in innocence, and he *did* flirt with her. She liked to make me jealous, and if she thought he was beginning to pay her less attention… If he'd started making up to Ann, all of a sudden…'

'This prophesying she did?' I interrupted. 'I've heard about that from a number of people. That was surely done to gain attention, not necessarily Gervase's. Do you not think she upset someone with one of her rhymes?'

'A few people, I suppose' he conceded, 'but 'twas all a lot of nonsense. She was play acting. Nothing anyone could take seriously. Unless…'

'Unless there really *is* something going on in this district, and she just happened to hit on it. Some nonsense rhyme including a word or two, or a name? That could have filled someone with alarm.'

'She never used names. 'twas all vague stuff about peoples' sins. Adultery, drunkenness, dishonesty and such. Things such as folks might well be doing in a general way. She never spoke of treason.'

'Gervase hasn't found anything. He's told me so. Yet information was laid before the Council of State. That's why he's been coming here.'

'I fathomed 'twas not just to eat us out of house and home.'

'You know what Mother is, Miles! Any stranger must be entertained as though he were a Lord. I think it's dawned on him that he should be paying for his board. If he offers money, take it.'

'I'll have to,' he said. 'I don't like to be thought a skinflint, and Mother will be furious, but I'll take it.'

'Gervase and Benjy are swilling out the byre just now.' I wanted to change the subject. 'What would you have me do this morning?'

'Nothing. Take that big horse of yours over to Lings, before he eats the grass here down to bare earth! Find out how they do. Mebbe take that great black dog back to them. The way Mother's feeding him scraps, and making a fuss of him, he's like to settle in and be another drain on the household!'

Since going over to Lings was exactly what I wanted to do, I took Miles at his word. I asked Gervase if he wanted to come with me, but he said no, he would stay and help Benjy, who was full of a notion to cut a drain from the cow byre to the midden pit, and line it with slates found in the barn. Gervase said nothing of leaving, despite what he'd said the day before. Evidently the order he'd been expecting hadn't arrived — or had perhaps been countermanded.

'He's got a practical turn of mind, young Ben,' he commented, leaning on his spade to watch Benjy marking out a route with a stick. 'We should encourage him to join up. He'd be a useful man in a siege encampment.'

'Are there going to be more sieges? Will the Royalists rally again?'

'I'm certain of it,' said my friend, rolling his sleeves further up his arms. 'And now, like what's-his-name in the Bible, I must labour seven years to gain your sister's hand! Digging trenches under Benjamin's instruction. I hope brother Miles will think better of me for it!'

'That may depend on the success of the enterprise!' I laughed, and went to fetch Caesar's harness. I didn't stop to ask Gervase what his father would say to his presenting his family with a humble farmer's daughter as his bride.

The dog, Claes, having formed an immediate admiration for my mother, had slunk back indoors and was hiding beneath the kitchen table. He was very reluctant to leave Lowflatts and accompany me to Lings, but I tied a rope to his collar and had him run alongside. Caesar, despite recent hard riding in the fells, was eager to go anywhere I pleased.

The Lune had risen after yesterday's cloud burst, so I rode down through Beckside, fording the river there. On the rough track that served as the hamlet's main thoroughfare I found Timmy Proctor, shying stones at a line of larch cones on a wall. Spotting the dog, his eyes sparkled.

'Major Rob, you found 'im! That's Clouse, the one as wus lost, ain't it?'

'He found us,' I told him. 'He turned up on the doorstep at Lowflatts this morning. I'm taking him back to Lings.'

'Can I bring 'im? I could hold 'im for yer!'

'Is your mother home?' A shake of the head. 'She's gone to Pardew's with the lile 'uns to help with t'washing.'

'And your father?'

'He's gone up t'dale with Saul and t'donkey cart to fetch wood. He sez there's that many dying, he mun stock up. He wouldn't tek me. He sez three's too many for t'donkey.'

So no one would miss the child, or worry about him, if I borrowed him for the morning. Arriving at Lings Hall with a grubby urchin in attendance had not been part of my plan, but I was also hoping to give Caesar his head, and gallop some of his fidgets out of him. Not a thing to be attempted with a dog on a string underfoot, so I handed Claes over.

The day, though grey and lowering, was dry. Despite yesterday's downpour the grassy ride on the far side of the Lune was firm enough to let Caesar have his head. It was good to be on the move, and free to think my own thoughts. Free to acknowledge, not for the first time, that Miles' love for Loveday had been truer than mine. What I'd thought was true love would never have endured. She'd been right to choose him, and if, by some miracle, I could have brought her back to life, I'd have done it for his sake and not for mine.

Then I fell to musing on yesterday's events. In the joy and relief of bringing Ann and Rachel safely out of that dreadful cavern, we'd given no thought to what had become of their captors. Matthew Garstang still lay dead in the stream bed. Perhaps the flash flood would have carried his body nearer to the mouth of the cave, but it hadn't been washed clear whilst we were up there. It was one of the things I needed to speak to Colonel Moreland about, sending someone up with Luke Proctor to retrieve the corpse. What of Zadoc and Job? I'd let them go, needing to concentrate on getting the girls to safety, and then banished them from my reflections. Now I pictured them again as I'd last seen them, scrambling over the rocks to escape. With Claes in furious pursuit. No one had seen them emerge into the ghyll, so they must have found a different route. Claes had emerged, whole and unharmed, and so, therefore, might they. And might, I suddenly realised, a cold knot forming in my stomach, have made their way down to Lowflatts, seeking revenge. Finding the dog in our kitchen this morning, I'd assumed he'd followed his original task, to find Ann. But does a dog think thus? He'd identified Zadoc and Job as his enemies. Might he in fact have followed those rogues to our farm? I nearly reigned Caesar in and turned back, but common sense told me that even if they approached the farm, Gervase and Benjy — and even Miles and Zeke, were there to keep Ann safe.

Caesar was lengthening his stride, his ears pricked. Scents and sounds that I couldn't yet smell or hear were calling him once again.

'Shame on you,' I grumbled, now catching sight of the object of his interest in the distance. 'I've seen you nuzzling the neck of Gervase's Venus! Now you are wishful to flirt with Mistress Judith's pretty mare! 'Tis as well you are gelded, or angry owners would be filing suits against me, come the winter, finding themselves with unexpected foals to feed!'

Judith Moreland must have caught sight of me at the same instant. She checked for a moment, but then straightened her hat, and rode steadily towards us. She was wearing the hat with the jaunty feather, but her face was set in a frown.

'Good morning, Mistress Judith!' I hailed her, for I told myself I couldn't, in common courtesy, pass by without speaking, although the set of her shoulders suggested that was what she wanted. Reluctantly, I thought, she reigned in. Tied in a shawl across her saddle bow I saw she carried a bundle, and I wondered what it contained.

'Good morning, Major Haddon,' she sounded, listless, formal. Yesterday she'd called me Rob. Hadn't she? 'I'm on my way to call at Lowflatts. I hope dear Ann is recovering from her ordeal?'

'Yes, she's up and about. My mother is cosseting her, you may be sure! We hope she'll suffer no long term effects…' I was going to say more, ask after her brother, thank her for her concern, urge her to speak to my sister on cheerful topics to raise her spirits, but Judith gave me no chance. No chance, either to ask what the bundle contained.

'You'll wish to know that Edwin is also as well as can be expected.' she said, frowning. Her lips parted for a moment as though to add something, but she pressed them closed, touched her mare's flank with her whip, and wheeled away without another word.

Well, so much for Gervase's theory that she had a partiality for me. So much for that moment of understanding I thought we'd shared at the cave mouth. Mistress Judith Moreland had no desire to consort with me this morning. Had Lady Brilliana come down yet more heavily on her daughter, forbidden all contact now and forever? Were we Haddons to be put firmly in our humble places from now on? What would be my reception at Lings Hall? And what would be Lady Brilliana's reaction to Gervase's offer to marry Ann, when she came to hear of it? Or Judith's for that matter? I wanted and needed to see the Colonel, but would I even gain admittance?

'Benson Moreland is a fine soldier,' I told Caesar, 'a master of men. But off the battlefield he seems to be a cipher in his own household.' Caesar flicked his ears at the sound of my voice, and lengthened his stride, although I had given him no signal to do so. Possibly he regarded me as a cipher also.

I found Lings Hall outwardly untroubled. Abel, the stable lad, came dawdling out to take Caesar's bridle.

'Timmy Proctor's on his way,' I told him, dismounting, 'bringing the dog, Claes. I take it you brought Piet back yesterday?'

'Aye. He's back there.' Abel jerked his chin over his shoulder to a closed loose box. 'Ah don't know what you want to bring t'other un back for. 'Twill be me that's landed with 'em.'

'Surely, once he is well again, Master Edwin will want his dog?' Abel shrugged. 'Most like he'll have forgotten all about it.'

'They're good animals. They found the girls, or at any rate Claes did. They're young dogs, and with a bit of training, they could be useful about the estate.'

Abel forbore to comment.

'Is Colonel Moreland at home?' I asked.

'He ain't ridden out.' I didn't doubt his loyalty, but as an obliging manservant Abel lacked something.

Joseph, the elderly indoor servant, was a touch more conciliatory, but not much. 'The Colonel is in his study, Major Haddon,' he told me. 'Shall I tell him you are here?' I held myself back from remarking that if I didn't wish to see his master I wouldn't have come, and stood, hat in hand, in the hallway, waiting to be summonsed. I waited a considerable time. The house was quiet. The door to Lady Brilliana's withdrawing room was closed. Somewhere in the distant kitchen quarters I could hear the faint echo of voices, the clatter of plates and dishes, and smell meat roasting on the spit.

'The Colonel will see you now, Major.' Joseph, reappearing, managed to convey through these few correct phrases that I was the recipient of a great favour. I handed him my hat, although he gave the impression (without saying a word) that it would soil his hands to take it. Joseph knew that I was merely the second son of Lowflatts farm, a country yokel, a nobody in society. I might have the title 'major' but I was an upstart in Joseph's eyes. An unfortunate consequence of our Civil war, which had raised me temporarily above my station. Yet, thinking about it, even when Gervase had been with me, his welcome had been cool. Did odorous Joseph have Royalist sympathies, or had he merely caught a sense of superiority from his mistress? I followed him meekly to the Colonel's study.

Benson Moreland's opening greeting confirmed my impression that my face was not the right one. 'Gervase Fenton not with you, Major? I'd hoped to see him. It would have saved me a ride over to your place. I really must see him.'

'I suggested he came with me, Sir,' I found myself saying apologetically, 'but he and Benjy Postlethwaite are working on some drainage scheme, and he was loath to leave it.'

'Was he now? His father would be astonished to hear it,' said the Colonel, dryly. 'I understand Gervase has not, in the past, shown much interest in agricultural matters. I met up with his father once, whilst we were in London, three years ago...' his voice tailed away. He (and Gervase's father) would have been in London for King Charles' execution.

'Gervase thinks, he believes... *I* think he thinks, that is, that Benjy's scheme might prove useful... might have applications for siege conditions...' I stuttered, not wanting to bring up Gervase's astonishing proposal to Ann, and my suspicion that he wanted to stay close to our house to protect her. If she needed to be protected. If she wanted him to protect her. The whole situation was confusing. I thought his offer of marriage had been genuine, but had it? Had he made it on the spur of the moment to help Ann feel more comfortable if gossip arose, as it almost certainly would, about the time she'd spent with those men in captivity? I really didn't know what was going on. They'd have to sort it out between them.

'We may be in siege conditions soon enough,' the Colonel was saying. 'Yesterday all was quiet. I urged Gervase to stay put for another day or two. This morning different information has reached me, as though I didn't have...' He didn't seem able to finish sentences this morning.

'I'm sorry, Sir. I haven't asked you, how your son fares? And Jem? That's why I came...and to return the dog, Claes, who turned up at Lowflatts this morning.'

Benson Moreland sat in reverie for a moment, tapping his index finger on the polished wood of his desk, and then shrugged. 'Edwin will recover. Two broken ankles and a blow to his head, but he'll live, God willing. God be praised indeed, that he suffered nothing more serious. Jem... my wife has been to see him and reports that he is no better but no worse. Again, it must be in the hands of the Almighty.'

He raised his shoulders and then lowered them again, his expression tired and defeated as I had never seen it on the battlefield. Not even, as Gervase had reminded me, after Edgehill, when so many were killed.

'So. You returned the dog. Abel will hardly thank you for that, although I hope Edwin may, in time. You came to enquire for Edwin, for which I thank you. And for all you did yesterday, Major Haddon...'

I'd been beginning to think, like Cousin Zeke, that some thanks would be appropriate, and now here they were, although Benson Moreland sounded too weary to put any vigour behind the words. Now he was pulling himself to his feet. 'I'll ride back with you. I must see young Fenton. This may be all another false alarm — but things seem to be moving. Not in the South West as we've all been expecting, but in Scotland. It's just rumour at this stage, but my information comes from a reliable source.'

'Scotland, Sir!' I said, surprised. 'Nothing of any moment was happening there when I left, two weeks ago.' Two weeks. It felt like a lifetime, so much had happened here. 'Edinburgh, the Lowlands, all's been quiet on the fighting front since Dunbar. A few skirmishes, but nothing of note. Oliver Cromwell hasn't been well, as you'll know, with this low burning fever that afflicts him. And the Covenanters, under Sir John Leslie, retreated to Stirling castle. Stirling is nigh on impregnable. There's no way through to take the Highlands. There was talk of trying to take the town of Inverkeithing, across the firth of Forth. An attempt to get men across, and so come at the Scots' army from behind and cut their supply lines. Cromwell wasn't keen. The last I heard was that he deemed it just a diversion.'

'It seems he's changed his mind. Or General Lambert's changed it for him,' said Colonel Moreland, pulling on his gloves. 'Come, let's ride over to Lowflatts.'

We rode. And found everything much as I had left it. Gervase and Benjy were getting themselves extremely dirty cutting the drainage trench and lining it with slates. Miles was leaning on the barn door watching them, wearing an expression that said he didn't expect to be enthralled with the finished result. Mother and Ann were in the kitchen tying puddings into cloths ready for the pot. Zeke was in the garth, perched on a three legged stool, milking the goat. I reigned in as we rode by, to warn him she was taking an unhealthy interest in his shirt tail.

'I imagine you'll be wanting to get back to Edinburgh as soon as possible,' said the Colonel, as we dismounted in the yard. We'd hardly spoken during the ride.

'Perhaps,' I replied, 'if this latest rumour is more than just that.'

I stood a moment, Caesar's reigns in my hands. And knew, in that instance, that I didn't want to go at all. Not to Scotland. Not to another campaign. Another siege. Another forced march. Another battlefield. I never wanted to be obliged to kill another human being. Miles was right. The whole conflict had been a stupid mistake. I met the Colonel's eyes, and knew that he knew what I was thinking.

'If you'd known what you know now, Sir, would you have joined?' I asked him, bluntly. He took a long shuddering breath. 'No, Major, I wouldn't. But what else could we have done? I threw down my glove, as they say. I backed my belief that Parliament had the right of it. I never envisaged the Regicide. I never expected the contention it has brought to families and communities. Men I counted as friends, who have chosen to support the other side. The damage to land and property. The resulting ruin to crops. Starvation for poor folk. You've seen it, I've seen it. Here, in the Lune valley we've been more fortunate than most. We *should* have found some other way. We didn't. And now I think we must push on to the end. Set up the Commonwealth. Appoint Cromwell as Lord Protector. I don't like it, I don't particularly like *him*. I didn't like what I heard about the Irish business. However, I believe we've got to make the best of it. He's proved himself as a strong leader, and without strong leadership we're lost. We cannot go on as we are. One last heave, up there in Scotland, one last engagement perhaps, here in England, and we can settle a peace? That's the best we can hope for.'

'Peace at any price?'

'Yes,' he said, after a long pause and heavy sigh. 'I believe we must settle for that.'

'You'll re-join the New Model?'

He sighed again, clear down to his high-topped boots. 'If it comes to it. As I suspect it will. Yes, I'd fight again.' He rubbed his great nose, flattening it, an unconscious gesture of his. 'I won't follow you to Scotland. I don't know the country, or what needs to be done there. I'd be a hindrance rather than a help. But if the Royalists rally in England again. Yes, I'll stand with Parliament and fight.'

We stood in silence, two men who knew what it was to kill or be killed, and would rather do anything else than have to do it again.

'These barges I'm hearing about,' he said, suddenly, 'what do you know of them? Have you seen them?' I knew what he meant. Up in Edinburgh we'd all heard talk of them, although I'd never set eyes on them myself. Parliament had had them constructed and towed up to Leith. The idea was that whole regiments could be ferried across the Firth of Forth from Leith to a landing place across the estuary they called Queensferry, in case we decided to take the county of Fife, and thus march on inland to circumvent Stirling and Leslie's redoubts which barred the way to the Highlands. Nobody outside London and the Council of State was very enthusiastic. As I'd already told the Colonel, Cromwell wasn't in favour. Or hadn't been when I left Scotland.

'I don't know much about the barges, Sir. I haven't seen them. I understand they're moored in Leith harbour. I don't even know how many men they could carry.' I was cavalry, nobody had told me much.

'Enough, I'm told.'

I shrugged. 'And we're to go forward into Fife?'

'The hope is, my informant tells me, that if we advance into Fife, and attack the garrison at Burntisland, it will tempt Leslie and Sir John Browne of Fordall out of Stirling. And thus force a decisive battle.'

I thought about this. 'It could work, Sir. Better than trying to take the Highlands. That country, believe me — Gervase can tell you — is wilder, the mountains more impassable, than our own Westmorland Hills. We'd be at a huge disadvantage against those Chieftains. Their clansmen are loyal unto death, every man jack of them. They'd hole up amongst the rocks and ravines, and pick us off like flies.'

'So Cromwell and Major-General Lambert have concluded. Fife, I understand, is hilly but with more rolling countryside. Stirling, as you say, is impregnable, but if the Covenanters could be tempted out…'

I blew a gusty outbreath, as men do, discussing the unknowable. 'The trouble is, the Scots want Charles, the son. He's a Stuart, he's one of them. As you know, they declared for him, three years ago. Apparently, although he's young, he's impressive. Men like Leslie and Browne have changed sides for him, as I don't have to remind you. And he's as smooth tongued when it comes to bribing people with promises as ever his father was. Apparently he's encouraged the Covenanters into believing they can have their Presbyterianism.'

'A promise I doubt he has any intention of keeping. Imbued as he is, with his mother's Catholicism,' snorted Benson Moreland. 'He's what, twenty-one years of age? A stripling who wants his father's throne at any price. He'd promise anybody anything to get it. Well, he's not going to, or not yet.'

'You envisage a time when he may, Sir?' Gervase, filthy, but apparently satisfied with his morning's labours, had strolled over to join us. He has the sharpest ears, and had probably caught the drift of our converse ever since we dismounted.

'Charles the son? I don't say it could never happen. But I'd have to see some pretty binding treaties in place before I'd accept it. You both know what Parliament went through with the father. Slippery as an eel! We could never pin the man down. First he'd sign an agreement, then within weeks he'd repudiate it. The whole thing was impossible. Anyway, Major Fenton, it would seem things are on the move, north of the border. I've had word from Edinburgh.'

'Edinburgh, Sir? That's a mite unexpected.' Gervase wasn't as surprised as I'd been.

'Edinburgh. Just when we thought the Scottish campaign was at stalemate, and likely to remain that way ...' The two of them walked aside now, talking in low voices. I didn't follow them immediately, but led the horses over to the hitching post. A cold stone lay in my stomach. The sun was making an effort to break through the clouds, lighting the Howgill fells, and nearer at hand I could just make out the blue of Lanty's smock as he moved across the hillside, guarding our little flock.

Ann came pattering into the yard with a bucket of grain for the hens. Her glance took in Colonel Moreland and Gervase, talking earnestly in the lee of the barn, and then her eyes sought mine.

'There's trouble?' she asked softly.

'In Scotland. Not here. All's well here, Ann, so far as I know, but Gervase and I may have to go north in a few days' time... what did Mistress Judith have to say?' Quite why I wanted to know, I couldn't have explained.

'Judith?' Ann was bewildered.

'Didn't she come? I met her earlier on my way to Lings. She said she was coming to see how you were faring.'

Ann shook her head. 'I haven't seen her today.'

# Chapter 26

Gervase broke the news to them all over the midday meal. He would be riding north on the morrow, despite the fact that it would be the Lord's Day. I had leave to remain to the end of the week ahead, to help Miles while he regained his strength, and resolve my affairs.

I said little. A sense of dread had settled on me. I'm not a coward. Which does not mean I'm unafraid. I joined the army to put my unrequited love behind me, and because I wanted to see the world outside our valley. Killing other men hadn't come easy, but when I myself was about to be killed, I'd done it. I just didn't want to do it anymore.

I thought back, sitting silently, as the conversation around the table focussed on Gervase's imminent departure (Mother was offering to wash and iron his shirts this very afternoon) to my previous leaving.

Six years ago I'd left to ride to Northamptonshire, heart heavy. Loveday's lovely face had hovered in my thoughts with every mile. Yet now, I realised, I could barely recall how she looked. When I tried, it was Judith Moreland's bright eyes that swam before me. The quick curl of her lips at the corners of her mouth, just before she broke into a smile. That hat, with the ridiculous feather! Oh, Rob Haddon, what a fool thou art! Doomed to fall into love with girls who are not for you.

Afterwards, I took myself off to inspect my gear, and clean Caesar's saddle and harness. Ann found me in the barn, struggling with needle and waxed thread, trying to repair my pack roll.

'Let me do that,' she said. 'You're making a mull of it!'

She flopped down on a pile of hay beside me, and bent her head over the canvas.

'Is Mother washing Gervase's linen?' I asked.

'She is, and Deb Snaith is come up from the village to aid her,' she replied. She sewed a few stitches, tugging at the greasy thread. 'I may be allowed to iron a shirt,' she added, giggling. 'Since he and I are betrothed.'

We sat in silence awhile.

'How do you feel about that?'

'I don't know.' My sister glanced at me, shyly, and then bent her head over the sewing. 'If he comes back… Will he come back safe, Rob? He says he's fought in five battles and never took a scratch —if he comes back, and he still wants to marry me — well, then, I think I will. I suppose that won't be before winter?'

'Most probably,' I replied, gravely. 'There'll certainly be no campaigning in Scotland once the bitter weather sets in, so then he'll be free to return for a while. But, Ann…'

'It's all such a surprise. I never thought to be *married*,' she continued, ignoring the doubt I'm sure my voice conveyed.

'But I've always liked Gervase,' she went on. 'He's always talked to me, talked to me by myself, not just when Loveday and the others were by. He's told me about his home in Huntingdonshire. Have you seen it? Shall I like it there? He says they have no great hills like our fells.'

'No, I've never been in that locality. Gervase has spoken of it, of course. Did he tell you his family are close neighbours to Oliver Cromwell? I daresay you'd grow to like it. I think the Fentons are more…socially prominent than we are. You'd be quite the lady, have your own carriage, and a fellow to drive it, I shouldn't wonder.'

'I'd like that,' said Ann, simply. 'Although I agree with Richard Hardcastle that we shouldn't strive too much after worldly things. But if I had a carriage, I could visit the poor, take foodstuffs to the afflicted, could I not? Gervase would allow it, I'm sure. I wouldn't look down my nose at the poor people, like Lady Brilliana.'

We sat in silence another spell, each thinking our own thoughts. Ann pushed and tugged at the needle, struggling to get it through the rough canvas. Even so, her stitching was a good deal neater than mine.

'The only thing is,' she said, slowly, 'having to leave Mama and Miles. You'll be gone, I know, with the army. That's your life for now. And I think Miles will marry again, don't you? Once he gets over grieving for Loveday. Hannah Postlethwaite would suit him very well, be a more comfortable wife to him than ever poor Loveday was. Mama likes Hannah, they'll deal well together. But I think she'll miss me. I know I'd miss her. She says she'd come and see me, but surely it must be three or four days ride to Huntingdonshire?'

'About that,' I agreed, 'but if Mother sets her mind to something, Ann, she'll undoubtedly do it.'

'She told me she has never been further north than Kirby Stephen, or south than Lancaster, in her life. But if I should have a child… she promised she'd come.'

I looked at her, and then away again, startled. My sister, sixteen years old! To me she was still a babe herself, yet here she was thinking to have children of her own. Gervase's children. The idea would take some getting used to. Had Gervase himself thought that far?

'It's big step to take,' I said, carefully. 'If you're not certain.'

'Well, he said I might have time to think of it. To accustom myself to leaving Lowflatts. Until winter comes a least. But I think I *will* do it. Who else would I marry, hereabouts? I won't marry Jem Robinson! I don't want to dwindle into an old maid like Mason Hardcastle's daughters.'

'Yes, I understand that,' I said. I hadn't thought of this before, because to me she was still my baby sister. Were Ann's choices so limited? Surely some young farmer further up or down the dale would be glad to have her as a helpmeet? I found I couldn't think of one. George Postlethwaite must be nearing forty and seemed unlikely to take a wife. Certainly not a girl of sixteen. Sam Woodley was spoken for — in a manner of speaking. Malachi too — in a manner of speaking also.

'When I come to leave the army,' I said, slowly, because I hadn't had time to give this more than a passing thought, 'I suppose I'll look into the running of this shop of Uncle William's. Has Mother told you he left it to me in his Will? You could come and keep house for me in Lancaster, Ann.'

Ann looked up and smiled. 'Oh, thank you, Rob! If… if something should happen to Gervase… which I pray it will not… I'd be glad to take you up on that offer.'

I saw that Ann was making up her mind. No, had made up her mind. I just hoped that Gervase had not changed his. Already I could hear it in her voice. A striving to be the bride he could be proud of. Ann's voice had always been soft, there was nothing strident in her speech, although she had the accent of our district. Now she was beginning to shorten her vowels as she must have heard Judith Moreland, and indeed Gervase, do. My sister was trying to turn herself into a lady. Well, no harm in that, I supposed. As Gervase's wife she would be expected to express herself clearly, to banish any harshness from her speech. Gervase himself had mixed these last years with all and sundry, had grown used to the speech of almost every region of the country. He had a good ear for all of them, and had never shown disdain for any. He even seemed able to understand the Scots, whose strange locutions had quite foxed me!

'Tomorrow is the Lord's day,' I said, rising to my feet, and stretching cramped limbs. (Sitting on a pile of straw on an earth floor was bad enough, soon I'd be lucky to be couched beneath a hedgerow) 'I don't know whether we'll have a sermon read in the church. It's surely too much to expect the parson to ride over from Barbon again, when he has his own flock. Jem Robinson is in no state to lead us. I'm thinking, once I know whether there will be a service or no, that I should go to Lancaster and return the dray horses Mother hired. I can pay off our debt to the hiring stables, and that'll be one less thing to trouble Miles.'

'If you set out early enough you could attend church in Lancaster. Then you should take a look at this shop of Uncle William's whilst you're there,' said my sister, sounding just like Mother. 'Surely you should find someone to tend it while you are away fighting. Else all those valuable spices could be stolen or spoiled?'

'I already have an idea about that!' I said, and strode away to find my brother.

'Miles, tomorrow I must go to Lancaster,' I told him, finding him looking over the orphaned lambs in the garth, all which seemed to have doubled in size since first I came home. 'I'll return the dray horses, and see that all's well with Uncle William's shop premises.'

'*Your* premises,' retorted my brother, scowling. 'Though what's to be done with the place once you go haring off to Scotland, I can't imagine. I've no time to go traipsing over there. Enough that I've dragged myself from my sick bed lest all here goes to rack and ruin.' Savagely he prodded the belly of one of the lambs, checking for worms, although the beast looked healthy enough to me. Trust Miles to resent what he saw as my good fortune, even though he himself had ridden over to Lancaster with all speed to claim the legacy on my behalf.

'My notion was to take Cousin Zeke with me, and put him in charge, since it seems to me that he'd be more useful minding the shop than getting under Mother's feet here.' I paused to let him assimilate this. He frowned, saying nothing, though his face grew dark. 'It doesn't seem to me that he has the makings of a farmhand,' I added, cunningly, as I thought.

'But if you put him in the shop he'll have it, for sure!' Miles exploded. 'He thought he should have it, though it was willed to you. If you leave him in charge, and then get yourself killed in this Scottish campaign, we'll never succeed in claiming it back! What I have not suffered for you, cast into that filthy gaol when he tried to claim it! And now you want to give it to him, or as good as!'

'He is to manage, not to *own*. I'll make it clear enough, never fear. If he's unwilling to do it on my terms, I'll find someone else. I realise my going, and taking Zeke, and with Gervase leaving at first light, will leave you short of help. Swallow your pride, brother, and ask Benjy to stay on. He isn't needed urgently at Highbiggens, and after all, Mother is feeding him meals fit for a prince.'

I didn't mention that I intended to slip some coins into Benjy's hand when Miles was elsewhere. The boy had worked hard for us and deserved a reward, which Miles was insisting he could not afford to give.

'Meals fit for a *prince*? No, fit for Oliver Cromwell, you mean,' Miles griped. 'Oh, very well, I'll speak to the lad. But you realise that for all your cleverness, you and Fenton never caught those wretches? The two fellows who held Ann and Rachel captive. How am I to manage if they should come trying to steal Ann back again?'

'I'll leave you my sword. If you see any sign of them, send Benjy running for George and Malachi — or if there isn't time for that, arm him with the scythe — though it's more than likely they've fled the district. They aren't complete fools. They'll guess that Colonel Moreland has ordered their arrest. I'm more likely to find them on the quay in Lancaster, trying for a passage to Ireland.'

'If you do, then for Heaven's sake Rob, give them in charge!'

Next morning we were all up soon after sunrise. Mother and Ann fussed over Gervase, urging food and extra clothing on him. Deb Snaith too, came hurrying up to the farm to press on him a leather bottle which she said contained some good beer of her own brewing. There's no doubt that Gervase makes himself agreeable to the womenfolk!

Once he was mounted on Venus (he would be selling the pretty mare before he reached Edinburgh, in exchange for a horse more suited to the battlefield) he seemed suddenly to recall, flushing and smiling, that he should salute his bride-to-be before he left, and leaned down to plant a clumsy buss on Ann's upturned nose. And so he rode away, grinning, and Ann stood, twisting her hands in her apron, gazing after him until he was gone from our sight. I wondered, as I knew my sister must, if we would ever see him again.

I had spoken to Zeke the night before, and got his agreement to take charge of the shop. 'In my absence I need a manager,' I'd told him, 'and who would I ask but you?' I did not mention that like my horse, Caesar, his appetite outweighed his usefulness on a working farm. Or that Miles, and probably Mother, although she would never admit it, would prefer his room to his company.

'I'll do it,' he decided, after screwing up his monkey face in thought, 'provided you don't expect me to ride astride one of them great hosses. To save your sister's life, and that of that hoity-toity lad Edwin, I was willing, but I'd as lief not do it again!'

I told him it wouldn't be necessary. I intended to harness them to the dray, and drive to the hiring stables on the outskirts of Lancaster.

'Then let it be early,' Zeke decided, 'because Aunty Sarah's threatening me with a dose of religion! That old fellow with the beard, Josiah Postlethwaite, is coming down from his farm to lead us all in prayer, as Auntie says is fitting on the Sabbath, your parson being dead. We carried a parson on shipboard now and then. I didn't at all care for being made to sing psalms — be it the Sabbath or any other day.'

Not being over fond of psalm singing myself, I shook his hand and sealed our bargain.

# Chapter 27

I took Caesar along with me, hitched to the tail of the cart. He sulked all the way. The indignity of it, forced to trail, captive, behind this pair of complete slugs!

'Your horse don't like this, do 'e?' remarked Zeke, noting the snorting going on behind us as we rumbled slowly into Beckside.

'Caesar has too high an opinion of himself. He is fortunate that you've agreed to stay behind in Lancaster, otherwise, once I've returned these two plodders to their owner, you would have had to ride up behind me on the return journey. Then he'd have something to snort about!'

'Why d'yer put up with the beast, then?' Zeke demanded. ''E's yards behind me, and 'e's still managing to blow down me neck!'

'He's a good horse. A cavalry horse. He's got me out of a lot of difficulties on the battle field.'

'You'll be taking him to Scotland?'

'He'd never forgive me if I didn't.'

'Strange…' Zeke began to say, and I thought he was still talking about Caesar's wicked ways, and my indulgence of them. Perhaps he was. But perhaps not, for up ahead of us, finely dressed as for some special occasion, and mounted on her chestnut mare, although the hour was still short of six in the morning, was Lady Brilliana Moreland. She raised her whip, hailing us in her familiar imperious manner. I reigned in.

'Good morning, Robert Haddon. Are you going far?'

'To Lancaster, Ma'am,' I raised my hat, inclining my head. It annoyed me that I felt obliged to treat her with such deference, yet she was a woman, and as such I owed her courtesy. She certainly expected it.

'Oh, I'd hoped you were not traveling so far. I'm riding out early to let as many in the parish as possible know that there can be no service at the church today. When I saw you approaching I thought you might save me riding to Lowflatts to inform your mother.'

'You need not in any case, Ma'am. She has already assumed as much, and has arranged with Josiah Postlethwaite that his family and ours will meet and sing psalms together.'

Lady Brilliana pulled a sour face. 'Well, I'm sure that's well intentioned, although I don't care for that form of worship myself. By the way…' she had already signalled her mare to move forward, and now spoke over her shoulder, 'your family may be relieved to know that they'll not have my silly daughter plaguing them for the present.' She smiled, the kind of smile that stretches the lips but goes no further. 'I sent her yesterday to stay with a relative of my husband's near Hornby. It was high time to put a stop to her forward behaviour. Your family have been very kind and patient, but really!'

With this, she gave her false tinkling laugh, and rode away.

'Who is that woman, the Queen of Sheba?' demanded Zeke. 'I seen 'er up on the hill, giving the Colonel a hard time.'

I laughed. 'No, she is Lady Brilliana Moreland! The Colonel's wife. A very proud woman. Her father was an Earl, and she despises us all, including, I think, her husband. *He* is a good man and a fine soldier.'

'But henpecked?'

'I fear so.'

'The daughter seemed a pleasant lass, not proud, and sweet on you, if I'm any judge?'

'She's pleasant enough,' I replied, making a show of urging the horses on, hoping to prevent him saying more. I'd grown to tolerate Zeke, but I didn't care for him sufficiently to want to share my personal affairs with him.

In truth, I was puzzled by the encounter we'd just had. Why was it necessary for Lady Brilliana to be out warning everyone about a church service that would not take place, at six in the morning? Surely, if the Colonel wanted it done he would have sent Joseph, or Abel, or both of them, after breakfast, and between them they could have reached every house in the parish in good time. And why had she then, almost as a casual afterthought, mentioned sending Judith away? I'd a strong feeling that it had not been an afterthought at all. I'd met Judith riding out yesterday. She had not appeared to be equipped for a stay with relative. Her bundle might have contained a few necessities, but not sufficient for a lengthy stay. She could, of course, have been planning a visit to Ann before she went, turning towards the river afterwards. She hadn't visited Ann. And, if she was journeying to a relative at her parents' behest, they would surely have found a servant to accompany her. Perhaps, since I knew them to be short-handed, they might have sent her brother, Nicholas.

I chewed on my under lip, vague anxieties clouding my thoughts. Where had Judith been going? Why would she tell me she was going to call on Ann, but then did not? Now, reflecting on that encounter, I couldn't help having the notion that she had been running away. But why? Where was she running to? Could the true reason her mother was riding out so early be that she was searching for her?

'You gotta bit of a weakness for women,' remarked Zeke, after I had been silent for some minutes, engrossed in these thoughts. 'First 'tis your brother's wife, now this Moreland wench. Still, I suppose if you're partial to the female sex you don't get many chances when you're away afighting them Cavaliers?' He slid his eyes sideways, testing my reaction. I set my jaw, determined not to give him satisfaction. I was beginning to regret, now, having offered this idiot the opportunity to run my shop. Miles was right, I was a fool. Fortunately for Zeke we'd reached the ford, so I divested myself of my boots and got down to coax the big cart horses into the water. Mother had warned me that they balked at getting their great hairy feet wet. Zeke balked at it too, so I made him hold the reigns while I seized their bridles and led them across, walking backwards before them. Several times I stumbled, and narrowly avoided a ducking. Caesar, behind, raised his roman nose, picked up his hooves with exaggerated care, and pretended that this whole undignified episode had nothing to do with him.

And so, safely across the river, we lumbered on, through the lush summer lanes, freshened by the recent rain. We were following the course of the Lune, as it flowed past Kirkby Lonsdale, Arkholme, Melling, Aughton, until the ramparts of Lancaster Castle, John of Gaunt's great fortress, huge and threatening above the town, reared up before us.

'Orrible place,' muttered Zeke, who, thankfully, had been silent for some miles past. 'I bin in prisons for a space, 'ere and there, Spain, the Low Countries, all over, and I niver seen one as filthy as that one. 'Tis no wonder your poor brother caught a fever.'

'He seems to be mending at last.' I was ready to call a truce.

'I'm right glad of it. I wus main sorry for what happened. Didn't mean 'im no harm. I gets me rag up when I've bin drinking. I'm a mild enough fellow in the general way, but drink brings out the devil in me.'

He seemed sincere, and so I humbled myself to ask, 'Do you know the whereabouts of Uncle William's shop?'

Zeke looked at me in astonishment. 'Ain't you never bin there?'

'When I was 'a lile' un,' I replied, using our North country word. Gervase told me once, when he heard me use it, that we men of the North got the word 'lile' for 'little' from the Norwegians. The Vikings, he says, must have taught it to us. As I spoke, I thought of Ann, who would be planning her bride clothes, and wondered once again if Gervase was serious about their marriage.

'Mother and Miles and I rode over with Father when he came to a sheep sale once in a while, but I don't recall exactly how we got there,' I told Zeke.

''Tis in Stoop Hall Street, below the castle. It's a narrow way, but we'll be on foot by then, as I take it?'

We left all three horses at the hiring stables. Caesar was outraged, whinnying his annoyance. I think he suspected me of selling him to a horsemeat butcher.

'Does 'e alus carry on like that?' the aged proprietor asked, as he bit the money I gave him, testing whether I was passing false coin.

'Take no notice,' I said, laughing. 'I made the mistake of naming him Caesar. He thinks he can behave like Julius of that name — the Roman Emperor.'

Mother had told me where to find the stables, but I hadn't thought to ask her for directions to the shop. I'd supposed that once I entered the town's grey stone streets, I'd remember where to go. Fortunately, since this was not the case, all I had to do was follow Zeke.

Stoop Hall Street was, as he'd indicated, a poky little lane off the main street leading up to the castle and the priory church. It was hardly more than an alley, lined by crazy old buildings, leaning this way and that, one side of the street nestling up against a grand old mansion, Stoop Hall, now very much decayed. By my reckoning it must have been built no later than the time of King Hal, if not so far back as John o' Gaunt himself. Behind it was a patch of open land, with cows and horses grazing on it, beneath the castle walls.

Uncle William's shop, though hard up against Stoop Hall, seemed to be in reasonable repair, all its shutters closed and barred. (Mother would have attended to that before she left) From what I could see, peering up from the street below, the Coniston slate roof was sound and watertight.

'Tis a good spot,' said Zeke, approvingly. 'Plenty of trade from the Castle as well as the townsfolk.'

I removed from my jerkin the heavy iron key ring Mother had given me as I left, and used the largest key to open the front door. Within, all seemed in good order, although a pair of mice, disturbed, scurried into holes in the wainscot, and there were other sounds, rustlings, above us on the upper floors, which I attributed to rats. I stood and let my nostrils assimilate the glorious smell of spices which pervaded every corner of the building.

'They're in this room,' Zeke said, watching me inhale. He pushed open the door to the right. 'This is the shop. 'Tis where Uncle did business.'

It was a small chamber, gloomy with the shutters closed, and lined with shelves above and oak wood cupboards below. The contents of the shelves, which were dimly visible, consisted of row upon row of glass jars, each labelled in the quavering hand of my late uncle. Above our heads, suspended from the ceiling, were bunches of dried herbs, amongst which spiders were busily weaving.

Zeke looked around, and, starting to the left of the doorway, began to recite. *'Anise, caraway, cinnamon, cloves, garlic, ginger, horseradish, mint, mustard seeds, nigella, orris-root, parsley, pepper, rosemary, thyme.* I disremember them that's in the cupboards.' He shrugged. 'Might be coffee beans. Them up above,' he jerked his head towards the ceiling, 'which he growed his self out the back, is all 'erbs. Uncle taught me the order of them that's on the shelves when I were knee high to a grasshopper. So as I could get 'em down for a customer if he'd stepped out to sink a jar. Eh, but it brings it back! There's t'old tall stool as I used to hafta climb on!'

I was taken aback. 'You lived here with Uncle at one time?'

'Mam kept house for him, after she was widowed — from my fourth year to my twelfth, or thereabouts,' he replied, simply. 'Then they 'ad words, and he turned us out. Or maybe Mam walked out. I disremember. Mam 'ad a temper on 'er too. Said he was a mean old nip-cheese, expected her to feed us all three on next to nowt. But I alus got on with the old man. He said he'd see me right,' he added, sadly, 'I thought he'd keep his word.'

'Perhaps the old fellow was wandering in his mind, towards the end?' Zeke was making me uncomfortable now, about this inheritance of mine. If it hadn't been for the scorn I would face from Miles, I'd have been tempted to give the shop over to him, lock and stock, there and then. I knew, however, that the gift had probably been in acknowledgement of Mother's regular parcels of comestibles, and her home cured bacon. This, she'd told me, she'd been sending to the old man, month in, month out, as he grew older and frailer. Uncle William must have thought 'Sarah's eldest will have the farm, I can repay her by willing the shop to the younger lad.' Had he just forgotten his previous promise to Zeke?

Zeke supplied the answer himself, 'Mam upset him,' he said. 'He tried to make it up her, get her to come and do his washing, but she wouldn't. They had a great 'up and downer' last Michaelmas tide in the market place. I suppose he made 'is Will next day, and cut us out! They both had tempers on 'em! Then she died, and then he died, and that was it.'

We unpacked the provisions Mother had sent, poured ale into two pewter tankards Zeke took down from the carved oak dresser, and sat at the bare and dusty dining table in the room across the hallway from the what he called 'the shop'. After our improvised meal, he produced from a drawer the ledger in which he said Uncle William had been wont to record all his incomings and outgoings. He assured me he knew how to keep it, and that he would lock any proceeds away each day in a strong box hidden in the principal bedroom, as William had always done.

I rubbed my jaw at this, realising I ought to be setting Cousin Zeke some kind of wage for his work, but I was at a loss to know what was reasonable. He would be living rent free, and if he cheated me, I'd be hard put to know it. Immaculately kept account books are just that. They don't tell you what 'passed under the counter' as the saying goes. I learned *that* lesson from a dishonest Quartermaster in the New Model. So, assuming that Cousin Zeke would certainly defraud me a little, I suggested that he take what he needed for his food and clothing, and keep a note of it in the back of the ledger. I think he was surprised by my trusting nature, but I'm not, after my years in the army, quite as green as I may be cabbage looking. Given an apparently open opportunity to cheat, it's been my experience that most rogues tie themselves in knots trying to prove their honesty, and end up cheating no-one but themselves.

'Show me this strong box of Uncle's,' I said, as we pushed our dishes aside. We mounted the stairs to the principal bedroom. The room was empty apart from a four-poster bed, draped in fusty hangings, with a crooked table standing beside it, upon which stood a wooden candlestick, thick with spilled wax. One wall was made up of oaken panels with cupboards set into the wall behind them. Zeke went straight to one of them and opened it up, revealing several grimy old coats of my uncle's. He pushed these aside, exposing the base of the cupboard which stood a foot off the floor. Then he held out his hand. 'Needs the key,' he said. I fished the ring out of my jerkin. He selected a small key that I'd hardly registered when Mother gave them to me, and inserted it into a recessed lock in the cupboard's base. The key turned smoothly, and he lifted out a small iron box. It was locked. The contents were heavy.

'The key for that should be...' Zeke began rifling through the inner pockets of one of the old coats he'd pushed to one side, 'here...!' he gave a startled grunt as the coats suddenly descended on him, smothering his head and shoulders. After them tumbled something heavier, a bundle of coats and blankets containing a human body.

A human body, which, dirty and dishevelled, gave a frightened yelp and began to disentangle itself from its wrappings. Judith Moreland gazed up at us, her face streaked with tears and dirt.

'Oh, 'tis you, Rob Haddon. Your house has rats,' she said.

I suspect, no, I know, I stood with my mouth open, unable to form words. It was Zeke, extricating himself from Uncle's old coats, who demanded, '*Rats?* What right have you, Mistress, to complain of rats? How come you're hiding in my cousin's house, dropping out of cupboards?'

He turned to me, 'A trap door to the attics. Uncle was afeared when there was all that trouble in '42. Wanted to be able to hide himself and his money if thieves broke in at night. He showed me once. What reason had you to be hiding up there, Mistress?'

Judith scrambled awkwardly to her feet. She was holding her left arm across her body, obviously in pain. 'I shan't tell you,' she said.

# Chapter 28

'I can't explain!' I'm sorry, truly I am… I can only crave your understanding.'

I'd escorted Judith Moreland downstairs, and now she sat huddled in my Uncle's tall armchair, cradling her wounded arm with its fellow. Her head was bowed, and she spoke without meeting my eye. I seated myself on the other side of the table. A silence followed, during which Zeke appeared, plonking one of the tankards on the table with an ill grace. I'd sent him to devise a soothing posset — after all he was the one who wanted to be a vendor of herbs and spices. I'd thought willow bark, my mother's chosen restorative, but Zeke didn't think Uncle William had stocked it.

'Uncle was a spice merchant, not an apothecary!' he grumbled when I suggested it. ''Erbs was a side line with him. Howsoever, we got some dried meadowsweet. That's a pain reliever, if I remembers rightly?'

I had to hope he was remembering rightly. After all, I was trusting that Zeke wouldn't poison too many of the good people of Lancaster whilst I left him in charge here.

Now Judith lifted the tankard with her good arm and took a small sip. 'Thank you. I'm sure this will ease it,' she murmured, her eyes still not meeting mine. 'It's just…a silly thing. It will heal. An accident.'

'When the rat in the attic startled you, and you fell through the cupboard?'

'No! I took no hurt from that. This happened before…before I left to come here. A stupid accident. But never mind that.' She took another sip. 'I'm sorry to be causing you trouble, Rob. I needed… to leave Lings. Something happened…never mind what. I thought, if I came to Lancaster I could find work, as…as a maid. I've heard people say how difficult it is to find maids, especially just now, if a lady wants to travel. They're afraid to take to the roads because of the war, you see?' She shrugged and winced, evidently feeling the pain in her back and shoulder. 'Afraid they'll be attacked by the Roundheads if they're with a Royalist family. Afraid of the Cavaliers, if their mistress's household is for Parliament.' She took another sip, grimaced, and went on, 'Mama had a letter from her sister, Letitia, the one who lives in Surrey, and in it she said not one of her maids would travel up to London with her — even when she threatened to turn them off! I thought I might hear of some lady here who wants to travel to Preston — or even to London. Or maybe to join her husband with the army? And I'd go with her, acting as her maid.'

'Why? Why should you need to leave your home?'

Judith placed her tankard down very deliberately. 'I'm not going to talk about it. I'm sorry, Rob. I owe you an explanation… but I can't give you one.'

We sat in silence for some more moments. These last years in the New Model, trying to get information out of someone, I'd found silence sometimes works. But Judith wasn't an enemy. Or was she? Just what was she about? Zeke had retreated to the doorway, but stood there, listening and glowering.

'So you came here, to my house?' I said, at last.

'Yes. Once again, I apologise. I needed somewhere safer than a common inn for a girl on her own, until I find the lady who wants a maid to travel with her. I thought...I thought you wouldn't mind? Ann said she didn't think you would.'

'You saw Ann? She told me you hadn't been there!' I recalled Ann, standing in the farmyard, raising those clear, innocent brown eyes to mine. My little sister, so modest, so good, revealed as a bare-faced liar! Gervase might be in for an unpleasant shock, when he discovered what a sly little deceiver he was proposing to marry.

'I told her to say I hadn't been at Lowflatts,' said Judith, unabashed. 'I needed the key. I thought no one would be here. I never imagined you'd come. That was stupid, wasn't it? It's your house, so of course you'd come to look it over, before you go to Scotland. I thought... I was stupid, stupid. I wasn't thinking clearly. Ann gave me the key to the back door.'

Whilst she was speaking, I had taken out the heavy key ring and laid it on the table. She glanced at it and then at me. 'The back door key. It's different.' She sought under her shawl and produced it. 'You won't let me stay, now, I suppose?'

'No!' growled Zeke. 'Tek the silly wench back to her folks!'

'No! I won't go!'

'I'm not shifting out so that *she* can bide here.' Zeke was adamant. 'You promised me a berth!' They glared at one another.

'Your mother,' I began, addressing Judith and ignoring Zeke. (Did he think I would turn him out to sleep in the street for this girl?) Judith flinched as though someone had slapped her, when I spoke. I went on, 'We met your mother, riding out early this morning. She told us you'd been sent to stay with a relative of your family at Hornby. Is that why you ran away? Because you didn't want to go?'

Judith's expression changed in an instant from distress to astonishment. 'Cousin Bess? My mother told you she'd sent me to *Cousin Bess*? But...Mama detests Cousin Bess!'

It was my turn to raise and lower my shoulders. 'That's what she said, although I think she was searching our neighbourhood for you. I wondered, though I may have been wrong, if she believed we were hiding you at Lowflatts.'

'Well, of course I did think of that,' said Judith, who seemed mysteriously cheered all of a sudden. She even managed a tiny smile. 'I'd thought to hide in your hay barn, now the hay's all in, and Ann would bring me food, but then your brother might be angry if he found out, and what was I to do with Moonbeam? If I turned her loose she'd probably go back to Lings, and then they'd guess I was close by.'

'Moonbeam? This one's all moonbeams if you ask me!' grumbled Zeke.

'I take it Moonbeam is your mare,' I said, continuing to ignore Zeke. Obviously the silly girl had quarrelled with Lady Brilliana. 'What *did* you do with her?'

'I turned her loose here,' she replied, nodding her head in the direction of the grazing ground beyond, under the castle ramparts. 'I didn't want to take her to a hiring stable, because I wasn't sure how long I'd be here, and I can't afford to spend too much. I...have only a little money.'

'And no one has stolen her?'

'You don't know Moonbeam! She won't allow herself to be caught by anyone, save myself and Abel Haythornethwaite.' Judith's manner had altered so much that she now appeared remarkably cheerful, although she continued to cradle her sore arm.

'I'm sorry,' I told her, thinking to shock her into telling the truth, 'but Zeke is right. I promised him he should live here and mind the shop in my absence. So, unfortunately I am obliged to turn you out. Would you like me to find you a place at one of the inns here in the town? If I take you to one of the decent ones, and put you in the landlady's especial care, you'll be safe.'

'No. I shall go to Cousin Bess!' replied this exasperating girl, blithely. 'If Mama is telling everyone that's where I am, that's where I'll be! Do you intend to ride back to Lowflatts today, Rob? Yes? Then you'll be passing close by. Let's ride together.'

It was after three of the clock when we set out. Zeke stood on the doorstep, arms folded, scowling, as we left. I think he couldn't quite believe that Judith was really going, and that he would have the place to himself. I worried that I ought to be leaving him with a long list of instructions for the care of my property and my business while I was away, but I couldn't think of any. As a soldier I was very used to knowing my business, and to issuing orders and commands. As a shop keeper, alas, I was nothing but the rawest recruit. Miles was probably right, when — if — I returned from whatever lay ahead in Scotland, wresting my inheritance back from Cousin Zeke might be fraught with difficulties. But what alternative did I have? None. I'd counted the money in the strong box while Judith was retrieving her saddle from the attic and catching the mare. Half the money I pocketed, and half I left with Zeke, letting him know I knew the amount to the last penny. What he did with it I had no choice but to leave to his discretion.

Nursing her mysterious wound, which obviously pained her greatly, Judith found the catching, harnessing and mounting of Moonbeam taxing, but she refused all offers of help, and finally scrambled onto her saddle by way of a stone mounting block which stood beside the old mansion at the end of the lane, Stoop Hall.

'It won't be an easy ride for you with that injured arm,' I warned, after we'd collected Caesar from the hiring stable. 'If you find yourself in difficulties, let me know and I'll slow our pace, but from what I see, clouds are building in the west. We may be in for a storm.'

Judith glanced back over her shoulder at the dark clouds massing above the ramparts of the castle, and set her jaw. 'I'll manage,' she said, 'Moonbeam is well schooled, she responds to the lightest touch.'

I thought it likely we would reach Hornby, eight miles or so distant, before the storm broke. I felt I must ensure that this mysterious 'Bess' was there to receive her cousin. Then I still had another ten mile ride to Lowflatts. It would probably be my fate to be soaked to the skin. Well, what was a mere soaking, compared to what was undoubtedly awaiting me north of the border?

To distract my mind from such thoughts, I asked Judith, 'Who is this Cousin Bess that your mother so dislikes, but that she never-the-less thinks to send you to visit?' Judith said nothing for several moments, and I assumed from the tightening of her lips that she thought me impertinent. This irritated me. She'd thrust herself into my family, and attempted to take possession of my house without so much as 'by your leave!' I considered she'd forfeited the right to decide now, that she was a lady and I was a peasant. Why should I not ask about her relative? However, it seemed she was only considering what to say.

'Cousin Bess… is Papa's cousin,' she said at last. 'She's a good deal older than he, and a Puritan. You know, the real old kind from the time of Queen Elizabeth?'

'She cannot be as old as that!' I exclaimed.

'No, but you'd think she was. She dresses all in black, and reads nothing but the Bible and other Puritan texts. She employs an elderly Divine to lead her household in prayer for an hour each day, and she thinks Papa is a backslider and too frivolous by far! Mama, she cannot abide at all. My brothers, she will not countenance to cross her threshold. She has nothing but contempt for the present war, which she terms 'the work of Satan.'

I felt my eyebrows climbing. 'So how will she react to finding you on her doorstep?'

'Oh, she likes me.' Judith winced as her mare stumbled slightly on the rough surface of the lane, jerking at her sore arm. 'As much as she likes anyone. You see, I was kind to her little dog. Rags —the little creature's name is Rags — is her one indulgence. He's a nasty, snappy little lapdog, overfed and indulged, and once, when we paid a visit of ceremony to see how she did, because after all, Papa is her nearest relative — what must my brothers do but tease him into a fury? So, it fell to me to rescue him, and he decided to like me. And therefore Cousin Bess thinks me the best of our family.'

'Yet your mother spoke of sending you to her as though this was a punishment?'

'I daresay,' agreed Judith. 'To her, an enforced stay with Cousin Bess would be the worst thing she could imagine. So she would think it a harsh punishment for me. I do not say I shall enjoy it, precisely, but it will serve.'

'Because you have quarrelled with your mother, and you don't want to go home. This must have been a serious quarrel?'

I kept my tone light, teasing, remembering Loveday — poor Loveday, not so many years ago — quarrelling with all of us, and hiding out in the barn, threatening never to speak to any of us again (until hunger drove her indoors, and she forgot why she hated us) but Judith set her mouth in a stubborn line and didn't reply. We rode on. Above us the clouds began to thicken, and the summer afternoon light faded to the gloom of evening, although it could not have been much beyond four of the clock. The leaves on the trees that now crowded around us began to hiss and rustle in the rising wind.

Presently Judith reigned in, some fifty yards before the gates of what I could just perceive through the trees, to be a solid stone building. 'That's Cousin Bess's house,' she said. As she spoke the first rumble of the approaching storm rolled over our heads, and a jagged flash of lightning lit the untidy bushes lining the road. As we began to walk our horses forward I heard Judith gasp, and knew I hadn't imagined it. That lightening flash had shown her, too, what I thought I'd seen. A band of men were waiting on the path ahead.

An ambush.

# Chapter 29

I would wish to report that I was the hero of the hour. A seasoned warrior, never caught unwitting. That I fought off our attackers single handed, but it wasn't so. It all happened so quickly that I never saw them clearly. I was unarmed, having left my sword with Miles. That had seemed like good sense at the time. Caesar did his best, rearing up onto his hind legs like one of those Spanish trained stallions you might see in a painting. He brought his hooves crashing down onto one of our assailants, inflicting, I hoped, a good deal of damage, but in doing so he unseated me, and I was cannoned backwards into those same bushes from which the ruffians had sprung. From this ignominious position, legs higher than my head, my coat was grasped and I was dragged forth and hurled forward, staggering and shouting to Judith to flee. Then my arms were seized and I was clubbed about the head as efficiently as a fisherman despatches a salmon.

You might be expecting that I woke (if I woke at all) to find myself on the hard and filthy floor of a rat-infested barn, bound and gagged. Be surprised then, as I was, to find instead that I was floating, pillowed, limbs lead-heavy but free. It was dark, true, but above me the stars glimmered, and a youngling moon emerged from a bank of cloud. My head hurt, but seemed to be fixed, bumping gently against something hard. Grit or gravel scraped at my neck. My body hung heavy but unconstrained, buoyed up. Water. My head and shoulders were grounded, the rest of my body was floating in water. My assailants, probably supposing they'd killed me (or not caring whether I subsequently drowned) had pitched me into the Lune. Only the air, trapped in my clothing, and the swirling current bearing me quickly away, had saved me. Unconscious, I'd not struggled, and the Lune, though wide here, was not deep. So I'd drifted, on my back, half submerged, until my head lodged between two limestone rocks against which the river had made one of those small temporary islands, created as its level rises and falls. An island of silted gravel, stones, weeds, and bleached driftwood, which lasts a few summer months and is swept away by the first Autumn storm.

The base of my skull hurt as though imps were pinching at it with red-hot tongs, but other than that, I was remarkably comfortable. I knew I should try to turn myself onto my front, crawl onto this fragile islet, and see how far it might be to wade ashore. I felt no particular urgency to do this. I conjectured, my mind itself seeming to float somewhere outside my body, that I must be cold. Even in late June, surely the water was cold?

I think I drifted, perhaps an hour, perhaps much less, in the river. Time seemed to be at a stand, and yet above me the clouds, the stars, moved across the Heavens. The sharp thunder shower that had marked our arrival before Cousin Bess's gate had evidently passed. Like a human baby held against its mother's shoulder, the infant moon peeked out shyly, now from this cloud, now that.

The river sang me a lullaby, and even the pain in my head seemed to beat a slow retreat. I was slipping down into death, wondering, vaguely, what the purpose of my time on earth had been, and yet… something roused me. Above the river's noise, some person, some animal, was moving about on the bank, crashing through bushes and undergrowth. Faintly, I heard a sound that chimed in my mind, and I half raised my head. A wave of pain went jabbing through my skull like a knife thrust.

Caesar! I could see him now, snorting and plunging as he pushed his way through tangled strands of reed mace to drink at the river brim. No, I didn't imagine he'd come to rescue me, but I was extraordinarily pleased to see him, and strived, as I hadn't before, to struggle to my knees.

'Caesar?' I called, and he raised his head, ears twitching, turning to identify where my enfeebled voice was coming from. I could see — for now the moon at last sailed clear — that his saddle had slipped sideways and hung against one flank, stirrups clanking together beneath his belly; the sound I'd heard. His reins were broken, their ends trailing in the water. I rejoiced. Any attempt by those scoundrels to catch or harm him had ended in failure.

'Caesar? Here, boy!' I scrabbled to my feet, wobbling on loose stones, annoyed to find I was barefoot. My attackers had failed to steal my horse, but they'd taken my boots.

A soldier's boots are a precious piece of kit. The fury that surged through me at this discovery was, I think, what aided me to propel myself forward across the broad expanse of water. As Caesar cautiously, but obediently, stepped into the stream, I was able to hurl myself at his neck, and cling on.

'Sorry about this, boy,' I gasped, gripping his mane to keep me upright. He snorted, lurching back on his haunches. 'I know, I know! This wouldn't happen on a well-conducted battlefield, but let's get out of this damned river before I catch a fever!'

Safe on the bank I managed to right his saddle, first loosening and then tightening the girth, and to knot the broken reins. By the time I'd achieved this, I was shaking uncontrollably, my teeth clattering together like an army of woodpeckers. It seemed so loud inside my head that I feared I'd be heard all over the district. I doubted I'd the strength to mount, so I led my horse along the river bank, pressing myself against his flank trying to absorb some warmth from his coat. Even though I was now fully conscious, I'd have given much simply to sink onto the grass and sleep.

'What happened to Judith?' I murmured. Caesar rolled an enquiring eye. He was a horse, he neither knew nor cared what had happened to Judith

Moreland. He wanted to know where we were going, where his next meal was coming from.

'Someone… guessed we might come that way,' I told him, trying to control my shivering. 'And lay in wait.'

'Whoever it was had no use for me, so I was disposed of. Could it have been Judith they wanted? Had she some knowledge which must not be revealed? Perhaps they supposed she'd already told it to me. Someone needed to stop Judith leaving home. Someone who knew her well enough to predict at her intentions. 'But why, Caesar, *why*?' None of it made sense.

Caesar snorted in my ear. I winced, head throbbing. 'Have they killed her, boy? Is she too in the river? Or are they holding her somewhere?'

Since neither of us had any answers, we plodded on along the bank until a gap in the vegetation opened onto the roadway. A hundred paces back from this lane I could see candlelight flickering in an uncurtained window. I was almost back to the spot where the ambush had taken place. Cousin Bess's house stood before me.

Should I go there? Judith hadn't told me a great deal about her relative. The impression I'd gained was of a formidable dame of enormous moral rectitude. Surely quite the last person to willingly involve herself in kidnapping an innocent girl? It was possible she knew nothing of the rogues who had been waiting just outside her gates. Though her servants could hardly have failed to be aware of the commotion.

It must be late. It was full dark on a June evening when daylight normally lingers hereabouts until nearly ten of the clock. Very like I would catch the household at their retiring prayers (and should offer some of my own for my deliverance and that of Caesar). I determined to call at the house and ask what they knew. It was a struggle to cover even such a small distance. The sharp stones beneath my naked feet almost made me abandon the attempt.

If I'd known what kind of welcome I'd receive, I would have abandoned it. My pounding at the door brought forth an elderly Cleric, who peered at me in disapproving silence over his spectacles for what seemed like several minutes.

'Whatever you've come for, your errand is fruitless,' he finally said. 'My mistress was greatly disturbed, *is* greatly disturbed by what happened here today. The whole household has been cast into turmoil, and we really cannot stand any more of it tonight.'

'I see. So your mistress is aware that Mistress Judith Moreland, in company with myself, was attacked outside her grounds?'

'Only too aware,' grimaced this old fool. 'If she had known of it before hand, Mistress Kenton would have taken steps to prevent it, naturally, but she did not.' His eyes moved away from my face, his lantern travelling down my sodden clothing to my bare, and now bleeding, feet.

'So they… carried… Judith Moreland away?' I was finding it hard to put words together.

'So we assume. You, young man, were supposed to be acting as her bodyguard? If so, you signally failed in your duty.'

I was too exhausted to argue. It had been pure chance that Judith and I had been riding together. I'd had no idea that she meant to flee to my house in Lancaster. When I told her she couldn't stay, she'd insisted that she'd be safe with her father's cousin. I'd agreed to ride with her, purely as a courtesy. Not having any reason to predict a likely attack, how could I have acted as a bodyguard? I ached with weariness. My limbs were fast stiffening from their cold immersion. I'd not even strength to lose my temper, and strike this idiot down.

Perhaps, however, he dimly recollected something he, as a clergyman, was supposed to understand. Something called Christian Charity. For he now said, 'It's late. I'll not disturb my mistress, but I give you leave to take shelter in the barn.'

Caesar and I settled for the barn. As we had done a hundred times before, on campaign, after battles we had won, as well as those we'd lost. The hay was in, fresh and sweet. I found a bucket half full of water. I removed Caesar's harness, stripped off, and wrung out, my own drenched clothing, and fell naked into a nest of loose dried grasses. There I slept until first light, slipping down into slumber to the sound of my horse, munching his way through Cousin Bess's hay. Before I did so I thought briefly of Judith, and what had happened. Was she living still? I was too dog weary even to grieve for her.

# Chapter 30

Caesar woke me. Well, a horse must piss as well as a man, and the noise and smell in the confines of a barn are considerable. Sometimes, on campaign, we have stalled our horses in churches. 'Tis little wonder many of the clergy are unsympathetic to Parliament's cause!

Still naked, I went outside to empty my own bladder, and found the sun just beginning to rim the summits of eastern fells with gold. A fine day in store, perhaps. I'd no exact idea of the time, but no one was stirring yet in the house.

Inside the barn once more, I found my spread garments, though damp, were wearable. Thanks be to the Lord Above that it was summer and warm. Should I call once again at Cousin Bess's house, and try for a little more information? And a spare pair of boots? Surely they knew more than the old Divine had been willing to divulge? And surely I'd a right to demand answers? This time I had no Gervase to back me up, to add an air of menace that would frighten them into conjecture about where those rogues had taken Judith, and why. And what they meant to do with her.

Caesar broke his fast with more hay, but the Lord God did not design man to exist on the grasses of the field. I was ravenous. Hearing a faint clatter of bowls and saucepans coming from Dame Bess's kitchens, I presented myself.

I suppose I made an unprepossessing sight, my clothes rough dried, hat and boots gone, hair wild, and full of strands of hay. However, I consider that the shriek the maid emitted when I appeared in the kitchen was needless. Still, it roused the household, and soon the Dame's chaplain was upon me once more, and presently the Dame herself.

Bess Kenton was a woman well stricken in years, a tiny creature whose bones seemed to have shrunk down inside her skin, so that all that could be seen of her face and tiny paws beyond the stiff black gown and starched cap she wore, seemed a interwoven mass of small wrinkles. Her eyes, though faded to almost colourless apart from the black dots of her pupils, still snapped with life and temper. She stood, glaring at me, her hands clasped tightly together.

'Well, young man! What dost thou want of me?' I eyed her with disfavour.

'As your chaplain may have told you…?'

'He did. Get on with it. What dost thou want?'

'Information and a pair of boots.' I can be curt too.

'I have no information. What happened here yesterday was an outrage. Thee wast escorting the girl, they tell me. Thee shouldst have been armed.'

'Possibly, Ma'am, but I was not, in any official capacity, escorting your relative. She'd thought to stay in Lancaster, but decided instead to come here. I was returning to my home further up the dale, and we agreed to ride together. She didn't indicate to me that she believed an attack was likely. I'd no reason to suspect an ambush.'

'You're an army officer?'

'Major Robert Haddon, Parliamentary Army, Ma'am.' I thought she relaxed, very slightly.

'Pshaw! If you're the best they can find to promote, then 'tis no wonder this war drags on! I know only what my servants have reported. That woman is very likely in it somewhere! My cousin Benson should never have married her. Fooled by a pretty face! Daughter of an Earl! He sold them off like a batch of heifers! 'Twould never surprise me to discover she's a *papist!*'

'Why, Ma'am, would Lady Brilliana kidnap her own daughter?'

'The Lord God alone knows. *I've* no idea.' As she spoke, a tiny white dog ambled into the room and, after sniffing at them, began to lick my bare and bloodied feet. This seemed to disconcert the lady. Perhaps it was something to do with the religious significance of the washing of feet. Perhaps it was the dog's evident approval — or her anxiety that he might fall ill as a result of ingesting my blood, who knows? She turned in haste to the chaplain.

'Sir Lawrence!' She used the old title for the clergyman. 'Find this fellow a pair of boots. He'll want to be on his way.' With this she signalled to an elderly maid to pick up the little dog, and together they left the room. It was only as she walked away that I noticed how her hands trembled. A formidable woman, but she was frightened. Of yesterday's intrusion. Of me. Our Civil War had never before managed to unsettle her peaceful kingdom. It had taken all her fortitude to face me down. I admired her for that. She was old, frail in body, but not in spirit. Her household relied on her, and she would defend them with her dying breath.

Sir Lawrence, who doubtless knew all this, flashed me a look of abhorrence. After mumbling orders to the kitchen girl who'd started the rumpus in the first place, he remarked, with a sigh, that he'd see what he could do about boots.

They gave me breakfast. Stale bread and watered small beer. Presently a youth with a hare lip, sweating visibly and totally silent, laid before me a pair of worn and patched boots. Now that I was somewhat recovered from the previous day's ordeal, I was even more furious about the boots. These battered substitutes would see me home, but where was I to get another pair before setting out for Scotland? Even if I could find a cobbler willing to make me some in the time, I resented the expense. In the station of life to which I belong, precious items like hats and boots are passed down through the generations. Mine had been willed to me by my grandfather, and had a good deal of wear in them yet. It was useless to think that the

Army would replace them. Parliament isn't made of money, as they frequently remind us. Many of the lesser ranks fight barefoot, but what respect would they have for a barefoot Major?

Champing my crust, I fell to wondering if I could go after the thief or thieves. I'd an idea, although not one I could substantiate, about who my assailants had been. It had all happened so quickly, in the shade of thickly foliaged trees, and in the midst of a thunderstorm. I knew there'd been four men of varying heights. At least one of them was armed with a club. I could hazard, of course, that Zadoc and Job had been two of them — how they must have exulted in their revenge! — but there'd been something so proficient, so deadly, about the way I'd been despatched, that suggested a true professional. Royalist Army? Thinking me dead, and needing to get rid of my body, what was more probable than that the 'Commander' of this little band had ordered Zadoc and Job to do it? He, whoever he was, must have thrown Judith across his saddle and ridden off, leaving them to tip my corpse into the river. My boots, those two rogues would simply consider fair recompense for the job.

I thanked the kitchen maid and left. I might have left a coin to compensate her for the fright I had given her, but didn't. She shouldn't have watered the beer. When I'd first put on my breeches, I'd been surprised to discover the money I'd taken from Uncle William's strong box was still wrapped in a damp handkerchief in the pocket sewn inside the waist band. Inefficient of Zadoc and Job to have missed it, but they would have been in a hurry. It would have been daylight once the thunderstorm passed. Even those two wouldn't have wanted to be witnessed robbing a corpse.

Caesar was as willing as I was to leave that place. I saddled up. Annoyingly, the knotted reigns were now too short. Having them repaired would be yet another expense, when I'd hoped to give most of Uncle William's money to Miles.

Some way down the lane I dismounted, and cut and trimmed a stout branch from the hedgerow. My clasp knife, happily, had been hidden in that same inner pocket. I sharpened one end to form a usable pikestaff. Caught unarmed yesterday, that wouldn't happen again. Of course that Royalist Officer — I had no evidence that my attacker was such a man, but felt in my gut he was — thought me dead. Whoever the fourth man had been, he too must think me dead. Standing in the lane, considering this, I suddenly knew who that man had been. Not because I had recognised him in that stormy light, but because I'd smelt him! A mixture of animal manure and some chemical smell. I recalled how surprised I'd been when I first encountered him — Joseph, the serving man at Lings!

A smartly dressed fellow, and yet this filthy smell hung about him. Thinking it odd at the time, I'd mentioned it to Gervase, who said he believed it to be some remedy for hair loss, a mixture of potassium salts and chicken shit.

Joseph had acted, to perfection, the part of the superior manservant, humble before his employers, but all the while looking down on the local peasants. But, it would seem, embarrassed by his thinning hair. It was unusual and surprising that the Morelands should tolerate this show of vanity. I was remembering, too, how confident and at ease he'd appeared on horseback, escorting Lady Brilliana as she rode into the ghyll.

'Mayhap Joseph is not what he seems,' I told Caesar. Caesar snatched at a bunch of yellow rattle in the hedgerow. 'Enough!' I exclaimed, 'you have already filled your belly in Cousin Bess's barn! You'll be too blown to make any speed.'

I rode on, towards Lowflatts and home. The day was fresh and so far fine, although clouds were massing in the West again. My immersion in the river seemed to have done me no serious corporal harm, praise God, but I wasn't at ease. I rode, my body taut with dread, fearing a new attack at each bend in the road. I've tried, these past years to convince myself that this sensation is not cowardice, but common sense. I knew my body to be bone weary still, despite my sound sleep. My bruised skull ached. In times of danger, the body, even more than the mind of a man, insists that every limb, every muscle, must remain on guard. Yesterday's attempt to kill me had been brutal, and these foes wouldn't hesitate to attack again. I kept turning my head, though my neck pained me horribly, thinking I heard hoof beats, even footsteps, behind me. However, I reasoned with myself, these men were probably miles away. Having, as they believed, murdered me, my reappearance would be the last thing they expected.

The trees that lined the road I was travelling, and the meadows beyond, looked newly greened by the recent heavy rains. Dandelions starred the grass. Foxgloves nodded in the shade. This was the peaceful landscape I'd ridden home from Scotland to find. There was nothing to affright me on this bright morning, and yet...

I'd nearly convinced myself when, as I rode out from beneath a canopy of sycamores, I saw a figure ahead of me in the road. I couldn't have sworn a Bible-oath he was newly emerged from a clump of bushes, but I had that impression. I reigned in. Caesar's ears flicked back and forth, a sign with him that he was alert to something unusual. The figure was seemingly alone, on foot, and wore a long, dun-coloured cloak and a wide brimmed black hat. Curiously, as I observed it — *him*, he seemed to shrink, to become very bent, progressing slowly with the aid of a stick. Yet when I'd first spied him, I was sure he had been upright, his step less feeble.

A ruse, a disguise? Or because, being a lone traveller on foot, he feared me? While I held Caesar at a stand, he continued to progress towards me, leaning heavily on his staff, his bent back arching higher than his battered felt hat. His face was hidden by the brim of the hat, and he held his cloak close. I could see that the hand that was free of the staff clutched something he evidently wished to keep concealed. From time to time, the hem of the cloak lifted in the morning breeze, and I caught a glimpse of his treasure. A pair of boots! I could swear they were *my* boots!

But how? How could this this old fellow have acquired them? Bought them from Zadoc and Job? Stolen them, whilst those two caroused in some ale house? Wild conjectures swirled through my thoughts as I urged Caesar forward and we drew level. I raised my improvised pikestaff and thrust it at him. 'Halt, fellow! Where's tha off to with those boots?'

He didn't reply, but clutched them to his chest and cringed away from me, apparently fearful. Yet I sensed there was something false here. This man was not as old and frail as he wished me to believe. I made a feint with my pike, and caught the edge of his cloak, whereupon he collapsed in the road and lay on his back, roaring with laughter, whilst his hat and staff rolled into the ditch.

'Gervase, you scoundrel!'

He lay there, clutching my boots to his chest, unable to speak for laughing.

# Chapter 31

'I couldn't resist a jape!' Gervase was saying. 'You looked so mighty fierce, Rob, and ready to run me through with that sapling!' He didn't say, though I knew it, that part of this giddiness was an expression of relief that I lived. Finding my boots in the clutches of a dead man, had made him fear the worst.

We were reclining in a small dell, back some distance from the road. I was listening to what he was telling me, and trying not to fall asleep. My body's rigidity had melted away. The sun was warm, the smell of crushed thyme soothed my aching pate. Bees buzzed in the harebells. A cuckoo called its cracked June note in the sycamores. I'd given him a brief account of my misadventure, and now he was explaining why he'd told us he was returning to Scotland, but was instead still roaming the neighbourhood disguised as a travelling preacher. And, more immediately, what he'd just discovered. A man, his throat crushed, in amongst bushes at the road's verge. It was from this discovery that Gervase had just emerged as I rode up.

'Poor little Job! A rogue, but I couldn't help liking him,' I'd found myself saying, when he showed me the pathetic corpse, carelessly thrust amongst hazel saplings.

Gervase snorted. 'Though he stole your boots and tipped you into the river?'

''Twas not he who wielded the club,' I replied, gingerly caressing my nape. 'Job, and with him Zadoc, I imagine — though I never saw their faces — were merely charged with disposing of me. Hired men, mercenaries, although I doubt either of them ever fought on any battlefield. My boots were just spoils of war, though I'm mighty glad to have them again!' I paused, forcing my tired brain to seek words. 'And now he has disposed of Job too.'

'He?' Gervase was all attention.' You never saw him, but you know who he was?'

'I think I do, and I surmise he's the man you have been looking for these last months.'

'You can name him?'

'I don't know his name, but doubtless you do. The Uncle. I — *we* — should have realised.'

'I should have realised! A messenger brought word late last night. He'd been seen on the outskirts of Lancaster, which is the reason I was making my way there, and not riding for the border. Now I've missed him again, damn it!'

I suppose it was the easing of fear. Now I was no longer alone, expecting to be set upon at any moment, I was finding it extraordinarily difficult to stay alert. I forced myself to continue.

'I knew there was an Uncle. Nicholas Moreland told me so, when you went to bring help for Edwin in the caves. Nicholas said his father wouldn't send them money to pay for their pleasures in Antwerp, and so they got it *from their Uncle.*'

'Lord Gilbert Delaunay, Lady Brilliana's royalist brother. Damn him!'

'Feathered hats and hunting dogs.'

'And horses. We were a pair of slow tops there, too, Rob! Those matched bays. The Colonel didn't buy those expensive pieces of horseflesh for his sons. We didn't question it either, did we, when the twins suddenly arrived home, apparently unescorted?'

I hitched myself up the bank, propped myself against the trunk of young oak and sat erect, to give this proper consideration. 'I just assumed this uncle was living in Antwerp. Lord knows, they say plenty of Royalists are hanging around in the Low Countries. Grumbling about the food, running fancy riding schools, fawning over the Royal Princes-in-exile, hoping for future preferment.'

'Indeed,' agreed Gervase, 'and Uncle Gilbert no doubt makes himself out to be one of those. But he's more than that, and now I know Edwin and Nicholas a trifle better, I doubt they travelled from Antwerp on their own initiative. Where did they get money for the crossing? No, Uncle Gilbert brought them! Delaunay's been travelling to and fro from the continent on a regular basis. And mayhap the twins' spending in Antwerp became too great a drain on his resources, so he returned them to their parents! Fool that I am, I didn't ask what route they took. I know now that they sailed from Antwerp to Cork, and from there across to Lancaster. Delaunay had need to call on sympathisers in Ireland on the way. Trying to raise money for The Cause. For King Charles the Second, our rightful monarch, he would no doubt say.'

'And not just the likes of Lady Brilliana's jewels, I suppose?'

'Whatever sympathisers can spare. Or be frightened out of. And, as I should also have guessed, whatever those scoundrels Matthew, Zadoc and Job could steal. What we saw in the caves was rubbishy stuff, but doubtless they stole other, more valuable, things. Matthew Garstang led that enterprise, but he was working for Delaunay.'

'Who found him in Ireland, discovered his history, and his knowledge of this district,' I supplied. 'Delaunay couldn't be here all the time to collect their pickings, but I know who was.' I removed my neck cloth, and rolled it to cushion my tender nape. 'In some sort, this Lord Gilbert is your counterpart, is he not? Riding up and down the country trying to whip up support for the Royalists, even as you are aiming to dissuade folk from so doing! I haven't told you that Joseph was one of my attackers, have I?' I described how I'd recognised the manservant by his stink.

'The Old Retainer. Someone who has served the Delaunays all his life. Turned off from the Earl's overstretched household seemingly, but taken in by Lady Brilliana because she "couldn't bear to see the old fellow in want." And the Colonel too easy going, and having been too often away from home to question it,' sighed Gervase. 'You have the right of it, I'm sure. Matthew and his band reported to Joseph between Delaunay's visits.' He pondered this for a few moments, chewing on a blade of grass.

'You're right too, I suppose,' he went on, 'that Lord Gilbert is my counterpart. Save that Cromwell is not so desperate that I'm required to be his bagman, and steal what people won't give! The Royalists need a mint of money to pay for men, arms, and supplies, if they're to have any chance of taking the field against Parliament again.'

He sounded quite elated by this. I continued to fidget, trying to find comfort for my sore neck. Gervase has always had more relish for warfare than I. Perhaps I'd relished it once, but it was hard to recall those days.

'So, someone informed on him, and now you know that he is currently in this district,' I stated. 'You found the informant?'

I was experiencing a stirring of dread in my gut. Despite having told Gervase of the previous day's attack, I'd said little about the kidnapping of Judith. I was feeling deeply guilty at my failure to foresee what happened. What must have been her fate?

'Was it, by chance, Mistress Judith?'

'Oh, no!' admitted Gervase, ruefully. 'I was a fool there, too, Rob, and wasted a great deal of time and energy on that missive sent to the Council of State. I sat through prayer meetings, listened to impromptu sermons, endeavoured to get samples of all your neighbours' handwriting. I even thought, for a while, that it could be your enchanting sister-in-law, Mistress Loveday, until I discovered she could barely write her own name, or understood which side she should be supporting! No, 'twas young Abel.'

'Abel Haythornethwaite wrote to the Council of State?' I was incredulous.

'He didn't write himself. I doubt if he can. But he's staunchly devoted to Colonel Moreland, who seems to have rescued him from destitution when his parents died. He'd somehow discovered, probably from a conversation overheard between the Colonel and one of the regular Parliamentary messengers, that the way to 'lay information' was to write to 'them up in Lunnon town,' but it had to be done 'proper like, and secret,' as he put it.' Gervase chuckled at the thought. 'When I appeared in the district, in various disguises I admit, the silly lummox dared not, until he was certain which side I was on! 'Twas only when I called in at Lings, after I left Lowflatts yesterday, to receive my last minute instructions, that he decided it was safe to confide in me.'

'Instead, he consulted Richard Hardcastle, but Richard was then about to leave on one of his preaching tours. He suggested this Biblically minded friend of his in Barbondale, and Abel met up with him at the Whitsun Hiring Fair in Sedbergh. The letter was duly despatched by a relay of travelling packmen. However, the resulting content, believe me, was so obscure, every sentence bound about in Biblical allusions, that no one up in 'Lunnon town' could make head or tail of it! Never-the-less, it did seem to contain what looked like a nugget of genuine information. So, since it was known that I was familiar with this area, I was chosen to investigate.'

'But what did Abel know? How came he to know, as I take it, that this Lord Gilbert was scouring the area, getting money by whatever means?'

'Well, he's a little sharper than he appears, and people do tend to discount the lad who mucks out the stables. I'm not sure, either, that Abel ever really saw Delaunay. What he saw was the horse. Heard it being led into the stable during the night hours. Abel sleeps in the loft overhead. Naturally, he shinned down and took a look at it. In the morning, it would be gone. Sometimes, he told me, he'd hear the rider walking towards the house, where he'd stay an hour or two. These times would be when Colonel Moreland was away. It shows, I think, the splendid purity of young Abel's mind that he never supposed this man to be Lady Brilliana's lover! Once the Colonel resigned his commission and came home for good, the visits ceased. At least, the horse came no more. Abel decided to say nothing. What could he say? That the Colonel's wife's brother used to visit her, but now did not? Even a poor toad like Abel understands where this war has left us. Whole families split asunder. He told me, most earnestly, that a brother and sister might surely still love one another though divided by family quarrels. This was another reason why, having sent the letter, he hesitated. Lady Brilliana had never been unkind to him, and he came to realise that there was danger, both to her, and to the Colonel himself.'

We sat silent a space, absorbing this. Then I said, 'Now we know what Loveday saw. *"She shall know the wrath of God, who meets her lover in the wood."* Only it was Lady Brilliana's brother she met in the wood.' Judith told me that little rhyme was one of Loveday's prophesies, but she claimed even Loveday didn't know to whom it applied. What decided Abel, in the first place, to send the letter?'

'That was the doing — though it must have been the last thing he intended — of Joseph. He, being an indoor servant, and believing himself highly superior...?'

'He does,' I affirmed.

'...was in the habit of treating young Abel disdainfully, regarding him, Abel says, as though he "ain't got no wits, and with no eyes in 'is 'ead." Thus he made an enemy, and also drew attention to himself. So when Abel spied him with a bundle of hay under his arm, and carrying a basket of provisions into Lings woods at dusk, he followed him.'

My mind went racing through Lings woods. Surely I remembered some place where a man might…? *The game hut.* A stone barn-like structure where deer killed in the hunt had formally been hung. A place for Lord Gilbert to hole up, when he could no longer visit Lings openly. The very place to store valuable goods between those visits. Much more convenient than the caves. Dry, and easily accessible. The Hardcastle sisters had seen Matthew and his band close by, pretending to collect firewood, but no doubt delivering stolen goods.

I was so busy retracing the steps of boyhood explorations that I neither saw or heard the man emerge from the wood we happened to be sitting in, until he was upon us.

# Chapter 32

Why the fool did it, I'll never fathom. For love of his comrade, Job, perhaps. Love flourishes, after all, in the breasts of the most improbable persons. The knife flashed and sank into Gervase's shoulder even as he leapt to his feet and turned. Without thought, I hurled myself at the assailant from a sitting position, landing on his shoulders and forcing him back onto the bank, where he lay, winded, his eyes rolling back in his head. I turned my attention to Gervase, who'd sunk to his knees and was plucking at the knife.

'No!' I bawled. 'leave it! You'll lose too much blood, 'twill come gushing forth. Leave it be, I'll get you to a doctor!'

The man on the bank raised his head at my bellowing, and looked across at us. It was Zadoc, Job's companion. I saw now that he was gravely wounded himself. Blood had poured from a chest wound down the front of his shirt. 'Beg pardon!,' he croaked, and fresh blood oozed from his mouth, 'Ah meant it for t'other.' His head flopped back onto the grassy bank, and his eyes closed in death. Gervase, now as white as a snow cap on Ingleborough, slid slowly to the ground in a faint.

Dear God, *now* what must I do? I'd a dead man on my hands and one who might soon follow him if he didn't get medical attention. Even as I fretted, I was plucking moss from around the tree roots to stay the bleeding. The knife was sunk deep, the handle jutting from Gervase's chest just below his collar bone.

'Pray God it went straight in, and so missed your heart!' I had no idea if he could hear me, but I kept talking in that hope, and of thus keeping him alive. I clasped his wrist as one of our orderlies in the New Model had shown me, and thought I felt the beat of his heart echo there, as the man had told me I should.

'I'll have to leave you to get help,' I babbled. 'I'll take Caesar and ride to Kirkby Lonsdale. There must be at least a barber-surgeon there! I daren't try to put you on Caesar, I couldn't hold you, and the jolting would enlarge the wound.'

All the time I was trying to reassure him (and myself), and forming these desperate plans in my head, I was pressing the moss close around the handle of the knife. Then I removed my own shirt and tore strips from it, binding them around Gervase's chest and shoulder to hold my improvised wound dressing in place. It was difficult to pass the strips of fabric around his unconscious body without jarring and opening the wound, but somehow I managed. I laid him down, his head slightly raised on a pillow made from his jerkin, and threw his preacher's cloak over him for warmth. The day was fine and warm, the dell a sheltered spot, but those worrying clouds were building in the west.

'Don't die on me whilst I'm gone!' I challenged his prone form as I turned to leave, 'Or my sister will never forgive me!'

I was sorely troubled which way to go, what to do. Kirkby Lonsdale was nearer than Lancaster, but would I find anyone there with a trained physician's skills? A barber-surgeon can set broken bones, or even sever a crushed limb if he must, but removing a knife from a deep wound is work for a trained physician.

I uttered up a prayer for guidance, and let Caesar have his head. It passed through my mind that it was strange that Caesar had made no fuss when Zadoc had come plunging out of the thicket, but perchance he was either sulking or stupefied. We'd tethered him to a tree away from the road, where Gervase had left his latest mount. Not the elegant Venus, but an ugly mule, with the largest teeth and the longest ears I'd ever seen. Gervase had explained that this was part of his disguise. No one would look closely at the preacher, he'd claimed, but would notice only the knock kneed stumble shanks he was riding. Caesar, understandably, was offended to be left in this beast's company. When I proposed to gallop all the way to Kirkby Lonsdale, he was perfectly amenable, and we set off at a raring pace.

I have become sceptical, since I grew to man's estate, about the efficacy of prayer. However, when I reflect back, I can name several occasions in my life, when, despite my paltry faith, the Lord God has shown His mercy towards me. Today was no exception, although at first, thundering round a bend in the road, loose stones flying out from beneath Caesar's hooves, I saw only a cause for frustration. A group of farm labourers spanned the roadway, rakes and pitchforks over their shoulders. They were walking along, five abreast, singing snatches of a popular ballad that had caught their fancy, and chaffing with one another. Evidently they'd come from one hayfield, and were moving on to another.

'Make way!' I bawled. 'I seek help for a dying man!' but instead of stepping aside to let me through, they ambled to a standstill, spread across the road, so that I could pass neither to the right nor left without colliding with one of them. Exasperated, but unwilling to run Caesar onto the tines of a pitchfork, I reined in.

'Tha wants t'doctor?' demanded a fellow so old and bent that I wondered what use he could be amongst the hay.

'I do,' I panted, 'my friend has been stabbed, and I must ride into Kirkby to get help.'

'Nah, nah, tha needn't,' said the old fellow, smiling upon me gummily.

'I must! 'Tis desperate!'

'Nah, nah,' repeated this aggravating old person, wagging his finger at me. 'See yonder?' He gestured back over his shoulder with his rake. 'See yon gate post? 'Tis Greenside farm, where we're come frae. Farmer's name is Crawshaw.' He peered from side to side to see if his companions agreed. The four louts nodded. 'And,' he paused like a play actor, or perhaps just for cussedness, 'not two hours ago Mistress Crawshaw was brought to bed with a bonny boy, and Doctor Stainton was with her. To see all went off well, d'ye see? — the Crawshaws having four lile lasses already. So, if tha was to hurry,' he added, maliciously, 'tha'd catch him without going ony further!'

At this, the haymakers did draw aside to let me pass. 'Reckon he's a good man!' one of them called after me. 'Trained in *I* -tally, they say, and has served with Old Ironsides too. He's the man tha wants!'

He was indeed. I caught him, but only just. When Caesar and I swerved in at the farm gate he'd climbed the mounting block, and was about to swing his leg over a dappled roan cob. I knew he was my man by the bulging leather bag he carried. Also, when he turned a startled face towards me as I pulled Caesar up, I recognised him.

'Preston,'48!' I gasped, too breathless to say more. Dr Stainton bowed. 'General Lambert's horse,' he acknowledged. 'Minor sword cut to your left wrist. I see you still have the horse. A fine animal. What can I do for you?'

For a moment, staring down at Gervase's prone body, I thought we were too late. His breathing was so shallow I could barely detect it.

'No, no, he'll do,' Doctor Stainton assured me. 'What does the bard say? "The thousand natural shocks that the flesh is heir to?" I studied in Padua, and they taught there that when the body receives a blow of this magnitude it's natural for it to close itself down. It tries to ensure that even the taking of breath involves as small an effort as maybe.' He knelt on the grass and opened his leather bag. ''Tis not often, these days, that I bring a child into the world and try to prevent a man from leaving it on the same day.'

'You worked with the Army for some time?' It was obvious that he was quite at home with serious flesh wounds.

'I did, but have retired from the fray.' He frowned. I said nothing. He removed my trifling attempts at bandaging, and threw the moss aside. 'Hmm. Gone deep, but the bleeding's contained.' He paused, frowning at the knife hilt, 'I'll not attempt to remove it here. No, we'll get a cart and take him to my house. Did you say there was a team of men working the hayfields hereabouts? Very like they have one, and we could transport him cushioned in a bed of hay. Farmer Crawshaw would be willing I imagine, since he's in mellow mood, having a son at last.' He gazed around at Zadoc, sprawled on the bank. 'And there's yet another corpse besides this one, you say?'

I indicated the hazel saplings amongst which Job lay concealed. 'As I told you, the two men must have been attacked yesterday.' I reflected that it was indeed fortunate that Dr Stainton had met me before, and knew something of my past, or he might have doubted my tale.

'I believe I know who the assailants were, but they're long gone. A falling out amongst thieves. Over money, I suppose, though I cannot know for sure. The man over there in the bushes was killed outright. This fellow,' I indicated Zadoc, 'must have crawled into the thicket gravely wounded, and after lying out overnight, become delirious. When he heard our voices this morning he must have imagined, in his confusion, that his foes had returned. He stumbled forth, and stabbed my friend. When he realised he'd attacked the wrong man, he apologised.'

'Not many do that. May his immortal soul be spared,' said the little doctor. 'My late wife was a Catholic,' he went on, his voice dropping almost to a whisper. Even in this lonely spot this was not something he dared say aloud. 'I didn't share her faith, but it was sincere. She was from an Irish family. A good woman. After the massacre at Drogheda I left tending the Army. I didn't hear any apologies issuing from Oliver Cromwell's mouth.'

'And will not, I fear,' I said, grimacing. 'He seems set in his belief that to be Irish and Catholic is to be less than human.' We stood a moment, deep in our disquieting thoughts.

'I'll go and find the haymakers and requisition a cart,' I decided. 'What think you we should do with the two dead men? We can hardly put them in the cart along with Gervase... though we do have the mule.'

'Splendid. Ask them for a coil of rope, if they have one.' Doctor Stainton looked appraisingly at Zadoc's corpse. 'I should like to have them both for a day or two,' he added, thoughtfully, 'for the purpose of scientific examination, if you understand me? The study of cadavers is an interest of mine, and I imagine these two scoundrels are unlikely to be missed? Afterward, I'd see them decently buried, of course.'

I was slightly perturbed at this, not entirely comfortable with the idea that the bodies of Zadoc and Job would be violated (though I owed them nothing) but understanding that a physician must study the dead human body, in order to aid the living, I went to find the haymakers.

# Chapter 33

I rode up the lane to Lowflatts in the early evening, almost too weary to think. Dr Stainton and I had delivered Gervase safely to his house, and I'd waited, taut with foreboding, while the little doctor extracted the knife. This he did with such speed and precision that it was over before I realised it was happening. Although blood seeped from the open wound, it didn't gush forth as I'd feared. Disturbed by the sharp onslaught of pain, Gervase had opened his eyes for a moment and frowned at me. He didn't speak, but I felt he was trying to communicate something. Then he sank back into unconsciousness. Once the wound was sealed and bound with clean linen dressings, Dr Stainton told me I might go.

'If he wakes I'll give him a poppy draught. Sleep and quiet are essential for healing. I'll sit with him myself through the first part of the night,' he assured me, and then my manservant will relieve me. I trust him to wake me if there is need. 'Twere best if you leave without rousing the town. I imagine the fewer people know he's here, the better.'

I'd told him very little about our reasons for being together in that wood, but he'd served with the army and was no fool. As I rode away I spared a thought for Zadoc and Job, dumped unceremoniously in an outbuilding behind the doctor's house. True, Lord Gilbert Delaunay and his henchman, and not Gervase and I, had been the cause of their deaths, but I regretted handing them over to Dr Stainton, and preferred not to think of what he would do to their corpses. In my head I knew that what he discovered might be of use to wounded men in the future, but my heart had turned delicate on me.

From this moment, I reflected, all depended on me. Gervase had identified the traitor. It was now my responsibility to deal with him. What should I say to my mother and to Ann? Was it best to leave them in ignorance, supposing Gervase to be half way to the border? And what of Judith? What should I, could I, do about Judith Moreland? I dared not contemplate her fate. She hadn't been the one to write that fateful letter to the Council of State, but her uncle might well have believed so. And if he did so believe, what would he do? Would he kill her as he had killed Zadoc and Job? Or carry her off to be imprisoned in some place where she could cause him no further trouble?

I approached Lowflatts, angry and heart sick. Doctor Stainton had quoted from the playmaker of past years, William Shakespeare. It had not been my lot to watch play actors perform, but I'd served with another man who was fond of quoting the bard. Hadn't he written, "a plague on both your houses?" I wouldn't wish the plague on anyone, but I knew how the playwright had felt (or how he'd supposed his character to feel.) This war of ours had gone on too long. Could the hatreds and injustices it had created ever be healed?

My head still ached from the bludgeoning it had received. It came to me now through a dull throb of pain, that which had not been clear before. Lord Gilbert's party had not, as I had assumed, been lying in wait for Judith at Dame Bess's gate. No, indeed. Our arrival had been fortuitous. He'd been there to demand money from the old woman and her household. Little wonder they had reacted with such dismay at my arrival, seeing me as yet another hostile rogue come to menace them, demanding money or goods. I pictured Bess Kenton, clutching her hands so tightly together, so that I should not see them tremble. Even those who sought only to live in peace were having that peace destroyed by this war, perhaps for ever.

Richard Hardcastle came into my mind. Benjy had told me how he intended to lease a smallholding and found a peaceful community. A worthy aim, but could it work? Dame Bess and her servants had lived in peace and contentment until yesterday.

I rode into the yard. By the slight faltering of his pace, I knew that even Caesar was weary. I slid from the saddle. Spots of rain began to splatter the cobbles. A young woman who'd been seated by the kitchen door shelling peas, jumped up hastily, depositing the bowl on her stool.

'Rob! Oh, Rob! Thank God! Thank God!'

It was Judith Moreland. She was wearing an old drab work gown, too short at the hem, a cast off of Ann's, and had one of my mother's sacking aprons tied around her waist.

'I thought he'd killed you!'

She came towards me. I took her hands in mine. 'I'm hard to kill,' I said, and my voice sounded like someone else's. 'I thought he'd killed *you*.'

Her mouth trembled and tears began to slide down her cheeks. I drew her to me, and she wept against my shirtless chest. The rain fell heavier and we stood there, unable to part, until we were both soaked through.

'I told your mother... that I didn't know what had happened to you,' Judith wept. 'I didn't know how to tell her the truth... *that I thought you were dead.*'

'That wasn't the truth,' I said. 'Thanks be to God.'

The back door opened, and Benjy Postlethwaite looked out at us.

'Hey! Them peas. Mistress Haddon's wantin' 'em. Oh!' he added, 'Tha's back. Better come in out of t'wet, eh? Ah'll tek t'horse.'

Mother had made lamb's tails pie, never a favourite of mine. It always feels strange to see the lambs skipping happily in the garth without them. However, I hadn't eaten since the crust I'd been given so grudgingly by Dame's Bess's kitchen wench, so I forced it down.

'So, how did you get here, Judith?' I asked as she scrambled to her feet to take the empty dishes away.

'Horseback,' she said, shortly. 'As I said to you before, no one can catch Moonbeam save Abel and myself. My uncle,' she grimaced, 'didn't realise that. So while he set on you, and one of his...accomplices... hauled me from the saddle, Moonbeam bolted. Then in the confusion, because they wanted possession of your Caesar of course, I ran. Caesar, naturally, lashed out at them, broke the reins, and galloped off. I ran into the coppice, caught Moonbeam, and rode away. I thought... I waited, at a distance, concealed in the trees, until I heard them ride by. They hadn't Caesar, but I couldn't see if they had you. I waited, a long while, to be sure they were gone, and then rode back, but... I couldn't find you.'

'No,' I answered, 'they didn't have me. I ended up spending the night in your relative's barn, with a sore head.' This wasn't the moment, with my mother and sister sitting open-mouthed and uneasy, forks suspended over their plates, to tell her what had actually happened. 'Then you came to Lowflatts?'

Judith whisked the plates away, brought a gooseberry tart to the table, and set it down before my mother. 'As I explained,' she said to me, 'when we...met in Lancaster, I've decided to find work as a maid. Earn my way in the world. Lowflatts needs a maid. With Zeke gone, and Rachel...and Loveday. Your mother has given me leave to stay.' She sounded angry, determined, as though she was daring me to question her decision, as I had in Lancaster. Mother and Ann looked unhappy. Judith was the daughter of the 'big house', and although they'd always accepted her presence amongst them, hearing her call herself a maid, and serve them at their own table, wasn't something they felt comfortable with.

'Tha'll need to learn, happen,' said Benjy, who hadn't taken his eyes off the gooseberry tart. 'Tha's too fierce yet, for a maid, Mistress Judith.'

Miles had entered the room while these exchanges were going on, and now took his place at the table. He was looking better, much more like himself, and as combative as always.

'Nobody asked my opinion, of course,' he grumbled, lifting his knife and fork to finish the pie congealing on his plate, 'but I suppose we must feel obliged to shelter Mistress Judith. Malachi Postlethwaite just came by, and told me he heard in Beckside that a Royalist squad are holding Colonel Moreland hostage.' We froze in our seats, speechless.

'That's what I feared,' said Judith. 'Mama will never repulse Uncle Gilbert.' She sank into her chair, dropped her head into her hands and burst into sobs. I placed my fingers on her arm, unable to think of anything of comfort to say.

'Yet you ran away?' my brother challenged her, though a mouthful of pie.

She raised her eyes and stared at him for moment. 'That wasn't the reason,' she replied, 'but no matter. Poor Papa. He's too trusting. He's been betrayed. But I hope my Uncle will not mistreat him.'

'Simply make a fool of hi'?' said Miles, who can never leave well alone.

After supper there were the usual tasks to be done. Benjy brushed and fed Caesar. Milking time was over. Lanty had penned the sheep and gone to his rest in the hay barn. Miles and Benjy set to, replacing the broken struts in a gate while the light held. The heavy rain shower had passed over. I ambled into the lane, pulling out bundles of green stuff from the hedges for the sheep. Judith appeared at my side, and without any discussion, we two wandered further, where we wouldn't be overheard.

'I've washed and dried the pots,' she said, 'and now, I believe, is the hour when a maid make take a little rest if her employer allows it. Which your kind mother does. What will you do now, Rob?'

'Are you expecting me to besiege Lings Hall? I would rescue your father if I could, Judith.'

'I doubt that's the most important thing,' she replied, her eyes dark pools of seriousness in the gloaming. 'Papa has been made to look a fool, as your brother pointed out, but as I said, I think my uncle is unlikely to do him bodily harm. I don't doubt that you could do it, Rob, even without a troop of trained soldiers at your command. The people here like Papa, I think. He's always been a good landlord, and fair in the dispensing of justice. If we called on all the men of the district, I believe most would come. But is it not more important to capture my uncle, and stop him from doing what he's doing here? Isn't that what Gervase Fenton planned to do?'

We stood in silence for a while. 'Perhaps we should do both,' I said. 'If we besiege Lings, we may smoke out this uncle of yours, and rescue your father at the same time.'

A siege, such as trained armies conduct, was not something I'd anticipated. Not here in the dale with raw recruits. I was reluctant, but I knew that I'd be expected to do something. Gervase could not have anticipated mounting a siege either, what would he have said to the idea?

'Who's there, at Lings?' I asked Judith. 'Your uncle, your mother, your two brothers? Your manservant? Abel Haythornethwaite? A couple of women servants?'

'My uncle has henchmen. Three, at least.'

'Two of those are dead.' I explained to her what had happened to Zadoc and Job. She expressed no surprise or sorrow at this news. 'There may be more. Surely he would not have risked taking Papa hostage unless he'd other men to call on? Edwin is no case to help him, even if he wishes to, and Nicholas is not...' She didn't finish her thought about Nicholas.

While we were speaking we had drifted back towards the farm. Miles looked up from his task as we approached.

'Well? What has your council of war concluded? Do you ride to the

Colonel's rescue?'

'It may not be so straight forward, Miles. Mistress Judith and I believe her uncle would not have taken her father hostage unless he had reinforcements. So we cannot simply ride to up to the door of Lings Hall and demand his release. We need reliable information.'

'Malachi mentioned a Royalist *squad*. I know not what he meant by that.'

'Us should have a proper council! To plan strategy!' said Benjy, his eyes shining 'With all of us as wants to see the Colonel free! Will Ah run and get 'em all here, Major?'

# Chapter 34

We assembled in the barn. Our neighbours were seated on piles of last year's straw, upturned buckets, or anything that came to hand. Lanty, above us on the stacked hay, slept throughout the proceedings, too deaf to be disturbed by the uproar. It was as well. We couldn't have explained to him what we were doing. Benjy had carried two kitchen stools through, one for Judith Moreland. I found myself taking the other, even Miles seemed to expect it. A table of sorts was created by placing a plank across two barrels, and Judith and I sat behind it. The womenfolk filed in, and crowded just inside the doorway. Mother looked worried, but mainly, I suspected, about whether she ought to have served refreshments.

While our 'council of war' was being set up, I noted who had come at Benjy's bidding. Josiah, George and Malachi Postlethwaite, Richard Hardcastle, but not his father, (for which mercy, the Lord God be praised), Luke Proctor, Sam Woodley, and two farmhands whose names I'd forgotten again, although they'd told them to me at the time of the cave rescue. Eight. With the addition of Benjy, Miles, and myself, eleven.

When I decided that all who were coming had arrived, I rapped on the surface of the improvised table and summoned them to their feet.

'We start with a prayer, asking for guidance from the Lord and blessing on our enterprise,' I told them. 'Josiah, will you lead us?'

Hats were hastily plucked from heads, eyes cast down, and feet shuffled in embarrassment. Well, they might as well know how we do things in the New Model Army. If I'd thought to disconcert Josiah, I was unsuccessful. The old fellow was intoning *'I will lift up mine eyes unto the hills, From whence cometh my help? My help cometh from the Lord,'* before the foot shuffling had ceased. This gave me time to form the words I was going to say. I wonder if that's the reason our commanders in the New Model like to proceed in this fashion? Certainly decisions made after the prayers are over frequently bear little relation to the appeal for guidance just expressed.

Once the 'amens' died away, I signalled my 'troop' to sit.

'The purpose of this gathering here tonight,' I began, 'is to decide whether it is reasonable and practical for us to make an attempt to free our neighbour and Magistrate, Colonel Benson Moreland, whom we understand to be being held captive at this time, within his own home, Lings Hall.' A hubbub erupted.

'Us don't *understand* it, us knows it!'

'Don't need to decide owt. Us should get on and do it!'

'No speechifying, lad! Let's go once 'tis full dark, and catch 'em napping!'

This does not happen when Oliver Cromwell addresses his forces.

What was I doing, in Heaven's name, supposing I could achieve anything with this rabble?

'Silence!' I roared. 'Mayhap you lot know different, but I have no idea how many men are holding the Colonel. Malachi, you spoke of a 'squad' of men being at Lings Hall. Who and what are they?'

'Ah only knows what Mistress Snaith told me,' mumbled Malc, scarlet faced. 'Happen she can tell yer herself.' All eyes turned to the women standing in the doorway, and Deb Snaith was pushed forward.

'Well, Mistress Snaith?' Was this going to turn out to be just some piece of women's gossip?

'May it please you, Sir, I mean Major Haddon, I went up to the Hall this morning to help with the wash,' Deb was flustered, pleating her apron between her fingers, but she stood her ground. 'but after we'd been working at the washtubs about an hour maybe, I saw these men ride into the yard. I think they came through the woods, they didn't ride up the drive. I counted them. There were seven. They waited a while, standing talking, very quiet like, amongst themselves. There's few windows on that side of the house, and I don't know as the Colonel would have known they were there. Then two more rode in, and joined them. I recognised one of them. 'Twas Joseph, that's a manservant there. He seemed to take charge,' she added, her tone indicating that she had been perplexed by this. 'He called for Abel, the young lad, to come from the stables, and lead the horses away. Then the men went indoors, all together. After a while the cook came running out to us, proper scared she was, and in tears, and she said as they were Royalists, and they'd pushed the Colonel down the cellar steps to keep him prisoner, and we should leave at once.'

Judith, who had been sitting silent beside me, spoke up, her voice sharp. 'Did you see my mother?'

'No, Mistress Judith,' Deb bit her lip, and her eyes filled with tears. 'No, nor your brothers. I didn't see any of the family. I hopes they're not hurt, Mistress.'

Deb Snaith seemed a reliable witness. 'Did you see any weapons?' I asked.

'Not to say for sure, Major Haddon. We were watching them from the wash house door, wondering why they were there. We never went nigh, nor they came nigh to us. I suppose they had swords. Yes, for sure they had swords at their sides.'

'Muskets? Firing pieces?' The grunts from my band of hotheads suggested that they might be cooling down a little at the thought of firing pieces. The Lord be thanked for that. What did we have? My sword, plus a collection of farm tools.

Deb Snaith shook her head, 'I don't think so, but I can't be sure, Sir.'

'We are eleven, and they are nine,' I told the assembly. 'The number of muskets, pistols, or other firearms they may have is unknown. So, nine swords against one sword and what?'

Pitchforks were raised, I counted four. Cudgels, three. Hay rakes, two. Stout sticks, one. Richard Hardcastle had nothing at all except a copy of the Bible, and was quite unashamed of it.

'Abel would join us, if we went, I know he would,' supplied Judith. 'that would make twelve.' I chose to ignore the 'we' and the 'us'.

'You're saying we can't do anything,' said Miles, disgusted. Trust my brother to lack faith in me.

'No, but I'm saying we need more information — if we can get it. It's no use our marching up to the front door and demanding they hand over the Colonel and his wife and sons. They won't do it. We need to surprise them, draw them away, if we can.'

A clamour of suggestions broke out, most of them downright perilous. Oh, for trained army men!

'Us could start a fire, burn 'em out!'

'Remember that his wife and his two sons, one of them on his sick bed, are inside the house.'

'Us could cause a… what-d'ye-call-it? A distraction. Set fire to t'stables and then they'd run out. Happen. The Widow tells us the horses are there.'

'Aye, first tek t'horses out, and then fire 'em!'

'Then what?' I asked, trying hard to hold onto my patience. 'We fire the stables. They run out, armed with swords, perhaps firearms. *Then* what do we do?'

'Tha'd better tell us,' said old Josiah. 'Tha's the soldier here.'

If I'd had a pistol to hand, I swear I'd have shot the old pestilence! I took a deep breath to calm myself.

'I suggest we go down there. Quietly. Separately. A mob approaching up the drive would immediately alert them. We go in ones and twos across the river and the meadows. We wait at some distance, preferably amongst the trees. Then we send someone — I glanced at Benjy — to make contact with Abel. We know, that is, I know, because Gervase Fenton told me this, that Abel sleeps above the stables. We discover from Abel what weapons these men have. Supposing they don't have firearms, or not many, we wait until we have reason to believe they're sleeping. Then we make some attempt to enter the premises by stealth and release the Colonel.'

''Tis a pity Gervase isn't here,' said Miles, gloomily, despite the fact that he had never previously had a good word to say about my comrade in arms. 'I'm sure he'd have come up with a better suggestion.'

It was indeed by the Lord's mercy that I'd no firing piece, or I'd have shot my brother too.

'What of the other members of the family? Are we to try to rescue them too, if way opens?' asked Richard Hardcastle, speaking for the first time.

'Don't assume that my mother will wish to be rescued,' said Judith. I glanced at her bitter expression, and understood that Judith's quarrel was not, after all, with Lord Gilbert Delaunay. That wound to her back and arm. Lady Brilliana must have beaten her daughter savagely with her whip.

Mine wasn't an inspired plan. Miles was right about that, but I'd defy General Lambert himself to come up with a better strategy, given the men, the information, and the weaponry at my disposal.

We'd passed the first twenty days of June, and the nights were already drawing in, but still a hour of dusk stretched before us. I dismissed my volunteer force once we agreed to make our separate ways to the edge of Lings wood, where it came closest to the Hall, at ten of the clock. Miles, of course, questioned the wisdom of this, saying half of them wouldn't return or would mistake the hour, but my mother was greatly relieved. As I'd guessed, she'd been afraid that she'd be expected to feed them all.

While the womenfolk (Judith had reverted to being a maid) busied themselves with household tasks, I sat at the dining table making a list of such necessities as we had.

My sword. A couple of pruning knives, usually employed around the farm to trim hedges. Four lanterns that could be closed to hide their light. Luke Procter had promised me his ropes. All the men had clasp knives.

I considered fastening these to poles to use as pikes, but doubted the effort to bind them securely was worth it. Stout staves can be very effective in close combat. Miles had the grace to find out for me some he had stored for fencing. Then I considered horses. Were we better on foot, or might we need to get away quickly? On the whole, foot soldiering seemed the wiser course. There could be no doubt that Gilbert Delaunay would know well enough who we were, and whatever the outcome, none of us had any intention of fleeing the district. As Josiah Postlethwaite had proclaimed (several times) our enterprise was righteous. Lord Gilbert was the felon, not we.

Ann came bustling through and ordered me to clear the table so that she could lay out some fabric she planned to cut out for a nightgown. Was she already at work on her bride clothes? 'Twas best not to ask.

'I wish Gervase was here,' she said, 'he would know exactly what to do.'

I grinned at her. 'And you think I don't?'

'Oh, I'm sure you'll do your best,' she said, 'but 'twould be better if he were here to aid you, would it not?'

'I wish he were here too,' I agreed, and suppressed a groan. I hadn't told her where Gervase was, or what had befallen him. I prayed my faith in Doctor Stainton was justified. If Gervase did not survive, it wouldn't comfort her much to know that his killer lay dead in Stainton's outhouse.

'You'll think me foolish,' my sister went on, 'but I wonder, is he really on his way to Scotland? Somehow, I can't say why, I feel he's near at hand. He told me he had information, that he had a name for the man he was looking for all these months. 'Tis hard to imagine he abandoned his task if his quarry is really close by.'

'When the army gives orders we have to obey them,' I said, hoping the guilt I felt at deceiving her wasn't written on my face.

'I suppose so,' said Ann, 'but somehow I feel I shall see him soon.'

I said nothing in reply. I prayed, most earnestly, that she would not see him soon. See him lying in a coffin.

# Chapter 35

Clouds veiled the hills. No sign of the moon which had witnessed my less than glorious adventures of the night before. The recent thundery rain had tugged cold breezes in from the Irish sea, and the air was chill. Not a night to relish lying prone in amongst damp undergrowth, waiting first for news, and then for the signal to attack. However, I'd suffered worse, much worse, on campaign. My companions had not, and it was obvious from their sighs and fidgets that they would have liked to complain, but didn't want to admit to being lesser men than I. Were they not hardy dales men, used to all weathers? They were, of course, but in harsh weather a dalesman keeps moving, and is frequently dressed in so many coats that the winds of winter don't penetrate. Here, tonight, crouched inside the border of Lings woods they needed to remain still and silent.

The only man overdressed for our enterprise was Miles. I'd suggested to Miles that he might not come, as he had been sick until so recently, but he insisted he was well enough, and then of course *Mother* insisted that he 'wrap up warm.' This he'd submitted to, with the result that he was so bound about with shawls and waistcoats that he could barely move his arms. I was praying he wouldn't have to, but could give no guarantee.

We sent Benjy to find Abel Haythornethwaite. There was never any question that he was the one who would go. Old Josiah prayed over his son, but he didn't query the decision. I justified it by saying that if he were caught he could claim he was just a young lad paying a visit to Abel, his friend. Since Benjy scorned Abel for a feeble-wit, and was wont to say so, loudly and often, I doubted he'd be believed if those he met with knew him. However, the hope was that he'd meet no one, or only those who'd never heard him castigate Abel's slow brain.

After an hour, when Benjy didn't return, it became apparent that he must have met with difficulties.

'Now what's t'do?' hissed Sam Woodley. 'Will Ah go, and see what's up?'

'We'll all go, as far as yonder tangle of bushes that grow against the stable yard wall.'

I'd decided that we were too far away, here amongst the trees. If one of us went to investigate he'd have no way of calling for assistance, short of bellowing, and revealing the position of our raiding party to the enemy.

'You can all crouch concealed there, and I'll be able to call on you quickly if I need to.' I was going to search the stables myself.

We skirted the edge of the wood, under the overhanging trees, the same route that Benjy had taken. Almost all the light had fled from the sky, but we knew we would be seen as dark figures, moving against the lighter grass of the meadow, if we ventured into the open. Reaching the outbuildings, we scurried, bent low, along the wall, until we were close to the entrance to the stable yard. All was in darkness. Beyond the yard, where it opened up to the lawns and the carriage drive, a few candles burned in the windows of the Hall, but within the stables no lights showed. I waited until everyone was hidden amongst the bushes, and signalled Sam alone to follow me. Recalling the skirmish at Hardcastle's farm, I knew he'd keep his head.

'Where does tha reckon young Abel sleeps?' he said, softly. I crossed to the doorway from which I'd seen Abel emerge when I'd last been here. The door was closed. When I tried the latch, it resisted, held by a wooden catch. We could hear horses moving in the loose boxes, but no voices. I'd assumed that Benjy had made his way here, but leaning against the door and peering through a knot hole in the wood, I heard and saw nothing. No voices or movement, no glimmer of light from flint or candle. Everything was deathly quiet.

'Happen they're not here,' murmured Sam. I sent him back to tell the others we were going forward, but they should stay in position until they received further orders. Then Sam and I began to make our way towards the house. I had my sword, Sam carried one of Miles' fencing posts. There was no sign of the moon breaking through the clouds, no shadows beneath the trees, yet an eerie light seemed to linger in the summer sky, too bright to risk crossing the lawns in the open. Instead, we dodged stealthily from tree to tree, waiting under each until we were sure no one on the watch at the hall had seen us. Colonel Moreland's lawns were not groomed like those of the palaces and great houses in the land. The grass was cropped by sheep, and the flock lay huddled beneath one of the ancient oaks. We passed close to them, but to my relief they seemed undisturbed. The scent of Sam probably reassured them. We found ourselves on a flagged pathway which brought us round to the kitchen quarters, and the washhouse Deb Snaith had spoken of. Sam tried the kitchen door. It was unlocked. Within, a tallow candle burned in a candlestick on the table. No one was there.

'Shall us go in?' whispered Sam.

'Better take our boots off,' I whispered back. We stepped inside, removed them, and lined them up neatly, toes pointed towards the door, in case we needed to jump into them and run.

'Chance is,' mused Sam, 'if this is t'main kitchen, cellar door ain't far off. Us could get t'Colonel out straight off, and none of these devils any wiser, if us goes cautious like. Then us can bargain for them two lads. If they've got 'em.'

He was right. Cromwell or Lambert would have offered Sam a commission on the spot, as would I, if I'd had the authority to do it. We stepped warily on to the cold stone slabs that lined the corridor. The door to the cellar was further from the kitchen door than I'd have expected, and it was that that caused me to make a serious error of judgement. We were now close enough to the entrance hall to see into it. Candles burned in a wall bracket. The hall appeared empty and silent, and I couldn't resist edging closer to see what was there. I'd caught a glimpse from the corridor. Muskets, a dozen of them, their long barrels propped upright against the wall! On a small table, the very one where Gervase and I had left our hats when we visited Lady Brilliana, lay an assortment of flintlock pistols. So, Lord Gilbert Delaunay had not simply been extorting money and valuables. Aided by Joseph, and Matthew Garstang's band of ruffians, he'd amassed quite a collection of firearms. All bound for use by a Royalist army of invasion.

There was no one visible in the hall. I stepped silently out, in my stocking feet, stupidly zealous to establish whether the boxes beneath the table contained, as I suspected, musket balls.

Joseph must have been standing watching from the landing above. From the corner of my eye I saw him angle the barrel of a musket, using the bannister rail to support it, dash the flint and fire.

'Down!' I yelled to Sam, and we dived to the floor. The noise of the gunpowder's explosion ripped through the hallway. There was a great flash like lightning. The musket ball destroyed the wall bracket, extinguishing all five candles as it fell. The ball, deflected, buried itself in my calf. Someone grunted in pain.

'Tha's hit!' hissed Sam.

'Glanced off me,' I mumbled in reply. 'Not serious.' I knew it wasn't, but it hurt as though a hellhound's teeth were clamped to my calf. 'Crawl backwards, Sam, into the...'

Before we'd chance to do so, the door to the dining chamber was flung open and Lord Gilbert, candle in one hand, drawn sword in the other, a crowd of men at his back, burst into the hall.

Now here is a difference between our two armies, our two *causes*, perhaps I should say. The Royalists, or at any rate their leaders, are skilled in sword play. It's a gentlemanly art, they tell me. Lord Gilbert would have been taught how to lunge, thrust, and parry, when he was barely out of petticoats. He advanced, weapon held correctly, blade at the proper angle, weight on the correct foot. Sam Woodley, however, like so many of the apprentices and farm lads who form the backbone of the New Model Army, had no such skills. Before I could scramble to my feet and unsheathe my sword, he'd rammed Lord Gilbert in his private parts with his weapon; one of the fencing-posts. A most unpleasant experience for Colonel Moreland's brother-in-law. It brought tears to my eyes, let alone his. He dropped his splendid sword with its bejewelled pommel, doubled over, and cannoned backwards into his followers. Two of them went down, dropping their candles. By this, I'd unsheathed my plain army issue blade, and was engaging with two more. Sam, meanwhile, laid waste to the two Lord Gilbert had inadvertently floored, clouting them with his post as they struggled to regain their footing. Suddenly the hallway was filled with struggling figures, flickering candles, the clash of steel, yells, groans, and grunts. I was holding two men off, but tiring. I'm a cavalryman, more used to thrusting downwards from Caesar's back, than hand-to-hand fighting. My wounded calf was bleeding into my stocking, sweat trickled into my eyes. There seemed to be more men pouring into the fray. I hadn't imagined, from Deb Snaith's description, that Lord Gilbert's party was so large. Then a pruning knife flashed past my ear, slashing my opponent's coat to ribbons, and a pitchfork tangled with a lace trimmed collar, tossing its wearer sideways into the path of Sam's fencing-post once again. It was *my* company that had suddenly enlarged. Miles, George, Malachi and the two farmhands, had got tired of waiting. Josiah Postlethwaite stood in the doorway, observing us with non-combatant enthusiasm. He was roaring encouragement, interspersed with fragments of Bible verse.

We were holding our own, or so I thought, but we'd forgotten Joseph. Long barrelled muskets are fiendish to reload singlehanded, but he'd done it, and now he was angling it over the bannisters once more, trying to aim where he had some hope of hitting one of us. I shouted a warning, and I didn't mean it just for my own people. This was a hopelessly dangerous manoeuvre in a crowded indoor setting. My humble fighting force suddenly stopped and retreated a step. Lord Gilbert, dazed, but on his feet, recovering from Sam's assault, lurched forward. At that very instant, there was a flash and a huge explosion above us, and the ball caught him square in the chest.

There was a long moment of silence. Then a howl of anguish as Joseph, the loyal manservant, realised what he had done.

It was at this dreadful moment that Lady Brilliana, in shawls and nightgown, appeared at the top of the stairs. Her fine eyes swept the scene. Joseph lay keening at her feet, grasping the newel post. She passed him without a glance, descending to where Lord Gilbert lay, and crouched beside him. Our opponents lowered their swords. We lowered such weapons as we had, and stood mute, heads bowed.

Lady Brilliana Moreland rose to her feet and turned to me. From the pocket of her gown she produced a pistol. She ran her finger over the solid brass cock on the top, and then locked her eyes with mine.

'Traitors, all of you! You have left me nothing!' she said, her voice grating with anger and sorrow mixed. 'Robert Haddon, you're the leader. I'll kill you, as I killed that stupid girl, Loveday! ' She raised the gun, cocked it, and fired. The ball stuck in the barrel. Mayhap the powder was damp. The gun exploded.

As the noise died, and we shrank from the terrible scene before us, we heard the tramp of boots outside, and a sharp rapping at the door.

'Open up! In the name of Parliament!'

George Postlethwaite shambled to open it, and suddenly the hall filled with buff uniform coats, helmets and pikestaffs.

'Cornet Ebenezer Perkin,' announced their leader, flourishing a docket. ''Ere on the h'orders of the Honourable Major Gervase Fenton, to arrest Lord Gilbert Delaunay on a charge of treason 'gainst the State...' He faltered, suddenly perceiving what he had walked into.

# Chapter 36

We didn't rescue Colonel Moreland. Or Benjy. Or Abel. Richard Hardcastle did that. While we fought a battle with fence posts and pruning knives, the man of peace had descended into the cellar and set the three captives free. Benjy had a black eye, and was in a furious temper. Abel was snivelling. The Colonel, despite chaffed wrists where he had been trying to free himself, seemed composed and very much himself, until he entered the hallway and saw his wife and brother-in-law lying dead. Then, though he remained upright, he seemed to crumple and grow old before our eyes. Nicholas Moreland, who'd wavered uncertainly at the back of the Royalist contingent whilst the fighting continued, now surprised me, firstly by fetching a cloth from the dining chamber to cover his mother's ruined beauty, and then by stepping to his father's side, and laying his hand on his shoulder.

'Come, Papa,' he said, husky with the effort not to weep. 'We can do nothing here. Let me take you to your study and have…and get… Brandywine?' He had, I think, been about to summon Joseph, but then recalled that the treacherous servant was in no state to serve.

Cornet Perkin began to ask questions, but before I could begin to answer them, we realised that the Royalists were melting away, disappearing out through an opened casement in the dining chamber, and the order was given to pursue them. The Lowflatts/Highbiggens contingent suddenly found ourselves too weary to follow. Let them away. They'd lost their leader, and all the firing pieces. If they got to the stables and saddled up before Cornet Perkin's troop caught up with them, good luck to them. Sam gathered up the prostrate Joseph and locked him in the cloak closet to stop his keening. Then, with one accord, we decamped outside and sat on the doorstep, breathing the cool air of the summer night, examining our wounds, and waiting for our hearts' beat to slow, and our limbs to stop trembling.

'So, Gervase knew about this Lord Gilbert?' Miles challenged me, 'and had arranged to have him arrested before he set out for Scotland?' Miles was still nursing on his lap the long pruning knife that had laid waste to some cavalier's favourite coat. He'd a bruise and a light cut to his forehead and was sweating heavily, but seemed remarkably cheerful.

'Gervase never went to Scotland,' I began. 'It's long tale. I met him as I rode back from Lancaster yesterday, and he told me he'd identified the man he was looking for.'

'So why isn't he here, taking charge?'

'*That's* the long tale. He was stabbed.'

'He's dead?'

'No. D'you want to hear it all?' I was almost too fatigued to make my mouth form words.

'No. I want to know what young Abel here is snivelling about,' Miles replied, turning to scowl at the boy, whilst peeling off one of his overcoats and several scarves. Mother would be furious, prophesying doom, and the return of gaol fever.

'One of them Royalists killed 'is dog,' said Benjy. 'Said it was rabid 'cause it bit 'im. But it weren't.' Abel's sobs grew louder. In the distance, across the park, we could hear shouts, and the clash of steel. A horse whinnied in alarm. Verily, Cornet Perkin was having his hour of glory.

'One of the Bouviers? Was that how you got your eye blackened, Benjy?'

'Piet, it was. This feller came to the stable while me and Abel wus talkin', and started looking fer summat in 'is pack roll. Didn't pay no mind to us, thinkin' we both belonged there, but then he stood back on Piet's paw, and Piet bit 'im, and then…' Benjy gulped, holding back tears of his own.

'Ah'd got right fond of 'im,' sobbed Abel.

'He ran the dog through with his sword. I see. You went for him, Ben, and got your eye blacked, and you both ended up in the cellar?' I summarised.

'Ah bit 'im too, and Abel tried to,' admitted Benjy.

'And the other dog, Claes?'

'He ran off, frit. Dunno where.'

'He'll come back,' I said, hoping to comfort them both. It is these incidental cruelties of war that are so hard to bear.

The front door creaked open behind us, and Nicholas Moreland looked out. That young man was surprising me tonight. Although pale as ghosts are said to be, he was calm and remarkably assured. 'Gentlemen,' he said, 'are any of you injured, and needing wounds dressed? The women are here at the kitchen door. My sister, and Mistress Haddon, Mistress Snaith, and Mistress Ann Haddon. They've brought baskets of salves and bandages and are anxious to be of assistance.'

Ah, I thought, as I dragged myself to my feet, so Ann hadn't been making herself a nightgown. She was cutting up an old one for bandages. Gervase little knows what a shrewd little dissembler my sister is!

'I've never had Mother dig a musket ball out of my leg,' I told the company, 'but I'm willing to have her try.'

We hobbled around the house to the kitchen. None of us wanted to re-enter the hallway where the bodies of Lord Gilbert and Lady Brilliana lay.

In the end, while the womenfolk applied bandages, salves, and compresses to cuts and bruises, it was Sam Woodley who flicked the musket ball out of my calf with the point of his clasp knife, just as he had proposed doing for Caesar. Then Mother came at me to bind the wound with a compress of boiled comfrey leaves.

'On the battlefield we use egg yolk, oil of roses and turpentine for flesh wounds,' I commented, drowsily. After a battle, I am always desperate for sleep, and I could feel that need stealing over me now. Josiah Postlethwaite had already succumbed, and was snoring in the inglenook, his bible in his lap.

'That's as maybe!' Mother snapped, 'but you'll put up with what I've got! Be grateful it's not boiling pitch!' She sounded angry, but I knew it was love and anxiety speaking. This was the first time she'd had to deal directly with the consequences of men fighting, and she must have been deadly afraid, for both Miles and myself.

Then two of Cornet Perkin's men tramped in, carrying an injured Royalist between them.

'Fell off 'is 'orse and cracked 'is 'ead,' one of them reported, as they deposited the unconscious man on the kitchen table.

''Tis 'im!' shouted Benjy, pulling away from Ann, who was trying to apply a compress of summer savory to his black eye. ''Tis the one killed Piet! Can us kill 'im?' That roused me from my lethargy.

'No, Benjy,' I said, rising, and going to stand at the man's side. 'What he did was wrong, but we treat fallen enemies with respect.'

'Huh!' said Benjy.

'No, Rob's right, we do, Benjamin, Parliament men and Royalists alike,' said a voice. Gervase stood in the doorway, pale and slightly unsteady on his feet, his arm strapped tight across his chest to keep the weight from his wounded shoulder. Ann ran to his side and clutched his good arm. 'Even if *they* behave like savages, we… well, we try not to behave like savages also. I gather I'm too late for the great battle of Lings Hall,' he went on. 'Well, done men, a notable victory!'

'How on earth did you manage to get here?' I asked Gervase later, when we'd ridden back to Lowflatts on the back of a cart, and were sitting round the kitchen table, drinking hot toddy. Mother and Deb Snaith had stayed behind to do what they could for the corpses of Lady Brilliana and her brother. 'When I left you, I thought it was touch and go whether Doctor Stainton could bring you through the night alive.'

'Evidently I'm tougher than you thought — than I thought, to tell you the truth, Rob! The good doctor didn't want me to attempt it, but when he saw I was determined, he got his gig out and swathed me in pillows and blankets. I'd alerted them to send a troop up from Lancaster, but I hadn't been able to give very precise instructions. I'd intended to meet up with them, naturally, and lead them myself. So I was afraid they'd get lost, or attack the wrong manor house. You and I both recall incidents when that's happened! Also, I thought you might tell your sister I was dead or dying.'

'He didn't tell me anything! I thought you were safe away to Scotland!' said Ann, furious that she hadn't known. Gervase circled her waist with his good arm, and laid his head on her shoulder. 'So you didn't worry about me. Good. As it is, no Scotland for me, which I'm sorry about. They want me at Whitehall to report on Lord Gilbert's activities.'

'How many of the Royalists have Cornet Perkin and his merry band caught?'

'Three, living I believe, now in the cellar at Lings. They're moving them to Lancaster Castle tomorrow. The one Benjy wanted to kill didn't survive. Fracture of the skull from falling from his horse.'

'Serve 'im right. Ah'm going to enlist,' said Benjy,' rousing himself, bleary eyed. His father and brothers had gone home to Highbiggins. Benjy had insisted on staying, but had, until now, been more or less asleep, sprawled across the table, his head on his arms. We probably shouldn't have let him drink the toddy. 'Then Ah can kill men like that. And Nicholas Moreland, he's going to join too. He told me. I'm for Parliament after this, he said t'me. Let Edwin fight for t'other lot!'

'Oh, Lord,' said Gervase, as we envisioned this. 'Twin brothers on opposite sides. Does Edwin want to fight?'

'Dunno. Reckon it'll be a while 'til he can, with his legs busted. He was laying upstairs whilst all that was going on, not able to get t'see what was going forward.'

'Edwin was Mama's favourite,' put in Judith, her voice barely audible. She had the toddy jug in her hand, but apart from asking us if we wanted fill-ups, she'd remained white faced and silent until now. Mother had sent her home with Ann, thinking it best. Nicholas was with his father, and two terrified maids were taking care of Edwin. 'He may feel he has to…avenge her. I pray not.'

Gervase and I both sighed deep. 'Vengeance,' I said, 'will we ever get clear of it? Create a realm at peace?'

'Not yet,' said Gervase, 'Lord Gilbert Delaunay is dead, and those weapons confiscated, but the Royalists have other agents, and access, I fear, to other weapons. I'll recommend to the Council that we send men into every county to gather up any that they find, from any house suspected of having the vaguest of Royalist sympathies, and that right speedily. No doubt the Royalists will send someone down from Scotland, or over on the next boat from the Low Countries to take Lord Gilbert's place. Do your best in Scotland, Rob. This new scheme of General Lambert's to tempt them out of Stirling — I think it might work. Subdue the Scots. Then, maybe one last fight in England, one last push, and we shall have peace at last.'

Miles came in from the barns, and caught this last remark. ''Tis pity I can't go,' he said, 'after tonight's doings I think I've a taste for it. That woman. She killed my wife.'

'It was all because of Loveday's rhyming,' whispered Judith. 'Mama knew Loveday had seen her meeting my uncle, and she believed Loveday was telling everyone, by her rhymes, that he was here, hiding out in the woods. Then she thought Ann and Rachel must know it too, that Loveday would have told them. So she sent those men, Matthew Garstang's men, to…silence them. Mayhap Jem spoke up for them, and so they were not …disposed of.' Tears rolled down her cheeks.

We sat mute, for a while. There seemed nothing we could say.

'You can go to Scotland in my place if you like, brother.' I said at last, only partly in jest.

# Chapter 37

It was early August when I rode down from the border, crossing the North York moors, making for my home in the Lune Valley once again. The year had moved on. Trees were heavy with summer foliage, becoming tired and dusty now. Grass was springing again in hayfields long shorn. Miles would soon be harvesting our field of oats. His field of oats. I must get used to the idea. Though Lowflatts would always be 'home' to me, my home, if I survived what was to come, must henceforth be the shop in Lancaster.

I had, tucked into the lining beneath the pommel of my horse's saddle, three letters. One was from my mother, giving me Lowflatts' news. Miles was much improved in health, and coping with the farm work. Saul Proctor had grown half a head since spring, and was helping him. Hannah Postlethwaite came regularly to help with the dairying. Ann was sewing her bride clothes and learning to cook.

The second was from my Cousin Zeke — every word misspelled except for the names of the spices, which I supposed he'd copied from the labels on the jars — telling how 'business' was going. Reasonably well, he reported, although the rumour that Charles Stuart and his Scottish army would soon be passing through Lancaster was making folks too nervous to go out. Many local lads were enlisting with the militia. He'd met Benjamin Postlethwaite and Nicholas Moreland in the street, all newly kitted out in the buff coats and helmets of the New Model Army, their chests puffed out with pride at being 'called up' by the Council of State in London.

'Thay sed thay wus goin to fite fur parlmunt,' wrote Zeke. 'Aye shul knot fite. Aye em a sayler. Aye wud fite at see, but knot on lande. Aye wull stik wiv yur shope fur th presnt.'

'Good to know,' I told my horse. 'I'm thankful Charles Stuart hasn't raised a fleet, or no doubt Cousin Zeke would abandon my 'shope' in a brace of shakes.'

The third letter was from Gervase, telling me what I already knew. The Prince was progressing south with his Scottish army. The Council of State were sending the trained bands out from London, marching North to cut him off. It was hoped that Cromwell would catch him up, but that couldn't be guaranteed. Also, that his, Gervase's, father had suffered a seizure, and he'd been at home in Huntingdonshire to attend to his affairs. He'd spoken to his father about Ann, and received his provisional blessing. 'I hope to send for her when all this is over,' he reported. 'Provided all goes in our favour in this last engagement, the Council of State want me to travel to Paris to make representations about trade to men there who are not unsympathetic with our cause. To make of it a wedding journey would suit my purposes.'

'I wonder what Ann will make of Paris?' I enquired aloud, but my horse plodded on, unresponsive.

We proceeded at a leisurely pace, both of us weary from taking a long and circuitous route down from Scotland to avoid Royalist outriders. We'd thrashed them at Inverkeithing, more by luck than skill, although General Lambert certainly showed some skilfulness in his deployments. Now they'd regrouped, though the Highland Clans were much depleted, and Charles Stuart was determined to fight this next battle (pray God the last) in England, and then march triumphantly on to London and claim his father's throne. Parliament was equally determined to stop him, once and for all.

It was late in the afternoon as I approached Lowflatts, and a young woman in a print gown and sun bonnet was driving our cows up the meadow from the river. She seemed to be assisted by a boy and a woolly black dog. Ann? Saul? Claes? Looking to the East, I caught a glimpse of the blue smock of Lanty Briggs as he moved down the fellside behind the Lowflatts' flock.

The dale looked as peaceful as it had the last time I'd ridden home. The day had been hot. Hips, haws, and blackberries were ripening in the hedgerows. Small white clouds floated above the fells. 'Nearly there,' I said, and my horse pricked up his ears. Perhaps he heard the relief in my voice. Apart from scratches sustained when I was hurled head first into a patch of gorse, I was in good health. Poor spirits, but good health.

It hadn't been easy to get permission to come. Cromwell was mustering, ready to march south when I left. By now he could be well on his way, hoping to catch the Prince's army somewhere in the Midlands. The Council of State were mobilising militias in every part in England, for fear he wouldn't get there in time. Even Tom Fairfax, it was rumoured, was coming out of retirement to lead the men of the Eastern counties. Tense and difficult days, although Zeke's and Gervase's missives suggested that preparations were well advanced, and the rumours I'd heard along the way indicated that few were choosing to join the Royalists as they marched south. They were said to be resting now, just north of Kendal. No one seemed sure how far Cromwell had got, only that he had taken Perth, left sufficient men behind to hold Southern Scotland, and was on his way.

Turning into the farmyard, I slithered down from the saddle. No one was visible, but I could hear sounds coming from the barn. Childish voices, chanting, *'Our Father, which art in 'eaven.'* Then the prayer finished, and a clear voice said, 'Thank you children, Class dismiss.' Whereupon the barn door flew open and a bevy of ragamuffins tumbled out, Timmy Proctor in the van.

'Major Rob! Ah'm bein' learned t'read!' he yelled. 'Our Saul don't want to, but Ah'm doin' champion! Mistress Judith's learnin' me!'

Judith herself stepped out into the sunlight yard. She was wearing a black dress and a sacking apron, a white cap covering her hair, a slate and a piece of chalk in her hand. She looked tired, but when she saw me her face lit into a smile.

'Turned instructress, Judith?' I said, not wishing to seem over pleased to see her in front of this swarm of imps.

'Yes. Papa always meant to start a school for the village children, but… Oh!' She stared past me to my horse. 'Oh, Rob, no!' Her eyes filled with tears.

'His name is Gideon.'

I was a big strong soldier. I must not allow my own eyes to fill, though I had certainly walked out of the camp and wept on the darkened brae, after that disastrous day in Fife. The children stood around us, wide-eyed, fingers in mouths, sensing something was wrong.

'Did yer Caesar get killed?' asked Timmy, his voice dropping to a whisper, his eyes enormous, as he took in what must have happened.

'He did, alas.'

'Damnation t'them Royalists!'

'No, Timmy. The Royalists weren't to blame. He was shot by one of our own dragoons. We workaday cavalrymen were being thrown back on the left flank, and the dragoons wheeled in to reinforce the line. You know what dragoons are? No? They're the heavy mounted troops, they wear armour, and fire their muskets from the saddle. Very skilled and effective men. Unfortunately Caesar, eager to compete with them, veered into the line of fire, and took a shot to the head. He was dead before he hit the ground.' Several lips began to tremble, including Timmy's.

'Don't grieve too much. Caesar didn't suffer. He never knew he'd been hit. And now,' I said, forcing a smile, and trying for a more cheerful note, 'I have Gideon, here. He lost his master in the same battle. The grooms rounded up all the stray horses after it was over, and our Master of Horse asked me to take Gideon. We were both sad, Gideon and I, so we understood each other.'

'Gideon. That's a name from the Bible, children,' said Judith, in the bright tone people use to younglings.

'I don't know if it really was his name all along,' I explained, 'but we had a reading from the Bible the next morning, about Gideon, who was a great warrior in Biblical times — I'm sure Mistress Judith will read the passage to you — and when I tried it on him, he lifted his head and looked at me, as though he'd heard it before. I'd the task, later, of escorting some of the prisoners to Edinburgh. One of them told me there's a Gallic name, Gilean, Gil-yan, so I imagine he's Highlander.'

I gave a passing thought then, as I had many times since that day, to the young clansman who must have been Gideon's master. Poor fellow, no doubt he'd turned out, as he was obliged to do, at his clan chief's bidding.

He may never have understood what he was fighting for, why it cost him his life. Once upon a time I'd thought I understood what I was fighting for. Now I was so weary of it I no longer cared.

'Him's a beauty,' said Timmy gruffly, stretching out a tentative hand to pat Gideon's neck.

'Indeed he is, and now you must all run home, children, or your mothers will wonder where you are!' Judith shooed her flock of little pupils out of the gate. Then she came back and stood beside me, stroking the white star on Gideon's coal black forehead.

'How comes it you're teaching the village tykes in Miles's barn, Judith?' There, I remembered to say 'Miles's', not *our* barn.

'Your mother's notion. It's not so far for them to walk from the village as it would be to Lings. Miles was quite agreeable.' She went on stroking Gideon's nose, eyes averted. 'Your mother understood I needed something to take my mind off …what happened. Mama and I never dealt well together, and I always disliked Uncle Gilbert. But when they died… Poor Loveday, She couldn't have known the danger she was putting herself in, when she made that rhyme. Do you remember, I told you, that day by the river? *"She shall know the wrath of God, who meets her lover in the wood,?"* She must have seen Mama meeting Uncle Gilbert, and thought Mama had a lover…'

'I remember,' I said. 'Loveday may never have realised who they actually were, but your mother must have been frightened that Loveday, with her rhymes, was alerting everyone to your uncle's presence in the neighbourhood.' I kept to myself the thought that Loveday might have stumbled on something darker even than a Royalist plot. Judith had enough to bear without the suspicion that her mother was in an incestuous relationship with her own brother.

'I suppose I was lost, devastated. It was *so horrible*,' Judith went on. 'I've tried to be a comfort to Papa, but I haven't been very successful. He loved Mama, even though he must have known she didn't return his affection, and to find she'd betrayed him, for her brother! She always said Gilbert was the one person of all her family who ever took an interest in her when she was little.'

'It was an arranged marriage, with your father?'

'Yes. Mama said she was sold to the highest bidder. Papa had — has still, I suppose — expectations. Cousin Bess! Although she seems like to live for ever! Mama's family had the name and title, but no money. Now I've not even that! No one wants a murderesses' daughter!'

'Surely no one blames you?'

'The taint's there. A husband would always be wondering, will she set about me, or our children, and crack our skulls as her mother did Loveday's? Don't you think?'

'I don't.'

'It's kind of you to say so, Rob,' she replied, stiffly. 'My father often speaks of you. Will you have time to call and see him, whilst you're here? He'd like to hear how Cromwell beat the Scots to flinders!'

'He didn't! Cromwell wasn't at Inverkeithing. Holed up in Linlithgow, unable to get past Leslie and the Scots in time. General Lambert and Colonel Oakey did it all. I'll call on your father. There are things I'd like to talk to him about. He's given up the idea of re-joining the army?'

She shrugged. 'He wanted to, but with Edwin still on crutches... Jem Robinson is out of danger, but unable to speak with his wounded throat... Here comes Ann with the cows. You know she has her bride-chest packed? She'd a letter from Gervase only two days ago. He may send for her any day.'

Ann waved to us across the yard, but passed by, following the cows to the byre, Saul and Claes at her heels. Miles crossed the garth, deep in conversation with Hannah, who was bringing in a basket of washing. They looked up, acknowledging my presence. Miles raised his hand, but didn't speak. Mother appeared at the kitchen door to take the basket from Hannah. She beamed in our direction, but turned away and went back indoors.

'Supposing Parliament prevails, as they surely must... what then will you do?' said Judith, tangling her fingers in Gideon's mane.

'Send Zeke on a long sea voyage, to fetch any spices I happen not to have in stock!...or...'

'Or?'

'Leave him where he is. I, too, had a letter from Gervase. In it he talks of what the Council of State is minded to do, once the war is over. They plan, he says, to send emissaries, men of good understanding, to forge, or re-establish, trading links in the various countries where we have allies, or with whom we've formally traded on good terms. He wonders if I'd be interested — in travelling to the New World.'

'The New World!'

''Tis a long way from our beloved Lonsdale, Judith, but I confess I'd like to see the New World. The war has turned some of we humbler sort into new men. I know I no longer feel entirely at home in this old world. The New World might be just the place for me.'

'I should like...to see it too.'

Gideon nickered softly, and blew down my neck, reminding me, rather more humbly than Caesar would have done, that he expected to be fed and watered. I took hold of his bridle, and began to walk him towards the stable.

'Let another month go by,' I called, turning to look over my shoulder. 'One last fight, by God's mercy, Judith! Look for Gideon and myself returning! Pray for us, every day! If your father says I may take you to Massachusetts, then I will.'

# Historical Note

The English Civil War (a misnomer if ever there was one, since many of the decisive battles took place in Wales, Scotland and Ireland) began in October 1642 and was finally won by the Parliamentarians at the battle of Worcester in September 1651. What began as a disagreement between King Charles the first and Parliament about the powers of monarchy, dragged on for nine years. However, many of those who had supported Parliament from the beginning were greatly dismayed by his execution in January 1649. Some retired to their lands and estates, others changed sides, believing that Charles' son was the rightful heir and should be given the throne, and after the Interregnum and the death of Oliver Cromwell, the monarchy was restored in 1660.

During the various phases of the war many ordinary people were caught up in events as the rival armies passed through their neighbourhoods, staged battles on their commons, or subjected their towns to crippling sieges. Also, many young men from humble backgrounds joined on either side, as foot soldiers or cavalrymen. Some did so from deeply held religious or political conviction, but many must have seen it as an opportunity for excitement and adventure, an escape no doubt from personal problems, or a chance to travel to other parts of the land at a time when most people lived and died within a few miles of the place where they were born. Some towns and villages experienced vicious fighting with many lives lost, others never saw anything of the war at all, living in peace and tranquillity throughout. For those who took part, as has been the case throughout history, the experience marked them in ways they could not have foreseen, and they returned changed men.

Made in the USA
Charleston, SC
29 November 2016